"A terrific, taut debut novel. . . . *The Story of Junk* is a grimly comic look at that underworld, the gritty workaday life of dealers and junkies, their loves and betrayals, and, finally, their disillusionments." —Jill Ciment, *Mirabella*

"A wonderful, shrewd novel." —Guy Trebay, *Village Voice*

"In the almost fifty years since William Burroughs's *Junky* appeared, one thing is obvious: women are no longer society's guard dogs. Yablonsky's women are vulnerable like men, have equal opportunity to 'vice,' and are equal prey to its pleasures and pains. . . . Yablonsky has written a bold, sometimes devastating, odyssey, a long night of the soul." —Lynne Tillman, *Bomb*

"Ms. Yablonsky is a provocative, gritty writer, and her rasping, intimate voice can be arresting."
—Sue Halpern, *New York Review of Books*

"Spare, jarring, and grimly fascinating. . . . An unblinking, occasionally comic description of the drug world and its lost-soul denizens." —Cathy Burke, *New York Post*

"Riveting. . . . This spare, elegant, and fascinating novel depicts the world of the downtown addict with an honesty and sense of authenticity that transcend the clichéd images of glamour and/or squalor." —Patrick McGrath

"Yablonsky's semi-autobiographical tale is so disarmingly life-sized, so inarguably human that it pulls you right into her bloodstream. She's a scaringly good writer, with prose so natural you are only occasionally stopped dead by the aptness of her images. It's not a book that asks your sympathy; instead, it compels complicity, identifying in the junkie's immersion and negation something that is sadly basic to the human condition."
—Jim Washburn, *OC Weekly* (Orange County, CA)

THE STORY OF

JUNK

THE STORY OF

JUNK

A NOVEL BY

LINDA YABLONSKY

Little, Brown and Company
Boston   New York   Toronto   London

FOR PAT
AND
FOR DAD

Originally published in hardcover by Farrar, Straus and Giroux, Inc., 1997
First Back Bay paperback edition, 1998

Reprinted by arrangement with Farrar, Straus and Giroux, Inc.

Library of Congress Cataloging-in-Publication Data

Yablonsky, Linda.
 The story of junk : a novel / by Linda Yablonsky.—1st
American ed.
  p. cm.
  ISBN 0-374-27024-4 (hc)   0-316-96808-0 (pb)
  I. Title.
  PS3575.A25S75   1997   96-48092
  813'.54—dc21   CIP

       10 9 8 7 6 5 4 3 2 1

                 MV-NY

           Designed by Abby Kagan

Published simultaneously in Canada by Little, Brown & Company (Canada) Limited

         Printed in the United States of America

For, while the tale of how we suffer, and how we are delighted, and how we may triumph is never new, it always must be heard. There isn't any other tale to tell, it's the only light we've got in all this darkness.

JAMES BALDWIN, ''SONNY'S BLUES''

PART ONE

KNOCK KNOCK

New York City March 1986

KNOCK KNOCK

There's a simple knock on the door, nothing special.

"Who's there?"

"Mailman," comes the answer. "Special delivery."

I open the door. Why did I open the door?

I see a mailman, six-foot, barrel chest, receding blond, blue eyes. No mail.

"Is your name Laura?"

"No, you must have the wrong apartment." I start to close the door. It's afternoon but I'm in my pajamas, rags I sleep in. I like to sleep in rags.

"Just a moment." He pushes back the door. "Your name's not Laura?"

"No," I say. "It isn't."

He takes a folded letter from a trouser pocket, opens it. I'm staring at his shoes, scuffed, pointy-toed, buff-colored western boots. Do mailmen wear western boots?

"Is this—?" He gives the address, the apartment number.

"Yes, but there must be some mistake."

"This is the right address but you're not Laura?"

"That's right. I'm not."

"Is this your apartment?"

"Yes."

"Well, who are you then?" Before I can make a reply, he pushes the door open wide. "Never mind. Federal agents, D.E.A. Step back, please. We're coming in."

Now there's a gun in his hand. He shoulders past me into the hall. Behind him, four men in plain clothes—no, five—are coming up the stairs. There's a woman, too, blonde, petite with a ponytail, wearing a tweed blazer. I see many hands on holstered guns.

I shrink back inside. My head is spinning. I sit at a table in the living room.

A man with a chin cleft, in a suit and trenchcoat, carefully reads me my rights. I stare at the floor. My cats are looking back at me, one gray fluffball, two tigers. I look away.

"Can I see some identification?" I ask. I'm stalling. I sound like a child.

The man in the trenchcoat shows me his badge and ID. While the others station themselves around the room, study walls, and peek out windows, I scrutinize the ID's photo and particulars without comprehension. My eyes won't focus. I see only "Drug Enforcement Agency." This one's name is . . . Dick.

"Now, what is your name?" Dick asks. He speaks softly. He's very patient.

I have to spell it out. It's painful. I'm not alone. A friend with whom I share this apartment is sitting speechless on my bed.

"Ladies, you're under arrest for the sale of narcotics, a federal offense," Dick announces. "We know you've been dealing heroin here. We've made several buys through an intermediary. Is there anything you'd like to say?"

"No." My friend shakes her head, pets one of the cats.

"All right, I have to ask one question: do you have any heroin here now?" The female agent and two of the men surround me at the table. Hands are still on guns. I'm in my pajamas. I might as well be naked.

"We'll have to search your apartment," Dick says.

"You have a warrant?" I'm all attitude. Do I think this is TV?

"No," he admits. "We don't have a warrant, but it won't be difficult to get one. It'll take about an hour, maybe two, and we'll stay right here till it arrives."

Then we'll wait, I say to myself. To the cops, I say not a word.

"Do you have any heroin in your possession?" Dick says again.

In another room off the kitchen, the tiny room that is my office, several grams of Pakistani brown, brought by the regular mailman, are sitting on a table-shelf in front of a scale. I'd been waiting for one of my better customers. Was he the rat? That one? You can never trust a junkie. I should have known.

My new source was here minutes before, left with all my money. In my pocket I'm holding nearly an ounce of his China White.

The woman agent makes a move toward me. I stand up, reach in my tattered pocket, hand a plastic sandwich bag over to Dick. It's not my lunch; it's my life.

The woman pats me down lightly, with nervous hands. She's more scared than I am. A rookie, I guess. They sent me a rookie. I almost laugh.

Dick looks at the bag, eyes its contents: white rocks the size of mothballs, loose powder at the bottom. It's the best stuff money can buy—pure. I've only had a taste. It's still in my nose.

"Okay, good," Dick says. A lock of dark hair falls over his eyes. They're gray. No, they don't have a color. "Do you have any more heroin in this apartment?" It's five rooms, light and airy, good location.

Miserably, I sink into a chair. "In there," I say, nodding toward the office. "You'll find it."

Unlike the rest of the place, the office is dark and gloomy, its floor worn out by heavy traffic. In three years I've had to retile it twice.

Dick sends the mailman to check it out. The others pair off to begin their search, but all that seems to interest them is our record collection—it's vintage.

"Please," I say dumbly. "Can I ask you not to make a mess?" As if I'll be there later and have to clean it all up.

"No problem," Dick says cheerfully. "We're not like your city cops. You're lucky you got us."

"Yeah," I say. "Lucky."

"Someday you'll thank me for this," he predicts.

"Not real soon," I say.

He laughs, says we can all relax. "She's cooperating." I freeze up.

When the mailman-cop returns with my Pakistani in his hand, Dick takes me in the office. He closes the door, seats himself at my desk. I take the plain wooden folding chair beside it that has always been the customer's. I've never sat in it before myself.

I look around. The scale is gone, the mirrors and the razors, the straws. I glance at the bookshelves extending up the opposite wall, and quickly look away. My remaining cash is hidden there, between the pages of several old books. I wonder if they've found it.

"So," says Dick. "How did a nice girl like you end up in a dirty business like this?" He gives me a silly grin.

"Look, I'm just a junkie, that's all." My shoulders sag. "Anyone can be a junkie."

"That so?"

"Yeah."

"I wonder."

"It's the truth," I say. It is.

"How does it happen?" he asks. "I'm just curious."

"It happens, that's all."

He tells me they've been watching me for several weeks, intercepting my mail, tapping the phone, making small buys. He asks if I keep my old phone bills. I do, I don't know why. Collecting was never my thing. The phone is ringing now, incessantly. We let it ring.

I stand up and reach for a cardboard briefcase on a shelf above Dick's head. "All my bills are here," I tell him. "Take your pick."

He lays a few pages on the desk and looks them over. I see a puzzled expression cross his face, disappointment.

"I never made any phone calls," I explain. "Everyone always called me." Same as they're doing now. Won't these people ever learn? The answering machine clicks and clicks, pleading voices asking if I'm home, when they can come over.

Dick cocks an ear, looks up from the bills. "You never made any calls? Then how'd you get your stuff?"

"It knocked on the door, like you."

"Come on."

"It did," I tell him.

It did.

Dick's still in his coat. He shifts in his seat. Can't tell his age, maybe forty. "I want to tell you something," he says, fingering the cleft in his chin, milky smooth, no stubble. "I can't make any promises, but I can almost guarantee, from what we've got here, right now you're looking at five to fifteen years in a federal prison."

Five to fifteen? I'm thinking, that means two, maybe three, if I'm good. I can't stand it. I stop thinking.

He asks if I know a certain guy—what should I call him? Angelo.

"Angelo who?" I say.

"Angelo something."

"I'm not sure."

"Listen," Dick says. Still patient, very deliberate, he tells me all about Angelo, a smuggler. He's been on this Angelo a long time but the guy keeps slipping away. Dick knows more about him than I do. He peers at me, searching my face, then the phone bills, then again my poker face. "Is Angelo a friend of yours?"

"I don't know who you mean."

"You know who I mean."

"Who set me up?"

"You can figure that out for yourself."

"I haven't got any idea." Actually, I have several, all of them wrong. I must've been too greedy, I think. *Never be greedy*, a supplier once told me. When you start to get greedy, it's the beginning of the end.

"You weren't that surprised to see us, were you?" Dick inquires.

"Of course I was!" I nearly shout. "I mean, I knew this day might come. I just didn't think it would be today."

"So, why'd you let us in?"

"I thought you were the mailman!"

He chuckles. "That was a good trick, wasn't it?" He offers me a smoke. It's not my brand and I demur. He lights one for himself, has one of the other agents bring me one of my own.

"You're not very tough," Dick says.

"Not at all," I agree. I feel nauseous.

"So, how'd you and Angelo meet?"

I don't answer. I can't. I look at the phone bills as if they're the Dead Sea Scrolls, cryptic and exalted.

"I have to ask you again: is this Angelo someone you know?"

"Maybe. I know a lot of people." I take a drag on my cigarette, drag deep. Dick looks at me, I look at the bills. "Angelo," I reflect. "I do know an Angelo," I say then. "I don't know if he's the one you mean."

"You get stuff from him, this Angelo?"

Time stops. There's no sound anywhere, no blood rushing in my ears, no sign from God, just heroin seeping through my pores. I need a bath. I need an out. There isn't one.

"Isn't Angelo your source for heroin?"

"I can't believe this is happening." My voice is small. Is it my voice?

Dick shakes his head. "Everyone says that," he tells me. "Every time. What about Angelo? You might as well tell me. It's going to come out, one way or another, in the end."

Will it?

"Yes," I say then, my voice smaller still. "Angelo."

It's over.

I'm going to kick dope in a cell. I can't *believe* this is happening.

"Who else is there?" Dick asks.

"Nobody."

"No one else?"

"No."

I think of all the "guys" who've sat in this seat over the last four or five years, the runners and stumblers, the dealers and smugglers, the Angelos and Franks and Eds, the Moes and Vinnies. Good-looking guys, fat guys, wasted guys; teachers, artists, carpenters, fathers: junkies. Nobodies.

"So, how did you and Angelo meet?"

"I don't remember. Junkies have a way of finding each other."

"How's that?"

"Listen," I say. "I'm no criminal. I'm addicted, I have a habit, and it's bad. I admit it. I get stuff for myself and sell some of it to my friends. Otherwise I couldn't afford it." Why am I talking like this? I can't stop talking. It must be the dope, the good pure dope. It isn't me. This isn't me. I don't do this. I've never done anything like this in my life.

"I don't expect you to give up your friends," Dick tells me. He looks sincere. "I'm not asking you about your friends. I can understand your wanting to protect them. But let me tell you what's going to happen next. When we're done here, we'll take you and your roommate to our office uptown and book you. You'll be fingerprinted and have your picture taken. We'll have to fill out some papers. Then we'll put you in handcuffs and take you down to Centre Street, to be arraigned. If you need a lawyer, the court will appoint one. This is a serious charge. I want you to understand how serious. Do you understand?"

"I can't believe this is happening."

"All you junkies seem to be on the same wavelength," he sighs. "You all think getting caught is your whole problem. It's never the junk, it's the law that's the problem. The law and the police. Is that how it is?"

I say, "It's a form of sickness."

"Do you want a doctor?"

A doctor? For years *I've* been the doctor, a medical dispenser. Not a crook.

"If you want a doctor, I can get you one. But let me ask you: if it was Angelo I was talking to now, do you think he'd be protecting you?"

"I don't know."

"Is Angelo a friend?"

"In a way."

"I don't think so. Do you know where he is?"

"No," I say. "This Angelo doesn't live in New York."

"Where then?"

"I don't know!" I insist. "I don't know where he is and I don't know where he lives. The guy shows up when he feels like it."

"Where do you get your stuff otherwise?"

"The street." I'm lying. I don't know if Dick believes me. He has to.

"When do you think you'll see Angelo again?"

"I don't know. I haven't heard anything from him in quite a long time." I don't have to lie about this.

The phone rings again, the machine picks it up. It's Angelo.

Dick's eyes dart to the phone. His lips part as Angelo identifies himself, names his hotel. Says to call him.

Dick gets to his feet, straightens his tie. "We're finished here," he says. "Time to go."

I'm to make the call to Angelo, but not from this apartment. Dick lets me go in the bathroom to dress. The woman agent watches. I peel off my rags and pull on a sweater, climb into faded black jeans. There's dried blood spattered all over the bathroom walls. I've never noticed it before.

Dick takes my elbow and draws me to the door. He's going to forgo the handcuffs.

"Just pretend we're your dates," he jokes.

"Yeah, right," says my friend. "You look exactly like the kind of guys we'd go out with."

The mailman-cop climbs behind the wheel of an unmarked car parked at the curb outside. It's brown and has a hole in the muffler. The driver's name is Tim. Dick puts me in back with my friend. She looks through me. I keep my eyes on the road.

We're going uptown by way of Tenth Avenue, under the ruin of the West Side Highway. It fronts the Hudson River and shields the greater city from view. Fire-ravaged piers stretch up the water side; transvestite hookers walk the other, past leather bars, auto-body shops, boarded-up warehouses, rusting diners. The sun looks cold on the water, traffic is light. Hardly any tourists at the Circle Line boat docks. Nobody talks much. We've seen it all before.

At Tenth and Fifty-seventh, we pull up before a white stone monolith too many floors to count, windows of blackest glass. "We made *awfully* good time," I observe.

"After you," says Dick. We get out of the car.

They take us in by a back door on Fifty-eighth adjoining a Pontiac showroom. "I figure you girls might not want anyone to see you," Dick explains. "Am I right?" Yeah, right. The mailman giggles. They shuffle us into a freight elevator big enough to carry a tank. I wonder how they would be treating us if we happened not to be "girls"?

The elevator opens on a long, well-lit corridor lined with dull white doors you need a code and ID card to enter. *The last mile,* I think. We walk it. Halfway down, the mailman slides his card through a gatekeeper, punches its keys. No doors open.

He punches the keypad again and a moment later we're in a large windowless gray room, empty but for a Steelcase desk, three wooden swivel chairs, and a drafting-table-sized fingerprint stand next to an industrial aluminum sink. Dick moves us into an adjoining room, toward a camera on a tripod opposite a wall hung with white no-seam paper. All the walls need paint.

A female agent moves behind the camera. She's only a few feet away but seems almost beyond vision, blurred. She jokes, "Which is your good side?"

"The inside," I say. I'm holding a slate clapboard with my name and a number on it under my chin.

I glare into the camera. White clamp lights glare back. I wonder if I should smile.

Dick sits me down at the desk. I have to sign papers now. One says I understand the charges against me: possession and sale of Schedule One narcotics. Another paper is, in Dick's words, "a kind of waiver." He asks me for my father's name, address, and phone.

I shriek. "You're not going to tell *him* about this, are you?" My father has no idea. This'll kill him.

"Nah. Not unless we have to."

"Have to?"

"In case something happens while you're in custody."

My eyes grow wide. "In case something happens? What's going to happen?"

"Nothing, probably. But you never know. This is just in case."

I fill in my brother's name. My father's moved, I don't know his address. I sign, feeling helpless.

The mailman-cop enters carrying my bag of pure, marked as evidence. It's the last time I'll ever see it; I feel like waving goodbye. Instead, I swallow. Hard. I'm sweating, the dope's wearing off, I'm going to cry. I look at my friend. She's pissed.

"Come with me," Dick beckons. He shows me through a door by the desk. It leads to a narrow corridor and two clean cells behind shiny black bars, each with a bare bulb and a bench. "In here," he tells me, indicating a room at the hallway's dead end. It's about the same size as my office but even more of a tomb. One desk, two chairs, no windows.

Over the next couple of hours, Dick continues to press me for names. He's got the answering-machine tape and also my phone book, a regulation-dealer pocket computer gadget. A password accesses all the "important" numbers—the sources, the money owed, the money owing—they're in a secret compartment Dick is not aware of. As we go through the names he does find, all I say is, That's a friend, and that's a friend. He presses harder. I say nothing.

Finally we pass back through the fingerprint room into a large outer office, where a couple of dozen agents sit at computers and talk on phones. They all watch as Dick sits me down at his desk and has me dial Angelo's hotel. My voice shaking, I ask Angelo to come by at seven. He can tell something's not right. I pray he can tell. I try to think of some code to warn him off, but with so many eyes and ears on me, I jam up.

We return to the big empty room. I'm clammy, a little dizzy, my calves twitch. My friend is sitting at the desk, toying with the black baseball cap in her hands. I wish we were both better dressed.

Dick disappears. We sit there.

Suddenly, he's back, smiling. Why shouldn't he smile? *He's* having a very good day. He tells us we're being released on our own recognizance, just for tonight. We're to go home and fix ourselves up. We're going to wait for Angelo.

I stare at him, disbelieving. Go home? Go home?

"You need cab money?" he asks.

"No," I say. I don't want any favors. "I have cab money." It's all I have.

In the taxi my friend turns her hat inside out, removes from the sweatband a bag of dope. My dope. She'd stolen it. She must have been keeping a stash all along. I've never been so grateful. I don't know how she got away with it—not hiding it from me but keeping it from the cops. I think she's crazy. We both are. We laugh, even though it hurts.

Just before seven, I'm sitting in Dick's brown government car, bundled in an old overcoat. Dick's behind the wheel, walkie-talkie in hand. I'm on the passenger side. Two agents are in another car somewhere behind us. Others are at Angelo's hotel. Still more are scattered elsewhere up and down the street, I can't see where. It seems very dark tonight. I've never seen it so dark.

We're parked in the shadow of a twelve-story co-op across the street from my apartment. On the other side, benches bolted to the sidewalk face the stoop of my building between spindly, weed-like trees—my outer office, so to speak. My customers call it the "waiting room." I'm the one waiting now.

The walkie-talkie crackles to life. "Subject is leaving the hotel," someone says. "He's with another guy. Should we take him?"

"No," Dick says. "Let's see where he goes." Where who goes? What other guy?

"Who's the other guy?" Dick asks me. Who could it be? I don't know anything. I'm shaking in my skin. "You okay?" Dick says.

"Just cold."

He says he'll turn on the heat and puts the key in the ignition. The engine sputters and dies. He tries it again. Same result. He floors it. With a shudder, the car roars to life. "Your tax dollars at work," says Dick. Tax? I haven't paid taxes in ages. "Better hurry," he teases. "Them I.R.S. guys are much worse than us."

"Yeah? What'll they do? Put me in jail?"

"Ah, don't be like that. You'll be all right."

"Sure," I say. "I'm fine."

Dick checks his watch, looks at the street. "He's late, this guy."

"That's nothing unusual. He's often late. Sometimes days late." I've waited on Angelo before.

"Where are they now?" Dick says into his walkie-talkie.

"In a deli," comes the answer.

"Jeez."

"These guys are splitting up," we hear from the radio. "They're taking separate cabs."

"Keep the tail."

"That walkie-talkie has a wide range," I comment.

"Latest model," Dick notes with satisfaction. "Wish I could say the same for the car." A quiet descends, dark as the night.

"I think we've lost them," an agent reports half an hour later.

Dick grips the wheel. "What?"

"I don't see them," the voice says. "They must be down there somewhere."

Two men are walking south on the other side of the street, coming our way. Dick asks, "Is that the guy?"

I'm slumped in the seat. Peering over the bottom edge of the window frame, I look through the dark. "No," I say. "Not him."

Static from the walkie-talkie. "Is this him?"

"No," says Dick. "Hold your places. We don't know who's carrying what."

I close my eyes.

While other drugs work to alleviate pain, excite the mind, or otherwise trick the senses, heroin plays with the soul—or whatever it is makes a person uniquely appealing and distinguishable. Like an enveloping shadow dissolving day into night, it sneaks across your vision and tries to put it out, whatever that joy is by which you live, it creeps inside and pushes you down, making you smaller and smaller, a tiny flame burning down. And when you're so small you're barely an ember, something happens, something comes at you and—

I've never felt so small as I do at this moment, in the car with Dick. Yet this thing, this drug that has brought me lower than I ever thought I could go, is the one thing I want to salve my soul. Just for a minute. Just for this minute. Not even a minute. Time's up.

"Is that the guy?"

I look again. Another stranger. And then, about a block away, I see him walking fast and alone, hands in pockets, head bent into the March wind. *Go away!* I want to shout. I'm screaming inside, *Just keep going!*

"You okay?" Dick asks.

Nothing I can do.

"Is that the guy?"

I glance up and shrink from my bones. He's close.

"Is that the guy?"

"I've never done anything like this in my life."

"Really?" says Dick. "I do this every day."

Bully for you, I want to say. Then I see Angelo enter my building. I choke on my tongue, nod yes. Fall to the floor of the car in a heap.

"GO!" Dick shouts in the walkie-talkie. "Move in."

Nothing happens for a minute. Then, static.

"Is he carrying?" Dick says.

"Affirmative."

"Stay down a minute," he tells me.

I no longer have eyes or ears; my mouth is twisted. I'm raging. I'm weeping. Then I'm like stone.

"Okay," Dick says. "Coast's clear."

I'm ready to go downtown.

"No," he says. His head wags. "I gotta deal with this guy

tonight. You go home and I'll be back bright and early. Get some sleep."

Sleep? He thinks I'll sleep? He thinks I'm too sick to run, but I might.

I can never tell anyone about any of this, I think, as I crawl on hands and knees up the stairs. Six flights. I could be climbing Mount Everest. My friend is waiting at the top, watching me crawl. When I see her face I know it for real: I can never say anything, not about this. I can never say anything, ever.

My friend backs into the apartment as I pass through the door. Our coats and hats hang double on their hooks in the hall— getting by is always a squeeze.

My friend's name is Kit. I can see her hands are trembling. Her hair is white, her eyes are red, black in the center, all pupil. Usually, they're blue, light blue, very light. You can always see the pins in them. Not now.

I toss myself into a chair at the table in the living room, next to the corner window. I pull the coat to my ears. My throat feels thick, like I've swallowed poison. "How does it feel to live with a rat?" I say hoarsely.

Kit's looking into the fireplace. It's cold, too. There's no mantel over its white brick, only a painting Kit made before I knew her. Her boot traces a path through soot that has fallen through the chimney. "Was it bad?" she asks.

"Awful," I say. "I can't believe this is happening."

"Did Angelo see you?"

I say no, I didn't see him either, I hid on the floor of the car.

"I saw the whole thing from the roof next door."

"All of it?" I'm astounded.

"Almost. I couldn't make out what happened in the doorway. I saw them take him away."

Oh God, I think. Angelo.

"I cried," Kit says. "I couldn't help it."

I stare straight ahead. Kit never cries.

I fix my eyes on the painting, a pair of cartoony green-and-yellow sea dragons scratched onto a splat of black paint like graffiti on a backyard fence. Purple drips inch down their middles, yellow beads radiate from their spines. They face off parallel to the surface, electric blue, their tongues unfurled, their tails curled into whips. It's impossible to know if they're dancing or just making eyes, if they're evil or good. They remind me of the way Kit plays guitar, how the sound creeps over your body and under your feet, inside your bones and out your mind. I miss that sound. There's been no real music at our house in over two years. The cats purr and meow, the phone rings, and the door buzzer bleats, but that's about it. People knock.

"I always kind of liked Angelo," Kit says then.

"Me, too," I allow. "Most of the time."

"Doesn't he have a kid?"

"Yeah, a girl. Three years old."

Kit slumps into a chair opposite, looks past my shoulder out the window. "Why did you do it?" she says.

"Why did he?" I counter. "I don't know. Don't ask me."

"I mean, why did you hand all our dope over like that?"

"They were gonna find it anyway," I mutter.

"You could have kept *some*. At least we'd have something now."

"Well, it didn't happen that way, did it?" I feel my toes curl.

Kit looks at her boots, twists a few hairs around her ear, a familiar gesture. "Well, are we gonna get anything tonight?"

"Are you nuts? We just got arrested! How can we?"

She shoots me a steely look. "I'm not going to jail feeling like this."

I'm too weary to argue. "Let's not fight," I say.

"Then call Daniel," she says. "He might have something."

"That frog?" I say, with too much disdain. Daniel is another smuggler—"importer," he likes to say. A friend. He never moved on Angelo's scale, but his stuff was about the same. "Well, maybe," I say. "Let me think."

We drift into the office without thinking. The cats follow us, settle into their customary places, under the lamp on my desk. They seem to think this is business as usual, but there isn't any business to do—no scale, no customers, no dope.

I sit in my chair and stare at my empty hands. Why *did* I give up so easily? Who is this sitting in my skin? That D, that devil D, it got in my life and it got in my mouth and threw itself over my senses. It thinks for me, it breathes for me, it fucks for me. Master and servant, it lives for me. It *lives*. It has no passion, except for me. Everything I want, it gives me, but it doesn't give enough. I want that devil to die. But how do you kill a devil? There's no part of you that doesn't belong to it. Everything you do to it, you do to you.

"We have to get *something*," Kit says again. "We have to. If we're gonna have to kick this stuff, we'd better get something to cut down with."

She sounds remotely reasonable. "All right." I relent, my defenses down.

She asks how much money we have left.

"I don't know." I shrug, though I know to the penny. "Enough," I say and swivel my chair around, ruffle through the pages of an old book on the shelf, a family heirloom, a prayer book. From between its leaves I pick out five crisp hundred-dollar bills, then button my boat. I'll have to make this call from outside. Kit goes with me. Up the street there's a pay phone on an alley, where I can watch the traffic in four directions. I don't spot any government cars, but I don't look too closely.

A couple of hours later, we're home, holding a gram. It's good stuff, not great. We take tiny snorts from the bag, just enough to put us straight. The rest we measure into a week's supply. By morning, it's almost gone.

Dick comes early. He sits in my living room and waits to see what gives. He's curious about me; I pretend to be flattered. Maybe I am. Dick's my new best friend. We talk about ourselves all day long while I sweat and jerk around, dopesick as hell. Somehow the idle chatter keeps me steady; otherwise I'd be screaming.

Kit slips out to go to "work" at a friend's studio over on Lafayette, where she's been designing costume jewelry. It's really a front for a coke house. She's really dealing base for the friend. Dick lets her go; he doesn't want her to lose her "job." He thinks our dope business was mine alone, that she doesn't know a thing.

It won't help to put us both away, but Kit's freedom makes me furious. Some friend of Angelo's could show up any minute, attack rifle in hand. Dick's stolid presence is no comfort. He's *hoping* another of my sources will stop by. The horrible thing is, one might.

So, we wait. Dick wants to know more about Kit. That's a story in itself. I tell it.

It's 1980, I say. I'm working nights in a restaurant, cooking. Kit's playing guitar in a rock band, her star is rising.

"What band?" says Dick. "I thought you said she was an artist." He's looking through her photographs now. At the moment we were popped, she was studying them too.

I sneeze, multiple eruptions in quick succession. "She is an artist," I say through a Kleenex, "and a musician." Kit's band has broken up, but I don't want to let Dick know about that. I have to convince him we do something besides junk. "A lot of artists are musicians," I explain.

"Are they all junkies, too?"

I struggle to fend off the yawns. "I told you," I say. "Anyone can be a junkie."

"That's right, you did." Dick nods, drumming his fingers on the table. "Is she any good?"

"Is who good?"

"Your roommate, Kit."

"What do you mean?" I say. "What do you mean, 'good'?"

"As a musician. You know, I like these pictures," he says and rubs his chin.

He likes the pictures. "Kit has a gift" is all I say. "Yeah, she's good." With her band, I tell him, she plays rhythm guitar, gets an itchy-jangly, nervous sound that catches your ear and doesn't let go. "It can be mesmerizing at times," I say. "Even if you're not on drugs."

"That so?" says Dick, wagging his head again, tsk-tsk. "Go on."

I go on. I don't know what else to do. I want the line of dope still tucked in the drawer of my bedside table. I want something else to think about—I sure don't want to think about Angelo—but it's hard keeping up this stupid chatter. I wish night would fall. Dick works only till five in the field, then he goes back to his office—to listen to his taps on my phone, I bet.

"This is still 1980," I say, sifting my thoughts for words that won't jail me. "No, that's not right. It's 1981. Where were you in 1981?" I need to buy a little time.

"I was working for the I.R.S," Dick tells me, a half smile sneaking toward my gaze. "Timmy, my partner, was delivering mail. That's how come he had the uniform."

"Oh," I reply. "How clever."

"We're all lifetime civil service," he explains.

"I wouldn't want to do what you do."

"It's more secure than your line of work." He chuckles.

"Writing, you mean? Or cooking?"

"You know what I mean," he says, loosening his tie. "So, it's 1981."

No, it isn't. It's 1986 and I've run out of steam. I don't have to feign illness. My joints ache something fierce, I might have rickets. My nose runs like a river, my head's full of noise.

"We don't have to keep talking now," Dick says, unconcerned. "I'll be around again tomorrow." He reaches for his wallet.

Is he going to *pay* for my cooperation now?

I'm not taking money from any cop. Forget it.

"This is the number for my radio phone and Tim's," he says, scribbling on some kind of card. "If you run into problems, call. If you know anyone besides Angelo who can lead us up the chain. Someone the government will find useful. I'll be calling you. The United States attorney will want another name. I'm going there now. I'll speak to the assistant. I'll tell him you're working on names. I'm giving you the number at the office, too. You can call it twenty-four hours a day." He tears the card in half and hands me the part with his scribble.

I look at the card. The words "right four fingers taken simultaneously" appear at the bottom. I'm chilled.

I let Dick out and lock the door.

I stare at the numbers scrawled on the card.

Another name?

I put the card away. You don't want to know names in this business; the less you know, the better. That was my big mistake. I had to know it all.

ABOUT DICK

It's a funny thing about Dick. Dick is a funny kind of cop. He didn't bust in with a crew of toughs and batter down the door. Nobody shouted, "Police! Open up!" Nobody put us in handcuffs. I have to admit, Dick was a gent. It worries me.

What did I tell him in that cell of a room in the federal building uptown? How much more will I have to say? If I tell him too much, I'll never live it down. If I say too little, he'll never let me be.

I can't sleep. I can't eat. I can't visit Angelo—how could I explain? I can't even look at Kit. But the customers, they still need me.

When Dick was gone, I started calling them from the pay phone up the street. "There's been a little trouble," I said. They asked if I'd deliver.

"No," I said. "Don't call me for this anymore, I'm done. I'm out of business for good." They all claimed I'd said that before. So the calls keep coming and the cops keep watching, and the days pass, slow and empty, and long.

KIT

When did drugs get to be a problem instead of a pastime? I'm trying to recall. Exactly when did I cross that line? I know it didn't happen in a day.

In 1980 I was sharing an apartment with a merchant marine I called Big Guy. He was six feet four and *big*, not skinny like most guys I knew then. He wasn't fat, he just had a lot of meat on him, a solid kind of guy with a sweet disposition.

Big Guy towered over everything in our little apartment, a tub-in-kitchen studio with a tiny bedroom at the back. He gave me the bedroom to sleep in, and when he wasn't at sea, he gave me heroin, too—long lines of clean white powder we snorted through sawed-off plastic straws. To him, it was a party drug. Big Guy didn't like getting high alone.

One of his pals was a pre-op transsexual who looked to be more woman than I—she didn't even need eye makeup. Her name was Toni. Men loved her jutting chin and easy pout, her extra-long limbs and baby-fine blond hair. Big Guy was dazzled by her whole situation, which he thought was too glamorous for words. She ran with the boho artists and rockers, worked a few seasons in Paris as a runway model. She had a mystique. She mystified me. Probably I was jealous.

The others in Big Guy's gang were waiters, cooks, bartenders, or doormen at clubs. His best friend, a waiter, was a lanky, dissipated longhair with the sloping gait of a practiced drunk. They had come from the same town in Texas. We called him Mr. Leather, even though he never wore any. He was a jeans-and-plaid-shirts kind of guy, with a nice set of lips and a droopy lemon-yellow mustache. Kind of handsome, really.

"Oh," he said when we met, squinting through wire-rimmed glasses. "I already know you."

This made me nervous. I squinted back. I was pretty sure Mr. Leather was gay—Big Guy was—but a lot of the time that didn't matter. "Did I sleep with you or something?" I asked.

"No, not that," he said with a laugh. "We used to work together. You don't remember?"

I didn't. He named a restaurant I'd worked at years before, a piano bar on Bleecker Street. He'd been a waiter there, his first job in New York. He liked me right away, he said. But he also thought I was scary.

"I'm not scary," I said defensively.

"No, no," he said quickly. "To me it was part of your charm."

I don't know why I didn't remember him. He seemed like the sort of person who would stay in my mind, the sort with a predilection for morbid travesty. He carried wallet-sized photos of himself modeling his favorite trash: macho motorcyclists, country bumpkins, tarts with big hair, sequined gowns, and hairy chests, all disheveled, some bloody. Posing was his hobby. He liked the look of pools of blood. Otherwise he was just another guy with a straw up his nose and a pocket full of Valium.

Big Guy was a bartender in the restaurant where I was cooking. Most of the time he was on the day shift, which made our living arrangement feasible. He slept when I worked and I worked when he slept. When he wanted to dry out, he'd load up on Valium and go to sea, then come back to work at the bar. On one of his returns, the day shift was filled and he had to join the crew on mine.

We worked six nights a week, five to three. I was the service chef, the grill girl, the expediter, and a prep, and when the sauté, fry, and cold-kitchen cooks were busy, I opened oysters, too. Big Guy worked the service bar. We were busy.

Just before work, he'd go to his dealer, a woman named Spider, or Web, I can't remember (we never met), and bought a little weight, which he measured into tenths and half-tenths of a gram he'd give me to hold till later. Friends pretending to pay for drinks slipped him money up front and, when they thought no one was looking, came back to the kitchen to see me. I passed them the drugs according to amounts Big Guy scrawled on cocktail napkins when I went to the bar on my breaks. I was usually cranked on speed and couldn't get through a night without a few Stolis. I pretended to be making sure the customers were happy with their food, but whenever I cruised the floor, it was more to get away from the kitchen's heat and noise. Besides, there was a party going on and I didn't want to miss it. In those days, making the scene was more important than making money. That came later.

This was not the sort of restaurant that earns a food critic's stars. This was the kind where the stars hang out, more like a private club. It was the size of a hotel dining room but much plainer, a big white whale of a room off Washington Square that had once been a Chinese restaurant. The entire room was hung with paintings and other works of art by the better-known clientele, who had sizable running tabs. This arrangement guaranteed the place a steady group of regulars whom the owner could count on to keep business at a boom. "Where the artists go, the world follows," he would tell me. "Always watch the artists."

Everyone called him by his nickname, Sticky. He earned it. This was a man who would have an employee arrested for stealing, then go down to the Tombs in the middle of the night to bail the guy out. He loaned money fearlessly and never believed the worst about anyone. Once you had him for a friend, he stuck by you. The restaurant had a name but no one ever used it. It was always, simply, "Sticky's."

Sticky was tall and shapelessly built on a long lanky frame. He had a prominently hooked nose and stringy black hair that fell over his eyes, two chestnuts. In the winter, he wore a raggedy boatneck sweater with a blue shirt under it. In the summer, he took the sweater off. Most nights, he sat on a stool between the bar and the dining room and decided who was hip enough to come in. If he didn't know you or understand your look, he'd say, "It'll be a few minutes," and leave you standing there. Sometimes, he'd tell you straight out to go somewhere else and lock a velvet rope against you. Other times, he'd have Lucky, the manager, get rid of the undesirables. The next night they'd be back. Sticky knew they would be. Eventually, he'd let them in, and either they liked what they saw or they'd weed themselves out.

In a single year, more than a few of the regulars had "accidents." First, a folksinging heartthrob of the 1960s, then an underground film star had fatal heart attacks shooting speedballs, cocaine and heroin, after a deeply drunken night at Sticky's. A drag-queen playwright overdosed on a combination of pills, whiskey, and heroin. Somebody else was murdered, no one knew under what circumstances. The fast life went by even quicker around here. We knew our time was borrowed, but nobody cared about that. What we couldn't borrow, we could always steal. It was in this atmosphere that the art of appropriation was born.

Sticky had two partners, Rico and Flint. Flint was balding, middle-aged, and had stomach cancer. Rico was plain nuts, a wiry Vietnam vet with a nervous twitch partially induced by cocaine psychosis. I didn't mind his jitters. Unlike the sour Flint, Rico had a happy-go-lucky demeanor, feverish, but I was attracted to heat. As Mr. Leather might say, that's why God put me to work in a kitchen.

Rico's quick hands and bad-boy intensity got my attention

the moment we met. He had a typically Italian, smooth olive complexion, smoldering black eyes, and sweet lips—characteristics I felt outweighed his perceptible flaws. Other women must have felt the same way: he was married to a former nun, and several waitresses seemed to know him better than she did. I didn't think anyone we knew in common suspected I would ever have sex with him—too proud—but every now and then, when the mood would strike, I did.

Of course I did. It was all about cocaine and fucking the night away, sucking the powder off our more sensitive parts, confessing our transgressions in the world, relaying our horrors, our pleasures, fucking again. His war stories were a little farfetched but his long bony penis always seemed to wear a smile. It gave me a wonderful ride. He enjoyed it, too. The whole thing was our little secret.

Except Sticky and Flint knew all about it. They tolerated my dealing partly because of this affair, but mostly because they liked the action. Rico dealt cocaine out of the office; when he had to, he bought a little dope from me. The other two just wanted to keep him happy: one of Rico's customers was a C.I.A. agent, another was an assistant to the mayor, a couple of the others were serious gamblers; one looked exactly like a pimp, all black leather, dreadlocks, and silver. There were other, more anonymous dudes in T-shirts and jeans who beat a steady path through the kitchen to the office. We never talked about any of them on the service line. We were cool. We had to be. Some of these guys looked bad enough to shut us down, on their way to the john in particular. There was always a lot of bathroom action at Sticky's, especially in the Ladies. Both sexes used it, and not just to wash their hands.

The front of the house was always jumping. On weekends, people stood six deep at the bar, forced up against it by an enormous twisted metal sculpture just inside the door. Sometimes there were fights and the bartenders had to double as bouncers, leaping over the bar to hustle out the drunks. If the police appeared outside, no one ever invited them in. We knew how to take care of our own.

We took them to the office or the kitchen, where friends seeking relief from the boozy climes of their tables came to watch me work, mostly to get a free meal. The kitchen was almost as big as the dining room, and wide steps by my reach-in gave my audience a place to sit. Having them there put me off my pace sometimes, but this was hot, dirty work and having friends around made it tolerable. When I had a minute to step away from the stoves, I'd take them, one or two at a time, into the walk-in fridge for a snort. Here, among the lobsters and lettuces, the sides of beef, was my own little private club, my sanctified place in the world.

One night, just before Christmas, the kitchen doors go flying open and who comes waltzing through but this big galoot of a girl named Betty. She was dressed in black leather pants, a tightly laced bustier topped by a studded motorcycle jacket, and high leather boots. After two minutes in that hot kitchen, her face began to flush and her eyes turned to glass. The guys on the line thought she was sexy, but to me she looked ready to fall on her face.

Betty was a wild girl, always stoned on something she couldn't handle. She had some weird problem with her equilibrium and was always falling down and making you take care of her. I didn't have the patience.

She was only seventeen the first time I met her five years before and she was already wasted then; there weren't enough Quaaludes in the world, not for her. Someone at a party had talked me into giving her shelter for the night. It happened to be her first day in town. I took her home with two other friends who were looking for a place to crash. Betty slept on the floor of my apartment that night, dead drunk, woke up with her head in the fireplace. I pulled her out. She treated me like a big sister after that, found me crystal meth when there wasn't enough speed in the world. She always had interesting connections.

Betty now claimed to have settled down some. She did seem happier than before. She was working two jobs, she said, a few days a week in a photo lab, a few nights in a sex dungeon. She told me she was living with Kit. "You know," she said. "The musician." I knew. Toast, Kit's band, had made a couple of records I liked. Their first had become a kind of local anthem of the streets and the new one had just hit the charts.

When Betty heard I had a source for China White, she started calling a few times a week. Every conversation went the same way. "Kit really wants to meet you," she'd say again and again. According to Betty, Kit had no friends outside the rock scene. It would be good for Kit to have a friend like me. Someone like a sister.

The day came when Betty brought Kit over to Big Guy's. It happened to be my day off. Her band was making a new record and they were on their way to the studio. It was going to be a long night. Kit sat on a chair in the kitchen looking at the floor, her legs crossed in red jeans so tight I wondered if she'd sewn them on, a boat-neck green pullover falling off one shoulder. Her platinum hair was short and spiky, half-hidden beneath a purple kamikaze headband. That was her aesthetic—white-girl midwestern punk.

A few other friends were already there. They dressed as Betty did, in bondage black, but Kit wouldn't say boo to them. I couldn't tell if she was shy or just a snob. A half hour later, she stood up and walked to the door. "Nice to meet you," she said, and left.

Betty called from the recording studio late that night. "Kit really likes you," she began.

"Oh," I replied. "I couldn't tell."

"Well, she does. She thinks you're cool. She says if you want to, you can stop by the session."

"I'd like that," I said. I've always been a sucker for music.

Then she got to the point. "Can you maybe bring us anything over here?"

Big Guy was at the restaurant, near the studio. "I don't know," I said. "I guess."

Kit came out to meet me as soon as I arrived, drawing me into a lounge. She gave me a guided tour. "This was Jimi Hendrix's studio," she told me, as if I didn't know. I looked around and tried to feel the vibe. The place had no personality whatever, just a few old posters on the wall. When I gave Kit the packet of dope, I saw her smile for the first time. Her teeth were capped, her round lips too small to hide a slight overbite. She was nice. Not a snob at all.

She introduced me to her band and their producer, the drummer from a heavyweight English rock group. He was coked to the gills. All of them were. Kit wanted the dope to smooth her out. The rest of them smoked pot. I stayed awhile and listened to them play, a girl singer named Sylph with a low drone of a voice and a red-haired bass player who pogo-hopped while she plucked. The only guy in the band was the drummer, a greaser with a nice sense of humor and the speed of a runaway train. Everyone called him Poop.

Next day, Betty phoned again and asked me to drop by Kit's apartment, which was around the corner from Big Guy's. It was late in the afternoon, just before I went to work. I climbed the six flights and knocked. The odor of cat spray greeted me at the door. Betty answered it. "Sorry for the mess," she said as I entered the hall. "We're doing the laundry."

The apartment didn't look lived in so much as run over—dirty dishes in the sink, furniture in disarray, broken floorboards. As I sat on a low couch in the living room, Kit appeared from somewhere at the back of the apartment. She had a guitar in her hand. Sunlight poured through the windows, a light breeze on its tail.

"Thanks for coming over," she said, looking pleased. "That was real nice of you, stopping by last night. We wanted to give you something for it."

"But you already paid me," I reminded her. Sixty dollars it was. Cost.

"We bought you a bag of dope," she told me. "It's no big deal, just a bag from the street."

I didn't know what to say. "I'll get it," Betty offered, and disappeared in the direction Kit had come from.

"We had a fight last night, after we got home," Kit volunteered. She showed me a few hairline scars on her arm. They'd been fooling around after the session, Betty tickling her with a razor blade in some kind of punk-flavored massage. Kit was too stoned to feel anything. When Betty started drawing blood, Kit smashed her face with a hairbrush. I was horrified.

"Did you know Kit's an artist, too?" Betty called out as she reentered the room. She was pointing with her nose to the dragon painting, busting her seams with pride.

Kit's eyes narrowed. They looked so light, I could barely see them. "You don't have to shout," she snapped.

"I'm not *shouting*," Betty whined. "I was just *telling* her . . ."

When she wasn't on the road, Kit took photographs. Not the kind with people in them. She used plastic dolls and all kinds of fetishes, Gumbys and trolls, assorted bubble-gum toys—bric-a-brac she composed into lurid still lifes and soaked in primary-colored light. She told me she'd gone to art school but no longer had time for painting. She was often on the road and this other kind of work she could do when she was home, late at night. She had a show in a gallery coming up, and something in a group show at a new museum.

I picked up the piece she was making, a photo-assemblage with a scarlet neon tube attached. This woman had an awful lot of energy, that was clear. I could feel her buzz in the room. She seemed to raise dust even when she was sitting down.

"You've known Betty a long time?" she asked when the girl left for her dungeon job.

"Since she was a kid," I allowed.

"She's still a kid. I don't know why I'm hanging out with her. She's crazy."

"She adores you," I said.

"It's a sick thing," Kit confided. "I don't know what to do about it, but she's pretty helpful to the band."

"They don't have to live with her."

"No, you're right," she said with a wistful shake of her head. "I wish Betty could get her shit together. She's a mess."

I felt sympathetic but it was time for me to leave. "It's good to talk to someone who has their shit together," Kit said as I was going out the door.

I felt embarrassed. I was a bigger mess than they were, but I guess it didn't show as much. I could always put up a front. It was my only natural talent.

"I'm not so together," I told her. I felt strangely compelled to be honest. "I started out a writer, I wrote plays. Now I cook in restaurants and sell drugs for my roommate. I don't do much of anything worth noticing."

"I bet you're a really good writer," Kit said with a confidence I never owned. "I'd really like to read what you've done." Her sincerity made me blink.

"I'll show you something," I promised. "Whenever I get around to doing it again." I didn't want to talk about that.

She brought me to a closet and pulled out a black brushed-velvet pinstriped suit that she said didn't fit her. Sylph, the singer in her band, had made it. She made a lot of their clothes. "Why don't you try it on," Kit said shyly. I thought it looked too small. "No, try it," she said. I did and it was perfect: snug jacket, narrow legs, totally rock 'n' roll.

"Keep it," she said. "I want you to have it." This embarrassed me, too. From what I could see, she didn't have much to give away, even if she was semi-famous.

Kit had come on the scene sometime in the 1970s, with a band that set a new standard for New York punk rock. She hadn't known much about playing guitar, but what she didn't know she invented. I'd seen articles about her in the *Times* and write-ups in every punk news rag there was. She was given featured roles in a couple of underground movies too—arty, low-budget, feminist super-8s. People were watching her. She had fans. Great things were expected. Now I was wearing her suit. Who says fashion is frivolous? Putting on those clothes changed my life.

JUST A CHIP

It was hard to go straight home after work, every night, alone. I had to unwind, and in the after-hours bars a girl could get pretty loose. Sometimes I stayed in Sticky's office, doing lines of coke while he and Rico counted money and talked about their wives. Their wives were always on their case; these guys were married to the store. Flint was a bachelor, but he had the cancer to deal with. It gave him moments of excruciating pain, so at closing time he'd give himself a poke in the rear with Dilaudid and go home to sleep it off.

I was there to give Big Guy a little space at home, but a couple of nights a week he went to the Mineshaft and the Anvil and the Crow's Nest, waterfront bars with steamy back rooms and unlit basements where a guy could get it on man-to-man. I never asked what actually went on there, I didn't want to know. There are rules of privacy I think roommates should respect.

On Saturday nights Big Guy and I went home together and sat up with the Sunday *Times* crossword, trading tales of the week about people at Sticky's. "I love New York," he'd say, whenever we called it a night. Then one day in the *Post*, there was a headline about the spreading "gay cancer," an infection that attacked homosexual men who took it up the ass. It was killing them by the dozen. I was certain Big Guy was more the voyeur, but this story made him squirm. He grew remote and forgetful. "I'm shipping out," he said at last. Every day he went to the union hall to wait for a berth and every night he came home to lay out those lines of heroin. The atmosphere changed for me, too. I grew sick of bars and sick of dope. I told Big Guy not to offer me any anymore, and he didn't. I withdrew.

After two weeks off the junk I felt more desolate than ever. When I looked in the mirror, I didn't see anyone I liked. I saw a loser, a writer who couldn't write, a cook who was out of control. I terrorized the wait-staff at Sticky's, working six nights a week for very little money and spending most of the seventh asleep. I slept all day alone in a bed that wasn't mine and drank my way till dawn. I didn't see how I could go on.

I had a small stash of knockout pills in a bedside drawer. On my day off I bought more in the park at Union Square and washed them all down with a pint of vodka. I went to bed with no intention of waking up, but wake up I did, late the next afternoon, and I answered the phone when it rang. It was a friend named Honey Cook, at whose apartment two years before I had taken my first sniff of heroin.

Honey was not a pusher. She was another would-be writer and sometime actress, mother to an eight-year-old named Mike. She knew Jayne Mansfield's life story by heart and never went anywhere without eyeliner. She worried about her looks, which only fascinated me: a toss of White Minx-tinted hair over blue-flame eyes that winked at the world; whore-pink painted lips under a Teutonic nose that snubbed it. One shoulder sported a moon-and-stars tattoo. Smaller tattoos graced the knuckles of both hands, which bore a number of filigreed silver rings.

She lived in the Village with a blues singer named Lute, a tough, striking blonde out of a film-noir comedy, if there is such a thing. There ought to be. Theirs was a house of mirth—everything for a laugh. This one night, I needed a laugh. I was broke and depressed, between jobs and intimates. Lute was out.

I sat in Honey's kitchen, a wallpapered and chandeliered affair, listening to her ideas on the subject of personal hygiene. She was convinced yogurt had healed her chronic P.I.D. and that parsley juice induced a period. She had also developed a solution for problem skin. The treatment was a lot like salad dressing, a vinaigrette for the face. "This really works," she told me. I thought maybe she should bottle it.

Honey had trouble keeping up with the rent. Once, in her youth, she'd spent a few months on a funny farm, after an unfortunate night on LSD. It wasn't the sort of thing that looked good on a résumé, so she collected disability and a few nights a week, after Mike had gone to bed, hired herself out as a topless dancer. "It's good for the figure," she said. Honey always looked at the bright side.

"Where's Lute tonight?" I asked.

"Oh, umm," Honey answered. "Visiting her mother." She was concentrating on her work. To pick up extra cash, she'd started dealing MDA, a speedy hypnotic we called "the love drug." This stuff was very Cloud Nine. It came in powder form, and packaging it for sale meant emptying vitamin caps and filling them with the drug. I was emptying the caps; she was filling them. "I never know how much of this stuff to put in," she said, scratching her head. "I suppose it's best to be conservative."

I didn't care. All I wanted was company.

She looked up. "You ever live with a woman, hon?"

"In college," I said. "I had roommates."

"I mean, as a lover."

"Not yet," I said. "Hasn't come up."

"This is going to sound weird—maybe I shouldn't tell you— but I've been thinking about getting married. To a man, I mean. I mean, Lute's really great and all. In bed she's like, *strong*, like an animal. But Mike could really use a father figure." She combed a hand through her hair. Her nails were sharp as teeth. "Oh, never mind," she said then, licking her fingertips. "Marriage is so middle-class. Still, I wish I could have it both ways." She looked me in the eye. "Do I sound really awful?"

"You sound modern, that's all. Is there someone you want to marry?"

"Modern? Not really. I was just thinking. It must be this drug, it's so toxic. Seeps through your fingers, gets under your skin. Want to try some?"

"Sure," I said. Fine with me.

She scraped up some loose powder and rolled it in toilet paper balls to put under our tongues. She said it dissolved faster that way. Then she wanted to spike it with heroin.

I remember how I snubbed it at first. I had already tried all the other drugs, but heroin, I felt, was out of my control. I didn't want to be an addict.

Honey batted her eyes at this. "One line doesn't make you an *addict*."

She was right. One line did not make me an addict. But one line once a week for two years did. Especially one of Big Guy's, not once a week but a little every day. I still wasn't hooked. I only had a chip—the beginning of a habit not yet matured. If I stopped now, I could kick it. It wasn't too late.

So Honey came over and made coffee. She sat with me for hours. She instructed me to drink a brewer's-yeast concoction she said I needed to keep up my spirits. It tasted like chalk. "It'll be okay," she said. "You're not depressed. You're just strung out."

"I'm not strung out," I protested. "It's just a chip."

"You can kick it," she said.

"Yeah," I agreed. "I can kick it."

The next day I was back at work, where they plied me with drinks and kept me too busy to think. I didn't feel sick but I didn't feel happy. I worked and watched TV and went to sleep. I was waiting for the chip to pass. I knew it would. I knew it would. It was just a matter of time.

BELLE

On the afternoon I started feeling better, I happened to see my friend Belle. She was moving to a new loft in SoHo. I went over and she made the coffee. I wore the pinstriped suit.

"That's a good outfit," she said.

I bragged about its being a present. Who from? Kit's name produced a frown.

"Isn't she a junkie?" Belle asked me right off.

"I don't know," I said, deliberately vague. "I mean, I know she does drugs, but so does everyone."

"But I think she's a *real* junkie," Belle declared. "Not like us."

I never argued with Belle. She wouldn't have heard me if I tried. Her mind was never at rest, in one mood and out the other, like quicksilver, the color of her hair. It set her apart, like her voice, a precision instrument marred by a consumptive cough.

Belle took drugs for the sake of entertainment, which was also the approach she took to sex. Her specialty was gay male erotica; the idea of fist-fucking gave her a charge. "Come on," she'd say. "Let's go up to that googoomaplex, or whatever it's called, on Eighth Avenue. They're showing a film about slave-training." Belle could never remember the name of anything and insisted on calling porno flicks "films." She thought they were "artful." I went along, but I'd go anywhere. I shared her sense of adventure.

It was Belle who first put a needle in my arm—speed, back in those days, we skin-popped. Now she was close to forty and sharp as the bones in her cheeks. Sexy too, in an eccentric sort of way. Her mouth had a certain intelligence. She carried herself tall in very high heels and didn't wear underwear after dark. "One shouldn't disguise the crease in one's buttocks," she would say. Hers were round and firm.

"Nice place," I said, looking around the near-empty loft. Belle wasn't the type to surround herself with clutter. As a young girl she'd had two sons by different fathers, but only one boy lived with her and only part of the time. Even her clothes were spare, but she didn't need help from decor. Her smile alone could light up a room.

At Sticky's, Belle drew people to her side like a magnet, sometimes just so they could talk about her later. She never ordered anything but fried zucchini and a side of broccoli with lots of butter. "I don't eat flesh," she always said. She was thin. She had a hunger for living, though, especially for living on the edge. She carried three vials of cocaine in her purse, one to share in the bathroom, one to sell to pay for the first one. The third was a backup in case she lost the other two before she got home. Belle was a study.

She coughed and waved a hand as if to shoo me away. "I thought you liked Kit's band," I said. We had similar tastes in music.

"I do," she agreed. "But that's not the issue. We're speaking of her purpose. Why would someone you hardly know want to give you their best clothes?"

I tasted envy in the air. "I don't know," I said. "She's just a nice person. Really."

"I don't doubt it. But she's a junkie, too. I know how easy it is to get swept up . . . in that sort of thing . . ." Her voice trailed off, her eyes staring into the distance. They were brown and set wide apart, so deep I was afraid to look into them. At their bottom was one giant slice of grief.

"Coffee ready?" I chirped.

She drew herself up, suddenly impatient. "You must have some better idea why Kit's been this nice to you. She must want something."

"She just wants a friend. I think that life of hers has her a little isolated."

"I don't think that's all she wants," Belle muttered.

"Don't *worry*," I said. I felt like I was talking to my mother. My mother resisted everything I ever did. We were never confidantes. She died young.

"Well, be careful."

"I'm careful," I said. "One thing I've always been is careful." The minute I heard myself say it, I knew it was a lie.

BETTY

Kit liked my cooking. She and Betty started coming into Sticky's just as Big Guy sailed for a six-month hitch in the North Atlantic. They offered me a bag of dope.

"I kicked it," I said, wiping the blood from a steak off my cutting board.

"Really?" Kit replied dully. "I wish I could. With Betty around, it's impossible."

"Hey!" Betty cried. "That's not fair."

"Pick up!" I yelled at a waitress. Kit stepped back. Betty fell down. We set her on a step. Pedro, a slight fellow with a long French braid who worked the station next to mine, asked if we shouldn't do something. I told him to turn up the radio.

Betty came to—the station we had on was playing a Toast song. When it ended, the DJ announced a gig the band had scheduled for the following night at Roseland. Kit asked if I would come as their guest. I would, but I had to work. Sticky's never closed, not for Thanksgiving, not for Christmas, not for anything. Not even when the previous cook was D.O.A. after a grease-fire explosion in the kitchen. Repairs were going on while Sticky was at the funeral, which he paid for. That's when he hired me. He was open for business that night.

Pedro wasn't just my kitchenmate; he was also Mr. Leather's

companion. We were buddies. He volunteered to work in my place. "Go on," he said. "See the show." He didn't have to say it twice.

The old ballroom was jammed that night. Bodies in black leather draped along the chrome rails of the dance floor in haunting neon light, a bigger crowd in the middle, in the dark, dancing, jumping up and down. I found Betty by the stage, hovering near the dressing-room door. When the band went on, she kept yelling in my ear, "Doesn't Kit sound *great*? She's great tonight, isn't she?"

She was awesome. The sound washed over the hall in waves, electronic arpeggios sailing over sudden squawks and harmonic bleats. She could have been playing three guitars, not one.

"How does she get that sound?" I asked Betty.

"Effects boxes!" she yelled. "Special effects!" She was in motion.

The sound of hip-swaying, finger-popping funk alternated with percussive, foot-stomping rock. I worked my body into it, but I didn't want to dance with Betty and I didn't like dancing by myself. I stood still on the dance floor and let other bodies bump against me, propel me where they might.

I fell into a distant region of my mind, where I saw my mother in her hospital bed, watching a teen dance show on TV. During the last months of her illness, she tuned it in every Saturday afternoon. For her, this was peculiar—my mother had cultivated her ears for opera. Every now and then, when I was growing up, I'd find her standing by the radio listening to jazz, but she always hated pop.

"Is this how you dance?" she asked me one Saturday near the end.

My mother knew how much I liked dancing. As a child, I went to dance parties every week, begged for opportunities to throw my own. Dancing was my first addiction. When I was dancing, I never had to tell anyone I loved them and no one had to say those words to me. The body said it all. Every turn of the head, every shrug, every sway, every snap of the spine was a buzz, the vocabulary of desire in the flesh.

"I enjoy watching these kids," my mother said. "Someday I'd like to watch you."

"I'll dance for you," I said. "When you're not so ill and can join me."

She said, "I'm getting better every day."

I shook the memory off and elbowed my way toward the stage. A string of beer bottles sat on Kit's amp and between songs she took quick, jerky swigs from one or two of them. She wore shiny tight purple jeans and long striped scarves. Strands of black ribbon hung from her wrists. She played with her back to the audience, all you saw was her arms moving and her legs. That's all you needed to see. She had a great ass—everyone said so. It was part of her celebrity.

As the band finished their encore, Kit set her guitar against her amp and turned up the volume. A high-pitched wail pierced the air. My hair stood on end. Sylph waved and said, "Goodnight, New York! We're Toast!" and the signal from Kit's amp grew louder. I couldn't stand it and I didn't want it to end, but a roadie came onstage and turned it off. The stage went dark and the DJ put on a record. My ears were ringing. I loved it.

After the show, Kit and Betty came home to my place and didn't want to leave. "The roommates," they said. "Too obnoxious." Kit had two roommates besides Betty, a man and a woman, not a couple, always drunk and stoned, she said, nothing but a shouting match, all confusion.

We sat on my bed watching a late movie on TV. I told them they could sleep in Big Guy's bed in the other room but they somehow never left mine. I didn't want to do the bag of dope they offered, but they were so sweet. One bag, I thought. A street bag. What harm could it do? I was used to stronger stuff.

Next morning I wanted to kill myself. My whole body ached,

I could hardly bend my knees. I vomited for hours. "I'm sorry," Kit said. "I guess that wasn't a very nice gift." She still seemed to be high. Normal, I mean. Junkies don't get high. They get "straight." I wasn't, but I was no junkie. I didn't have a name for what I was. I didn't want one.

Later, on her way home from rehearsal, Kit stopped by my place again. She had another bindle of dope for me, if I wanted it. The name "Toilet" was rubber-stamped on the glassine bag. "This'll take the edge off," she said. I knew it would but I turned it down. She said she would save it. She stayed a few minutes more to talk about Betty, whom she didn't think she could live with any longer. They'd had another fight.

"You could ask her to leave," I said.

"I know. But she makes herself so useful."

"Maybe there are too many people living in your apartment," I said.

"Yeah," Kit nodded. "I know, but that's how I pay the rent. Usually, I sublet and move out. I've had that place for five years, but I've hardly lived there at all."

"You're making money now," I pointed out. "You don't need roommates."

"Well, these drugs get expensive," she said, her voice quiet. "I wish I could quit. Maybe if Betty moved out, I could."

"Maybe," I agreed.

"She'll never move."

"I've never known her to stay anyplace long."

Kit stared into space, scratching her ear with a few strands of hair. "Was Betty always this fucked up?"

"I hate to say it, but yes."

"You know," Kit told me, "she's really a nice kid, but she left home too soon. Her parents were always fighting. She ran away. I'd feel pretty bad if I kicked her out now."

"Are you lovers?"

She nodded slowly. "I think big women are really attractive," she said. "Betty was sort of a groupie, you know? Always hanging out at our rehearsal studio. My apartment was sublet and I was living with two people from my first band. All we had was a shower in the kitchen and I wanted a bath. Betty said I could use her place. It was right across the street. While I was in the tub she shot me up. You know the feeling. The warm water and that rush? It was the best thing I ever felt. Ever. Then she told me it wasn't her apartment we were in. She was just staying there. I told her she could come live at my place and we moved back in. What a mistake." Kit looked truly miserable. "What a mistake."

"I don't know what to tell you."

"She'll never move. I know she won't."

"Well," I said, before I thought it through, "if you want to stay over here some night, it's all right with me."

"You really wouldn't mind?"

"Not at all. I've been kind of lonesome lately, to tell you the truth."

"All right if I stay tonight?"

"I work till three," I said.

"I'll pick you up at the restaurant," she said. "Will you make me dinner?"

"Anytime," I laughed. There were worse things I could do than feed people.

She woke me at seven the next morning. Her pupils were unnaturally large, her hands shook. Her skin was clammy, the color of the sky before a snow. Immediately she was on the phone to Betty, ordering a couple of bags of D. At seven-forty-five the girl was back from the street, putting a needle in Kit's waiting arm. I felt sick, too, but for a different reason. The long red tracks on Kit's arm, the degree of her sickness, the girl's willing servitude—all of it turned me off.

Betty had to go to her job in the photo lab. When she came

into the kitchen, she looked so hurt and angry, I felt ashamed. "Nothing happened," I told her. "Really."

Betty tossed her head toward the bedroom. "Then why is she here?"

"I think she just wanted a break."

"You know," Betty started in, her whine rising to a full-moon pitch, "I was really *glad* that you and Kit were getting to be friends. I was *really* glad. I always thought you were one of the *best* people around. Now I'm not so sure."

"Chill out, Betty," Kit called from the bedroom. She still had the needle in her arm.

"I'll see you later!" Betty yelled, and stormed out the door.

I pulled aside the curtain leading to the bedroom, a vintage 1950s palm print Big Guy had brought from Texas. "I feel bad," I said.

"So do I," Kit sighed. "But I'm not going back home with all of them there."

"If you're going to stay here," I told her, "I'm going to get you off this needle."

"I hope you can," Kit said. I remember she said that.

Before I knew it, Kit's clothes were hanging in my closet and her cats were fucking in my kitchen. So were we. That's where it happened—in the kitchen. In the tub.

I'd had a hard week on the job and was taking a long steamy soak. I must have been high. We were both feeling giddy. Kit was splashing me, then she was rubbing my neck. Before I knew it, she was in the water on top of me, and I was getting hot. It wasn't a very big tub.

Somehow, with all our splashing around, the plug in the drain came loose and let the water out, but we didn't get out of the tub. As Kit moved against me, she bumped a faucet and turned the water on. It poured out behind me. It was scalding. When I cried out, Kit thought it was from pleasure and kept on at me harder. By the time I got her off me, I'd been badly burned—my back, an elbow, a hand, completely scorched.

At the emergency room they gave me a burn cream and sent me home without anything for the pain. My skin grew hotter with every passing minute; it hurt like hell. There wasn't any way to get comfortable. Kit handed me a hairbrush.

"What's this for?" I said.

"Spank me," she said. "I've been bad."

"I can't do that!" I said, appalled. "It was an accident."

"Go ahead, spank me," she said again. "It turns me on."

You never know what a person's really like until you've showered together, I thought. It's even more binding than sex. I took the brush in my good hand while Kit dropped her jeans. I felt ridiculous doing it, but I spanked her. After a moment, the pain in my burned arm seemed to subside. "You really like this?" I said.

"It must have meant something to me when I was little," she said. "Right now, I don't care."

I laughed. Looking at Kit's body was like seeing my own, same narrow hips, same champagne-glass breasts, same sex, except she was blond and I was dark. It was easy to get familiar.

"I love you," she whispered.

"You hurt me," I said.

"Same thing," she retorted. We've hardly been separated since.

THE DAWN

In the weeks that followed, the hairbrush took up residence in the bedroom. Whenever Betty called to ask when Kit was coming home, Kit explained she had to stick around to "nurse" me. Betty's calls were troublesome, but we put them out of mind.

We had sex every day and went shopping. I brought Kit to clothing stores on Prince Street and she took me to guitar shops on Forty-eighth. It was exhilarating, having a woman friend who wasn't a rival, who didn't compete. A new world opened up, a world of music and art, a universe of private delight, whose orbit inevitably converged on Sticky's.

To make me presentable for work, Kit ripped up one of her scarves and tied a remnant around my wrist to hide the bandages. It was a junkie's fashion ploy. Many addicts wear wrist bands to hide their tracks, but mine were Kit's stagewear. At Sticky's, they did me proud.

She also brought me a daily bag of dope, dope Betty thought she had bought for Kit, with whom she was certain she would soon be reunited. I knew she was hurting while I had no pain, but standing in front of a 500-degree broiler for eight hours was no picnic, even without an injury. If it wasn't for that heroin in my blood, I wouldn't have been able to work. No work, no pay. No painkiller.

As the days went by, the burn on my arm became infected. I didn't go back to the doctor, though; doctors don't know shit. I went up to two bags a day. Six months later, Betty and her roommates were gone and my old needle habit was back. So was Big Guy. It was May 1981.

I moved in here. This is two three-room apartments put together, really, a shower in the kitchen, toilet in a narrow water closet that once opened onto the outside hall. The walls have been knocked out in one half of the place, to make one large room and three smaller ones, not counting the kitchen, windows in every room. The largest room, the living room, is where I sleep. The corner window overlooks Sixth Avenue and down a side street to a piece of the Hudson River. The Hoboken waterfront lies beyond, the World Trade Center towers to the south. The small bedroom next to the toilet we use as a walk-in closet. It has the same view. The little room I call the office, next to the kitchen on the other side of the hall, has a window on an air shaft, a desk and two chairs, a side table under a clothes rack, and bookshelves up two of the walls. The room behind the kitchen is Kit's. When I first came here, I slept in there too.

That was the dawn of my addiction; Kit was twenty-six and I was thirty-two. I gave up on my life and decided hers was the more important—she was the one with the budding career. In restaurant parlance, I was the back-of-the-house person, she was the front.

Kitchen work had given me pop-up veins in a couple of places on my arms, and Kit took pleasure in poking them with a spike— a syringe. I hated watching the blood, my blood, surge back into the chamber—it scared me—but the rush that came with the boot of the plunger was another story entirely.

ALL DRUGS ARE POISON

Dick again, day two. Can he really have nothing better to do than sit here and watch me kick? He's actually getting paid for this. I'm glad I didn't pay taxes.

My father called around the middle of the day. Now I know where he is—in a hospital. He needs an operation, a triple bypass. What did he want from me? Same thing he's always wanted: me. I can't worry about him right now, I have Kit. I have Dick, for God's sake. I have shit.

Still, I do worry. He's my father, after all. What would happen if I had to tell him about the bust? At least Dick already knows. In some respects he reminds me of my dad. Revolting.

Dick wasn't around for Dad's phone call, thank God. He was out for lunch. The agents downstairs got him a sandwich and they all ate together in the car. I could see them by going up on the roof; they were parked across the street. It's weird, the way they leave me alone. How soon will they take me away? Let them eat, I don't care. I hope they eat a lot. As long as I don't have to cook.

Dick was after me to talk about my drug connections. That's all he wanted to know—how a nice girl like me got mixed up in a dirty business like this.

It doesn't matter how I started on heroin. What matters is

why I stayed. The answer to that is sex. Heroin made sex more exciting. No, exciting is too dull a word—this drug is not for the faint of heart. Once you've done it, there's no such thing as going too far. Heroin is a trip, an adventure in desire. When it smiles at you, you can't refuse it. I couldn't. I didn't. I don't. I have a large capacity for desire. Too large. Only heroin cut it down to size.

When I moved in with Kit, I no longer cared what the world found socially acceptable. Two girls together? Of course. Could we have sex standing up? Fine with me: heat rises—where's the fire? There was hardly a moment that didn't get us wet. Could she turn me on my head and prop me on a wall? I was down with it. Squat with my hands in restraints? I'd play.

It was the physical thing that hooked me. I wasn't looking for God. I thought I'd seen enough. But the prospect of a life of pure sensation—that, I liked. Heroin was another way to see the world, from the other side of the glass, another way to free it. It's a world you don't have to enter; it enters you. It makes you feel sexy—good for something. But this life isn't about feeling good; it's about feeling better. However good or bad you feel, heroin makes you feel better. It's a short leap from there to feeling nothing at all. For that you pay a price. Not five hundred dollars a gram—that's just money. For heroin, you pay with your life.

All drugs are poisons, my dad used to say. A necessary evil, he called them. He was talking about medicines. In his youth he had been a pharmacist's apprentice and then, after the war, a drug salesman—like father, like daughter, ho ho.

Dad pushed pharmaceuticals, eye, ear, nose, and throat. I grew up on a cough syrup made of two ingredients, codeine and alcohol—my first cocktail and still my favorite. Dad didn't know that, of course. When there's a poison in the body, he said, your best weapon is a stronger poison. The trick is to kill the intruder without killing yourself. I have yet to get the hang of it.

PART TWO

HEROIN HONEYMOON

HEROIN HONEYMOON

May 1981.

"I've been watching you sleep," I hear Kit say. It's my first week in residence at her apartment. "I like watching you sleep," she says. "You've been dreaming."

I don't believe it. "I never dream," I say.

Kit's kneeling on the floor beside me with a bent spoon and cotton, preparing a syringe. "You're on your heroin honeymoon," she tells me. "You sleep with that heroin honeymoon smile. You don't wake up sick, like me." She holds out a hand mirror lying by the bed. "Take a look and see."

I sit up and take the mirror from her hand. I don't look.

"You went out and copped already?" I ask. I've been dead to the world. I can smell the coffee.

"I had to," she says. "Rehearsal's in an hour."

"How is it?" I nod toward the spoon. Sun fills the room. I feel pale.

"Put out your arm."

I pump it. She ties me off with one of her scarves. "You have such good veins," she says. "I used to have veins like yours."

"Don't give me too much," I say. "I'm not ready."

Her eyes graze my arm, her voice is gentle. "It's only one bag, don't worry."

I hear music coming from the living room, it's jarring. "I don't like loud music so early in the morning," I say.

"I do," Kit retorts. "Anyway, it isn't morning." She holds a lighter under the spoon, dissolves the dope in the water. This is tricky. If the water boils, she's lost it.

"What *is* that you're playing?" I ask. Don't know why I'm so irritable. "Can't we listen to your music, at least? This is dreadful."

"This," she says quietly, "is a tape of yesterday's rehearsal."

I'm still nervous about the needle. I don't know how to inject myself. I don't want to know. I like the way Kit does it. I like her touch. My eyes lock onto her hands as she draws the liquid into the barrel of the syringe, taps out the air. Here it comes. I don't want to watch but can't help it.

"There's that smile again," she says after a moment. I look in the mirror. There it is, right on my face, a smile of saintly serenity. It's odd to see—I never smile. I've been pissed off about something or other all my life. Now I look like a dark Ophelia floating in her pale river of dreams, all my worries over, love sealed in my heart at last.

I lie back on the pillows and take in the sun. The bedroom windows at the rear avail a view to the east, a maze of rooftop water towers wide as the horizon in the sky. I'm in heaven. My legs curl under me. I'm warm, my skin tingles. I listen to my heart beat. It's slow and easy. I don't move but I can see myself dancing. My mind races. I'm excited. The music—I wonder if I did the right thing, giving up Big Guy's apartment. Well, it wasn't mine to keep. Isn't it better not to pay two rents? After all, we're a couple now, Kit and I, aren't we a couple? High time I tried something new. New life, new kind of sex, new apartment. This place is big, filled with light. The cats are happier here, too. One of them is pregnant. I've cleaned the house, everything neat and tidy, but there's one thing I missed: Betty's presence. It's here. I can smell it. I can feel her eyes at my back. Then, in my mind, I see a grave. It's covered in weeds and sits near a road down a slope beside a bridge. I kneel at the grave, pull at the weeds. I hear a voice say my name. It's my mother's. Then my mind empties, and everything is different.

It's not easy to describe this euphoria—a sublime nausea, a flushed meeting of mortal and immaterial all at once, a leap beyond fate, a divine embrace. Heroin gives the impression you've gained a level of self-knowledge closed to other pursuits, and the moment you recognize the place where you stand, it blots you out as if you'd never existed. Nothing in the world can hurt you then. Nothing can touch you. And nothing can satisfy your hunger for more: more love, more pain, more sex, more excitement. More *more*.

Everything happens, if you let it, sooner or later, all the things you've left undone come back to claim you. I feel safe here. Heroin doesn't rattle any skeletons. It's sweet. It can't get any sweeter than this. Everything is as I remember it, as I want it, as I need. I own it, the great, the pure, the impossible. All mine.

"Which dope is this?" I ask. I sound far away.

"Something new," Kit says. "Black Mark," she reads from the stamp on the glassine paper. "I'll walk you over there later."

She lies down beside me, her face pressed to mine, my lizard, my lover, my waking dream. Isn't this love? It must be.

COPPING

With Betty out of the picture and no one else to run, Kit has to go out on the Lower East Side to cop drugs for herself. "Come with me," she says, pulling on her boots. They're black velvet suede, cut low, pointy-toe—very King's Road, London.

I'm not interested in buying from the street. Too risky. And the stuff itself is dirty—cut with quinine and strychnine and God knows what else. It's the color of wet sand. White dope is much more refined, closer to pure. Like me.

"You're such a snob," Kit teases.

"You think I'll put any old shit in this body?" I challenge her. I don't eat processed food, or animal fat, either. I like feeling lean.

"Come on," she pleads. "I don't like going out there alone."

What the hell, I think. The exercise will do me good. Muscles gather strength with repetition; so does mettle. I have to sharpen my wits—it's New York. A flabby spirit never cut it around here. My mother grew up in a Second Avenue tenement; my father was born on Avenue D. I'm just going back to my roots.

From SoHo, it's a twenty-minute walk across town, maybe thirty, every day to a different spot. The Lower East Side's made a comeback. It even has a new name: Alphabet City. It's no less wretched than when it was the Lower East Side, just more colorful and illicit. Away from the splendor of upper Fifth Avenue, re-moved from the bright lights, the tawdry novelties, human or otherwise, for sale in Times Square, it visibly sags under the weight of housing too many different kinds of people with too many different ideas of fun: immigrants, bikers, poets, punks, self-appointed priests, a decrepit bohemia buzzing with capitalist cheer.

Big-time Latino drug entrepreneurs have built a model cor-porate structure in the body of the condemned. Every day new drug "stalls" sprout from the walls of abandoned buildings and the grasses of rubble-strewn lots. An incredible din fills the air: blaring sirens, running feet, lookouts shouting *Bajando!* (the Man), or *Todo bien!* (all clear). Hawkers stand on corners calling out the brand names of "houses" they represent: Poison, 57 Mag-num, Colt 45, Toilet, Star, President, Executive. It's big. To a tourist, it must look like a casbah from hell.

Even at eight a.m. the streets are crawling. Avenue B reminds me of a drag strip; transactions are a blur. By midafternoon, it's a swarm, bodies slinking in and out of guarded doorways, diving through holes punched in concrete walls, wiggling into gaps in the sidewalk deep as wells, shooting up in empty lots, nodding on the hulks of abandoned cars. Everyone's slumming. Everyone, from the unwashed to the unwed to the unbelievably rich. They're not residents. These streets are home only to the cun-ning.

"It's the new Gold Rush," I observe as we go. These derelict buildings with their broken windows and missing floors, these dank peeling shells with their dimly lit corridors to oblivion, these are our mines. "We're not breaking laws," I say. "We're working the *mines*."

Kit gives me a look. "Try and tell that to the judge."

We know the cops can't haul everyone in, but at random moments they load a hundred people in buses, take their drugs, book them, embarrass them, and let them go. When the police can't handle it, the politicians campaign to tear the buildings down. Most of them are owned by the city. Some days we have to dodge bulldozers as often as we do the law.

Cops aren't the only hazard. If some desperado wants our stuff, he'll get it. Around here they pull the rings right off your fingers—with their teeth, if they have to—if your money's not good enough. If the thieves don't get you, the beat artists will—sellers who tap out a hit for themselves and sell you a bag filled with sugar or baby powder, or worse. Then there are the undercovers. Every now and then a pair of them will pull you aside and snap on the handcuffs. If one of them wants a kick, he'll trade your freedom for a suck-off in his car. If a cop doesn't do it, one of the *flacos* will. A *flaco* is a cop-man, it's what the dealers call themselves. They all have the same name, they do the same things. They take you.

It's all a stupid game run by creeps and fueled by assholes, but we accept it. The danger is part of the draw. Life isn't easy, not for anyone. Heroin is a finger up its nose. It's got a life of its own and that life is ours, we don't have to plan or think it out. There lies the beauty: I'm done with thinking. All it ever did was make me cry.

Kit is my guide on these daily excursions across town. Our safety depends on our sticking together, and we're together most of the time, copping, getting high, going home to fool around. If sex is the main attraction in our friendship, heroin is the glue. Then food.

One night I bring home a box of overripe strawberries and slip a few inside her while we're in bed. "Here's fresh fruit for dessert," I say, giggling. "You can make the cream." Usually, all I do with Kit is laugh. Not this time.

"I don't like dirty talk," she says, her face white. "It makes me feel weird." I shrug and eat the berries. It's the only disagreement we've had.

Over the summer, our routine falls into a certain rhythm. We hear it from boom boxes at every step. "Everything's rap now," Kit says one afternoon. We're sitting in bed eating ice cream. "My band better write one or we'll never get a record contract."

I pull out a notebook and hand her a pen. "They're simple rhymes," I say. "We can write one."

"I'm no writer."

"I'll start," I say, and it comes: *I don't want to stand in line, I don't need to waste my time. Six flights up and no way down, so many creeps for just one town.*

"Your turn," I say, and Kit writes:

I watch TV from nine to noon, waiting for miracles that don't exist. Up so high, lay down in bed. One day I'm gonna wake up dead.

"That's awful," I say.

Kit likes it.

Back out we go to hunt for the dope du jour, the bigger bags, the better high. The dealers keep moving, like so many country doctors crisscrossing the fields to treat their neighbors. The police bust them out of business all the time, and then they turn up a day or so later in a new location, often in close proximity to the last, sometimes in the same place. One day we get over to a spot on Rivington in time to see a police bulldozer ram the front door of the building. Next day, business is brisk as before—there's even a hot-dog stand parked in front. We keep walking.

We walk past broken stoops, sealed doorways, and gaunt savages, looking to buy works—syringes. "Blue tips," we call them, like the matches from Ohio. Works, kits, points, rigs, gimmicks, spikes—they're a long way from the eyedroppers junkies used in the 1950s. Those were bebop; this is no jive, just more disposable. Except everyone uses them again and again, till they're too dull to pop the skin.

Kit shows me how to sharpen our points on the side of a matchbox. We rinse them out with bleach. You can never be too careful. A man with one arm has sealed works for sale in the parking lot of an abandoned gas station on Avenue B, but he's only there at night. Days, we stop into a bodega on Forsythe, where they sell cheap, under-the-counter wine to Bowery bums and clean blue-tips to dopers like us. Here, they cost only a dollar apiece. At most other spots, they're two.

We carry our money rolled up in our sleeves, pockets empty, walk close together at a steady pace, and watch all the faces that pass. I learn to differentiate the junkies from the users. Here's the difference: users travel in packs; junkies are always alone.

Big Guy calls. He's back, and what's-her-name—Spider's—source has gone dry. Are we going out to cop today, and can I get a couple of bags for him? He'll buy one for me, he'll be glad to.

Sure, I say. We'll be out there. A couple of other friends want something too, so yeah, I'll go. No problem.

"I don't know how y'all get away with it," he says. "Goin' over there. Just the *idea* gives me the shakes."

"I don't know," I say. "I guess someone out there likes me."

"It must be true," he says, and I agree. It must be.

The real truth is, I no longer stand out among the living ghosts in the streets. I like the look; it makes me interesting. I'm not the same person I was, and that's the way I want it. Some days, though, it's too much work—days we feel sick, days it rains, days when our money is low. Those are days to drink methadone.

Methadone is legal, but only to those in a state-run program. It's supposed to help you kick, but your body doesn't know that. Kicking methadone is harder than heroin. There's only one difference between the two drugs: methadone you can't shoot up. If you do, they say, the sediment will clog your veins and kill you. If it doesn't, you just want to throw yourself under a train.

Kit has a private methadone connection, a white woman over on Tenth Street, across from the Russian Baths. She's got a black jazzman husband and two schoolage kids. Every time we go there, she's folding laundry or moving furniture. The apartment's small. She sells the juice in two sizes: forty and eighty milligrams, twenty bucks for one, forty for the other. We figure her husband works in one of the clinics. He doesn't seem to buy from junkies in the program. They're supposed to drink the stuff on the spot and return for a refill each day, but many hold it in their mouths and spit it back in their bottles once they get outside.

Our connection insists her juice is clean, no spit. It tastes so horrible I wouldn't know the difference. Kit thinks the husband is really getting the "biscuits," the orange meth tablets the clinics break up and dissolve in water or Tang. Kit would rather have the biscuits—easier to take on the road—but the woman says it's juice or nothing. Her skin is the color of bone dust. With sharper teeth, she'd make a perfect vampire. Kit says it's the effect of long-term meth use. It sucks your blood, rots your bones. "Shit," I say. Shopping here may be safer than on the street, but the street, at least, has a life.

As the weather heats up, so does the market. The police pressure, too. Nearly every day we get locked inside buildings while the cops pass by outside. Same thing happens while the sellers re-up—resupply the house. When traffic is thick, the houses sell out faster than the baggers can put bundles together and quicker than the runners can trade on the money, some say upward of eighty thousand dollars a day.

That's all anyone talks about on the drug lines—money and drugs. Sometimes sex or weather, but it always comes back to drugs: what brands are "on the money," where else to cop. Sex, drugs, money—it's all the same. It's got the same look and it's got the same hook, same same. We see it in telephone operators, Con Ed repairmen, shop owners, cabbies, and clerks. We see it in people who look like us, white middle-class users for whom copping is simply hip, avant-garde behavior; in hookers from Third Avenue, some of them women we used to know; and in no small number of drag queens, out of drag. Down here they don't look too fabulous. Midday, it's the lawyers and traders from Wall Street, out to lunch. Their partners have no idea, their wives and husbands can't find them, their bosses are oblivious. We're out there for the world to see but nobody knows what we're up to. That's what everyone thinks—that no one can tell. I know they can't see it in me. Rico's always saying how amazing it is I can "pass."

I'm careful how I look. Kit says it's better not to appear too prosperous, but I put on my makeup and clean clothes and walk the streets as if I own them. God knows I'm spending enough money on them. No one bothers us. Oh, occasionally some jerk will yell at us, "Yo! Punk rock!" It's better than "Fucking dikes!"

"You'd think women weren't allowed to be friends," I say.

"Do I look really dikey?" Kit asks.

"No way," I say. "You're a star."

She says, "You look good to me, too."

We laugh together but we don't hold hands, not on Avenue D. Not anywhere. Too tacky.

By the middle of summer, the junkie grapevine has been usurped by working journalists. Every night on the news and every week on the front page of the *Times* there are detailed reports on the activity of the East Village drug trade. It's as if the neighborhood had its own Dow Jones. They give the locations and the brand names and the best hours of the day to make the best buys. They cover the police activity, too.

It bothers me to see the name Executive—my brand of choice—emblazoned on the front page of the paper. Executive is white dope. Now everyone will go there. The wait-lines are already excessively long.

At the stairs, a bouncer asks to see our tracks. This guy always gives me grief. I don't have tracks, only a few pricks in the crook of my arm, no larger than a bug bite. Kit rolls up her sleeves: she has scars from her knuckles to her elbows, and because I'm with her they let me in. Another creep stands at the "window," the mail-type slot they've cut in the wall of a locked apartment on an upper floor, telling everyone to have their money ready. You put your money through the slot, and a minute later, out comes your stuff. You never see the guy inside. You don't get to check the bags to see if they're beat and you don't read that in the *Times*. Reporters never get this far. Not unless they're junkies.

One very hot day we're locked in at Executive two hours. "They must be re-upping," says Kit, when we hear the all-clear and the line doesn't move an inch. Suddenly, we see Lucky, Sticky's house manager, races down the stairs and heads for the door.

"This is too much for me, man," he gasps. "I can't take it." He's heard about a new place on Tenth Street and B called Lareda. He'll see me at work. But in the middle of my shift, it's Rico who runs in the kitchen, his eyes wild, snot running from his nose in glistening green strands. I don't have to ask what the trouble is. I've seen this happen before.

"You busy?" he says, checking the orders clothes-pinned to the line in front of me, switching his bony hips from side to side, wiping the sweat from his brow. He's agitated.

"Yeah," I say. "Steady rush all night." I cut a finger slicing a steak for a sandwich but it's Rico's appearance making me ill. "Wipe your nose, man, will you? Pick up, damn it!" I yell at a waitress.

"Pipe down," she says—one of my favorites, Tina. "This table's too drunk to remember how to eat."

"What about Kit?" Rico mutters, giving Tina the once-over. "She home?"

"No," I say, wrapping my hand in a dish towel. "She's playing a gig in New Jersey."

"I need you to go out there for me," he says, nodding toward the Lower East Side. "Take a cab. Go quick."

"I gotta finish these orders."

"Don't make me crazy," he says. "Finish what you're doing, then go. Quick."

I give Pedro the nod, lay a red snapper on a plate, turn some steaks, pop a French fry in my mouth, and duck out to run over to the spot on Tenth and B. It hasn't yet made the news. I leave the cab at Avenue A and walk along the park, where I can watch the action in front of me. I see a renovated, fully occupied residence at the corner. A yellow-skinned guy with close-cropped hair is standing on a landing in front of it, wearing a sneer. At my approach, he gives a signal and disappears inside the glass-enclosed vestibule behind him. "Yeah?" he says, as I follow. "What's up?"

I hand him forty dollars, he goes inside. "Wait here," he barks. A minute later he's back with four bags folded into tiny rectangles of lined yellow legal-pad paper. No glassines here. I like that. Not so sleazy. In the park, I sit on a bench under a tree and undo one of the papers. I cup it to my face and take a snort. Baking soda!

I race over to Executive, blood dripping from my nose. I still have money for a deuce. On my way out, the door to a shooting gallery under the first-floor stairs swings open and I look inside. It's a dirty cubicle of a room with a ratty mattress on the floor and a bunch of hard-assed junkies with spikes in their arms, their legs, their necks, their cocks. It's sickening.

When I get home that night, Kit tells me she's had an awful gig. Gloria, the bass player, showed up only minutes before show-time, so high she could barely play. She'd been arrested, copping on Eighth Street. Kit's disgusted. I show her my folds of yellow paper. "You went *there?*" she says. "Alone?"

NOT THE USUAL THING

As the seasons change, Kit gets sick. It's not the usual thing. Do I know a doctor? Kit wants a doctor. Doctors have pills. I call my friend Paul who used to be a resident at the local hospital. "Doctor Paul," I say, one professional to another. "Kit has hepatitis." I know what it is. I've had it.

He wants to see for himself. We go to his office. I'm right, it's hepatitis. Paul tells Kit she has to get off the needle. He knows better than to suggest she get off the drugs. The medical profession has the highest incidence of drug addiction of any in the country. But the needle has to go, he makes it clear. Gay cancer has been identified as AIDS and junkies are at risk. Kit is slow to give in. To her, snorting drugs isn't even getting high. She'll listen to Paul, though. He's got stories.

"I'll never forget the night an ambulance brought a woman to the E.R. complaining of severe pain in her uterus," he says. "She'd been masturbating with a light bulb—the three-way kind, you know, the large size? She tried to pull it out but it wouldn't budge. Too slippery, she said. She tried applying pressure through abdominal contractions—still no go. She contorted herself into all kinds of crazy positions to get it out, but just as she got a firm hold on it, the bulb exploded inside her. She was bleeding quite a lot."

"That sounds really bad," says Kit. "I don't know why I'm laughing."

Paul smiles. "You wouldn't believe some of the things we see. The things we do. That was nothing."

"Tell us."

"Well," he answers slowly, "I probably shouldn't, but I've got to tell someone. Did you know that old cook at Sticky's—Mr. Blue?"

"I remember him," I say. "Died in the kitchen fire. Very sad. Everyone liked him."

"It wasn't the fire that killed him."

Kit sits forward. She nudges my foot. It's pointing toward a counter behind Paul, where I see an open box of syringes. The label says it's a gross.

"The paramedics," Doctor Paul continues. "They made an error. A serious error. They inserted a catheter in the wrong pipe. Blue wasn't burned, he choked to death."

I can't believe this.

Paul's shaking his head. "No reason that man had to die. We tried to tell the family. I tried. The hospital hushed it up. I thought the family would sue, but all they wanted was to bury him and let it rest. I felt so bad, I went to the funeral. They were a very religious family. They said it must have been God's will."

"God's will."

"That is totally fucked up," Kit says. "It makes me wonder about my brother."

Kit's older brother had died of cancer in San Francisco a few years before. He was barely thirty. She was with him at the time. Afterward, she collapsed. The family doctor prescribed Valium. By the time she came back to New York, she was hooked. She takes Valium every day now, I don't know how many. She's not as open about it as she is about the dope.

"Most cases aren't this bad," Paul explains. "Believe it or not, we've got the best E.R. in the city."

I clear my throat. "Now you know why we prescribe our own drugs—you have to be stoned just to go there."

"I take them now and then, to relax me," Paul admits.

"Gee, I take them every day and I'm a wreck."

"But you're an addict."

It shocks me to hear him say it. No one's ever said that before.

Hepatitis is supposed to lay you up, but Kit spends most of her convalescence on the road with her band. Several times I have to send her drugs in the mail. They go overnight express in cassette boxes to various clubs and motels in the west, wherever she happens to be. When she gets home, the hep is gone. "It wasn't so bad," she says. "Nothing to it."

"Heroin cures everything," I say. "It's the only known cure for the common cold. You don't hear much about it from doctors, because it would put them out of business. All you hear is how addictive it is."

"Yeah, well I don't care. It's cheap enough—ten dollars a day to keep you feeling good. People spend more than that on candy and toothpaste."

"We're spending a lot more than ten dollars a day."

"Well, we don't have to buy food."

"What would you do if I didn't work in a restaurant?"

She looks at me calmly. "I'd deal."

DEAD OF WINTER

The kitchen at Sticky's, February 1982. Dead of winter. One of the guys who hangs out with the bosses, Marty his name is, approaches me. His blue eyes seem sad, maybe scared. I've been warned away from him by wait-staff gossip, which I always take for fact.

Marty's supposed to have done time on a drug charge. Some say he was a rat in jail, gave up his pals and got out. Others claim he made parole early. I don't know, he's never revealed anything of himself to me. Our longest conversation was, "Hi. How are you?" But Marty's a handsome guy, the kind who knows it and likes to show it. A preppy ladies'-man type: white smile, long legs, nice chest. Waspy nose. He draws me aside, away from the line, pushing his hands in the pockets of his jeans.

"Listen," he says. There's a wince in his voice, a nasal baritone. "D'you think you could go over the East Side and cop a couple of bags for me?"

I look at the time: two a.m.

"I can't go over there," he explains, his cheeks going red. "I'm too shaky." He stutters a little. Marty's a cokehead, he's been blowing coke. He has to bring himself down. Like, *now*. "I'll buy you a bag and pay your cab," he offers.

It's freezing outside, plenty of ice on the street. Do I want to go over to the Lower East Side in the bitter cold to buy drugs for a guy who has no other interest in me? I pretend to think about it but I know I'm on my way. He looks so helpless, it makes me soft.

I tell Marty he'll have to buy me a bag for each one of his. I'm thinking about Kit. I can hear her voice in my head, complaining that I would cop for a guy like Marty and not get something for her. He hands me forty bucks for the dope, ten more for the cab. I have to close the kitchen first. He retreats to the office.

Rico comes out a minute later. I haven't been seeing much of him—his wife has adopted a baby. Some nights he actually stays home. He walks behind the line and casually nuzzles my shoulder, like old times. I hope he's not going to start telling me how he was a bag man for the C.I.A. chief in Cambodia. I've heard that one. It's his favorite bedtime story, how they were running dope to disperse opium lords in the Golden Triangle who were selling scag to American soldiers. I look around. Maybe he can tell it to someone else. But these cold nights don't bring in much work and most of my crew has gone home. The rest mind their business, as usual.

"Hey, you goin' over there?"

"Yeah," I say. "I must be crazy, but yeah."

"You mind getting a little something for me?" He'll turn me on to some coke for the favor. Okay okay. I'm going.

A little before three, my coat thrown over three sweaters and a fur-lined cap pulled over my eyes, I go out and hail a cab. The air sparkles in the cold, the park looks barren, the streets are deserted. Even the homeless have gone inside. My cab's all that moves for many blocks. I give a vague destination. I don't know exactly where to go, what's open this time of night. I decide to try Executive, even though I've heard it's been busted.

The cabbie drops me a block and a half away and I walk fast

toward Avenue D. On the far end of the street, I spy a lookout standing in front of the steps. The police have nailed a metal sheet over the door to the building, but the sellers have cut away the bottom half of the metal. "Watch your head," the lookout says. He's friendlier than usual. I duck under the sheet and find myself standing in a pitch-black hall. In the distance, I hear the shuffle of feet. As I edge toward the stairs, I see the light of a burning candle. A worker is standing there warming his hands over the flame. "Tracks?" he says.

"You gotta be kidding!" I'm not about to peel off any clothes—I want to cop and get out of there. "Straight on up," the guy answers, breaking into a laugh. "Shit's good tonight, all right! G'wan up."

There's another guy on the landing, blowing his breath in his hands and jittering. No waiting line—that's a relief. I pull out Marty and Rico's money with twenty of my own and hand it to the seller. He passes the money through the hole. While I wait, I'm thinking, For another twenty dollars I could buy a bundle, ten bags. Nobody messes with bundles.

Eight glassines emerge from the hole. I stuff them in my sleeve and hustle down the stairs, hugging the wall. When I get to where I think the door is, I lunge. Something hits me hard, knocks the hat off my head. I get ready to fight but I think I'm blacking out. It's so dark, I can't see the metal sheet over the door and have forgotten it was there. I steady myself, pick up my hat. Then I flee.

Moving fast, sliding along the icy sidewalk, not stopping to look around, I hurry down three long, frosty blocks west, when I spot a cruising taxi. It must have dropped some other desperado nearby. I jump in the cab and go back to the store, deliver the goods, and run home.

It takes me several minutes to thaw. When I get off my hat, I see a lump forming over my eye—a mark of honor, perhaps, like the Red Badge of Courage.

"I can't believe you went over there this time of night," Kit says, taking her share from my hand. "How is it?"

"It hurts."

"I mean, the dope."

"Same as usual."

"Anyone out there?"

"Couple of guys. Maybe it's better going over there in the middle of the night. Safer. The workers are a lot nicer and there's no one in the street to give you the eye."

"I wouldn't do it too much."

"I don't really want to do it at all."

"People like getting drugs from you," Kit says. "Maybe we should buy larger quantities and sell some. It would save us money. I hate paying for this stuff all the time."

I know what she means.

"Dickie Howard knows someone who has China White."

"Who's Dickie Howard?" I turn on the TV. There's a movie ending. The sound-track music rises to a crescendo.

"One of Sylph's friends. You've met him—the Vietnam vet, the war poet. Maybe you should get to know him better."

"Maybe."

"We know enough people who like getting high. We could do it."

"I don't know . . ." I change the station—another movie about to end. "What've you been doing all night?" I ask.

"Waiting for you. Did you bring anything to eat?"

"I forgot. It's awfully cold in here." Still in my sweaters and jeans, I get into bed and pull up the covers.

"You didn't bring any food at all?"

"I brought the dope."

"I wish you wouldn't get into bed with those clothes on. You smell like garlic and oil."

I throw off my jeans and climb back under the quilts. "I like the smell of garlic."

Kit goes to the refrigerator, opens the door. "I wish there was something to eat," she says. "Can you go down to the store and get some chips? Maybe I'll make nachos."

"You're asking me to go out to that wasteland again?"

"Well, I'm not dressed."

"Neither am I!"

"You're half-dressed." She comes back in the bedroom and gives me a pleading look. "I'll cop for you tomorrow."

"I already copped for tomorrow."

"Next time, then. Come on. The dope'll keep you warm."

Before I know it, I'm back on the street again, copping tortilla chips and jack cheese at the all-night grocery around the corner. I don't know why I'm doing this, except I'm a little keyed up from the earlier run, and maybe Rico's coke. I might be hungry now, too. I never have time to eat at work, and cocaine always makes me want to chew.

Kit makes the nachos, and we sit in bed with the cats and talk about our future. We're a family now. When the sun comes in the window, we find ourselves watching an aerobic exercise program on TV and smoking. Kit gets a kick out of the chirpy blond instructor, who's not very graceful, considering.

STICKY'S

When Kit leaves for a tour of Europe, I work two weeks straight before I take a night off. I feel pathetic when the only place I can think of going is Sticky's. There isn't any other place. At his tables sit the great haircuts and shiny suits of the day, the bar filled with noisy chatter and bright ideas and everyone in it stoned. Everyone but Sticky. He never even takes a drink. Maybe a brandy, now and then, at last call.

I find him on his barstool, watching the door. He isn't surprised to see me. "Your friends are here," he says, grinning at a spot on the floor. He never looks at me directly. "And Rico wants to see you," he whispers, leaning past my ear. "In the back."

First, I scan the room. Honey Cook is holding down a center table. She's sitting with two other women, one in a flesh-baring dress. This is Magna. The other one's wearing a man's suit. That's Lute, Honey's girlfriend.

"Hi, Granny," I say. Lute's older than the rest of us, though not so anyone could tell. Not with those freckled blunt cheeks and sapphire eyes, that mop of yellow curls and puckering mouth. She has a body that seems to square itself at every turn. No wonder Honey likes her. Lute's dramatic.

" 'Bout time," she grunts. Her eyes flash. "Where you been, sweet thing? We thought you'd *never* get here!"

"We can't seem to get our drinks," Honey explains, as I take an empty chair. "Can you do anything, hon?"

"If you can, I'll buy the first round," Magna offers. Having a bar for a second home does come with certain advantages. A waitress is already at the table.

"We've been talking about Whit," Magna tells me. "I'm considering him as a possible boyfriend."

"Whit?"

"That's him over there by the bar." I crane my neck. It's three-deep in male agendas. None stand out. "I'm trying to imagine his mouth on mine," she says, "but somehow I just can't GET it."

"Child," Lute says. "You keep looking over there like that. You'll get it."

Magna likes the strangest guys, the runty ones with scars. No denying her own sex appeal. Unlike most of Sticky's clientele, she has the plump of genuine health. Her proportions are large and perfect, with more curves than a winding river. She's young, too. And rich. Her dark eyebrows appear to have been pasted on her porcelain complexion, each in a high, delicate arch. It's hard to pin down the color of her eyes. They change from blue to gray to green quicker than you can say "Fuck me." But it's Magna's mouth that really draws attention. It, too, looks appliquéd to her face, drawing up in a thin red line even when she isn't smiling. I can't help staring whenever I see her. I love a mask.

"I don't know," Magna says, burying her face in her hair, a peekaboo veil of golden brown falling to her chin. "All Whit ever talks about is what he DOES, but he never asks me anything about myself. Isn't that peculiar? I know he likes me."

I look to the bar again. "Those LIPS," she says. "Do you see them? I think they're GOOD."

"I see them," I say. "They're good."

"Kissing is so important. Don't YOU think so, Honey?"

"Absolutely," Honey hisses. She isn't angry. She has a lisp. "Cupid misses without good kisses."

That's our Honey, quick with a quip. Now she writes a personal interest column for a downtown weekly about the art world, and deals a little cocaine on the side. She can't afford to give up the dealing, but the column is the first job she's ever liked. If she's smart, she'll do for the crowd at Sticky's what the writers at the Algonquin Round Table did for their time—create a legend. If I know Honey, she'll be it.

We hear laughter behind us. It's Toni, Big Guy's transsexual friend. She's with Calvin Tutweiler. He's obsessed. Almost never appears in public without wearing Toni on his arm. When he's home he lives with Bobby D., a composer who sweats too much. Big Guy says their domestic life is pretty interesting, but I'm always working when they're receiving, so I don't really know what that means.

One of Cal's canvases is hanging opposite where we're sitting. He practices what our group, privately, likes to call "mineralism," because he works with the elements of Mother Earth—red clay and quartz and precious metals. This painting looks as if it's been plucked from a tomb in Byzantium and seems to be oxidizing before our eyes. It's so ugly it's actually interesting. To my eye, it's almost supernatural, but so is Cal; he's something of a mystic.

He takes a glance at the painting but keeps his attention turned to Toni, whom he calls his "demon princess." With her pale skin and platinum hair and his long legs and priestly clothes, they make quite the couple.

"You're all coming to Cal's opening, right?" Toni says with a deep-throated chuckle. "Saturday night?"

"Yeah," he agrees. "You should see my new paintings—I've been working in gold. They're really great."

"They're in a new *penthouse* gallery," Toni adds.

"Isn't that special?" he says.

She nods. "Too divine."

"Come, precious," he says. "Let's take a walk."

I'm glad when they don't try to sit with us.

"But they're fabulous," says Honey.

"Maybe," I hedge. "But a woman who's never had a period always makes me feel like a freak."

"Mercy!" says Lute, running a hand through her curls. "Can you cheer up? Take a pill or something?"

Honey seems nervous. "Another depression coming on, hon?"

"I'm not depressed and I like Toni fine. She's too beautiful, that's all. It isn't fair."

Magna downs her drink. "Maybe we should get some food."

Lute waves her arms in the air, her eyes rolling. "At this place? I cast no aspersions on your kitchen," she tells me, "but it's a pain in the butt to get waited on here."

"I don't care," Honey says. "I'm so hungry I could throw up."

Magna wouldn't mind another drink. "Maybe I'll walk over there," she declares, her eyes still on the bar. "I think that bartender's cute."

"Poor Whit," I say.

Magna's cheeks puff out. "I am NOT going home alone tonight," she pouts. "You can all understand that. A person should not have to live without the pleasures of the flesh—human beings were not meant to sleep alone." She gives me an intensely meaningful look. "Sex for one simply doesn't CUT it in my house."

"Maybe you didn't know, but I don't live alone."

"Where *is* Kit, anyhow?" Honey asks.

"On the road," I tell her. "Germany."

"Really?" she squeals. "I'm going too! To Berlin, to the film festival. I'm a judge. Does Kit know Udo? Of course she does, she must. Tell her she has to look him up. He's really great, if you're in Berlin, though he's kind of an asshole here. Anyway, he knows everyone—he's really fun. You should come with me, hon. Why don't you? Oh, come! We can stir up all kinds of trouble there."

Of this I have no doubt. "Excuse me," I say. Rico's signaling me from the kitchen. "Daddy wants to see his girl."

Lute gives me a poke in the side. "When are you going to make up your mind which sex you like?"

"I don't see why I have to," I object. "I like them all."

This is not my favorite topic.

Where I grew up, no one talked about sexual identities. More attention was paid to class. This was just north of Philadelphia, an all-American suburban town, a house and two cars and a pet for the children. You were middle-class white or blue-collar white, mostly Protestant. The Catholics went to their own schools, the Jews were the ones who took fashion seriously. I was one of these: a style queen. We were tolerated. There were a few black people in the area, but they lived in another township, on the other side of the tracks. The richer white people lived on the other side of another set of tracks, in large homes overlooking a riverbank. We were in between, not working-class but not professional, either. Truly middle—just where I hated to be.

Middle meant ordinary. Middle meant safe. I wanted excitement and excitement meant sex, but it was never a question of gender. If you were a boy, you were a boy, and if you were a girl, you were a girl, and that's all. There was no confusion over who wore the pants, who the lipstick. Boys had crewcuts or long greased-up hair and sideburns. Girls set their hair in rollers every night and lacquered it with hairspray. They shaved their legs and padded their bras, they made jokes about sanitary napkins. It was all in good fun. No one took drugs. No one mentioned them. We lived among dairy farms and monuments that commemorated the Revolutionary War. We drank beer and milkshakes. We were wholesome.

You had to be a good kid or you were bad. Good meant smart; bad was lower-class. Bad meant you got pregnant while you were still in school, you smoked in the bathroom and got drunk in the parking lot, and you had more style than the good kids, who would say you didn't know how to dress. If you were bad, you dressed for sex. That wasn't so bad in itself; what ticked people off was being obvious about it. It didn't make you more boy or girl, but it did make you more available. All you wanted was to be popular. And that's how it is in the world today; sometimes it seems we never got out of high school.

My school was just a stone's throw from the birth of the Bristol Stomp, but it bored me. Everyone wanted to get married. I only wanted to get out. Freedom lay on the other side of the world, in Paris, Rome, New York, San Francisco, or in the back seat of a car. We all had cars. It was important to stay mobile.

I drove to a summer job in another county, where I was an usher in a country playhouse. The actors all came from New York and they were always having sex, some of the men with other men, the others with girls like me. They showed me a world that separated me from the kids I knew at school. None of them had ever seen a queer. Older women had not propositioned them, and they didn't blow married men in small hotels. These kids had no idea what I was up to, and having a secret knowledge of the truth gave me a sense of entitlement. It was the same feeling I was soon to find in drugs. In the sixties, we called it enlightenment.

I watch Honey pick the ice out of her drink. She's femmier than I am, softer, loose. I'm all angles: pointy hair, bony hips and Peter Pan tits, sharp jaw, tense. I've always been bashful about my appearance. I ought to be grateful for the times we live in—androgyny's the height of fashion—but I hate getting caught in a trend. I didn't invent this look but I didn't go out and buy it, either. This is the way I was made.

I let myself in the office behind the kitchen. Rico's at his desk in front of a postal scale and two Ziploc bags fat with powder. One holds Peruvian cocaine; the other has the cut.

"Listen," he says, balancing the cocaine in the one bag with the mannitol in the other. "You know Dean? He's always in here. Dean, with the beard. You've seen him. He's coming over with some Downtown I thought you'd like."

In Rico's personal code, 'Downtown' means dope; 'Uptown' is coke. I guess he's been uptown all night. His right knee is bouncing off his chair like a proton lost in an atom smasher. He asks me to stick around.

"I'm around," I say. "Kit's out of town on tour."

He raises an eyebrow at this, scratches a lip. I know that look. I don't meet it. He hands me a straw and I help myself to a line off the scale. It whizzes through my brain like a bullet. "I don't know if I'm into anything tonight," I say. "It's my day off, you know. I'm tired."

"Have another hit," he says, scooping yet another powder into the mix.

"What's that?"

"You know," he says, pulling at the air for the word he wants. "Methedrine. Speed."

"You're cutting this coke with speed?"

"Yeah. It keeps you from getting a headache."

"Does it?" I ask. "I've never heard that."

"Sure, it does. Of course, you knew that. You're the one who told me."

"I'd like to taste the crystal," I say, reflecting. "I've already had the coke."

A smallish guy with sandy hair and a closely trimmed beard appears in the doorway. This is Dean. He clears a space next to me on the couch, which is spread all over with papers. The office is never too tidy. There isn't much room for hanging out, though that's all anyone does here, between two desks pushed against opposite walls, on either side of a safe.

After a few torpid pleasantries, Dean reaches in his pocket for an envelope. It's the dope. He draws a few lines on a mirror with a razor. We taste it. This stuff is so smooth and clean it's like not even doing a drug. I feel perfect. Maybe it's getting help from the coke, but this dope has a taste all its own. Nothing like it.

Dean says there's plenty where this came from. If I know anyone I can split it with, he can get me a gram. "How much?" I ask. It's six hundred dollars.

"It's worth it," Rico says. "You can step on it with an elephant and it'll still be better than what you get in the street."

"Why don't you buy it?" I say. He's the one with the six hundred. It's about two weeks' pay to me.

"I just invested in this shit," he says, snorting a big one. "No, really, I can't handle having quantities of Down. You can do it, though. You have some control. You can do it."

People like buying drugs from me, Kit said. I'll wait for her return. Then I'll see.

"Kit's away?" Rico asks, wrapping some coke in an old dinner check. "Oh, yeah. You said. So, what are you doing tonight? You don't want to stay here, do you? I'll be done soon. We can go to your place."

"I'll be outside," I say. Best thing to do now is humor him.

He's snapping his fingers, scratching his cheek, bouncing his knees. "Too bad Kit's out of town," he says, snapping away. He's crackling. "We could really get something going, the three of us, huh? Kit looks like the type who could, you know, party all night, you know what I mean? A cute ass like that has to know how to party."

"Right," I say. "I know." What must we look like to him? He's never said anything about Kit before. I know she would never have a threesome with him—men don't turn her on—and threesomes make me feel lonesome. In any case, she'll be home late tonight. I wink at Dean. By tomorrow, we'll be in business.

When I return to the table, the girls have been joined by a wan scarecrow in white jeans and a black silk jacket. He's Prescott

Weems, an opera buff, and a very *buffo* guy. He's also a critic. And a poet.

"*Mon dieu!*" he yelps at my approach. "Doesn't she look happy!"

"I hope so," says Lute. "She's been a bitch all night."

"I'm not a bitch," I say gently.

"Darling, of course not. And I'm the king of Prussia. You'll order me a drink, won't you? You're so good."

Lute clasps his hand. "You know what, m'dear? Men are pigs."

"But look at her! Look at her!" Weems won't stop pointing at me and shouting. "Her eyes are little pin spots. Teeny *tiny*. She's *loaded!*"

"Says who?" I ask, but at the same time I'm thinking: here they are, my first customers.

"Darling," he says, "if I had your look, I wouldn't be sitting *here*. I'd be Salome. I'd be Aïda. I'd be in love."

"No," Lute says. "You'd be quiet."

"Isn't that someone we know?" I inquire, nodding toward the opposite side of the room—another customer?

"Uh-oh," says Honey. "There's trouble."

Magna looks interested. "What kind of trouble?"

"Big trouble."

"How big? In inches?"

"Oh, my dear!" Prescott howls. "Who is this babe? Where did you come from, where have you been? We should have known each other years ago."

"I was in school," Magna tells him. "In Europe."

Prescott moves his chair beside her. "Girl? We have to talk."

I've known Prescott Weems a long time, ten years. He's spent his life yearning to be a socialite. His dad was some kind of gangster, died in jail. Heart attack, they said. Prescott suspected foul play. His brother went schizophrenic. Prescott couldn't wait to get away. He came to New York and met a few painters. In spite of, or because of, a compulsion to drink himself blind, he became a notable interpreter of new movements in art. Poets are like that; Prescott more so. "These young painters," he likes to say. "They're *sooo* cute. But they're *no one* until I've written about them. No artist is anywhere in this town without a poet to write them up. Without me." He says this often. That's what he's saying now, to "big trouble," to Claude.

Kit knows him, I think. He has that band, what's it called? Red Cross or something? Blue Whale? White Duck? Some color of something. They're all painters who play or sing, after a fashion—echoey, vibrating stuff, music you can dance to, if you put your mind to it. They're appearing later at a place called The Scourge. We're invited.

"You know Claude, right?" Honey says. Her eyes are locked on his, eyes that burn holes in your heart. "This is Claude Ballard, Prescott's new *find*." Claude nods self-consciously in my direction. He's a twenty-something guy with creamy pumpernickel skin and Brillo dreads. "Come to the gig," he says. His smile's as wide as the Atlantic. "I'll leave your names at the door."

Yes yes *yes*, I think as he departs. A customer.

Tina, the waitress, reappears. Magna leans forward in her seat. Claude's visit has left her panting. "Let's have something CHOC-OLATE," she says, her lips moist. "There are SOME desires only chocolate can satisfy."

"The food of love," Honey agrees.

The waitress suggests oysters. "Great idea!" Magna brightens. She orders a dozen, along with chocolate cake and more drinks all around. A busboy piles our empties in a tray. "I'm sure that boy has a thing for me," she muses, watching him walk away. "Did anyone check out his MOUTH?"

Prescott picks up her drink and drains it. "It wasn't his mouth that caught *my* attention."

"That's Belle's son," I say.

"Go on."

"No, really."

"Talk about what's not FAIR," Magna pouts.

Lute cups her hand to her mouth to stifle her shout. "Lord, give me *strength*," she says. "Cal Tutweiler—will you check out the *hat*?" Now he's wearing a dark cape and a flat black fedora. "He must've died and gone up to his next *life* or something!"

"Ladies," Cal says as he brushes by.

Weems replies with a soigné drag on his Camel, blowing smoke through both his nostrils. There hasn't been any love lost between these two. Actually, there's been a lot of love lost. They both have a thing about Toni. Weems thinks Toni is a goddess. Cal, on the other hand, he says, is an ass.

"Where'd you go?" I ask. "What's happened to Toni?"

"Oh, darling," says Weems. "Isn't it obvious? She has to be looking for a new pot to piss in."

Cal presses my neck. "We got really high."

"*No*," Prescott says. "Really?"

"Heh heh."

Well, well, I think. Another customer.

"I've never done heroin," Magna confesses.

"Why not?"

"I'm afraid I'll like it."

"Hello there," says an unmistakable voice. It coughs.

"Why, Belle!" Prescott calls. "Do sit. Sit here, girl. Sit." He swipes a chair from a nearby table.

"I'm not a dog, you know." Belle sits.

Magna gives her a smoldering look. "I had no idea you were the mother of that delicious boy over there."

"Oh, yes," Belle replies, her eyes picking him out from the crowd.

"Do you happen to know if he has a girlfriend? He seems to have an eye on me."

"I'll have to speak to him," murmurs Belle.

The food has arrived, more drinks all around. Magna heads for the john, where we can see a crowd spilling out of the hallway. Belle mouths the words "Is she doing drugs?"

"Magna doesn't take drugs," Honey notes.

"Nobody takes drugs anymore," Belle says, peering into my drink. "We just sit around and pray for money."

"Magna doesn't need money," Lute points out. "She needs love."

"Of course," says Cal. "Money is love in action."

"Magna takes drugs," I say. "She doesn't do smack."

"She doesn't need to," Belle submits.

"We all need a little," I say. "Now and then. That's why I'm going into the business."

Belle looks at me, aghast. "You can't."

"But I can."

"But scag? It's so *sordid*."

"It's the Lower East Side that's sordid," I reply.

Belle's cough is so violent it startles the silverware. "The East Side isn't sordid. It's merely provincial."

Hard to please, Belle is. She's a drug snob. If it was cocaine I wanted to sell, that would be all right—I could move to the head of the class. Cocaine is a social drug; it brings you such interesting people, such bright and radical ideas. But conversation on junk? That's something else. It lacks luster. Still, it would put a stop to that cough.

"Do be sure you have a good, safe connection," Weems says, speaking barely above a whisper. He's in earnest. "A good connection can make you *rich*."

Belle reaches in my pack for a smoke. "Let's not prattle on about this," she says. "It's so boring."

I think she protests too much. I think she's a customer.

The discussion turns, as it always does, to what's going on in the world of art: who's doing what, where, and to whom, and how much they got paid for it. As I listen, I realize what's left for me to do: to make an art of dealing. It's not such a foreign concept in this crowd. Always watch the artists, Sticky says.

So I'm watching.

THAT DICK

That Dick was here three days. Then he started calling.

"So," he said. "What've you been doing?"

"Breathing."

"I mean, you lookin' for names?"

"I thought I was lookin' at five to fifteen."

"Not yet. We're still working on Angelo. It's taking longer than we thought. You might want to find yourself a job."

"I'm kinda weak for that," I said. Get a *job*? There isn't a soul on this earth that would hire me now. Except, maybe, that Dick.

"If you were legitimately employed," he said, "it might sit well with a judge."

"You're better legal aid than a lawyer."

"You don't need a lawyer."

Right. Then why do I need *him*?

"Maybe you should think about going back to work at your restaurant."

I shuddered at the thought. "No," I said slowly. "It closed."

"That's too bad, but you can get a job. Look in the papers.

Restaurants are always hiring. Even my guys have a crew working one."

Why tell me? Was he bragging?

"I'm not sure I know how to cook anymore," I said, feeling weary. "I don't know what I can do. Everything I know is history."

PART THREE

THE ART OF DEALING

THE ART OF DEALING

It doesn't take a lot of know-how to know how to deal drugs. You learn as you go along. You buy, you mix, you weigh and measure; you bag, trade, and sell. It's a business, like any other religion: same dependence on faith and ritual, same promise of deliverance, same foundation in fear. Same flow of tax-free cash.

But this is not an easy business to profit by; the product can tempt more than the proceeds. It's all about turnover and control, same as restaurants. Restaurants can't depend on serving food alone. They have to have personalities. That's how it is in drugs: a dealer can't be too honest or too devious; attitude counts the most. It might be nice to have a patient, kind, and understanding nature, to be close-mouthed and mature, but none of that is really very useful. It takes a bitch to be a dealer.

Advertising is out, except by word of mouth, and that's a double-edged sword. The word can easily reach the wrong ears. I can't let myself sell to just anyone; that's the business of the street.

Besides, I'm no kind of pusher. Pushers are the "nifty Louie" types you see in movies, extortionists with an evil glint in their eyes and the monkey on a taut, stinking leash. Private dealers like me do not remotely resemble these Hollywood lowlifes. We're respectable, and selective. When I drop hints around

Sticky's, it's all very furtive, very hush-hush. Kit does the same at her gigs. And before long, people start calling.

The needleheads come first. That's natural, I can't complain. They're the steady customers. *Knock-knock, ring-ring, beep-beep: Are you in now? Are you in? Okay to stop by now? Got anything to drink? How is this stuff? How much should I do?* This is the usual drill. *Can I pay you later? tomorrow? next week?*

I prefer the less regular customers, chippers and partyheads, overachievers, friends—filmmakers, poets, painters, musician friends of Kit's. Not all of them are into drugs, but the ones who aren't have husbands or girlfriends or sisters who are, and they all come together and hang out. It's not a big scene but I enjoy it. I was always such a loner. I have a community now.

On nights I have to work, I deal the way I did for Big Guy, weighing out tenths and half-tenths of a gram from a green plastic miniscale that fits in the pocket of my grill jacket. The walk-in refrigerator is my place of business. Pedro calls it the Food and Drug Administration. Everything coming out of Sticky's, he says, is FDA-tested and approved.

At home I deal from the living room, salon-style. If they're very good friends, Honey and Magna, or Big Guy and Mr. Leather (Belle comes by only when no one will know), I work out of the bedroom, where Kit and I actually live. It's the one comfortable room in the apartment: a carpet and two armchairs, a small table and the bed, a raised platform. Kit and Betty had been sleeping on the floor, but I couldn't put up with that. Too slummy.

Dean's all right, though. He delivers, but he's slow, a little slow. He teaches shop in a high school downtown. Every day after class he comes by to pick up money, then he goes to his source while I wait. I wait and so do all my friends, outside on the benches, at home by the phone, in bars. I don't like to keep them waiting, but what can I do? When Dean finally arrives, he lays out a taste, then he wants to stay and talk and I have to listen.

It's the biggest part of my job, listening, or pretending to. Having a private dealership is like sitting in a confessional—that religious aspect again. Sometimes it's more like therapy. People are supposed to tell a shrink everything on their minds, but who ever actually does that? No one I know, not when they can spill to a dealer. A dealer has to keep mum.

I don't know what Dean thinks about besides drugs and money. Every now and then he mentions an ex-girlfriend, emphasizing the "ex," but mostly all I hear are vague references to his supplier, and Rico.

Was it Rico who set him up with this connection, I wonder? Maybe it's someone Rico owes a favor and Dean is someone he promised a favor and now they're all making out, through me. They make the money and I do all the work. I work just as hard at this as I ever have in a kitchen. Then how can I be serving so many people and not come out ahead? I keep strict control of Kit's intake, am even harder on my own. The problem is the cost to me: I must not be close enough to the source. Yet the dope is pure, not stepped-on, not cut to shit by having passed through too many hands. Nobody's touching it but me, a little, I don't want to spoil anyone. This might not last.

I ask Dean to cut me a better deal. Impossible, he says. Why? I'm turning it over fast enough, building a regular clientele. "It is what it is," he says. This is the way we talk now, the language of self-evidence: it is what it is, truth is truth, Ruth is Ruth. When you're looking to get high, when you're looking to get over, you don't waste time looking for words.

I have to find a way to keep our expenses down. If we didn't indulge ourselves, this would be a piece of cake, but if we didn't indulge, I wouldn't be dealing in the first place. I'll have to work harder. I can't work any harder. I'm taking in more money in a day than I do in a week at my job, but it all goes back into buying more. Kit complains about this; half our investment is her money. What's the point of dealing dope, she says, if you can't get it when you want? We get it when we need, I say. Sometimes when we want.

Finally, when the winter is nearly over, I make enough profit to buy a warm coat, which I don't already happen to own. It's a gangster-style thick navy wool with deep pockets and subtle red stripes in a windowpane pattern—sixty dollars at an East Side thrift store. Some profit. Now I really look like a dealer—good thing I have a job. But I don't want to depend on drugs for a living. Dealing is just a sideline.

Listen," Rico confides one night. We're hanging out on his office couch. "Be nice to Sticky," he says. "Okay? He's having trouble at home. His wife is threatening to leave him and he's really depressed. So be nice."

He lays a line of coke on my belly and snorts it. It tickles but it doesn't turn me on. Rico doesn't do much for me anymore, not since I've been with Kit. She does it all, and then some.

"Nice?" I say. "I'm always nice, especially to Sticky. I love that guy." And I do. We've never touched, not a hug, not a handshake, but for six years our lives have been lived in each other's faces. He hasn't just been tolerant. He's been swell. Forget about the dealing. When I was sick, when I broke my foot on the job, when a former cook in a drug-induced rage punched me bloody in the face, Sticky was always there, paying the expenses, covering my ass. Unlike the grumpy Flint, Sticky never got temperamental, not with me. Fuck his wife—Angie is her name. She's his second, and not much older than his oldest child. I'll be nice to him, of course.

Rico puts some coke on my tongue and sucks it. In spite of myself, this turns me on. "I don't like Sticky doing dope," he says.

"Man his age, with his bad colon—he's not up to it. But you know how it is. He says a little goes a long way."

"How long?" I say, reaching into his drawers. "In inches?"

The next night business is very bad, nothing doing in the kitchen. Pedro and I amuse ourselves by creating new dishes no one is there to eat. Then I see Sticky by the coffee machine, glumly pouring himself a cup. His head is bowed, his shoulders slump. I follow him to the office, where I find him at his desk, a shot of brandy in front of him and a bag of dope in his hand.

"Can I come in?" I ask.

"Sure," he says. "Have a seat."

"Sticky," I say. "I don't mean to get personal, but are you all right?"

"I'm just bored," he says. "If I could, I'd close this place and move on. Once I get bored with a joint, it's time to go."

"It's just boredom?"

He picks up the brandy, looks through the glass. "You really want to hear this?"

Not really. But I love this guy. I'll listen to whatever he has to say.

He hesitates. "I'm terribly shy around women," he murmurs. Well, I knew that. In all the years I've known Sticky, this is the first time he's ever looked at me.

"How'd you manage two marriages?" I ask.

"I don't know. The wives—they helped. I was always kind of a nerd." He strokes his hawklike nose and gives a smile. "It's funny," he snorts. Sticky's asthmatic. "My restaurants have always attracted the crazies, the drunks, and the drug addicts, and I was never into any of it myself. But drug addicts are some of the best people I know. Sure, they've got problems, who doesn't? They don't take life the way it's handed to them. They put on a show and the town comes to watch. And I make all the money. Or I did." He flips through the receipts on his desk with a sigh.

I wonder what's happened to the money. "Oh, you know, two wives, four kids, alimony . . ." He lifts the glass of brandy. "I never expected to go into this business," he goes on. "I have a law degree, but I never practiced. I tried it for about six months, and hated it." He smiles as his eyes fall on the bag of dope still in his hand. I offer him a line of mine. He takes it.

"I was always more interested in art," he says then, "but I wasn't much good at making it. I already had a wife and two of my kids—I had to do something. We were living in a small apartment on East Tenth. A lot of artists had studios there, they were my neighbors. They wanted a place to hang out. There was an empty storefront on the block. The rent was cheap, so I took it. I built the place myself, poured the drinks, did the cooking. Hamburgers mostly. Peanuts on the bar. When it was busy, one of the artists or their girlfriends would come in and help out. A couple of them hung their paintings on the wall, so I gave them tabs. I wasn't making any money anyway. But the word got around, and it drew people in. Good people. Nice paintings." Now he's smiling. He puts down his glass, lights a smoke.

Soon, he says, he moved to a bigger space on the other side of town, a steak house in the Village, taking the artists and the peanuts with him. This place was a mess. The floor was bad so he threw sawdust and peanut shells all over it and they became a symbol, somehow, of the good life. When he got restless, he moved again, this time to an even bigger place, three glass-fronted stories on lower Park Avenue.

It was at this place I first set eyes on Sticky. I was still in school, but his bar offered a better education, not to mention a higher life. Pop artists, poets, rockers, flaming queens and macho cowboys, black, white, gay, straight—you didn't see that at the malls. I was dazzled. Reporters were always writing about the faces they saw there, the things people said other people had done. It had glamour—good bodies, big hair, wet lips. Especially on the waitresses. Half the guys in the bar came in just to pick up waitresses. Sticky got one, too. Angie.

I offer him another line. He takes it.

A week later Rico disappears. No one knows where he is for days. Then, suddenly, there's a commotion by the coffee stand in the kitchen, where he's yelling at a waitress for neglecting to freshen a pot. He stands there, one arm shaking behind him, as he waits for the liquid to drip in his cup. I almost duck when I see him turn in my direction.

"I'm really worried about Sticky now," he tells me from the other side of my prep table. He doesn't speak so much as puff. The dark circles under his eyes are black as coal, his face a mass of competing sharp planes. I can hardly make out his form beneath his clothes. He's wasted.

"Well, I'm worried about you," I say, though I don't entirely mean it. "Where you been?"

"I'm fine," he says, swaying. I reach out to catch him but because I've been boning chickens, I'm holding a knife. It clatters to the table as he steadies himself, grips my arm.

"I'm all right," he assures me. "It's that Agent Orange shit, comes and goes. I can deal with it."

Rico thinks he's been affected by wartime exposure to toxic chemicals, but the stuff caked around his nose looks more like cocaine. He's been in a blackout, he says, but he's okay now. Woke up sitting in his car at a stoplight in a strange town in upstate New York. Doesn't know how he got there. Isn't sure how he got back. Drugs weren't the only reason I ever climbed into bed with him, but right now I can't remember what other reason there was.

Next thing we know, Sticky ends up in the hospital. He's got intestinal trouble complicated by a liver thing, don't know what.

He needs an operation. A pall falls over the dining room. Crowds keep coming, but they're thinner. "How's Sticky?" they say. "Is Sticky back yet?" The room's the same, the food's the same, or better, but the customers seem lost without him. Even after he recoups, slow nights run equal to busy ones. The art world's not that big. New clubs are opening, new bistros. The same people are no longer in the same place at the same time. They come, they go. They go. *Where the artists go, the world follows*. And Sticky's is no longer the only game in town.

In April, with spring in the air, I ask Flint for a raise. He fires me. I'll collect unemployment, I don't care. Rico's upset about it, though. He cares. After some discussion, back and forth, I agree to go back part-time, prepping on the day shift, doing lunches. I'm working with Big Guy again, but it's not the same. I have a business of my own now. Drugs are no sideline. Mainline.

MY NEW LIFE

Morning. Well, noon. Kit's making coffee. Her needle and spoon lie by the bed. "You awake?" she calls from the kitchen.

"Mmmm," I say, reaching for the tobacco tin where I keep the dope. Kit comes in and picks up the needle. I put a little dope in the spoon, she adds a little coke. I've never done a speedball. Kit says I have to try it. What kind of dealer am I, doesn't know her drugs?

Kit cooks the coke in the spoon with the dope. It bubbles and foams. She taps my arm and finds a vein. What a feeling! Like the downhill run of a roller-coaster, like mountains rising suddenly out of a mist—whoosh! The top of my head seems to rise, my limbs grow strong, my feet tingle: I'm weightless. My heart pounds, my eyes snap to attention. I've never known such excitement. It's too good.

The phone rings. It's Ridley, a woodworker, somebody's boyfriend. Okay, I say, c'mon by. The phone again—Matthew. He works in an office across the street, it's his lunch hour. Can he "eat" with us? Sure. The phone rings. This is Steve. Which Steve? Steve who? Steve we-met-at-CB's-last-night. Am I in? I pull on a bathrobe. I'm in. I pour a cup of coffee.

"Who's coming?" Kit asks. I tell her. "I hope they don't stay," she says. "I have to take a shower."

"They won't stay. It's their lunch hour."

"They always want to stay." And they do.

My day, my new life, begins. I stop, once, to consider its merit. I look out the window and watch people with jobs disappear into the subway, their postures defensive, their faces empty of expression, jaws set. Not for me, the weekly pay check. You have to take bigger risks to call your life your own. I'll take one. I'll answer the phone and open the door and then I'll take up my pen. Why should I worry? I have my wits. Cunning alone has brought me to this day. No, not cunning. Cash.

VANCE

June 1982: I quit the job at Sticky's and go into business full-time. My cover is gone. I'm a drug dealer with no visible means of support. I know it's madness: if the cops don't get me, the customers will. Their claim on my confidence is monumental. So's the cost. But heroin buffers pain and stress same as it works for pleasure—fast. That's the drug's finest point: its efficiency—how quickly the world falls away. Poof! And the unbearable becomes entertainment.

I dispense with store-bought papers and glassines (I'm watching my expenses), and in my idle hours, such as they are, I make my own bindles by cutting up the pages of art magazines, something my customers can appreciate. I trim all the cutouts into triangles, which I then fold into envelopes and seal with decorative press-tape. I found a whole store of it in a carton Betty left behind. When I run out of art stock, Prescott brings me fashion magazines from Europe, circa 1965.

"That is so cool," Magna says, opening a package I made from the crotch shot of a yellow vinyl mini. I know it's cool. If I'm going to make an art of dealing, I'm going to do it right. Heaven knows I had a good teacher.

My father wasn't the only one in my family pushing palliatives and pills. My mother dealt in mail-order vitamins. She bought capsules from a wholesaler and printed labels of her own. I glued them on the bottles myself. She took ads in the back of selected magazines and rented a post box. Then she went about her usual household affairs, talking on the phone and waiting for mail.

Her business got off to a very slow start. Even family friends and neighbors needed convincing. At the time, most people thought of vitamins as a late form of witchery, suspect and useless. This was when fast food was just taking hold of the nation. You could hardly find a community uninfected by the smell of cheap burgers and fries. Pizza was practically table d'hôte. At school, my friends ate "lunch meat," whatever that was. Talk about suspicious. Most kids I knew went to school skipping breakfast, but I was never allowed to leave the house until I'd had my egg and downed my multiple.

The vitamin business failed, but my habit certainly stayed with me. I've hardly begun a day of my life without some kind of pill or powder. It's no different now, but I could use an alternative source of supply—Dean isn't always available, and the way he does business is a chore. I'm tired of all the waiting. Kit wants to call Sylph's friend Dickie Howard. Maybe, she says, he can turn us on to his connection.

"That's easier said than done," I brood.

"Want me to call?"

I call. I let him know I'm holding. Soon, he's at our kitchen table.

I weigh out a thirty-dollar fix and he boots it. "Yeah," he says. "Oh, yeah."

I ask Dickie about his dealer. He's sort of living with the guy, part-time, doing housework to pay for his dope. He'll ask if we can meet. Later on, he calls with the address. There's no bell, he says. We have to call from the corner and he'll come down to let us in.

We cab it to a building in the flower district, where Dickie's dealer holds court in a second-floor loft beneath a massage parlor.

Dickie leads us through a clutter of cameras, tripods, light racks, and rolls of no-seam paper at the front of the space, most of which is covered in a carpet of dust. Taller ceilings open up the back, but it's dark there. The windows are all in the front, and they're shaded.

The dealer's name is Vance. He's about my age, good-looking, black hair, Italian, but sexless. I have a weakness for Italians, nonetheless—look at Rico. Vance claims to be a filmmaker. Up to now, he says, he's only made commercials, but he's working on getting himself a feature. The dope, I gather, is his banker.

A galley kitchen with a potted palm and a six-foot cat scratch leads up a couple of steps to Vance's living quarters: a bed, a TV, a pitted wooden table, and a couple of modular armchairs. In an L-shape behind the bed are bookcases filled with videocassettes. Dickie stays in the kitchen, earning his keep, talking to Vance's girlfriend, Marcy, and two Abyssinian cats. Kit coos over the cats. She says she would have been a veterinarian if she hadn't gone to art school. She loves animals. At this, I have to laugh. "I'm sorry," I say. "But we live in a zoo."

Vance moves to the table and lays out a sample taste for us to snort. He squirms when Kit wants to shoot it. We snort. The dope is just like Dean's, but it's a hundred dollars a gram less. I buy one and we get acquainted, stay another couple of hours to watch one of the movies in Vance's collection. Videocassette players are still a new thing. No one else I know has one—this is a treat. But Vance has a suspicious vibe—too friendly. Vibes are very important in this business. Intuition pays off. Nevertheless, when I sell everything I've bought, I call him again to re-up.

He's pleased I turned the stuff around so quickly. Now he advances me a gram on the one I pay for. I hesitate. Vance is a pusher, I think. Go slow. He wants us to watch another movie, but no. Time I was getting back.

I go home to mix the dope with a little mannitol, not too heavy, just enough to give it some stretch. The phone rings, the door buzzes, it moves. By nightfall, I'm glad I quit the job. I'll have more time to myself now, more time for my friends and for Kit. Now I can go to her gigs. I love Kit in a lot of ways, but she's never more impressive than she is onstage, when I love her all the more.

At a show in a college hall uptown, Poop breaks one of his skins in midset. People mill around; I'm on the nod. A screeching guitar run raises my head. Kit's improvising a melody. I've never heard her play a melody; her job is rhythm and fills. Sylph stands off to the side, smiling, wondering where this will go. It goes into what sounds like a rocket in reverse, thunderous, grinding, propulsive. Gloria isn't sure what to do. She's looking for a place to go in. The crowd hollers and Kit soars. She drops her pick and plays her guitar with maracas, with Poop's drumsticks, with her feet. It's wild. Poop goes back into action, finds her rhythm, and Gloria picks him up. Sylph moans into the microphone and they jam, picking up speed and taking off into one of their hits.

"That was beautiful," I say to Kit when they come offstage.

"Really? Was it?" she says. She's so modest. "I was just fooling around."

We go home and dye our hair, both of us. I need a new look. Then Kit wants to play with her toys. I watch her arrange plastic trolls, beads, and lights on her work table and busy herself taking pictures. I try to write, but nothing comes. I play with my makeup, redesign my face. We listen to music and dance, move slow.

I like the way Kit dances. She's funny. Her head bobs like a dashboard doll, her fingers mark the beat as if she were testing the wind, north-south, east-west. "You're a goof," I say and take her in my arms while the cats pad around us and snuggle. The dawn breaks. Then the bell rings. It's Vance.

"I thought you might be up," he says. He's brought a guitar, a pre-CBS Fender Stratocaster, worth plenty to a collector. Vance has taken it in trade from some hard-luck customer. "What d'you think?" he asks Kit. "Can you use it?" She can have the guitar, he says, if it'll help make us better friends. Consider it a permanent loan.

I don't like this. Selling drugs to people with money is one thing; taking their things when they run out of it, another. I'm not going to be responsible for anyone's sad life—I don't want it on my mind. Kit doesn't, either. "Thanks," she says, "but the neck's too big for me. I'll never be able to play it."

I'm impressed: that Strat is equipment she'd die for. I seem to be only just getting to know her. In the weeks that follow, I come to know her band better, too. They're an amusing bunch, and they've taken a liking to me. They even invite me on a tour.

I don't explain why it's so hard for me to get away. Impossible, really, but I can go out on the town. There are lots of new clubs. The best one isn't far from where Kit and I live and we go there a few nights a week.

The doorman waves us through the crowd stalking the entrance, hands me a pass to the lounge for VIPs. It's like this wherever we go—red carpet. It's Kit's celebrity, my private cachet. Drinks don't cost me, either. One of the bartenders is a customer. So's the DJ and some of the crowd. "Oh," Belle will whisper, or Honey, or Cal. "You holding?" But I never carry anything in the clubs. I'm there to drink and dance.

When I do go home, the party comes along. Sometimes Vance is in it. He can't get enough of our scene. First I think he's looking to steal my action, but all he wants to do is hang out. When Kit plays in one of the rock clubs, we invite the other bands on the bill. Vance wants to know them, too. They come from England, Australia, California; white hair, black hair, blue. Neither Kit nor I sleeps much or eats much but I don't seem to care. I'm not tired and I don't feel hungry. I don't feel anything. That's the idea.

TRUST ME

On a night in late December I get a call from Ginger Snaps, a photographer I know from the clubs. She wants to stop by with her friends Duke and Earl. Earl's okay but he ODs a lot and Duke's into total nodding. They bore me. Ginger's a little more responsible. She'll make them behave. "Don't you trust me?" she squeals. "We've been getting so close—aren't we friends? I *live* for my friends. You can trust *me*."

Trust? This is the first time I've ever had Ginger in my house. She's usually tending bar in a saloon near Times Square—that's how she pays the rent. I like Ginger well enough, but sometimes she gets too personal. She's making a photographic record of her life and wants everyone in it to play themselves—fucking, shooting up, looking for love, and acting natural. That's her thing—naturalism. Spontaneity. Ginger goes for the gut. There's no telling where she'll turn up: at your party, on your blanket at the beach, in your bedroom. She takes that camera everywhere, like the family dog. She makes me feel exposed. I don't want my picture taken by Ginger or anyone else. That's all I need—proof of my existence.

We sit in the living room, listening to music. I do the thing, and Duke and Earl tie off. Ginger whips out her camera.

"I can't have pictures," I tell her.

"I can," she says, and takes one.

"Not here," I say. "Please. I have to keep the profile low."

She wanders into the dressing room next to the john. "Can I try some of this?" she says. My new lipstick. I go into the room and Kit follows, so does Duke. "Oh, let *me* see," he says. He wants to try some, too. Earl stays in the living room.

"Gorgeous," says Ginger as she tries the various cosmetics on my bureau. Then she starts rooting through my jewel case. "What are *these?*" she breathes, picking up an oversize ring with a gargantuan paste diamond and a glittery bracelet I wore last New Year's Eve. She stands in the mirror to fluff her frizzy red hair, tucks in her ample boobs. She's distracting. Then I remember I've left the dope tin lying out on the coffee table. I turn, but Duke's standing in my way. I make a move to pass but he's thumbing through my clothes, lost in thought.

"Can I get by?" I strain to see over him. He looks at me as if he doesn't understand. "I want to change the record," I say.

"But I *like* this one," he says.

"I have a better one," I tell him and push past. Nothing seems amiss in the living room. Earl's looking through the records on the floor, the tin is where I left it. I pick it up, slip it in a pocket. When I turn, they have their coats on, then they're gone.

The phone wakes me in the morning. It's Ridley. He's just back from California, where he used to be a surfer. Even his hair is wavy, kissed by the sun; his voice speaks of coastal mists and easy living. He wants to come by right away. Okay, I say, but I'm not dressed.

"So?" he says in his misty way. "That's exactly how I like you."

I go into the tin for our a.m. dose. My heart stops. It's empty. "What's the matter?" Kit says. I don't answer. My brain pushes against itself. When Ginger left with Duke and Earl, we watched the end of two movies on TV and fell out. Where did I put the stuff? Did I stash it? Yeah, that's what I did. I'm always hiding it somewhere. You never know if the cops are going to surprise you in the night. You never know who may walk in. Better safe than sorry.

I go back in the closet and look through everything I own. I look in the oven and under the floor. Then it dawns. Those creeps. Those fuckers. What a sucker I am, what a fool. How could I not have known? They're a tight little clique, almost a ménage. It's a conspiracy, they did it together. Earl took the dope and the other two provided cover. I'm furious.

Now Ridley's at the door. I let him in and tell him what's gone down. "I know those guys," he says. "Never liked them much. They're slick."

"They're junkies," says Kit.

"They're friends," I insist. "They know I'm not rich. I have nothing."

"You have drugs," Ridley says.

"Call them," says Kit.

"Call them? What are they going to say? Oh yeah, we were stoned, we didn't know what we were doing? They knew."

"You're too trusting, maybe," Ridley says. "Too nice. They're not."

"I thought they were." I think of the time I gave Earl a kitchen job, when he was on the skids. He's always saying how much I mean to him. Ginger's friend or no, I'll kill him.

"You did leave the dope lying out in the open," says Kit. "In a way, I can't blame them."

"Maybe they didn't do it," Ridley says. "Maybe it'll still turn up."

I call Ginger. "Wake up," I say. "We have to talk."

She doesn't know a thing about it. This is shocking. She can't believe Earl would steal with her there. She'd be over him in a minute, and they've been friends since childhood. He worships her. She'll speak to him, she says. She'll call me back. Keep looking, she says. Maybe I put it somewhere and forgot.

Vance calls. "I gotta see you," I say, knowing I do, but what'll I tell him? Yesterday we were eating popcorn together and watching movies. Now I owe him a thousand bucks.

Kit's feeling sick now, she won't stop grumbling. She wants me to go back on the street. Ridley offers me money to go. "I'd come with you," he says, "but I'm a sissy out there." I look him up and down, six feet four inches of milksop. I should specialize in macho wimps, I think. I'd be in clover.

I look out the window. It snowed during the night. I look for my clothes. They feel gummy. "Don't go away," I say to Ridley.

"I'll make coffee," Kit sniffs. It's cold in the apartment.

"Just keep looking," I say. "That stuff has to be here somewhere."

I get a cab and head over to Eighth and C. There aren't many people out, it's too cold. Even the dealers are lying low, not all the houses are open. The sky is gray. As more snow begins to fall, I follow a couple of likely prospects across an empty lot and into the back of a building missing all its doors and windows, no protection from the wind. The interior's been gutted, but parts of the top floor are visible, mostly the beams. There's a guy up there straddling a rafter, holding a bucket attached to a rope. A dozen or so shivering fools like me are waiting on the ground below. There's no floor under us, dirt and rubble only. The only light comes from a single emergency bulb and whatever daylight penetrates the gloom from outside.

I watch the people in front of me put money in the basket. The guy on the beam hauls it up and sends it back down to a "spotter," who tips the basket just enough to let the customer take out the dope.

How does the guy get up there? Talk about no visible means

of support! I marvel at this enterprise for a minute, then it's my turn. I put my money in the basket and watch it rise. After too long a wait, the basket descends. I lift out the dope. "Next," growls the spotter. I move on.

In the shadows along the edges of the space, I can make out a few lurking figures heating their cookers over low-burning candles. I walk to a wall and open one of the bags. I can't wait to get out of this frozen cave but I can't stand the way I feel. I snort a line, fast, some of it misses my nose. Damn. I start to walk. It tastes all right, may even be good. At least it's not beat. I find another cab and run up the stairs to the apartment.

Ridley and Kit are in the kitchen, exactly where I left them, both of them jiggling their limbs.

"How is it?" Kit asks.

"Not bad," I say. "It's the new Black Mark."

"Maybe we should get more."

"You go."

"Let me get straight first."

"I really admire you girls, copping like this," Ridley says. God, he's smarmy. "I don't know why, I just can't."

"All you big guys say that," I tease. A lighter mood has hit me. "You're nothing but chickenshits in gorilla clothing."

He offers to stake me to a bigger buy so I can make up some of the money I owe Vance. "I may be chickenshit," he admits, "but you can't say I'm not a good guy."

"I wouldn't say that," I agree. But you never know.

Kit leaves to go cop and Ridley goes with her, to a bank machine for the cash. I don't keep money in the bank, only enough to cover the bills—no paper trail for me. I sit in bed and answer the phone. By afternoon I've made up a third of the money, but we haven't enough dope to get us through the night and I can't keep this up much longer. My business is young and Vance isn't going to wait while it grows. He needs what I owe him to buy more material for himself. He's already called three times. I keep hoping the stuff from last night will turn up. Some-times things like that happen.

It sort of happened to my father once, I tell Kit later, when he was in Paris during the Second World War. He told me the story on one of our drives to see my mother, who was then in the hospital and not doing well. Neither my dad nor I wanted to think about what might happen next, so I asked him about the war—the only other time he'd been separated from my mother. A funny thing happened while he was at the front. There had been a lot of killing at Bastogne, but Paris had been liberated and Dad was given a three-day pass.

Before he left camp, he said, the men in his company who had to stay behind gave him money for things to send home. Nine thousand dollars, it was, all told. "Combat pay piles up!" he said. He didn't say he was bright. Dad had lost his wallet some time before and had picked up a European-style billfold. He stuffed the money into it and pushed it into a back pocket.

Somewhere between Verdun and Paris, bouncing along in a troop truck, the wallet must have fallen out. Dad didn't notice until they were driving into the city. He'd been infiltrating enemy territory for some time but he never felt as afraid as now. If I go back and tell them I've lost their money, they'll kill me, he said to himself. They've got guns, after all. They'll *kill* me.

Some of the guys on the truck owed him money. They paid up then, so Dad wouldn't have to be in Paris without a sou. Two thousand dollars, he collected. He could still recall the dinner he had that night: bottle of wine, soup, salad, main course, dessert, all for twenty francs. A franc was worth two cents, American, then. He said it was fantastic.

After dinner, he was strolling down the boulevard with two of the other men, when someone approached from behind and slapped him on the back. He wheeled around swearing, "You S.O.B.!"

"Well," Dad explained, "it was Jacques Perrier. He and I had worked the hedgerows in Normandy together, after the beach. We did sniper patrols. He was with the underground, the F.F.I.—you know, the Cross of Lorraine? He wants to show me a good time while I'm in Paris. I says, Thanks, but I don't have any money, and I tell him the story of losing the wallet. Gee, he says, you have *anything*? I says, Yes, and I show him the two thousand, which, out of nine, isn't enough. So he says, Look, leave it to me. I'll get you some money.

"He takes me to a gambling house. Pick out whatever game you want, he says. I look around. I don't know what to do, I never gambled. Just look around, he says. So, I'm lookin'. And I'm lookin' at the roulette wheel.

"Now, these gambling houses were not legit. They were an open secret, like a little underground. So, this character goes and talks to another guy and comes back and says, Why don't you play some? I realize I'll be shot dead for what I've got left anyway, what's the difference? I put some money down. And I win.

"They're letting me win, of course. When I'd won another two thousand bucks, I quit. I probably could have stayed there all night and won all I needed but I'd had enough, I'm just not a gambler. I says to Jacques: Look. You literally *gave* me this money. I know what you've been up to. But now, I'm out.

"He walks me back to my hotel, it's pretty late, and then he says, You have any cigarettes? Any salt? Chocolates? So I says, Yeah—I'd purposely brought these things for trading—I had a carton of Luckies, a dozen Hershey bars, and four bars of Lux soap from the Army PX, which travels with you. You can get anything in combat, it's all free. So he takes the stuff, everything I have. I says, Jacques, don't get me in trouble for this. He says, No, no—I won't get you in any trouble. I'll get you more money.

"Cigarettes were going for a dollar-fifty on the black market— they were supposed to cost twenty cents. So fifteen dollars a carton was a lot of money. I don't know what he got for the soap and the rest—I gave him some tobacco and a box of cigars, too.

I figured, well, he helped with the gambling thing. Let him keep it. I didn't expect to see him again.

"Next morning, after breakfast, I'm walking down the boulevard, you know how wide they are in Paris, and this guy across the road is waving a fistful of money and yelling at me. Yelling my name! I'm pretending not to see or hear—MPs are everywhere. I can't be caught doing business on the black market. He comes running over, shoving money in my face. Don't bother me, I says. Just walk behind me, willya?

"So he gets behind me and follows me back to the hotel. He pulls money out of a bag and I take it, peel off about a third, and give him the rest. No, he doesn't want it. I says, Look, how much do you make? He's a captain in the French army and the guy's getting a lousy twenty dollars a month. I says, Look, I'm a lot wealthier than you are. Take it. I had to shove it in his pocket and throw him outta my room!"

So Dad went shopping in Paris. He bought perfume for Mom, a new wallet for himself, and as many of the items on his company's list as he had money for. He went back to his outfit expecting to be flayed, if not killed, and distributed the goods, explaining what had happened to the money. "I knew they didn't believe me," he said, "but they didn't say anything, not a word. That disturbed me." He said he still remembers that silence.

A few weeks went by, during which he earned the rank of lieutenant. This made the situation worse. Not only did the men distrust him because of the money, now he was their superior and they had to salute him.

"Well," he said, "they 'sirred' me to death, but before we went on another mission, I explained that if anything went wrong, it was my ass, I'd take the blame. That's all the lieutenant's bar means. Otherwise, I'm eating and sleeping with them as before, probably dying with them, too. So, anyway, it worked out. They warmed up.

"Two weeks later, I get a letter from an MP detachment outside of Verdun: a wallet has been found on the road. Will I please reply by describing the contents and how they should dispose of it? Who would return a wallet with all its contents? I mean, I grew up on Avenue D. It must be a chaplain, I think—one of some stripe. I ran around the whole outfit showing off that letter. See, I says, I really lost it!

"I returned a letter with a description of the wallet's contents and asked that the finder be given a reward, returning the balance by money order.

"Then we're on a drive, and I'm in my jeep at the end of the column as usual—tanks first, jeeps and trucks in the rear—and a mail jeep comes rolling along and tosses me a bundle. I open it. There's my wallet, with everything in it. They never took anything out."

"This is a true story," I say to Kit, who doesn't believe me, and though I know I'm my father's daughter, I also know nothing like this will ever happen to me.

IT SUCKS

This sucks. I'm lying in bed, knees to my chest, staring out the window. It's night. My genitals pound, I'm swimming in jelly. Kit lies coiled beside me, rolling from side to side.

"Must you jerk around like that?" I say.

"Oh, leave me alone. Why do you think they call it kicking?"

I know why. I sit up, legs over the side, feet on the floor. My knees leap into my face. A sour odor finds its way to my nose. B.O.

I stand beside the bed, tear at my clothes. My skin feels like papier-mâché. I have hot flashes, then I'm chilled to the bone. My calves twitch inconsolably.

A venomous rage snakes through my veins and lodges in my throat. I can't contain it. "I don't know how you talked me into dealing," I tell Kit. "If it weren't for you, I would never be like this."

"You fucked up all by yourself," she retorts. "If you'd let me take care of the dope once in a while, things like this never would happen."

I'm a shit. My hand finds its way to my crotch, hungry for sex I can't bear. I shove my fist between my legs and press. That's worse. I slap my cunt to keep it quiet. It makes me shudder. I stare bleakly into the closet. Nothing left but to lie down and stink up the room.

I want to know how long this will last. Kit's the expert.

"Thirty-six hours," she says. "If we're lucky."

"Where are your pills?"

"I took them."

"What a pal." The bitterness in my voice makes me angrier still.

"I thought you didn't like pills," she says.

"Christ!" I say. "Where's Bernie?"

Bernie is Kit's pill connection. He was one of her roommates in the Betty days, a young guitar player who holds her in high esteem. It's mutual. Bernie has a druggist for a father. On blank 'scrips Bernie steals from his father's store, he writes prescriptions for whatever she needs: Valium, Darvon, Darvocet, Percocet, codeine. Kit calls him whenever she goes on the road. What about now? Can he stop by? Yes, but not right away. His father's getting suspicious. We may have to wait a day or two. Or, at least, till later.

We can't wait. We can't. I'll call Dean. He's made enough off me by now to advance me a stash. I can turn it over, he knows that. It's the one thing I'm still good for.

I dial his number. No answer. This sucks very bad. This really sucks a big one.

"Never mind," Kit says, pulling herself to her feet. "Somebody will think of something."

I could cry.

I wish I was driving a fast, heavy car, speeding down a mountain road with steeply banked curves and sudden drops. I wish this road could be long and unpaved, I want to feel every shudder in the wheel. I want to see cinders fly, I want to see a crack in the earth. I wish a large animal, a bear or a deer, would cross my path so I could ram it. I want to send it up in the air and crush it under the car. I want to kill it and feel it die. Just so I won't kill Kit.

I look in her eyes. They're murderous.

The phone rings. It's Vance. How'm I doin'? Fine. Do I want to come up and see his new "photos"? Maybe later, I say. Prob'ly later.

I sink back on the bed and the phone rings. "Anything happening?" says a treacly voice—Earl's. My rage grows enormous.

"I can make something happen," I say through my teeth and I improvise a plan. If the scumbag will front me some cash, I'll make a run for him, sure. I'll get some D on the street and I'll beat it. He'll get a short count and a sour one. I'll spike it with baking soda and sugar and salt and seal it in Kit's old glassines. She saves them.

"I'm coming with you," she says as I pull on clothes. This is not a simple task. I can't stand upright, my hands won't get a grip. An involuntary tremor accompanies my every labored move. I don't bother with my makeup. On my way out the door, I heave.

We ring the bell at Earl's apartment and I go up. Kit wants to wait outside. Duke's up there with two other a-holes who have runny noses and dark circles under their eyes. I see no signal from anyone, I hear no attempt to explain a thing. "You look funny," says Earl. Do I? He looks blasted. These guys, these fucking *guys*.

I run with Kit straight to Avenue B, moving with caution. This dopesick, anyone could take us, but it's Isabelle who shouts us down. She's an old girlfriend of the Toast's roadie, a methadone goddess, all smiles. Does she have any juice? No, she sold it. Where'd she cop? "Black Mark," she says, "but they were busted just before. You look bad." We look bad? She's like a starved albino rat. We're standing in front of the building where she lives, shivering. After we cop, she says, we can come up and get off at her place.

Someone I recognize from Sticky's says they're selling good

shit on Fifth Street. We walk over to a tall, grinning black guy standing alone. "Yo!" I say. I think I'm shouting but he barely hears me. He grins wider. Not only am I sick, I'm white. Uh-oh.

"Give me six," I say, my voice fuzz.

"Thirty bucks," he says.

Is he playing with me? That's half-price. I look at him. No change of expression. I hand him the money, take the bags, turn on my heel. Kit buys two more and scrambles after me.

"I don't know about this," she says. "Why is it so cheap?"

"Cops are everywhere," I say. "Maybe Flaco is having a sale."

We push Isabelle's buzzer and climb a flight of steps to her apartment, one room and a half, sturdy gates on every window, all two of them. I plead with Kit: "Do me first?"

"I don't know why I should," she grumbles. I'm sicker than she is—first time that's happened. She loads the spoon, stares into the powder.

"I don't know," she says. "It looks weird."

"Just do it," I say, impatient. "We can complain about it later."

She boots it in my arm and sits back to watch my face. I wait, looking back at hers. I don't feel any different. Then I do. "God-damn the pusher-man!" I gasp. "It's coke! We've bought fucking cocaine!"

There's only one thing worse than kicking dope, and that's kicking dope on coke. Usually, nickel bags of street coke are packed in rectangles of aluminum foil. This stuff was in the same glassine bags they use for dope but without an identifying rubber stamp.

"Is it good coke at least?" Kit says.

"For crying out loud! How am I supposed to be able to tell that?"

"I think maybe you went the wrong direction on Fifth Street," Isabelle says calmly, taking a sip from her beer. "Try the next block going west."

A minute later we're back outside, walking up Fifth Street. My legs are still rubbery, but at least I can move. Kit's having trouble keeping up. Near Avenue A we see a gaggle of kids standing on the sidewalk in front of a jagged hole cut into a cinder-block wall, a couple of jitterbugs pacing alongside. We stop and peer into the hole. A short line of junkies is waiting dog-faced before another hole, in a candlelit cavelike space that once must have been a basement.

"Hey, good-lookin', whatchu want?" says a kid about ten years old. He's standing too close to me, he's pressing my arm. An older guy, a seller, is in front of me.

"Aren't you up past your bedtime?" I ask the kid.

"Give me your money," says the seller. "How many?"

Do we have any money left? Kit passes me forty dollars of her own and I watch as the kid runs to a garbage can on the corner. He lifts out a brown paper bag and counts out four glassines. "The narcs been comin' roun' here all day, man," explains the seller. "But they don't mess with kids."

Buying drugs from a ten-year-old—I don't care how smart— upsets me. I walk away shaking my head. "This is really the end," I say. "I won't do this even one more time, no matter how desperate I get."

"It's pretty disgusting," Kit agrees.

"We have to develop more sources," I say. We have to.

"Piss, shit, fuck." Kit is kicking the door—Isabelle's not answering her bell. We make our way to Second Avenue. Part of our street habit, or custom, has been to eat right after we cop, usually at one of the Ukrainian diners that are on nearly every East Village block. The best is a banquet hall on Second Avenue, where the bathrooms have stalls big enough for two. No one notices us go in and shoot up, and soon we're sitting at a table. Kit's hungry but I've never felt less like eating in my life. I just want that shithead Earl to stew. That Earl.

A waitress in a peasant costume hands us menus, her smile

too sugared for my taste. She says, "Don't you want to use the ladies' room first?"

I feel my cheeks flush but Kit's expression remains neutral. "I already washed my hands," she says, just as sweet. "Can we order?"

"We have to stop coming here, too," I say when the waitress has gone. We're having hot borscht and sharing a plate of boiled pierogies—all we can pay for. An accordion player steps up to the microphone at the other end of the room. He nods in our direction. The whole staff is giving us the eye.

"I wish we had enough money for rice pudding," Kit says.

"Eat the bread. It's just as sweet." I want to run out of there, quick.

Kit's fiddling with a spoon. "Why don't I do the dealing for a while?"

"You're in a band. You're too public. You're always out of town. We need another connection, that's all."

"I'm not sure I like that white dope," she says. "It's too expensive. It's too clean. It doesn't give you any rush."

"Who cares about a rush?" I nearly screech. "The stuff gets you straight, doesn't it? That's what counts."

She puts down the spoon and leans toward me. "I *want* the rush. Why do you think I do this?"

I'm exasperated. This dope has not altered my mood. The coke must have done some damage. Turning over what's left to Earl should pick me up. I'll be gone before he opens it.

Kit's eyes, so pinned. Incredible eyes. "We need a new connection," I say, "and that's that."

She tears a thick piece of bread and dunks it. "Why don't we try Brooklyn Moe?"

BROOKLYN MOE

Brooklyn Moe is a beer-bellied friend of Bernie's. He deals cocaine. Kit likes him. No, she appreciates him. He brings us an eighth and a half ounce of pot whenever her band has a gig. Moe idolizes Kit. Like most guys I've met from Brooklyn, he's cool enough but he's always stoned. I mean, *stoned*. Excessives make me nervous. And I wish he'd do something about that stringy brown hair. It hides his eyes. They're quiet.

Moe drives us out to deepest Brooklyn, I don't know where. He's taking us to some drug kingpin, a mob type, or a Persian, or a Turk, some immigrant from a place with an opiate-sounding name who he says can sell us quantity for cheap. That's what I've been waiting to hear: quality dope at low cost. Moe says you can get anything cheaper in Brooklyn.

Now we're lost. Brooklyn is vast. I never come here. Who can understand the layout? It's not a simple grid like Manhattan. It's shaped like a chunk of meat. We could be roaming the Amazon, for all I know, the streets are so dense and foreign. We've been in Moe's car quite a while.

Then he turns into a road that looks exactly like the suburbs. The surrounding housing projects, brownstones, and mosques have evaporated. Tall trees line both sides of the street. Otherwise, it's empty. No dogs, no strollers, no toys scattered over yards—just rows of parked cars and small houses, big lawns. Christmas lights are on every house, and not a sound from one.

"Where *are* we?" I ask. Moe answers with a word I don't catch. Most of what he says is unintelligible: *Gzeezer m'buh-buh ovah y'ar*—that sort of thing. Neanderthal.

"Dis izzit," he says, pulling up to the curb. "Ai don' tell awn." *Excuse me?*

"He shouldn't be long," Kit interprets. She gets him, somehow. It's weird.

"Do you see that?" she says, poking me in the ribs. "What's that about?" Moe is feeling his way across the lawn, crouching in the dark like a marine under fire. His shadow is that of an ape. He knocks on the side door of a single-story white frame house. The door opens and he stumbles in.

In the car, we snort some very icy C, compliments of Moe. "He does get good coke," Kit says. Then we grow impatient. "I know he's getting high in there," she grumbles. We might be sitting out here all night.

A patrol car approaches. My feet grip the floor. We stash the coke under the seat. The patrol car slows. The cops look us over as they pass.

"Be friendly," I say under my breath and slide behind the wheel.

"How friendly?" says Kit.

We smile, give a wave. They stop.

One cop rolls down the window of his car. I do the same. "Don't tell me I was speeding, officer," I say, girly as can be. "Everyone's been passing us by." He's a young one, this cop, could be he just started shaving. Likes his aftershave, that's for sure.

He shines a flashlight directly into my eyes. "This your house?" he says.

"Uh, no," I say. Brilliant.

"You ladies lost?"

"Ain't that the truth!" I let my eyes blink a few times. That still works with some guys. "We were going to a friend's house for dinner in—" Damn! I can't think of a name. I don't know Brooklyn neighborhoods. I steal a look at Kit. She's fishing in the glove compartment. What's she looking for? A map?

"Bensonhurst," she mutters.

"We're looking for Bensonhurst," I say. "Are we close?" The flash doesn't move from my face. He better not ask for my license. I don't have one.

"Nice car," says the cop. "You don't see a lotta these any-more." It's a stupid car, an old Chevy Nova, gray inside and out. An old-lady car. "Kinda late for dinner," he says.

"Is it! We've been driving around a long time."

He gets out and pulls something from his belt. My blood goes cold. I'm fighting for control of my mouth—my tongue is stuck to its roof.

"Have you ever been arrested before?" *Fuck all.* They couldn't have seen that coke!

"You're kidding me, right?" I say. It's a ticket book in the cop's hands. A ticket for what? Loitering? Write the ticket and go.

He leans in the window, averting the flash, looks around the car. "You sure you're not ladies of the night or sumpin'? Not waiting on your pimp in there?" He gestures toward the house.

"Aw, c'mon," I say. That ape better stay inside.

Kit leans across me, looking at his badge. "Capoletti?" she says. "I know a drummer in the city named Capoletti."

He points the flash at her. "Hey, yeah—that's my cousin from Flatbush! You know him?"

"Well," she says, turning to face the windshield. "I'm in a band."

"No kiddin'—which one?" We tell him, Toast.

"Get out! Hey, Tony," he yells to his partner, more seasoned by the look of him. "These ain't no working girls. They're from the Toast! I seen you play! Last year. My brother-in-law took me. Yeah, I remember you now—you play pretty good. Guitar, right?"

He turns off the flash, studies my face. "And you must be the singer. You're great, man. How about this! And I thought you were hookers." Yuk yuk.

"When you gonna come play in Brooklyn?" the other cop shouts. "We like the girl bands out here."

"There's a guy in our band," Kit says.

"Don't listen to him," Capoletti mutters. "He's not too hip. But I know a guy might want to book you—my cousin owns a coupla clubs over here, and in Queens. I'll give you his number. He could use a new act, and you can tell him I said so. Listen," he says. "Can I get your autograph? For my baby sister. She's sixteen." He opens his book and passes it through the window. "Here," he says. "Sign one of these."

I sign Sylph's name on a summons and hand the book to Kit. Are they watching us from that house?

"Listen," Kit says, very buddy-buddy. "Anytime you want to come to one of our gigs, just let our manager know and we'll put you on our guest list. I'll write down his number, too."

"Can you point us back to Manhattan?" I ask in clipped tones. The coke has me grinding my teeth.

"Yeah, yeah, sure, I'll draw you a map—hey, why not?"

The door to the house opens and Moe comes lurching out.

"Who's that?" says the cop. Moe stands there, not moving. "He with you?"

Kit leans over me for Capoletti's map. "That's our manager," she says. Cocaine makes her quick. "He went over there to see if he could use the phone."

The cop hauls himself back in the patrol car. "Tough stuff about your dinner," he says. "But Bensonhurst's where you go for Italian ice. You wanna eat good, you gotta go to Sheepshead Bay."

"Thanks a bunch," I say. "Sure am glad you guys came along." Kit kicks me.

I roll up the window and they drive on, too slowly, about the speed of Moe. He's moving in our direction. I roll the window down.

"Fuzzeesh?" he says.

"It's okay," I tell him. "They thought we were lost. Let's go."

"Uh," he replies. "Fug." He looks down the empty street. "Them g'zuys, man," he says, shaking his head. "Mo' bread, y'know whu' I zayne?"

"The stuff is more expensive than he thought," says Kit. How much more? A hundred dollars more. I groan. Shit, I'm beginning to sound like him.

"Look," I say. "Hey Moe! Did you at least bring us a taste?" He wipes one palm with the other. Oh, right. We have to pay for it.

"This is ridiculous," I say. "How long did it take us to get here? An hour? My people can't wait. I can't sit here and dilly-dally all night. I'm coming in."

Moe shifts his feet, hangs his head. "Uh, don' know." Fucking dummy.

"Whack," he says. *What?* "They've got a gun," he says loud and clear. "There's three of 'em," he adds. "Okay people, bu' y'know, ner-vous."

"Did you sell them some of this coke?"

A goofy smile. "Don' fly," he mumbles. "Patience." He slouches back to the house.

"I'm going in," I say after a minute.

Kit says, "I'm not staying out here by myself. This neighborhood gives me the creeps. And what if those cops come back?" I think she can handle that.

We turn up the volume on the radio and Moe returns high as a kite. His smile looks triumphant. The reason: he's brought us a taste. We snort it out of the bag. It's not worth the trip, but it's late now and I have to get something—my troops will be panting at my doorstep. I order the minimum—a gram.

"They ain't gonna like this," Moe growls, I think. "You wanna make any kinda bread, you gotta buy weight."

I start to roll up the window. "Some other time," I say. "Tell them it's bad form to keep a lady waiting. You hear me? Now let's go or I'll change my mind."

Late that night, I go to Vance and cop to the truth. He grew up in Brooklyn, too.

"Shit," he says, scratching his cheek. "You gotta be more careful." He counts what money I have and shakes his head. "You'll never catch up to what you owe dealing piddly. You might as well get a job."

"Never mind that," I say. "What do we do?"

"Look, we're friends, right? I take care of my friends. I'm not gonna be hard with you girls. I'll advance you another quarter. Step on it, turn it over, and we'll be even."

I have to acquiesce; he's got me. He pulls a video off the shelf. Marcy's mulling cider. If only I could be in the movies: I wouldn't have to do drugs.

It's six a.m. when we get home, and the world is powdered white. White inside, white outside. White. "From now on things will be different," I say. "No more dealing from the living room."

"The bedroom, either," says Kit.

I'll move the business to our spare room next to the kitchen. The junk room, we've been calling it. So be it. It's been housing Betty's storage since the day I moved in. She'll never come back for it, I don't think so. She went hooking on Third Avenue, we heard. She didn't have a place to put her things. Still doesn't.

Some of Betty's things are useful. There's a nice table among them—her mother deals Early American. It'll make a good desk. I go to a headshop and acquire a brass counterweight scale—no more plastic minijob for me. I need something accurate. At a housewares store in the Village, I buy a small table to rest the scale on, a white aluminum folding number that attaches to the wall. Ridley installs it. Mr. Leather brings a black Formica sheet to place on the desktop and I get a sleek black lamp to sit on that. Next I acquire a sifter to grind the mannitol into the dope. Vance has given me a recipe. I taste it. It's slower to come on, but nothing can stop the power of this baby. I'm ready to go to work.

I work all day and into the night, when Dean comes by unannounced. "I thought I'd see if anything's happening," he says, and I use the money for Vance's stuff to buy a gram from him. I haven't got time to go and sit through another movie; Dean's *here*. To break even, I'll have to cut the dope even more. Instead, I raise the price. Isn't this the best dope money can buy?

Okay, then. Let money buy it.

NICE GUYS

I'll say one thing for Dick: he's persistent. I can't get him out of my mind. *Someday you'll thank me for this.* It bugs me. What is he—a fortune-teller, or a cop? I hate that my fate has taken his shape. It's demeaning. Dick isn't the one I'll ever have to thank— it's heroin. Heroin brought me this. It put me under its spell. When the D.E.A. knocked, the spell was broken, and my world came crashing down. I sit here and watch it fall. Is this better than a cell with a bare bulb and a bench? I can't even tell.

That Dick. He wants to be a nice guy. He wants to understand. He's asked a thousand questions and still he keeps calling. Has anyone threatened me? Tried to shake me down? Any of Angelo's buddies? "I don't know about his friends," I say. I don't even know about mine.

It's tough getting along in this city. Opposing forces don't always act like the enemy—most of the time they're your friends and neighbors, people of similar sympathies whom you wouldn't begrudge a thing. You don't want to believe they'd turn you in. But alliances huddle and break apart, stars rise and fall. To stay alive, you have to keep a few secrets. Half the population has gone underground just to pay the rent.

Who set me up? Dick refuses to say. I know he's just looking out for me, the way all dicks like to do. It's pathetic. Oh, Dick

. . . Dick . . . Dick. He's waiting for me to tire, to slip, to give someone else away. It's bad enough one guy's gone down for me; I'm not about to send in a second string. Dick thinks I'll cave in if I have to, but I don't. I've been to a lawyer and I know.

"You decide if you want to cooperate," the lawyer said. Co-operate—the very word made me wince. "Frankly," he said, forcing a smile, "I think you've done enough. But I can tell you this," he added quickly. "If you can stay away from your drug buddies, you'll have a much better chance at getting off."

He looked at Kit. He looked at me. "I don't need to see them again," I said. Kit looked over at the door.

"The less you know, the less you can tell the cops," the lawyer explained, as if everyone knew this but me. "You want the cops off your back and the D.E.A. wants information. As long as they think you can give them what they want, they'll keep coming back for more."

"I wouldn't want that," I said.

"Then," he said, "you don't have to worry."

This advice cost me every penny I had. "This isn't drug money," I said, when I handed him the cash.

"I don't want to know where it came from," he replied.

"Well, I earned it," I said.

"That's good," he said, and slipped it in a pocket.

He didn't wear a suit, this lawyer. He dressed in a beige cashmere sweater, a pair of pressed chinos, and tasseled loafers. He'd helped a friend of Kit's escape a smuggling charge two years before. He was a deal-maker, rich and relaxed. Judges knew him well; politicians too. He'd never lost a case. Like Dick, he didn't make any promises, except for a day in court. "Until then," he said, "just stay honest."

"I'm honest," I told him. I believed it.

"You did break a law."

"Look at me," I said. I was dressed up and sweating. "Do I seem like a criminal? What good would it do to put me in jail?"

He folded his hands across his chest. "You've been lucky so far."

"Yeah," I said. "Lucky."

I once knew a guy who went to prison for a murder he didn't commit. He was given a life sentence with no chance of parole. He kept himself apart from the other prisoners, refused to be lumped in with convicts. "I'm not a killer," he always said, "so I can't be a convict." He was in jail fifteen years before a judge finally agreed. I got caught red-handed and here I am walking away. There can only be one explanation: I am not a criminal.

"I talked to those detectives on the phone," the lawyer related. "They seem like unusually nice guys."

"Yeah," I agreed. "Too nice."

Kit twisted in her seat. "Can we go now?" Her voice betrayed nothing.

The lawyer stood up and extended his hand. He had very long fingers that brushed a hair from his sweater. The sweater was the same camel color as his hair, which receded high above his pug-like brow, and every time he ran those fingers through his hair he lost a little more of it. "You'll be okay," he promised, and forced another smile. "Especially if you can clean up your act."

"That's all I want in the world," I said. The one thing I couldn't get.

At the elevator I said to Kit, "That was the last of our money."

"Not all of it!"

"Yes, all."

"I don't understand you," she said. "First you give the cops all our dope, then you give the lawyer all our money. What are we supposed to do now?"

"We have to get clean," I said. "Now we have to."

"No, we don't. I know we can't sell drugs anymore, but I don't see why we should have to stop doing them."

"It's illegal."

"It's a stupid law."

"So, it's a stupid law. Are we gonna change it? Come on. Cal Tutweiler knows a doctor we can call."

"What kind of doctor?"

"A shrink who makes house calls. He'll give us pills. We can kick."

"You kick," she said. "I'm going home without you."

PART FOUR

THE FAMILY OF JUNK

New York 1983

DAD

Kit isn't too excited when I tell her my father's coming to visit. He called. Dad doesn't call often; my stepmother and I are at odds. All we have in common is the content of her medicine chest. Every time I go to their house, I cop some of her painkillers, sleeping pills, and ups. That's why I go to their house.

"Do they have to come here?" Kit complains. She's standing before the mirror over the kitchen sink, snipping at her hair.

"Why are you doing that?"

"These ends," she says. "This *hair*. I don't know about this hair." She lays the scissors on the sink and comes in the office, where I'm weighing what's left of the day's dope. When I start to get low, I make packages ahead, mostly to track our own doses. Also, it's something to do.

"Really," she says. "Can't you take them someplace else? I mean, this *is* 1983. No one stays home anymore."

"It'll make more trouble if I tell them not to come," I say. 1983? It is?

The phone rings. She glances at the scale. "What about the business?"

"I'll have to tell the day shift to come later on."

I answer the phone and make my own calls and then we clean the apartment. We're careful to close the bedroom and office doors. We've never discussed our living arrangement with our families. Kit's parents know her brother was gay but they aren't pleased with the information. When he died, he left all his money to his lover. They didn't understand.

"Parents," Kit says as we sweep up the dust. "If you marry a man, they give you money and a big wedding and all that furniture, those gifts—they give you the moon. But if you want to live with a woman, they only give you shit."

Kit thinks her parents would disown her if they knew about us. They already have suspicions. My father probably does too, but he's a different case. He refuses to believe any child of his would go "wrong." He lives by a set of unwritten rules that make anything outside of his experience unacceptable. We only connected when we cooked.

Everyone cooked in my family. I knew how to scramble an egg before I learned how to lace my shoes. My father was our breakfast chef, the grill man at our summer barbecues; my mother oversaw the rest. When company was coming, I made the soup, stuffed the chicken. My brother baked muffins and bread. He could turn out a respectable peach pie at a very tender age. Every now and then we'd go out for Italian or Chinese. Otherwise, we cooked.

What drove a stake through the heart of my family was God. My parents were strong believers, but I found religion restrictive and synagogue services uninspired and obscure. I didn't like praying in groups in language no one could feel. I didn't want anyone putting words in my mouth; I wanted to write my own. "That's not how it works," Dad would tell me. "Not in this world." I didn't listen. This upset my mother; she didn't want me to lose my faith. She didn't want to lose me. I liked that but I also resented it. That's how we got along. I wanted to know the world and she wanted me closer to home. "Stick with your own kind," she always said. "We're the ones who love you."

I wasn't sure what my kind was back then, and she never said. She never said much about anything important. Like Belle, she played it close to the chest. I resented this as a child because it left me out. It did teach me one thing, though: you never get to know a person if all you do is love them. You never get to know yourself. Affection may make you feel safe and secure but it's enmity that wins you respect. That enmity was what kept our family together—it worked better than religion. Faith doesn't need visibility to exist, but you can never let the enemy out of sight.

One of the last times I saw my mother alive was a Sunday afternoon in spring. There were a lot of people in the hospital, visiting. My mother was in a room with an older woman who was a member of a Bible-study group, all female, all dressed in black. The group was there that day, gathered around the woman's bed with their Bibles open in their laps. They spoke in murmurs—I guess they were praying. We were quiet, too. My mother's brain wasn't getting enough blood and her blood wasn't getting enough oxygen. It was difficult for her to speak. My father gave her some insurance papers to sign but she had trouble writing her name. "Stupid!" she cried. "There's no ink in this pen!" and she threw it across the room. My father and brother and I exchanged glances. We did our best not to sob. The Bible sisters were staring.

"We know you're not Catholic," said a woman with a wizened face. "But would you mind if we said a prayer to Jesus for you?"

My mother turned her head. "I believe in a God for everyone," she said, a weak smile parting her lips. "Thank you. I don't mind a bit."

She looked back at me then. I must have seemed surprised. "I don't mind if they pray to their Jesus for me," she said. "I need all the help I can get."

At that, I had to turn away. I knew nothing was going to save her. I looked out the window and listened to the women on the other side of the room. Those poor sisters, I thought, those misguided fools. I said a prayer for them.

"We didn't have any religion," Kit says. "I don't even know what that's like. And I don't like hearing you talk this way. It's depressing."

"Sorry, it's the way I am."

"It doesn't matter to me if you believe in God. I want you to believe in yourself."

I see a bird at the window.

"Are you going to cry?"

"I don't know." I pick up my dust rag and go back to work.

"I wish I could tell my parents we're together," she says. "I wish we could have kids."

I look up. "Wait a minute."

"Well, I do," she says. "I'd really like to have a kid and I'd like to raise it with you."

I take out the dope. "Let's do this now," I say. "Before they get here." I need it to clear my head.

The doorbell rings around three, Dad and my stepmother. It takes them several minutes to get up the stairs.

"Whew!" says Dad. "I couldn't do this every day."

"You get used to it."

"I never want to do this again," says his wife. She has back pain and a heart condition. She's not in shape.

"It's good cardiovascular exercise," I tell her.

She lights a cigarette, king-size. "I've never exercised in my life."

"My daughter was a great swimmer in school," Dad informs her. Is he trying to embarrass me? I'm a businesswoman, after all, but I can hardly tell him that.

We sit in the living room. They don't want tea, or coffee, or a drink. They don't want anything. They just want to sit.

"I don't understand how you're living," Dad says, resting his elbows on the table. He rubs his palms back and forth, slowly. "What are you doing for money?"

"I freelance." It's an effort to keep my voice bright. "I don't have to work every day, so I have time for my own writing—it's okay. We don't have many expenses." Oops. I said *we.*

"Where do you sleep?" he says, looking around the room.

"Here," I say without expression. Oh God, the phone! I meant to turn it off. Kit answers it from the bedroom. A moment later, it rings again.

I stand up. "Why don't we decide where we want to have dinner?"

"We only just got here," says my stepmother with a loud exhale.

"I may have to reserve a table," I explain.

"Oh," she says. "We can't stay that long. We're having dinner at your brother's. Maybe you want to come."

Kit walks in with her guitar case slung over her shoulder. "Hullo," she says. "I'm sorry I can't be here for your visit, but I have a rehearsal with my band."

"That's okay," says the wife. "Nice to see you."

The phone again, damn it. "You certainly are popular!" says Dad.

"People call here for your daughter all day long," Kit explains. "They tell her all their problems. She's like the village shrink."

"Really," says the wife on a puff of smoke. "How interesting."

It happens to be true. So many of my customers seem to be living lives of tragedy: couples with recalcitrant children; sons and daughters whose parents or brothers are dying; people with jobs getting harassed at work; junkies losing their apartments, or their teeth, or their lovers. I don't know when I became such an expert on human relations, but all I seem to do besides drugs is give people counsel. Even more amazing, they follow my advice.

"You always were a good listener," Dad says. "You were a quiet little kid."

I never thought he noticed. Dad always seemed to take more pride in household acquisitions than he did in us kids—the new dishwasher, the stereo, the fiberglass roof over the porch—but he was a child of the Depression. I grew up in a different world. I shut myself in my room. I listened to records. I read books. Lots and lots of books. I dreamed. I had fantasies. One was about writing books. In another, I was being raped, not by a single man or woman but a circle of molesting shapes, faceless figures who stroked me and stretched me and opened me wide. They pored over my flesh, lifted and puckered me. I watched, horrified, elec-trified, as they tunneled within. I thought they could see inside. I tried to fight them off, but the more I struggled, the more alive I felt. I wasn't afraid they would hurt me; I just didn't want them to see inside.

While Kit says her hellos and goodbyes, I slip into the office and turn down the volume on the answering machine. "What's in there?" says Dad when I return.

"Oh," I say. "My workroom. I'd show you, but I've been kind of busy and it's a mess."

"Next time, then."

"Why don't we go for a walk?" I say. "Let me show you around the neighborhood."

They like that idea. They're ready to get up. My stepmother wants to use the bathroom. She's horrified when I show her where it is. She takes a long, glum look at the peeling walls, the gaping toilet at the end of the hall. "This is a bathroom?" she whispers. I guess it's embarrassing; the neighbors might hear.

"It's an old building," I say. "I like living in a place that has a history."

"History, we've had. Give me the modern, give me the new."

"Look, it flushes and everything," I say.

"But where's the sink?"

"In the kitchen."

"What a setup," she says, shaking her head. "I don't see how you put up with it."

HONEY

March 1983. Another night, just Honey and me in the office. I can't believe it—she's written a book! It's kind of a beauty book. Sixty pages, illustrated, stories that culminate in her recipe for a healthy complexion. Ginger has taken the pictures. I'm trying not to be jealous.

"I wish we could write a book together," I say, knowing this might be the only way I'll ever write one.

She looks uncertain. "What kind of book?"

"We could write a manual for drug dealers," I say then. "About the art of dealing."

She claps her hands. "That could work!" she exclaims. Her bracelets jingle. "That could happen." She still looks unsure.

Well, I say, all in a rush, look: we both know the same people, don't we? Share the same customers? All day long they beat a path between her house and mine, or Bebe's, another coke-dealing friend who lives around the corner—Kit's over there now. Between us, we know all there is to know on the subject; what's more, I've already taken notes, in my journal, enough to get us started, anyway . . . So, what does she say?

"I think I hate writing," she tells me. She says it doesn't pay.

"It'll pay, it'll pay," I insist. "Lots of people are dealing," I say, passing her half a tenth—that's her usual—"but hardly anyone does it right. We need to establish working guidelines. Living with these drugs is hard enough."

"Yeah," she says. "There oughta be a *law*!"

"I'm working on that one," I hear myself say. "I'm writing the book that will legalize heroin."

"Really!" She regards me with awe. I'm kind of surprised to hear it myself.

"If anyone can do it," she says, "it's you." I've just published a two-page story in a downtown anthology—one of my customers was the editor. Honey's got a story in it, too. Hers is about a road trip to Florida in search of some phantom cocaine. Mine's about unrequited love on dope. We both believe in writing what we know. Collaborating should be easy.

"I don't know how you make anything on dope," she says, taking a snort from the bag I've just sold her. "It's so much easier with coke. You get much more volume for the money."

"I don't make anything much," I tell her. (I never say I turn a profit—people take advantage.) "But," I say, "it gives me material, you know, for writing. People do this dope, and suddenly everything that's ever gone through their minds is coming out their mouths."

"It's interesting, sometimes," she says.

"I don't know about that. There's such a thing as knowing too much about a person."

"It's ten times *worse* on coke," she tells me. "A *hundred* times worse. People never shut up, and then they repeat themselves, endlessly, the same shit over and over. I don't do that, do I?"

"I wasn't talking about us," I assure her.

"We should get Bebe in on this too," she suggests.

I'm not sure I like that. We don't exactly compete, the three of us, and we don't exactly not. Honey sends me some of her coke customers when they want a different high and I do the same for her with mine, some of them.

"Bebe's my main connection," Honey says with a shrug. "She's the only one who'll give me any credit."

"All right," I say. "We'll ask her."

"Maybe that's not such a good idea," she says then. "Keep it simple. Bebe won't have all that much to add and then we'd have to *split* everything. It's so insane—we've all got the same people, the same stuff. Bebe deals Downtown sometimes, you know."

"Yeah, I know," I say, though this is news to me. "It's really the same?"

"Well," she says, watching me, "maybe not exactly the same."

I ponder this. If Bebe's dealing dope, she must be getting it cheaper than I am. She's got that coke over there, too, and a boyfriend who ships pot by the bale. It's one-stop shopping at her house. This could cost me. And Bebe is Kit's best friend.

"Don't you think women make better dealers than men?" Honey says, freshening her lipstick. "Let's put *that* in the manual. Men have no guts when it comes to drugs. Nothing but ego, you know what I mean? No pride of purpose. Men are so *needy*, especially when they're on drugs."

"All junkies are needy," I say. "There isn't a time when they don't have a need."

"And then they want to sit around and get high with you," she sighs. "I just don't have the time. Of course," she adds, "that depends on who they are."

"You mean," I say crisply, "they could be Duke or Earl."

"Oh," she says. "I *heard* about that time they ripped off your stash. Earl even brags about it, if you want to know the truth."

"He *brags* about it?"

"I know you think Ginger had something to do with it, but I don't think she knew what was going on. She's embarrassed she was with them."

"She knew," I insist.

"You really think so?"

"I didn't see any of them bring any of it back."

"Well," Honey says, carefully reopening her packet and peeking in. "No one does that." I watch as Honey slips a fingernail inside the bag and lifts the powder to her nose. "I don't want to get into this stuff too much tonight," she says. "I'm sure I'll need it tomorrow." She searches my face. "I'm getting my eyes done," she confesses.

Here's a touchy subject; I smoke a line myself. I usually don't get high with the customers, but Honey isn't just any customer. We've been getting high together for years, one drug or another, this night or that. There isn't much I've done she hasn't been a part of.

"You can't talk me out of it," she says, "Don't even try."

There *is* some puffiness under her eyes, but to me it's just part of her face. It doesn't look *bad*. Well, maybe it looks a little bad right now, but it's the end of a weekend, she's tired. She picks up the mirror I keep on the desk for shaping lines and gives herself a glance. "I've had these bags since I was little," she says. "God, they're hideous!" She brushes a finger across the mirror, checks it for powder. "I'll never have to wake up to these hideous bags again. We'll all be better off."

"Honey, you're gorgeous. You don't need surgery." I'm wondering how she's gonna pay for this. With the kid and all, even with the sideline in coke, Honey's just scraping by. She's a junkie, like the rest of us—nothing to spare. "How can you afford it?" I ask. She was facing eviction the month before.

"I found a place that does it cheap. I mean, they don't do cheap work or anything, I checked. They're licensed. It's all right, believe me. I've done a lot of research. I went to this one place yesterday and talked to the doctor and he showed me exactly what he'd do. It's like liposuction for the eyes—it's no big *deal*. He agreed I was doing the right thing."

"Of course he agreed!" I say. "It's how he makes money." I sneak a look at myself in the mirror. I've got bags, too.

"Sometimes I think you're too cynical," she says. "It's not

healthy, you know? Anyway," she says, tossing back her hair, "it takes, like, twenty minutes, hardly anything, but it changes *everything*. I've read about it. All these women say their lives improved after plastic surgery. Not just their appearance—their *whole lives*. Every single one. If you feel better about your looks, it gives you confidence. You make more money. They all say it happened to them."

"I guess it makes sense," I concede.

"I wish I could buy a little more of this," she starts to say, peeking again in her package, then closing it. "But I don't want to get strung out. If only I'd been a painter instead of a writer!" she says, gathering up her papers. "It's so much *easier*, don't you think? Painters have all the fun, especially now. They're all getting *rich*. It's taken me a year and a half to put together even this little book and all I'm getting is a few hundred dollars. You can make a painting in a few hours and sell it for thousands."

"Honey, come on. Most artists aren't rich at all. You're talking about a handful."

"You don't get out enough, hon!" She opens her package, takes a snort. "Oh, I don't know why I had to be a writer! Art is where it's at."

Art? I don't want to hear about art. The most important thing happening in our culture is drugs, that's what I say. Drugs rule the world, because drugs rule the mind, and drugs are the law of the body.

She looks at me strangely. "Is this what you're putting in your book?"

I light a cigarette. "It's as good a place to start as any."

"I can't say I agree with you," she says, looking me in the eye, her voice firm. Her lisp has disappeared. "People everywhere are buying art, and they're not all on drugs. Not that many are. Some." She takes another look in the mirror. "Do you have any eyeliner I can use? I have to get ready to go out."

"What are we talking about?" I say. I want to keep her mind on the manual. "Art is a very small corner of the world, just another business. Books are the real foundation of ideas. Not art. It just seems like it here, 'cause that's what everyone around us does."

"It doesn't matter," she says. "Everything that happens, happens here first. New York is the center of the world and the art world's the center of that, and that's where we happen to be. What we do, the whole world watches."

"The *world*," I say—are we having an argument?—"is focused on the price of beans. It's about money, not art. Money. And wherever there's money, there's drugs. And wherever there are drugs, there's more money. *Drugs* are where it's at."

"You *gotta* get out more, hon! See more different kinds of people. When was the last time you went anywhere?"

"I haven't," I admit. "I see the news on TV."

"Don't watch," she says. "It's not real."

I want to change the subject. "What about your eyes? They're real. Is this surgery going to be painful?"

"Not on your stuff, it won't be," she laughs. "Your dope is the best." I'm proud of this, I have to admit.

"You want a line?" I say, laying it out on the mirror. I can see her bindle's empty.

Her eyes go wide. "Really?" she says.

"Mmm . . . don't tell Kit."

The next night, Honey's back early, her face swathed in a wide silk scarf. She's had the operation. Ginger comes with her. Prescott, too.

"How was it?" I ask. "A success?"

Honey takes off the scarf and starts to peel the bandages.

"Oh," Prescott says, spinning through the kitchen, waving his hands in the air. "This is so exciting! Just like the movies. It's like a movie, isn't it, Kit? Let's have some music! We must have music! Come," he says with a sobering stare. "This is a major *moment*."

"It's a party!" Ginger shouts. She's acting pretty friendly, but I'm keeping an eye on her anyway. Kit guards the bedroom door.

"Darling," Prescott calls to Ginger. "Where's the *camera*?"

"I'm way ahead of you," she says, a strobe in her hand. "Okay, Hon, let 'er rip."

Honey moves to the mirror over the sink and delicately lifts the gauze.

She looks the same as she ever did.

"Gorgeous," says Ginger.

"I can hardly see the stitches," I say, admiring.

"There's still some swelling," Honey explains. "But you can see the difference, can't you? I can. This is a face I can *love*—don't you love me?" She flashes us her Hollywood grin.

"Oh, Honey," says Ginger. "Oh, baby."

Honey's eyes mist over. She shakes her head. "This mascara," she says. "It always makes me cry."

ALLOVER DRUGS

Ever since I came to this city, it's been the same: drugs all over, allover drugs. Once they find you, they stalk you, like Dick. The city's full of them, drugs and dicks, they chase you, and that's the truth. The search for bliss never ends. There's no better high than rapture, except the ability to sustain it. Each return to the spoon or the straw holds that promise, or that threat. Enterprise is all it takes to access this condition—dollars and cents, which by the spring of 1983 are in ever greater supply.

A junk-bond boom on Wall Street is flooding the underground economy with a steady flow of disposable cash. "Discretionary income," they call it, and some of it trickles down here. The world seems made of junk: junk money, junk food, junk stores, junk powder. I got into junk at just the right time. Boning chickens never earned me any bonuses, that's for sure. High time I did something real.

In the daytime and early evening, I deal to the customers. Nights the suppliers come in. I pay for one with money from another—I'm always juggling books. Not that I keep records. As long as money keeps changing hands, everyone's happy. Everyone but Kit.

"We never do anything together anymore," she complains.

"We live together," I say.

"But we don't *do* anything."

Not together. I see most of my clients alone. She stays in the bedroom, or she's out. Her public image makes her self-conscious, though most of our friends are just as visible. She doesn't think of so many of them as her friends. This is my territory and it's taking up space in hers. What can I do? I had a life before junk, and some of these people are holdovers. One of them is Bill, an old non-drug friend of Belle's who also befriended me.

Bill's sick. Bill has AIDS. Bill's dying. Belle sees him now and then, brings him food, gets him medicine. I've been meaning to go but my hours are so strange and he has to rest; I just haven't found the time. Belle keeps me up on his devolving condition while I dial in occasional visits by phone, but one day while Kit's at rehearsal, he gives me a call on his own.

"You know my situation," he begins.

"Yes," I say. "I'm sorry you're so sick. I hope you're not too uncomfortable."

"I have some money," he says. "I was hoping maybe you could help me."

"What do you mean 'help you'?" I'm sitting at the scale, there's someone with me—Belle. Out of the corner of my eye, I spy one of the cats, my skinny tiger, perched high on a shelf near the ceiling. He's listing to one side, eyes half-closed—I can't believe it. He's nodding! How did he get into the stuff? What a question. How could he avoid it?

"I want to sleep," Bill says. His voice is muffled. "I want to sleep a long time. You know what I mean. I don't want to say it on the phone. Can you help me out? How much to put me out of my misery? You don't have to come here, I'm not a pretty sight. I can send someone. There's someone here now. That all right?"

This is more than I bargained for. Do I really have to do *this*? This stuff that turns men into monsters and monsters to mush, this drug that makes shadows look like dreams and desire feel like loathing, what does it make of me? An angel of mercy or an executioner?

I lower my voice to speak. I don't want Belle to know who this is. She'll turn on me, she'll freak. "I'm sorry," I whisper to Bill. "I can't have anyone I don't know coming here right now. I just can't."

"You know *me.*"

My God, this is difficult. The guy's in terrible pain. I can hear it. When I got into this business, I knew I was taking my own life in my hands. I didn't know how many others would give me theirs.

"Let me think about it a bit," I say

"Will you call me?"

"Yes."

"Soon?"

"Well, I'm working right now—"

"Please, can't I send my friend? I can't even describe how awful this is."

"Isn't there someone else you can call?" There has to be someone.

"Not Belle," he says. "Please don't tell her, okay? I know this is a hard thing to do. I wouldn't ask you but . . . I'm asking."

"Can I call you back? I'm sorry, I can't talk right now. I'll try to come see you later myself."

"Not too much later, okay?"

I hang up and turn back to Belle with a shiver, spilling the dope in my hand on the table. Some of it falls to the floor. Belle moves to catch it, her eyes meet mine. "I'll get it," I say. But I don't.

She sits back in the chair. "What's up?"

"This guy," I say, busying myself at the scale. "Friend of a friend, has AIDS. I think he's dying. Wants some of this," I tap the table, "to die with."

"How awful," she says, her mouth active, her breathing long.

"This horrid disease. Deeply sad. And frightening. It's not always possible to know what you need to about a person, is it? And always to remember where you've been—there are so many reasons one might not want to."

"I suppose we ought to get tested," I say.

"I suppose," she concurs, and purses her lips. "Have you heard anything about Honey?"

"I heard she had her eyes done."

"Well, I heard she has HIV."

"Why would anyone say a thing like that?" I feel my temperature rise.

Belle lays a hand on mine, the hand now holding the dope. "Because of that guy," she says, in her fill-in-the-blank way. "You know who it is. The one who made that devotional movie, what's it called—?"

"*Thrill Sucker?*"

"That's the one. He died the other week."

"Did Honey have an affair with *him?*"

"I don't know, I didn't ask. I think she shot up with him or something."

I never know whether to slap Belle or give her a hug. I hate her for telling me this.

"This is a drag," she says with a shake of her head. "Can we not think about it anymore?" She asks if I feel like a movie.

No, I say. I have to think about this. It's not going to go away. The first time a guy with AIDS came here and asked to use the toilet, I wanted to refuse him. Let him sit on my throne? I knew kissing didn't kill, but those lesions on his ass—I didn't know about *them*. I let him use the toilet but I scrubbed it down afterward with bleach. I felt bad doing that, but I just didn't know. The next time he called was from a hospital bed. He had the dementia and I couldn't make out a thing he said. I think he wanted me to bring him dope. I didn't want to go near him.

"I don't blame you," says Belle. She looks ashen. I'm beginning to think drugs don't affect her well. She does them for fun but they get her so *down*. I wonder why she keeps it up.

"I hardly do drugs at all," she says, her eyes falling again on the dope. Tell me another one, I want to say, but I don't get the chance. "I'm too occupied trying to work out how to make money," she tells me. "Even you seem to have figured it out."

Even me?

"I realize you're making a living at this, but it's not what you were meant to do."

Whoops. She's hit an open wound. "I'm writing," I say, avoiding her gaze. "Every night after business. I can hardly keep myself in notebooks."

"That's all right, then."

No, it isn't. What I have in my notebooks aren't quite stories, or ideas. They're more like swallowed cris de coeur, the scribbles of a mind in half-light. "I'm not especially proud of what I'm doing," I say. "But I couldn't stay in any job."

"Then you have to stop."

"It's not so easy."

"It's going to get you in trouble," she says. "You'll get sick."

"Yeah." I stare at the wall, thinking of Bill. I know I won't call him back.

"Look," Belle says, anxious to change the subject. "I hate to ask you but . . . well, you couldn't get some of the other thing?"

"Sure, I could." She's talking about cocaine. Belle never calls drugs by their names. Too specific.

"Can you get it tonight? An eighth?"

"No problem," I say. Brooklyn Moe should be available.

"I'd ask Honey," she confides, "but her thing hasn't been so good lately—and please don't tell her I said that."

"Like I said, no problem." I do my best to dredge up a smile.

"I wish you were selling *it* instead of this," she says, packing up to go. "This stuff is so low-class. By reputation, I mean," she adds quickly. "The way it makes you have to live—you know." She takes a quick parting hit off the dope, gives me a self-conscious look. "I want you to promise you'll never sell to my son."

This is a problem—a conflict of loyalties. He's already been here several times.

"He'll pressure you for it, I know," she goes on. "I'm not entirely sure he's interested in drugs, but I have reason to suspect. He may have got involved with a junky girlfriend and I don't want it to become an issue. Can you promise?"

I promise, but a knot forms in my chest. As soon as Belle leaves, I take a quick hit, too. Dear Belle . . . Poor Bill. If I had a prayer, I'd say it. If I had a heart, I'd beat it.

RICO

It's the middle of April when I hear from Rico again, calling from Sticky's office. This is awkward: Kit has never wanted him in this apartment, I can't see him. I say, "Want me to come over there?"

"No . . . Ah, no. Can't talk. Explain when I get there."

"Rico's coming here?" says Kit.

The phone again—Rico. He doesn't have the address. "Kit there?" he says. "Okay, good."

The next call is from Lucky. He's managing a rock club in midtown now. Somebody famous must be playing there tonight, unannounced. This happens now and then.

"Did you hear?" Lucky says.

"No, what?"

"I'm just going to say this the way I heard it. Sticky's dead."

"What?" I hold my breath.

"He OD'd last night."

"My God, no. At the joint?"

"No, he was home. One of the kids found him."

"I can't believe this." Sticky, an OD?

"Believe it. It's terrible. I just called to say, watch out for the wife. That Angie. She's telling everyone he got the stuff from you."

"That's ridiculous!" Am I shouting? "I haven't seen Sticky in months."

"I didn't think so," Lucky says, his voice steady. "But watch out. She's got a *mouth*, that one. She could make *trouble*."

"She's full of shit."

"You know that and I know that, but other people think other things."

"Sticky OD'd," I say to Kit when I get off the phone. She's in the kitchen, putting on hair dye.

"Is that why Rico called?"

"I guess." I can't say more. I choke up.

When Rico arrives, he makes for the office as if he's been here a thousand times. "You okay?" he asks, giving my shoulder a nudge.

"Not really. You?" His face is drawn, his skin sallow, his hands never at rest. They tug at his clothes, scratch his legs, rub his nose.

"It's been a weird day," he says with a sigh.

"So I hear. Lucky told me."

"Yeah, shit. You holding?"

I put out a line. Least I can do. How many has he given me?

"How is this stuff?"

"You'll see. What's all this about Angie?"

"Oh. Angie, yeah. That's why I wanted to see you." He takes out a hanky and hocks up a good one, picks up a straw and vacuums the line whole.

"Can't you shut her up?" I ask.

"No one can shut that bitch up. That fuckface. I knew it was a mistake for Sticky to marry her. She's a goddam two-faced fuckin' bitch."

"He was in love with her."

"I know, I know. Damn! If the Down hadn't killed him, she would have. Did."

"She didn't force it down his throat. She wasn't even living there."

"No, she was. She went back."

"She was there when it happened?"

"No, of course not. Out somewhere with her mob friends."

"A boyfriend?"

"I don't know! I don't know nothin'. Sticky's dead, that's all I know. The service is tomorrow night." He gives me the details, the time, the place. "You comin'?"

"Of course."

"Maybe you shouldn't."

"I have to."

"Maybe you should sit in the back."

"I don't have anything to feel guilty about!"

"I know, I know. But Angie—"

"She won't be the only one there. Must've been some rotten street shit Sticky copped."

"Yeah, sure. Listen, what I came to tell you—"

"Something else?"

"Your phone. I think it's tapped."

"Come on."

"No, really. I checked it out. There's something wrong." He lays a hundred bucks on the table. "Let me buy some of this off you, okay?"

While I'm weighing it out, he tells me there's a number you can dial to check the phone line for bugs. Repairmen use it. So do cops. He gives me the number, says not to write it down. We dial. If it rings busy, I've got trouble. If it beeps, the line's clear.

It's busy.

"You think Angie dropped a dime?" I ask.

"I don't know if it was her, but she does know . . . people. You get into this business, you can piss people off."

"My people aren't pissed. My dope is beautiful. My life is

beautiful. My packages are divine. When my people leave here, they go happy."

He takes another snort. "When was the last time you saw Sticky?"

"Come on, Rico! It wasn't me."

"Okay. I was just making sure. Things can happen. Don't worry about the phone," he says. "I can have it fixed from the office. I know this guy, y'know, he works downtown, for the city. You know. I'll ask him, he'll take care of it. But stay off the horn for a while."

When he leaves, Kit takes his chair. She's overheard the whole conversation. "I don't get why you believe anything Rico says. You know he's crazy."

"I guess."

She looks thoughtful. "You really used to have sex with him? He's so fucked up."

"Well, he used to be more attractive. Anyway, he had cocaine." I take out a couple lines of D. Kit lifts a set of works from a drawer.

"You don't even like coke."

"Okay. I got off on him."

"You're weird."

She thinks this is weird? Wait till she hears about Ned.

Ned is a boyfriend I had in college. I met him one day when my roommate left for class. He'd spent the night with her. In those days, Ned was living for his dick. I guess I was too, for a minute. We never really got along, except when I blew him, except when I licked his ass. He never complained about that. I would. To him, I was nothing but a drive-in window. He's been living off women as long as I've known him, never even had an apartment of his own. I don't know why I let him keep coming around. So what if he has good pot? *Pot?* Give me a break. I never told him I'd moved on to dope, he wouldn't get it if I had. On top of all the other indignities, he's a square.

Ned's been here a few times when Kit happened to be out. I've said nothing about it to her; he's been dropping in on me so long, it seemed more normal than disloyal. I want to put an end to it once and for all, though Ned does have a magnificent dick and Kit has none of any kind. Doesn't matter. He doesn't know what he's missing. He'll find out. When I played him Kit's records he wanted to meet her. He promised to come over later. I tell her about it now.

She gags. "I'm a monogamous person," she says. She can't live with the knowledge I'd have sex with anyone else, even if it's a man, even if the man is Ned.

"Monogamous? What was that with me and you and Betty?" I ask, then I drop it. Not fair.

I make Kit a promise: no more sex with Ned. That feels strange. I've had other boyfriends and a girlfriend or two, some were lovers, some housemates, but I was never with them for the long run. I never thought I'd have a long run. Now here I am with Kit, for however long time will tell, doing what our bodies tell us, dressing in each other's skin—the skin of the High House of Heroin, in the mythical Land of Grim.

On the next night the phone still rings busy when I dial the secret number, and I know: it isn't Angie who put the heat on me; it's Rico. He resents me, and Kit, doing this, living here, I can tell. That business about fixing it for me . . . he fixed it all right. It was Rico.

I go to Sticky's funeral with Pedro and Mr. Leather—the first time since we met I've been anywhere without Kit, not counting when she was out of town. When I reach the chapel, I'm glad Kit hasn't come because the first person I see is Betty. She's with Angie, of all people, and she doesn't look good.

Betty gives me the evil eye. We don't speak. Angie couldn't be nicer. She even apologizes for that nasty rumor about me doping Sticky, though I'm sure if Betty has her way, I'll never hear its end.

At the restaurant after the service, drinks are on the house. It's a sad occasion, but I'm strangely giddy throughout. Mr. Leather is deep in his cups, jerking his head to the music playing. He's had a letter from Big Guy—sorry, he meant to tell me. In all the excitement, he forgot. The letter is postmarked Hawaii, and includes a note addressed to me.

It's a warning. Big Guy is glad I quit Sticky's, the atmosphere's so unhealthy, but it pains him to know I'm still dealing. He's heard about Duke and Earl. I should get out while I can—please, get out. He's clean now, he says, and he misses us.

Mr. Leather tells me not to worry, not about Betty or Angie, or Big Guy, or Kit. Everything's fine, where's a waitress?

At home, Kit tells me Vance has been calling every half hour. He's run dry, what can I do? I could call Dean, but I don't trust his tie to Rico. What I need is to develop an inventory and soon, find yet another source of supply.

As it turns out, I don't have to do anything. One of my customers has a friend with "work" for me to see. I look heavenward and think of the note from Big Guy, then toss the thought aside. If I wasn't doing the right thing by my friends, the right thing wouldn't be coming back to me.

AMSTERDAM BROWN

Maggie is the mother of a baby girl, Peter is the father. Maggie is the dealer. Peter is the mule. The baby is something of a passport.

Maggie's heroin is brown. She brings it from Amsterdam, where she lives. My customers don't like it at first. "But this is brown," they say. "It's good," say I. "You smoke it," and I show them how.

You put the powder on a piece of aluminum foil, roll up a straw with another piece. That's your pipe. Holding a lighter under the foil, you angle the foil, put it to the pipe, and inhale. As the dope starts to bubble, you move the lighter under the foil and keep inhaling through the aluminum straw. The dope slides across the foil as it burns over the flame. This is called "chasing the dragon." It's heaven. It even gives you a rush. Not like the one you get from a needle, but close enough. "I don't know," Kit says. "Smoking this stuff seems wasteful."

"You can shoot it," Maggie tells her. "Just mix lemon juice into the water before you cook it."

Kit tries it. I try it. We're back in business.

Some of the customers prefer the brown. They like that low-down, dirty-bottom feeling. They also like my price. Brown dope is cheaper than white and I've decided to pass on the savings. I make it up in volume sales to other dealers. Their money is always green.

Maggie comes over with Peter and the baby every day. She also brings cocaine. She smokes both drugs, so she doesn't have tracks, but her face, her hands, her forearms are mottled with dried scabs and festering sores. When Maggie's high, which is always, she thinks insects are crawling under her skin. She digs through it to get them out.

"Maggie, really. Please stop that," I say one afternoon. My living-room table is littered with burnt foils and pipes, ashtrays, beer cans, and diapers. I can't bear watching her scratch. Can't she stop?

"No," she says, ashamed. "I can't," and commences to pick at a particularly ugly scab as if I'd said nothing at all.

Sometimes, while I'm doing other things, the image of Maggie's arms comes to mind, and it upsets me. That business of smoking the coke, freebasing it's called, is the most obsessive act I have ever seen anyone perform, but Kit finds it has a certain allure. She's started picking her face, too, and cutting off her hair. She's already shaved the sides of her head behind her ears and is slowly snipping away at the spikes on top. Onstage, it looks fabulous. At home, it looks insane.

In June, I begin to miss the white. This brown dope may cost less, but you have to do more of it to get the same effect. It's harder on the system, too. A couple of times, when Maggie is nowhere to be found, I get sicker than I've ever been in my life. More disgusted. It makes me sour, like the lemon.

Brown dope has also given me a hankering for brown food—chocolate milk, for instance. Days go by when that's all I can get down, chocolate milk and chocolate ice cream. I've never liked chocolate this much; I didn't eat candy as a child. I'm smoking more cigarettes, too. Something about this dope requires tobacco.

I'm up to two packs a day, unfiltered. Periodically, I have to run to the sink or the toilet to spit. I'm coughing up green-and-black goo, but I don't want to give up smoking; it's keeping me off the needle. We know now how needles put us at risk for AIDS. I don't want the customers fixing here, either—one of them is already dying—but I can't really stop them, not with Kit banging away every few hours for all the world to see.

When Maggie and Peter go back to Amsterdam to re-up, I give the Lower East Side one more try, going directly to the projects on the river and buying quarter-grams or half-grams through a homeboy I've met in the street (I'm trying to save money). The dope's not as potent as Maggie's, but it's cleaner than the strychnine-laced bundles from the other buildings. White dope is like health food by comparison. Same poison, but no chemical additives. No fat.

When my runner is busted and ends up in Rikers, I'm forced to turn again to Dean. In a way, I'm relieved. I'll never have to set foot in the East Village again. Except that someone's decided it's a great place to open an art gallery—Belle—and it's not "provincial" anymore. It's *posh*.

How does this happen? One day a neighborhood's a war zone; the next it's a fucking town square. Dozens of new shops and galleries have opened in spaces where, not so long ago, people shot dope, not art. Here, women and minority artists can be the stars, they're creating a whole new market. Openings are like parties at hip-hop clubs—paintings in the front room, drugs in the back, art dealers in the alleyways with money in their hats. Collectors are coming from all over town. The street-dope sellers have had to move south a few blocks but they haven't disappeared. If anything, they're more numerous than ever.

I worry about the competition this scene is stirring up. If everyone's on the Lower East Side every day, who will bother coming to Sixth Avenue? Everyone, as it turns out, thanks to Prescott Weems. I don't mind giving Weems a line now and then.

He's a scene all his own, twittering through the door with a parade of artists and anglers for whom heroin is a medium of discovery, succulent and boundless. Business is almost too good; Weems never brings the same person twice. Most nights I hardly have time to get out of my chair, and Kit has to take over the door.

One of Weems's pals is a pizza-faced guy by the name of Davey Boxer. He offers Kit a fall show in his gallery, another new spot on a corner near the Bowery. His family's in real estate and they've bought him the space. All of his artists are people he gets high with, and most of them buy their stuff from me. The rest see a tiny blonde named Sylvia, who's no stranger here, either.

Kit is consumed with work, making new photos, running to the lab with one of our customers, a color expert, printing through the night. She's going through massive quantities of drugs, which we happen to have on hand. Bebe's coke is always just around the corner and Dean has gone to Europe for an extended vacation, leaving me with a summer's worth of dope. There's money stashed all over the apartment; I have to pay up on his return. I'm more nervous about the money than the drugs. The money takes up more space.

I run out of stuff long before Dean gets home. So does Vance. He's waiting for a fresh supply. We can get by a few days on pills, but I can't let the business slide. That's out of the question. I find a new alternative in a guy named Massimo, I don't remember how—through somebody someone else I know knows, most likely.

Massimo's an ex-skier from Switzerland, comes from the Alps—born to be high. His connection's small-time but at least it's Italian—on the money. In September, Maggie returns without Peter—they've split. Now she's always in the company of suspicious men. I don't like her scene at all, but Kit's and mine really isn't much better.

We've both developed a tolerance for dope that's hardly cost-effective. Every week we need more and more. We ought to get away, bring the tolerance down. Anywhere will do—a beach, a hot tub, a hotel room, anything. Trouble is, Massimo can't extend me much credit and I'm low on ready cash. Who's gonna front us a vacation?

I remember a place in Montauk where the off-season rates aren't bad. It's the farthest place on Long Island we can go and still be on dry land. The beach is beautiful this time of year, let's go. Kit agrees. "Sounds good to me," she says, but she can't leave till after her gallery show. That's not soon enough for me, so when Sylph suddenly books a five-day tour for the band, I go along for the ride.

WE HIT THE ROAD

With my customers and dope from Massimo temporarily in Honey's hands, we hit the road. We're going north, to Boston, Detroit, Montreal, Toronto, and Buffalo. Toast is used to these one-night stands; I'm depending on pills and nerve. I've offered to help drive the van—the only way I can get a comfortable seat. Otherwise, I have to make do on an amp like the rest. We're seven all told: four band members, a roadie, a road manager, and me.

The band has to keep touring to make any money. They're still taking offers for a record contract but they can never agree on terms. Meanwhile, there's no getting away from the fact that their audience isn't growing—it's been too long since they put out a record. Some of the places they have to play are god-awful clubs that smell of beer and sweat. Boston doesn't give them a bad reception but Detroit is a ghost town—some diehard fans and a few dozen stragglers who happen to be drinking in the bar. The band still puts out at every show and their humor never flags. At each gig they play better than at the one before—in Montreal, to a crowd of Quebecois punks who can't get enough of their music. Spirits are so high I don't even notice the edge I've got on, not till we reach Toronto. That's where I run out of pills and Kit finishes the last of her dope.

In Toronto, they sell smack in vitamin capsules the way Honey used to sell MDA. We can't get many—the kids who take us around don't know the scene well enough to score. I let Kit have the pills but I do take a taste. It's nasty. But there's over-the-counter codeine for sale in every drugstore. Not to worry.

None of us have had much sleep when we get to the border. Customs agents order us out of the van while they search it. They look under the seats, in the engine, in the instrument cases and amps. They read every word of the band's working papers, the fine print on the tax forms. When they start on the luggage, we're confined to an office, can't even get permission to go to the bathroom. Sylph sits on a bench clutching her kidneys, a pained expression on her face. The rest of us stand aside and smoke.

Two hours go by before they get to Kit's duffel. That's where she packs her electronics. Her shoulder bag contains twin black nylon makeup cases. One holds her makeup, the other a few cotton swabs, a blackened bent spoon, and a syringe—enough to get us all arrested. We hold our collective breath as an agent unzips the first bag. It's the makeup. He examines the compact, removing the mirror and tasting the powder. It's hard not to laugh. Kit's foot taps the floor. The guard picks up the other bag, then looks at his watch. "All right," he says. "I've seen enough. You're gone."

We scramble back in the van and peel out. I'm behind the wheel. "Shit man," says Poop. "Was I sweating bullets or what?"

"Really, Kit," Gloria says. "That was too close."

Kit wants to know where she was hiding her stuff all that time.

"They didn't look in *my* bags."

"You mean, you do have drugs on you?"

Gloria looks out the window. "Pretty landscape," she says. "Isn't it?"

"Pull over," says Sylph. "I've really *got* to take this piss."

We arrive in Buffalo with only enough time for a sound check and a quick bite to eat before showtime. The club is a skanky bar that smells of varnished vomit, the stage in a small back room. "Jesus," says Poop. "Who booked this gig?"

"You did," Sylph reminds him. Buffalo is Poop's hometown.

"Oh, yeah—sorry," he says with a sheepish grin. "This ain't the way I remember it."

It's a gray, depressing town, nothing but smokestacks and dull red brick, hardly anyone on the street. We're beat, but there's no place to rest. After the border search, we decided to cancel our hotel and drive back to New York after the show. Sylph lies down on the stage to catch a few winks while Poop stays at the bar; he's found a girl to make out with. Kit can't do anything but stew. Gloria's shot the rest of her dope and is floating on a cloud of superiority. "Fucking Gloria," Kit says through her teeth. "Why couldn't she save me a line?"

"Sorry, Kit," she says. "It's just not the kind of thing you share."

"I can't play," Kit says. "We'll have to cancel."

Sylph's eyes flutter open. "Kit, you're not serious."

"I can't play. I'm too sick. I'm sorry, this place is a hole. We're not gonna make any money here. Let's get in the van and go home."

"There must be *someone* around who has *something*," Gloria reflects. "There's *always* someone."

There is—a derelict who's been watching us from an unlit doorway at the back. He sidles up to Kit, who can barely tune her guitar, much less play it. He tells her he has some pills that are something like methadone. They won't get her high but they'll straighten her out. He quotes an outrageous price. I pay it.

There are barely fifty people in the bar when the band begins their set—the smallest crowd they've ever played to. Kit turns up the volume on her amp. The sound is nearly deafening. I sit in the back with the road manager, listening in awe. I've never seen Kit look so grim onstage and never heard her sound better. She makes pain seem almost desirable. I don't care what Honey says: *this* is art. Too bad no one's around to hear it. Damn shame.

GOOD CONNECTIONS

Dick just threw me a curve. He showed up without any warning. "What's that you're taking?" he asked, indicating a prescription bottle in my hand.

"Clonidine," I answered, licking my lips. Clonidine gives you dry mouth. "Or Catapres, for high blood pressure."

"How long have you been taking these?"

"Not long," I told him. "You want one?"

He looked at me intently. I was twitching. Actually, I was about to throw up.

"Listen," he said, "do you want to go to a clinic?"

"I don't have insurance," I said. "I can't pay."

"That's no problem." He smirked. "We can get you into any rehab, any institution. We do have good connections that way."

Do you? I thought. Me, too!

Cal Tutweiler had sent over his doctor the night before, a balding man in his fifties, dressed in rumpled tweeds. Have 'scrip pad, will travel—that's him. He's helped *everybody*, Cal said, meaning the celebrity underground. My kind of people, he implied. The kind who deliver.

Kit could hardly wait for the doctor to arrive. She couldn't stand to be sick. She was in the customer chair, bouncing one of the cats on her knee. The other two were sleeping on my desk. I led the doctor in the office and began telling him our story. He didn't wait to hear it all.

"I suppose you know what you want?" he said, producing a prescription pad and a pen. "Or do you want me to recommend something?" He seemed very nice.

"I guess I know what works for me, yeah."

"I want Valium," Kit said gruffly. "Valium and codeine and methadone."

"I'm sorry," said the doctor, his eyes lighting on a drawing Cal had given me. "I can't write for methadone. You need a special license for that."

"What I really want is heroin," Kit remarked.

He chuckled. "Valium, Darvon, that I can give." He scratched out the 'scrips with his pen. "I'm giving you three refills," he told her with a very slight smile. "That should hold you awhile. Long enough."

I ordered clonidine for myself, to relieve the leg cramps, sinusitis, and twitching, and some Ativan to calm my nerves. As an afterthought, I got some Lomotil, a bowel-binder whose composition nearly replicates morphine.

The doctor wrote the 'scrips and asked if we knew how to use them. We all had a laugh, low in the throat. *Do we know how to use them?*

We hardly know anything else.

PART FIVE

CRUSHER

CRUSHER

October 1983. The world is in *desperate* condition. It only looks like a mountain of cash. Honey just left here in tears, on her way to another party. She was upset about her breakup with her new boyfriend, Julius, an intellectual part-time dope dealer. Brown, like himself. He was Honey's idea of a potential husband, a man who could build her a ladder to the straight world—an artist. He made rickety, columnar assemblages out of detritus he picked up from the street. "Space junk" he called it. He pleased her. They were together only a few months, long enough for Lute. She's left town, she clicked her heels together and went straight to New Orleans, where she's making a career in the blues and carrying on with a Cajun singer, genus: male. "I'm so *jealous*," Honey said. "Lute always gets what I want."

It's all for the best. Julius was kind of a mess—a smart enough guy but he hardly ever took a bath. He said the dope kept him clean. "Junk doesn't let you perspire," he once told me. "There's nothing to wash off."

On Honey's heels came Brooklyn Moe. He was *very* unhappy. Not because of me. Someone stole his Chevy Nova. It was parked across the street from here—a safe place, I thought. Not anymore, not for Chevy Novas. Moe says they're collector's items. I didn't know that. Poor Moe. How's he gonna get back to Brooklyn? Subway? Poor Moe.

Then came Rhonda Kay, a guitar player from a female blues band. This is a time of funk women and funk love. Rhonda Kay imagines herself a real hipster; her dad was into jazz. She came in drunk as all getout, squawking like a rooster, knocking things over, and babbling about the insane relationship she has with whoever the hell it is, I never did get the drift. She totally freaked out Kit, who was already on edge, troubled by the imminent demise of her own band.

And Vance, my madman dealer, he was here, too, bloody and bruised and stitched up in the face, his lower lip hanging off after some "accident" he had last night copping from *Russians*, he said.

Bo Brinks, now there's a case, a painter who makes a living copping hard drugs for wealthy middle-aged women. He says he's "building a collector-base," and comes here with his boyfriend for comic relief. I accepted an air-conditioner from them in exchange for a tenth of D—my turn to laugh. At last.

Then Toni stopped in, very squirmy, stroking those long legs and brushing his/her hair while she/he asked if maybe I'd like to give her forty dollars worth of dope in return for this black moiré pantsuit she just modeled in *Paris*. She knows it'll fit me—aren't we the same size? Sure, give or take a few feet. Anyway, it's divine. She was sorry she didn't have money, they paid her in clothes.

Before you could say "designer dress," Prescott was on the phone from an airport in Rome wanting to know will I have what he needs when he lands in New York seven hours from now? What have I got here? A home or a halfway house for the bummed? I'm surrounded by the wicked and the testy. Do normal people have days like this? I doubt it.

Then Honey comes back with Bert, a painter I know from the bar at Sticky's. He's a mineralist like Cal. I didn't remember Bert ever being into dope. "Well, every now and then, you know—something different," he says. I can't believe Honey would have sex with him—he's so bourgeois. *Are* they fucking? Well, none of my business. Some questions you just don't ask. Most of them, really.

As soon as Bert has a snort, he starts speculating on the way Sticky died. He believed that story Angie was telling about me selling lethal dope. "I would have been here before," Bert said, "but I never knew if I could trust you."

Trust me? Trust *me*? How am I gonna control *him*? Loose of lip, he is, that one, Norbert, that's his real name. Norbert Fluss. What a cheap bastard. He nickels-and-dimes me all over the place, slumping in the chair like he's ducking blows.

While he's grousing, Bo calls to say he's run into some kind of major life-drama he can't explain. Would I, could I, tide him over with something on credit? He did so much of the dope he copped for one of his rich lady-friends, he had nothing left to sell. He'll tell them he was mugged and they'll give him more money, and then he'll pay me. Later.

How powerful must be a substance that turns otherwise well-behaved, levelheaded, hardworking professionals and loving sons into two-bit hustlers, liars, and thieves with disgusting personal hygiene and no sense of humor? Very powerful. And what happens to the person holding the strings?

Let's see.

Ginger arrives with the left side of her face under gauze. She's had surgery. Her boyfriend got drunk and beat her up in a hotel room in Germany, where she was having a show. She had to fly all the way across the Atlantic with her eye hanging half out and now she's feeling vengeful. In certain circumstances vengeance is a girl's best friend, better than diamonds ever were. Maybe not better than heroin.

Ginger could lose her eye. She won't say what the fight with the boyfriend was about, but it doesn't matter here; none of us thinks it's cool to beat up a lady. She has some painkillers but they don't do much for humiliation. She wants dope. My dope. She also wants female company, so she's brought along a quiet woman-friend who has huge and sympathetic watery blue eyes. Now that she has what she wants, Ginger goes back to being jolly, sort of. When she isn't making jokes, she's making a list of fifty ways to kill a lover.

That's when Claude Ballard stops by with his head in the clouds and wanting to go higher. Last year he was doing graffiti in the subways; this year he's the most celebrated artist in town. And the most stoned.

What do ordinary people do for fun? Do they come home from work, buss the spouse, plop themselves in front of the tube, and feel that their lives are complete? For me, it just goes on and on.

At five a.m. the phone blows again, three, four times, junkies in trouble. One's half out of his mind on cocaine, another has a sick friend on his hands, can I do something?

Bo shows up with the money he owes. Now he needs some weight to take to a party in the Hamptons. He has to get there before breakfast. He doesn't want to rush me, but hurry, hurry. Can't talk now. See me later.

Nearly everyone who comes talks about cutting down, getting out of this life once and for all. They've gotta come up for air. Oh really? What's the *air* got to offer? No, it's too hard, they say, really too, too hard. What, this life? This is my life. What about that?

Kit crawls home from a gig with bone-crusher symptoms, mild but scary. A bone-crusher is what you get when a piece of cotton from the spoon slips inside your vein. It induces cold-turkey chills, fever, cramping, and retching, but feels even more intense, as if your bones are crumbling and you're going to die, soon. Only another shot can put you out of your misery. If you're steady enough to hold the needle and have something left to shoot.

"It's not a bone-crusher," Kit says. "It could be arthritis." Her mother has arthritis. She knows what it's like. "It's in my shoulder," she says. "I need to get some sleep."

Her left arm hangs limply at her side, it hurts to move it. The fingers on her right hand are numb, she has a splitting headache and a fever. She downs half a dozen aspirin but has trouble getting out of her clothes. I give her a line to help her nod off. She looks sort of all right but not really quite. Her eyes are dull glass. I want her to see a doctor. She turns to the wall and says, "Mmf."

I don't like this, not at all, but I don't know what to do. Suddenly the apartment feels empty. No, not the apartment. Our life. From now on I'm going to have business hours—must I be on call around the clock?

Tomorrow, everything will be different. Its promise fills me with hope. I wish I could wake Kit. This will come as good news. I'm sure she'll feel better when she hears it. Maybe I'll go for a walk. But Kit's lying so still, I can't leave her. And I can't stand being with myself.

I decide to shoot myself up, I ought to know how by now. In spite of everything, or because, I want to try it. I pick up the spoon, add dope, add water. I'm careful with the flame. I tie off, hit a vein in my wrist, except I miss it. My skin balloons out the size of a Ping-Pong ball. An abscess—ugh. Good thing I deal. Good thing I have more. Good thing I have plenty.

I load up another spoon, take another shot, this time in one of my usual places. Bingo, a rush—not of chemicals but ideas. My head floods with stories, characters, speeches. I envision an entire scenario, beginning, middle . . . I'll know the end when I come to it.

I move to my desk and start scribbling in my notebook, scratch, scratch. I have to work to keep up with my mind. I light a cigarette and scrawl out a paragraph. My pen suspended over the page, my head swinging like a trapeze, I sit at my desk and bless my night and feel the heat drain out of me, going, gone. It'll be back in a minute. Concentrate.

When Kit wakes up, we talk about kicking. It's time to cut down, cut back, clean up—we're no different than anyone else. We promise ourselves a few days off. We'll go somewhere nice and chill, but not today—tomorrow. Tonight, Kit's flying to Washington to play a gig. She dreads it. No one's getting along in her band. They bicker all the time: over money, managers, bookings, arrangements, set lists. It never stops. She's afraid of what's coming. Oh well, she says. She's getting too old for rock and roll, anyway. Time she went back to painting.

She takes her guitar into bed and forces one hand across the strings; the other falls off the fret board. "How can you do anything with your arm like that?" I say, the voice of reason. She calls Sylph to gauge the reaction to her possible cancellation. They're all broke, Sylph says. They can't do without the money from this gig. They're counting on Kit to play. There's no chance of finding a replacement.

Early the next morning, I'm sleeping when the doorbell sounds. It's Kit, back from D.C. She needs help getting up the stairs, please come down. I find her just inside the downstairs door, slumped over her bags. "Kit!"

"I'm all right," she says, straightening. "I can't carry all this stuff by myself is all."

I pick up the guitar, the duffel, the bag of effects boxes and cords. "What happened?" I ask.

"Bad gig," she says. "We broke up." We mount the steps in silence.

"What about the arm?" I say, once we're inside.

"Don't ask."

"How did you play?"

"I got as high as I could and let my hands do it without me. Anyway, it was a very short set. Gloria threw a fit and stomped offstage in the middle of a song. Then, of course, the club didn't want to pay us. Give me something. Please."

I cook it for her while she ties off, the rig in her teeth. "Got any coke?" she asks.

"No."

Will I get some?

"In a minute," I say, but as soon as she's finished I take her head in my hands and tell her it's time she saw a doctor. This can't wait.

She won't go.

I wait.

Kit's sure whatever's causing the paralysis in her arm will pass. She doesn't feel sick or anything. It's just a . . . just a *thing*.

"It's not a *thing*," I say. "You can't move your arm. You have pain in your shoulder. You play guitar and you can't use your hand. This is *something*."

I call Doctor Paul, but he's out of the office. He may not be back all day. I leave a message, say it's an emergency. "If it's an emergency," the service says, "perhaps you should go straight to the hospital."

Kit says it hurts to move. She has to rest. We can talk about it later.

By nightfall, I'm going over the edge. I've been giving her dope all day, and when she's too high to argue, I get her dressed and into a cab to the hospital.

"You don't look well," says the nurse at emergency admitting.

"I feel all right," says Kit.

"Her arm's paralyzed," I say.

"Are you a relative?"

"Friend," I say. "Roommate."

"Does your friend have insurance?"

Kit produces a card and calmly sits down to answer questions while the nurse fills out papers. It doesn't take long and they walk her inside.

Years of experience with knife cuts and other calamities incurred while cooking have made me familiar with the operations of this hospital. I know Kit might have to be there for hours, and I have business to conduct. Before I leave, I make sure the nurse knows to call me when they find out what the trouble is. I leave Paul's name for good measure. Kit will get better treatment because of it.

A block from home I see them: a half dozen of my favorite customers, sitting on the benches in front of my building, waiting. It makes me nervous to know they've all been out there pacing, but they do look happy to see me. I start to feel like the Pied Piper as they follow me down the street. I turn and look behind: a few couples, a few loners; long-legged guys, sexy girls. So this is what it's like, I say to myself, thinking about all our artist friends who were bums one day and stars the next, never able to go anywhere without an entourage of "guests." I'm humbled.

Upstairs, I work up a sweat serving so many people all at once. "Kit's in the hospital," I say. "I can't ask anyone to stay. I may have to go back any minute." The truth is, I have to re-up but I don't want to cop till I know more about Kit. If I go up to see Vance, it may take a long time. I'll try Massimo. We still don't know each other well, but his apartment's in the Village, near the hospital. I call the emergency room first. The nurse says she was just about to call me.

"Your friend is very sick," she says.

"How sick?"

"You'll have to talk to the doctor about that. I can't discuss a patient's diagnosis on the phone."

I want to be prepared.

"I think it's best if you just come here. Your friend is a very sick young lady."

Now I'm prepared. I know what that means. When my mother

was dying, that's what everyone said, those were the words they used—my father, my parents' friends, the nurses. "Your mother is a very sick woman," they said, and then their mouths would twist and their eyes would cloud up and their silence said the rest. If a person is ill, it means they'll get better. If they're sick, they're going to die.

The nurse ushers me in the moment I appear at her window. I don't find Kit right away. All I see is a maze of white-curtained hospital beds, thin sheets of muslin fluttering the antiseptic air. I see a guy wrestling with his bed, his wrists taped in bloody bandages. I see a woman who hasn't shit in a year. Where's Kit? Then she's walking toward me in one of those silly cornflower-print gowns, dragging an IV stand behind her.

"I'm not sure what to do," she says. "I want to go home and be with you and the cats, but the doctor says if I leave now, I'll be dead within twenty-four hours."

"You're not sure what to do? You're not sure?" I feel wild. Then I laugh. I live in a comic world. It's tragic. "Kit"—I have to steady my voice—"I think you have to stay."

"I guess so." Her bewilderment is somehow touching. "It's just, you know, I mean I understand I'm sick, but I don't feel all that bad. I don't see why they can't give me medicine and let me go home."

I'm not surprised she doesn't feel bad. She's gone through five hundred dollars' worth of pure heroin in just a few hours. She's walking on air. I grasp her arm. I'm afraid she'll float away. "What is it they say you've got?"

"It's called endocarditis," she says. I've never heard of it. She explains what the doctors have told her. It's a nasty infection of the heart, a bacteria that lives on the surface of the skin and enters the body when the prick of a syringe opens a passageway to the heart, where it lodges in the walls of a valve and nibbles its way through. That's when the valve collapses. That's when the heart explodes. Apparently, Kit is near detonation.

"Don't you want to sit down?" I say.

Then Doctor Paul appears, drawing up a gurney. "The standard treatment for endocarditis is six weeks of intravenous antibiotics," he tells me.

Six weeks?

"If all I'm going to do is lie in bed for six weeks with a needle in my arm, I'd just as soon do it at home," Kit pouts.

Paul shakes his head and sighs. "First we have to see if the treatment takes," he says, sounding none too sure it will. "We'll be watching you for the next three days. We'll have to do a lot of tests. If the fever comes down, if the antibiotics kick in, you'll get better. If they don't, we'll have to operate—take out the valve and give you a new one. The success rate there is about fifty-fifty. Maybe a little more on the success side. There's something else. We aren't entirely sure if this *is* endocarditis—if it's only endocarditis. You're an intravenous user of heroin. I won't lie to you. Some of your symptoms . . . there's a possibility . . . you might have AIDS."

Nobody moves. "I have symptoms?" Kit says.

I'm too shocked to speak.

"Maybe I shouldn't have said that, since I'm not sure," Paul concedes. "But it is a possibility we have to face."

It is. But we can't face it.

It's one a.m. before they have her in a bed upstairs. It's a private room. Paul thinks it's best. Most of the other patients on the floor are old, in a lot of pain, and all doped up. It's the quietest corridor in the hospital.

"Don't leave me," Kit pleads, when we're alone.

"I won't." She grips my hand and my eyes fill, and my heart. I'm not nearly as stoned as she is. This is all too real.

"I hope it isn't AIDS," she says.

"I don't think it is." I don't. I don't know much about it but I know what it looks like. Not this.

"I wish he hadn't told me that," she says. "I'm depressed

enough, what with the band breaking up and all. That would be a little too much."

"It's not that."

"But it could be. Betty's new girlfriend came to the studio the other day and told me Betty's sick. I shared needles with her, you know."

"But that was before AIDS."

"No. I'm sorry. I couldn't tell you before—I got high with her a couple of times when you were mad at me for—I don't know what for. Doing too much dope, probably. Not washing dishes."

I'm holding my head in my hands, I'm putting them over my face. I don't want to scream. I don't want to cry. I don't want to know this is someone I love. How am I supposed to feel?

"You'd give me enough dope to OD if it was AIDS, wouldn't you? You would, right? No way I'm going through that."

"Let's talk about you getting better," I say. *Man, this life. Doom and gloom, no glory. I hate it.*

"Before you came back—why were you gone so long anyway?—Paul said they'll detox me on methadone while I'm here. The antibiotics might not work if I'm on all these other drugs."

"I'll cut down too," I say. *I hate it.*

"Promise me you'll stop using needles," she says.

"I like smoking better anyway."

"If I'm going to live, I can never shoot up again. If I see you do it, I will, too."

"I don't need to use a needle. I don't need to do so much dope." *If only it didn't love me.*

"Will you bring me something tomorrow?"

"You'll be on methadone."

"Not right away. They say I can't have anything until they know if—if the antibiotics are working."

"Kit," I say, a sob swelling in my throat. "Please listen. Can you do what they ask? I'll come every day, I promise. I'll bring you whatever you want. But I can't bring you anything yet."

"It's not bad enough I have to have these antibiotics every minute. It's not bad enough I have a fucked-up valve in my heart. It's not bad enough I'm facing surgery, or fucking AIDS. Now you want me to kick cold? Can you see sitting in this hospital bed, in this stupid gown, cold turkey? You can leave. You can go home and wear what you want. You can go back to the dope. I'm in here. I have to kick. You know what it's like for me. You know how sick I get. That's what you want for me?"

I don't want that. And I don't want this.

"I'm sorry," I say. I'm no angel, no kind of saint. What am I supposed to *do*?

"I'm scared."

"I am, too."

A nurse carrying a blood-sample basket comes in with two orderlies and an electrocardiogram contraption. They smear jelly over half a dozen places on Kit's torso and attach electrodes to each place.

"What's this rash?" asks the nurse.

"It's the fever," Kit says. "I always break out in a rash when I have a fever."

"You have fevers often?"

"Do you have to do this now?" I ask.

"I'm afraid so," the nurse replies. "We have to take blood every four hours."

Kit looks miserable. Her temperature's a hundred four.

"We're going to watch you very closely for a while," says the nurse, starting to pack her in ice. "You're one very sick young lady."

I stay another hour, when Kit finally falls asleep. I'm tired, too, but I'm afraid to leave. "Are you the family?" the nurse asks me. I say yes. She tells me to stay as long as I like. I should call Kit's parents but what can I say? Your daughter might be dying? How can I say that? I've never even met them. I'll call later. Bad news is always easier to take when it doesn't come in the middle of the night.

Kit's eyes open. "I'm freezing," she whispers. "I'm freezing to death."

I tiptoe down the hall to find the nurse. Kit has sweated through her sheets, they're soaking. I help the nurse lift Kit out of bed. She leans heavily against me, her arm dangling by her side, the IV tube from it. She grasps my hand. What's that she's saying? I can't make it out. The Toast set list? She must be delirious; she thinks I'm Sylph, that we're about to go onstage. I put my free hand to her head. It's burning.

"Let me know if this happens again," says the nurse as she repacks Kit in thermal blankets and the bed in bags of dry ice. I feel drained. I need sleep, but I'm restless. Then I remember: Massimo. Can I call him now? Why not? Nobody cares what time it is when they want to call *me*.

"Are you up?" I say timidly.

"I believe so," he says. His cat just had kittens he'd love me to see. I let the nurse know I'm going home to get some sleep, to call if there's a crisis. She's been amazingly kind, considering she knows Kit's a junkie. She never said, "Well, what did you expect?" or "You made this bed, now lie in it." She made the bed. And now she'll sit beside it. A jewel, she is. A real gem. She loves Toast, thinks Kit's the best. The nurse gives me a hug. I don't know why, but I want to kick her.

I ring Massimo's bell with Gestapo-like force. He answers the door holding two of his kittens.

"How's your Kit?" he asks, smiling, a proud father of five, three black ones, two gray, half Persian, half Russian Blue. I start to crumble.

"Not so good," I say and stammer when I tell him what's

happened. He's worried. Of all the dealers I know, Massimo comes closest to human.

"I'm sorry," he says. "That sounds bad. I'll go over and see Kit tomorrow."

"Thanks," I say. "She'd like that." But then I have second thoughts. Massimo's too good a guy to stand up to Kit's craving. I know she'll ask him for drugs. I beg him to wait. He can't bring her anything, no matter what she says.

"I understand," he says slowly, gesturing toward his brood. "I've got my hands full here anyway." Kittens are crawling over every piece of furniture. One catches my eye and I pick it up, the sweetest little kitten I've ever seen: fluffy dark gray with deep jade eyes, a square head, and pointy ears. It purrs the moment I touch it.

"I have dibs on this guy," I say, pulling it to my chest. I need to put something there.

"I can't decide which is cutest," he says. "That one, or his sister." He cups her in his hand and we stand together there a minute with these babies in our arms, not sure whether to laugh or weep. At this point, it all feels the same.

When I call the hospital in the morning, I take it as a good sign they haven't called me. Kit's about the same, or worse; she's in withdrawal. Her chest hurts, she says. Her arm's completely useless. She's having trouble breathing. They come in at all hours and stick her with needles. She can't sleep. "These people," she says. "I have to show them where to find my veins. I do it better than they do."

Vance seems upset by the news of Kit's illness. "What about you?" he says. "You all right?"

"I guess."

"Six weeks she'll be in there?"

"Yeah."

"No drugs?"

"They're putting her on methadone."

"Well, you'll make some money." I know what he means. There are some advantages to this situation. For one, I no longer have to stick around and watch movies with this crazy man. Kit's the real reason he wanted us around—he's star-struck. But he wants to make it easy on me, and he wants me coming back. Vance knows I have other connections now. Whenever his source runs dry, he comes over to buy from me.

He advances me a larger quantity than usual and insists I take home one of his VCRs as well—movies will keep me company for the time I have to be alone. There's a laugh. When am I ever alone? It's an occupational hazard.

I don't stay long in the hospital that night—Kit's out of it and things are busy at home. When finally all is quiet, I sit in bed with the cats and feel afraid. Her bed, her cats, her apartment. She saved me from myself once. How often can a person count on that? I don't want to lose her. This is hard.

I retire to my blade and mirror. With a small jeweler's hammer, I pound the white rocks and crush them, chop them into powder fine as Turkish coffee. I take my time. I've hooked up the VCR, but this is my evening's real amusement. I like the blade. I like the feel of it on my tongue. It tastes of dope, bitter and sweet. I think casually about infection as I chop. I think about my health, my sanity, the shape of my kidneys, the possibility of my getting AIDS. I watch the rise and fall of my chest, visualize my lungs. They don't look so good. I chop and push the powder into decorative lines, abstract doodles. Wish I could draw. I try to read the lines, between them, as a fortune-teller does a palm. I pick up a spike I've been saving—haven't had time to toss it. I put a pebble of dope on my belly and wait for it to melt. I'm wasting it. It's wasting me. I consider the blade, reflect on its affinity for my tongue. I consider the edge of night, the razors at my elbow. I tie off, load the spike, find the vein.

Blood. Blood everywhere. A gusher. I forgot to loosen the tie, so it doesn't last long. While I'm cleaning up the mess, the phone rings. It's Kit.

"What are you doing?" she asks.

"Thinking about you."

"I want to come home." Her melancholy tone feels threatening.

"I guess that's not possible," I say.

"I know, I know. But I wish. Are you high?"

"Not especially."

"Don't lie. You sound stoned. Is anybody with you?"

"No, I'm alone."

"I don't like the idea of you being with someone else."

"I'm not with anyone," I say. Just the dope.

Back in the days of my heroin honeymoon, I happened to see a man I knew in college. "How do you stay so young-looking?" he asked. "Heroin" was my answer. He was a newspaper reporter and was accustomed to asking questions. He wanted to know what the drug did for me. I told him it calmed my nerves, relaxed my features, and lifted my spirits—in other words, kept the aging process at bay. "Wait a minute," he said. "Are you telling me *heroin* is the fountain of youth?" "Well, yes," I said. "Heroin cures everything." "What's it *really* like?" he asked. "What does it feel like to be on heroin?" "What's it *like*?" I said.

This is what it's like.

THE WORK COMES FIRST

Vance was right. With Kit in the hospital, I do make more money, customers in and out. They talk about all the usual things: opportunities for love they missed, work they haven't done, places they haven't been . . . places only heroin can reach, love only heroin can warm, work only heroin can form. There's always a longing for things that never touched them. Makes me feel sad. Also useful.

All day long I sit and serve. Then I go to the hospital and stay till they throw me out. Then it's back to business. Ginger's here almost every night, sometimes with her girlfriend Vivian. We watch movies on the VCR and don't say goodnight till we see the sun.

I don't know what I'd do without Ginger now. She's really a terrific person. When you need a friend, she's there. When you need an idea, she has one. When you're having a long night, she makes it pass. She's smart as a whip and likes sexy clothes. She reads books and can gossip with the best of them. Ginger cracks me up.

She has this theory about a third gender and what it will do to break down the sociopolitical power structure, no scandal, no shame. It's interesting, listening to her ideas and ambitions—until she asks about mine.

"What are you writing these days?" Ginger asks. Vivian lies on the floor and smokes.

"Writing?" A casual question, but it stuns me. "I have no time for that."

"But dealing can't take up your whole life—you're too *driven*."

"All I ever seem to be doing is changing channels," I observe.

"Well, that's something," she says, a weak smile curling her lips. "What about Kit? Her pictures at Davey Boxer's are wonderful."

"I know," I say. "But now she's in the hospital. And her band broke up. She's feeling pretty discouraged."

Vivian sits up from the floor. "Toast broke up? That's *awful*."

"Listen to me," Ginger says, her eyes so penetrating I want to crawl under the bed. "You have to snap out of this. Kit, too. You can't lose touch with your work. The work comes first. The work always comes first."

"No," I say blankly. "Life comes first." Vivian blows a smoke ring.

"No," Ginger says, her expression somber. "It doesn't. It can't. It's too short, especially now. So many of our friends are sick with AIDS, and other things. How many are already gone? We're not going to outlive ourselves. There's nothing more important than the work. Get back to work, girl. It'll save your soul."

She's too stoned. I shake my head. It's not my soul I want to save. It's Kit. Besides, dealing is work. Talking is work. Turning on the lights, taking showers, buying groceries, waking up—it's all very demanding work.

I don't sleep at all that night. Next day, I get to the hospital early.

"How much is that?" I hear Kit say as I step inside her room. Doctor Paul is giving her the methadone.

"Sixty milligrams," he says. "You shouldn't need more than forty."

"It's not enough," she replies. "I need eighty."

"Forty's what they call a blocking dose," he explains. "That's what the experts say is required to take you off heroin without putting you into withdrawal. Anything over forty won't get you high, it's just icing on the cake."

She glares at him. "They don't know what they're talking about."

"The idea is to bring your tolerance down so the antibiotics will be effective," he says. "I don't want to detox you too quickly, but this isn't a maintenance program. It's all I can offer for now."

"Are you sure Paul knows what he's doing?" she asks when he's gone.

"I think he's a good doctor," I say. "But, you know, I met him at a disco."

"Can't you bring me some dope? This meth will never keep me straight. I'm sick enough as it is."

I hesitate. I'm running low on patience. "Let the methadone go to work first, will you?" I plead.

Anger crawls over her face.

"All right, all right," I say. "I'll get it." Goodbye profit, I'm thinking. Hello grief. "Will you take the methadone or not?"

"I have to," she says. "They make me. Don't be so mean," she says then. "I'll get better faster that way."

A SUNNY SPELL

Doctor Paul reports Kit's AIDS test is negative, but she's slipped into some kind of new crisis. The infection's more virulent than they thought. Her skin is gray, there's no life behind her eyes. I'm terrified.

Some things have to hurt, that's all. It's the way life goes. We don't have to like it. I wonder if miracles really happen. But drugs were made for people to believe in miracles. Chemistry is magic: it can turn shit to gold and gold to shit, just like that. Nice work, if you can get it.

I sit by Kit's bed until Sylph stops in with Poop. They take over the watch and I race home to work, weighing out dope in a robotic haze. "This batch is especially strong," I say to the customers, but it's only the same old shit. "Promise you'll be careful."

Admonishments get them buying more. Oh wow, they say, after sneaking a taste. I wasn't kidding, this *is* good. Am I gonna have this stuff tomorrow?

Tomorrow? *Tomorrow?* I have to think. "Tomorrow," I say. "Yes, I am."

Kit's awake when I return to the hospital, where I find Bo Brinks slipping her a bag of street dope.

"Well," she says. "*You* wouldn't give me anything." He looks flustered.

I don't say a word. I close the door after Bo and hand Kit a straw and she takes up the dope in my hand. If it hasn't killed her yet, it's not going to. By nightfall, her condition stabilizes and it's safe to take a break. Her good mood allays my fear. Maybe also my guilt. I'm still smiling when I run into Massimo outside, edging down the street with a large, heavy package. Can I help?

"I believe so," he says. He and his girlfriend Cherry are getting married. He's moving out in just a few days. This is sudden.

"I believe so," he says again. "But I like it." Cherry's at his apartment now. Why don't I come over to meet her?

She's labeling boxes when we arrive, wedding gifts and personal belongings: skis, a pasta pot, a drawing board, and a new stereo, computer, and radar detector. Massimo's into gadgets. Cherry puts on a tape. "Sounds good," she says. "I'm happy!"

Cherry's a cheerful sort, like Massimo. Clear, freckled skin, red hair, and blue eyes. We crack a few beers while she makes spaghetti and tosses salad, moving to the music. The kittens run around our feet, play in the empty boxes. I relax.

After we eat, Massimo unveils his package, a large oval mirror for Cherry. She cuts hair for a living and offers to give me a trim. Why not? It'll be therapeutic. A person can't live by dread alone.

A friend comes by as she's finishing, a handsome frog named Daniel. I assume he's Cherry's coke connection—the salon where she works is famous as a candy store. He takes a seat on a carton beside the kitchen table and starts shaving the sides of a golf ball–sized rock with one of Cherry's razors. The lines he draws are anything but generous. When I taste one, I find out why: it's not cocaine. Daniel is Massimo's new source for smack. He's letting me meet his man.

Daniel's a virile, matinee-idol type: square jaw, strong arms, straight nose, bright smile, a curl of dark hair over smoldering eyes. I sit beside him and study his ear. Somehow I find it seductive. That jaw line: it works so easily into a smile. His mouth looks so pliable, his chest inviting as a plush welcome mat.

What am I thinking? I can't think this way. Cherry is his girlfriend's hairdresser. They all met on a double date. But this is how connections are made, through family and by hairdo.

I know I should give Kit a call, but she's all right where she is and, after all, the work comes first and the work is here. I flirt like crazy with Daniel and don't let up till we come to terms. I shouldn't come to his place, he says. The girlfriend disapproves. He'll deliver.

We do a few lines and help Massimo and Cherry with their packing. What a domesticated crew we are—and what a nice night it's become, too nice to spend alone. When I leave, I take Daniel home with me.

I like his craggy French face and black hair, his accent, and his dope. His mother smuggles it from Turkey to Marseilles. His mother! I like that, too. "Doesn't she know what she's carrying?" I squeal over coffee. It's morning. We didn't get much sleep.

"Oh, sure. She just likes to travel. I could get away with it once or twice, but they never search her at the borders. She's a *bourgeoise*, you know, but she looks like an aristocrat. They think she's trading jewelry from abroad. My mother is very chic."

I can believe that. Daniel seems to have more than the usual measure of vanity, for a man. Maybe it's a French thing, maybe a dope thing, I don't know. Drug addicts tend to fuss.

Kit's condition improves with the upswing in the quality of our dope. Daniel's a boon to the business. The customers remark on the difference.

"You're in such a good mood," they say. "My, aren't we chip-per!"

"I'm having a sunny spell" is all I say. They can figure out the rest.

THE BOOK

November 1983. I prepare for the book I'm going to write, the one that will legalize heroin. "It's so NEEDED," says Magna. She'll bring me a book to help with my research—*Diary of a Drug Fiend*, by Aleister Crowley. A classic. But, she says, it's OLD, and a downer. She's counting on me to bring us up to date.

She's not the only one. Books come in from others, too—whatever anyone can find on narcotics laws, drug trafficking, or addiction. I have to ask Ridley to build me a new bookcase. I put the books on the shelves, certain they say nothing I don't already know, but to please my friends I read snatches aloud while they're here in the chairs. To their nods and grunts, their muttered amens, I read about the romance of drugs and the nightmare of addiction. I go through the history of the world.

There has never been a day people didn't want a drug, not since the beginning of civilized time. Prohibition's never worked, how can anyone think it will? Aren't the jails and hospitals full enough? Drugs are financing films, revolutions, art projects, businesses large and small. They generate millions of dollars in research, not to mention hundreds of hours of entertainment value. What would television writers do for material without drug dealers and drug users? There's hardly a show on today whose plot doesn't turn on some aspect of drugs. Clinics provide employment for I don't know how many ex-addicts and paid killers society is happy to keep off the street. Policing the borders is no good. Drugs are the biggest business there is. Even back in 1870, so many Persian farmers were growing opium there was a famine, and it didn't stop them then. In China, chandoo was practically the national stimulant, much more profitable than rice. You can grow opium anywhere there isn't excessive rainfall and the labor's cheap. It says so right here, in one of these books.

Cal brought it over. He wants to paint my portrait. I'll think about it, I say. How about Sunday? Come Sunday. (It's my day off; the phone won't wake me.)

When he shows up again, it's with Magna. Now *they're* a pair. A drug couple. NO sex. That's what Magna says. Cal's legs aren't right or something. Too long. She likes his arms. Cal has effeminate arms. She thinks they're SWEET. He says she's his "precious light," but he must be referring to her trust fund. Toni's left him for Davey Boxer, and Magna is filling the gap.

Magna. She's the touchy-feely type: snakeskin boots drive her wild, chairs with suede cushions give her goosebumps, most of her clothing is silk. She can't keep her hands away from Cal. Her father, the son of a lumber baron, died when she was only eight and left her all his money. I gather she loved him a little too much, albeit from afar. She spent most of her childhood in boarding schools, kicked out at sixteen for drugs. She went to Europe and met a man her father's age. She moved in. She came back at eighteen and married a musician who was also a junkie and a car thief. When she dumped him, she moved to Paris to finish school, came back to New York and enrolled again, this time for graduate study. She still has a hankering for older guys. Any guys, from the look of it.

After they get high, we sit in the office with the *Times* Sunday crossword, the way Big Guy and I used to. Heroin is the perfect puzzle-solving tool. Words flow and connect in a dazzling stream;

obscure references come to mind as if they were common slang. We're hooked.

Those people were here an awfully long time," says Kit on her first Sunday home from the hospital. After six weeks apart, we have to make adjustments.

"It's just the crossword," I say. "We had a hard time with this one."

"You'd rather be with them than me."

"That's not true." I reach out to give her a hug, but she turns away to look for the cats. The kitten Massimo has given us is all that delights her. I don't want to say I don't love her. I don't want to say that.

Daniel phones. He's coming to pick up money.

"I'm going to bed," says Kit, clasping the kitten to her shoulder.

"But I want you to meet him."

"Are you going to get high with him?"

"Probably."

"Wake me when he gets here."

They hit it right off. Guys always like her. The next time Weems visits, she doesn't make any noise. He's here to look at her pictures. He's seen them at Davey Boxer's and now he wants to buy one for a French collector. But Kit doesn't trust Prescott. She thinks he's a flake. Drug addicts tend to be flaky. It doesn't say that in any of the books, not in so many words. I rethink my collaboration with Honey. It's not dealers who need a manual; it's junkies who need a book of etiquette. I reach for the phone but it rings in my hand.

It's Betty.

"Put Kit on the phone," she commands, the voice of doom. "And don't try to tell me she isn't there."

I motion for Kit to pick it up in the bedroom and close the office door. I have a book to write.

This call could only mean trouble. I know Betty still wants Kit back. Has she got some sort of plan? Is she going to drop a dime on me? No telling what's on her mind. Not the crossword.

"She's coming over," Kit calls out. "She wants to get her things."

Oh, no. Moments later, I hear Betty whining in the hall. I stay in the office, pretending to be out, but when the decibel level rises, I pull the door ajar.

"You!" she yells when she sees me.

I don't know what she means. She looks awfully thin. She was always so voluptuous.

I step into the kitchen, she makes a move toward the office. "Your stuff's not in there anymore," I say, blocking the door. "We moved your things to the closet."

"I already looked," she says. "It's not there. What did you do? Sell it all?"

"Everything you left is still here, come on. You're the one who abandoned it."

"I told Kit I'd be back to pick it up."

"But that was two years ago," says Kit. I'm glad to see she's on my side; for a minute, I wasn't sure.

"I know what you're doing in there!" Betty shouts, pointing at the office. "You think it's a secret? Everyone knows! Everyone talks about you, and what they say isn't *nice*. You don't want to fuck with me, I'm telling you . . . see?"

She's got someone with her, a stocky older man in a plaid shirt and chinos, with a brushy mustache and silver hair. "This is a cop," Betty says, grasping his shoulder. He gives her a wary look. "That's right," she says. "A cop. I came here to get my stuff, so get out of my way and let me get it."

"Betty," I say. "Calm down, okay." I'm lookin' at this guy, Kit's backing into the bedroom. He could be a cop, he certainly could. He could also be Betty's pimp. Pimps might easily look like cops out there in the suburbs, where Betty lives now. She's moved back in with her mother. Maybe this is her mother's friend. Maybe I'd better do what they say.

But I don't. Betty's sick and I'm sorry about that, but it's my house and they're not welcome. "Get out of my way," she says, and moves to push me aside. The cop stays where he is, leaning on the kitchen table, watching. Betty barges into the office and shrieks when she sees the desk.

"My table!" she cries. "My mother's good table! Get your shit off. I'm taking it out."

"That's my book there," I say, indicating the papers I've spread to hide the mirrors. I've put away the scale. "I'm writing a book to decriminalize drugs."

"Ha! Ha ha! That's very funny," she says.

"Look," I say. "I'm serious. Read my notes."

"You're crazy," she says. "You are really nuts."

"Look, Betty," I say. "How much do you want for this table? I'll pay you, even though you did leave it behind."

"I don't want your dirty drug money!" she yells. "I don't want to look at you another second! You ruined my life, goddamit. And you totally fucked over Kit. You did that, not me! You! If it wasn't for you, I'd be—"

The cop moves to settle her down. "Betty," says the man.

"All right, I'm going! Let's go! But I'm coming back, I tell you. I'm coming back to get my shit."

"You think that guy was really a cop?" I ask Kit when they slam the door.

"I don't know—maybe. It doesn't matter. She's dying, can't you see? She won't do anything to hurt us."

NO ORDINARY SUNSET

I'm standing in the living-room window looking down toward the river. Over the water I can see the sky. This is no ordinary sunset. It's beautiful. Beauty is power—more powerful than drugs. Beauty makes you forget you live in a sixth-floor tenement walkup the police have just closed the door on.

They've taken Kit out in an ambulance. Over the last few days, she swallowed ninety Valium. She said the first eighty didn't do anything. She was taking them by the handful. After the last ten she started convulsing. Maybe she'd done some coke, I don't know. Must have been something.

We've both been kicking, bad. Punched all the feathers out of our pillows. Kit thought it was a good idea to call Mr. Leather. Kit wanted him to go out and refill her 'scrips, but he saw through her. Mr. Leather's quit drugs for AA. He picked up Kit's prescription and then he called 911. Kit punched out another pillow.

The two EMS workers, a woman and a man, walked in through a shower of gently falling feathers. I didn't try to explain. Didn't have to. A couple of dumbfounded uniformed cops were with them, a man and a woman. They didn't stay long—about as long as Kit stayed in the E.R. Not very. They couldn't find anything wrong with her. As a matter of fact, they ignored her. She walked home and fell asleep.

Poor Kit. It's all those pills. Pills are much worse than heroin. They get into the liver and they don't come out. Heroin's pretty safe, as drugs go, in tolerable amounts. Too bad it isn't legal.

Dick says heroin will never be legal. "This country's at war," he reminds me. "The President says so—the war on drugs? I'm part of the solution to the drug problem."

"The problem with drugs is they work," I explain. "They work a long time, then they don't. That's the problem."

"Shouldn't the question be *who* is the problem? Is it me or is it you? The government or the dealer? The junkie or the junk?"

"If I knew the answer to that question," I reply, "the drug problem in this country would be over."

PART SIX

I WANT OUT

I WANT OUT

Christmas 1983. Kit's been in an awful funk since the endocarditis. The antibiotics have zapped her strength, the demise of her band has stripped her spirit. The dope has done the rest. Most of the time she stays in bed. Now she's hooked on soap operas.

I'm sympathetic at first. I cook the meals, pay the bills, sit with her and watch TV. In three months, she hasn't improved. Paul says there's been no damage to her heart but he doesn't know it the way I do. My sympathy turns to resentment.

I never have a single moment to myself. When Kit isn't here, the customers are. Sure, I make money, so what? I spend it—on a new guitar for Kit, a typewriter for myself, new clothes. When the linoleum on the kitchen floor wears out from the hallway to the office door, I have the whole thing tiled over, carpet the other rooms, buy new chairs. I never care what I spend; what goes out one day comes back the next. Yet, I wake up every day feeling robbed.

Kit isn't to blame but I blame her. We have a fight. It isn't just an argument; we come to blows. That is, I throw dishes and she kicks the walls. We never have physical contact. That's over.

"You wish you could be with a man again, don't you?" she says, her eyes cold as the air.

"No," I say, my voice flat. "I don't want anyone else."

I want out.

I'm tired. Junk makes me tired, Kit makes me tired, dealing is exhausting. I'm out of it. Not my mind, my body. I want to eat and it doesn't. I want to sleep and it won't. I want to fuck and it isn't in the mood. There are days when the sadness of this life weighs so heavily I can't see the sky. I don't lift my head to look. The winter air snaps at my teeth, the wind burns my face. The apartment's so cold I live in my coat. I never really sleep. The darkness tucks me in and I go missing for a while. When I wake up, it's dark out again.

Maybe, I think, maybe it's the season. The holidays are numbing. But I feel something: boredom. I'm hearing the same things too many times; I don't want to hear them anymore. I don't want to know who steals what to get money for their drugs. I don't want to know who they lie to or why. I don't want to know who's dying or who's getting famous, who they're fucking or how, if they're shit-eaters or thumb-suckers or virgins or witches. I'm sick of it.

Doctor Paul comes but not to check on Kit. His girlfriend wants something for New Year's Eve. It's been a heavy week with her patients. She's an AIDS nurse. He's in love.

"This is probably the last time I'll see you," he says, but I don't pay him any mind. They all say that, at least once. "We're getting married," he says then. "Leaving the country. The atmosphere now is depressing. I want to do work that has some meaning and I don't have it here. People are too paranoid and suspicious."

He's talking about AIDS. Doesn't AIDS work have meaning?

He shakes his head. "You can't help people with AIDS," he says. "They're dying. People don't want to help and I can't fight it alone. Besides," he says, biting a nail, "you can't help people with AIDS." He's going to Ethiopia, where people are starving, where he can lay on hands. Those people can be helped.

AIDS is keeping Big Guy away, too. He's bought a house in Honolulu. Mr. Leather called to say our old apartment's up for grabs. Do I want it?

Kit and I could use some breathing room, but what happens to her if I leave? Maybe I could use Big Guy's place as the office. Maybe we'd both feel better. No, I can't afford that, get real. I'll wait. Kit will get better someday. Someday a record contract will come. Someday we'll be off drugs. I'll simply have to wait.

I wait till April, counting money, marking time, my head bent over the foil, couching myself in the dark. I have a room of my own, Kit says. Why can't she have one, too? We move the bed to the living room, behind a shelving system that acts as a screen. The old bedroom is now her studio. People really like the necklaces she wears; maybe she'll make some jewelry. Maybe she'll do some painting. Maybe she'll do some drugs.

Little by little, Sylph draws Kit back to work. In May they start recording a demo with a new drummer and bass player—Poop and Gloria are gone. On the new band's last night in the studio, Kit asks me to come along.

I go and sit stoned in the dark, drinking beer with the band. We're passing lines of cocaine, smoking pot. I listen to the music. Every song seems to end with a death wish. Kit turns up the volume on her guitar tracks; the producer turns it down. He wants to hear the drums. Sylph says he's burying her vocals. Kit thinks the lyrics sound like shit. Why should they take up more tracks than her guitar? I find this all very tedious. What am I doing here? Kit doesn't need me.

Next thing I know, I'm sitting up in bed and it's the middle of the afternoon. Magna's in the armchair by the television. Mr. Leather's sitting on the floor by the bed. Kit stands in the doorway while Honey talks on the phone.

"Listen," Magna's saying. "Don't worry about the bill. I can take care of it. GLAD to."

"What are you talking about?" I say. I feel groggy.

"The phone bill," she says. I see it in her hand. "Weren't you depressed about not having money to pay it?"

I don't understand this. I pay all my bills when they're due.

"You all right?" Mr. Leather asks.

"I'll get it," says Kit. The doorbell.

"What's going on?" I say, bewildered. My God, the dope is lying open in its bag beside me. What *is* this?

"You've been kind of out of it," Honey says. "Maybe you should think about taking time off." When did she get here? I can't remember. What about the others? Why can't I remember?

I hear Kit walk someone into the office. She comes back in the bedroom for the dope. "You swallowed all my Valium," she says. "A whole bottle. You didn't even leave me one."

Valium? I never take Valium. I hate pills. These drugs—there's no getting away from these goddam miraculous drugs.

Kit puts a newspaper in my lap. Three days have come and gone since that night at the studio, and all the while I've been weighing packages, counting money, giving out advice. That's what they tell me. Three *days*?

"Why don't you get dressed?" Magna says, gesturing with her elbow in a peculiar fashion, like a piston, or an upset chicken. "I'll take you shopping," she offers. "You can use a new sweater, right? EVERYONE needs a sweater. How about a jacket? Or some shoes?"

Honey has another idea. Her business has been pretty good of late, lots of visiting Europeans. She's subletting her apartment for the summer and renting a villa on the Amalfi Coast. It's just a few hours south of Rome, easy to find. Why don't Kit and I come and stay? It's really great, she says. She adores it. There's a guy there she met on a vacation the summer before and she's been thinking about him, just thinking, but a lot. Prescott will be there, and Davey Boxer—maybe Ginger too. All kinds of people. Lots of room.

How can I get away? I can't even get out of bed.

Later on, in the evening, alone with Kit, I'm still trying to remember what happened. She's sitting in the chair opposite the bed, her eyes soft, her face open, placating, contrite.

"I know I was sick a long time," she says. "I know it's been a strain on you. I know I can be demanding and possessive and jealous, and I'm sorry." At this, we both reach for a cat.

"When I was in the hospital," she goes on, "I really felt close to dying. I thought I didn't care and I'm still confused. I don't know the answers to life. But I want to live and I want to live with you." She stops talking a moment. I can't return her gaze. "I don't know how you feel about any of this," she says, her voice husky. "I hope you feel the same."

How do I feel? I don't know. How should I feel? I don't feel *good*. I know she loves me, but she's always saying that. What's it supposed to mean?

"I wrote a song for you," she says.

I pull myself up. "You wrote a song? Actually wrote? For me?"

"Want to hear it?"

I almost say no. Whatever it is, it represents a kindness and to my mind, kindness always kills. Right now I'm glad I didn't die. Listening could be dangerous.

"When did you write this?" I try to look expectant.

"Oh," she says with a sheepish grin, "I've been working on it for a while." Kit has never composed without her band before. A song for me—I can't believe it.

She puts down the cat and picks up her guitar and I listen, reaching back in my mind for three days. I don't know how I could have taken those pills, what was going through my head. I should never do cocaine.

"I love it, Kit," I say when she's done. "It's a hit."

"It needs words," she says. We feel fine, and then I know: there isn't anything wrong with Kit or me. The trouble isn't us.

I call Daniel.

"What do you think of this dope?" I ask when I have him alone in the office. "Doesn't it seem a little off?" I think he's going to punch me out. His face is red and I see his teeth, but not because he's smiling.

"Are you saying I cheat you? You can't get away with that again."

There was another day, a few months before, when I was convinced there was something wrong with his stuff. Some of what I had when I went to sleep wasn't there when I woke up. I told Daniel I'd left the bag open on my desk overnight and that some of the dope had evaporated. The big pussycat, he bought it that time.

"This stuff is really no good," I say now, hesitant but calm. "I think you should replace it."

I've never seen Daniel so mad. "You must be the most stupid woman alive," he says, spitting out the words. "How can anyone do business with a person like you? I front you every time you ask, I let you owe me money. I know what you're trying to do— you forget how well I know you."

My head feels hot, my eyes are clouding. "Ssh," I say, embarrassed. Kit's only in the next room. She still needs quiet. She needs a lot of rest. "I'm not trying to take advantage," I say, my voice beginning to crack. "I know I've been a little messed up, but this stuff really made me sick."

For a moment, he doesn't respond. I can see his mind working away. "You cut this last batch, didn't you, Daniel? Tell me the truth." I still think he's attractive.

"Your problem is you smoke everything you do, you waste it. You don't even know how *much* you do, sitting here all night with your aluminum foil—it's stupid!" He shakes his head. It doesn't matter what he thinks of me; he can't afford to lose my business.

Finally, he admits this is not the usual stuff—there isn't much profit in argument. His supply is low and he's been scraping. He'll let me slide on this one, but I won't get away with it again. He's leaving for France in a couple of days—he has to meet his mother in Marseilles. Meanwhile, I should give Massimo a call. He has something.

Instead, I call Vance, I don't know why. Maybe I don't want a cocaine haircut. "You'll never get ahead this way," he says, when he's sitting in the chair by my desk. "You really should go to Thailand—you could make some real money as a mule. I know a guy who can hook you up over there. Put away some cash, you won't need a lot. You should go."

"I will never do that," I say. I would never take that chance, not for him, not for anyone. I'd rather pay more and stay here.

But I do save some cash and I don't stay here. Magna has a private doctor in Queens who has a license to dispense methadone. Kit and I take a cab there every morning through the middle of summer. We drink his juice and take his vitamins, skim the dope only late at night, when the meth is wearing off.

In July, I turn my business over to Bebe and Daniel over to her; Kit sublets the apartment. We get on a plane and fly to Rome.

We get out.

ITALY

In our rented Fiat, the four-hour drive from Rome to Positano stretches on for eight. We get lost in Naples. When we finally reach the Amalfi Coast, it's at the opposite end from our destination. Traffic inches along a narrow road, the Mediterranean to one side, mountains to the other, curling up toward Ravello and down through the white flats of Amalfi, twisting through tiny resort towns that emerge every few miles from limestone hills. It's beautiful but it goes on too long. We can't enjoy it. The methadone isn't holding, at least not for Kit. She's cranky. First she wants to drive, then she doesn't know the way. She wants to stop and swim, then she can't be bothered. She wants to stop and eat; then she won't. She wants to look at scenery, then she looks away.

It's dusk when we pull in to Positano. People spill from cafés, hotels, and shops, flooding the single road that loops through the town around two steep hills dotted with villas and pensiones. I don't see Honey on our first pass. "We're *easy* to find," she'd said on the phone the night before, when I called from our hotel in Rome. "Ask anyone."

I drive through the town once, twice, a third time. Traffic moves at a snail's pace. There's no place to park. It's hot. At last I pull into a space reserved for some official and get out to look for Honey on foot. Kit stays with the car.

On the phone, Honey had given me directions to her villa. Now I walk back and forth along a narrow stone path in the upper part of town. It's flowing with bougainvillea. This seems to be the street she'd described, but I find nothing resembling the doorway she'd said was hers—a weathered green wood without a number. A mother and her six children stare as I go by their house. A dog barks, but Honey doesn't show her face. On my third trip down the alley, a man steps out of the kitchen of a modest pensione. He's wearing a bright red shirt open wide at the collar, a friendly smile above it. In halting Italian I've picked up from Massimo, I ask if he happens to know an American named Honey. The man's face lights up at the sound of her name. "Si si!" he says, with a grin, and then in English, "Every-body know Honey!"

"She's my friend," I say. "I came from New York to visit."

"Ameri-cane!" he says, emphasizing the last syllables, the word for dogs.

"Do you know where she is?"

He calls a young boy out of the kitchen, his son, I suppose. Out comes his wife, joined by several other women. Together they discuss the matter, and me, while I stand there and sweat. Darkness falls. Then the man points in the direction I've just come from. I make a sign that Honey isn't there. He takes my arm and draws me to a door I've already decided is wrong. It has a faded number and a tile embedded in the doorpost reading CAVE CANEM, Beware of the Dog.

"Oh," I say. "This is it?"

He knocks to prove it is. No answer. "Not there!" he says, the smile taking over his face. If Honey's not home, he says, she must be at a café down the hill. It's where she goes to use the phone.

"Can I drive there?" I ask.

"You have a parking place?"

"Not a legal one," I answer.

"No problem," he tells me. "You . . . New York!"

I start walking down the road in the direction he points me, picturing Kit sitting sick and alone in the car at the top, having a fit. I've been gone nearly an hour. I turn round a bend and there's Honey walking toward me, barefoot, in a black skirt and black leather vest, her dog scampering on ahead.

"*Veni qua!*" she's saying to the dog. "Glory, *va via! Va via!*"

"Your Italian sounds pretty good," I say, relieved at the sound of her laugh.

"Yeah, but I don't think Glory knows it."

"I can't believe I'm finally here!" I say.

"What took you so long? Where's Kit?"

I tell her we have the car parked illegally at the top of the hill and that I've been looking for her house for an hour.

"Gee, all you had to do was come to the bar," she says. "Grigorio's there now with Prescott."

"Can't wait to meet him," I say.

"Maybe we should go rescue Kit."

I'm not sure what she means by "rescue," not till we reach the car, where a smiling Kit is surrounded by three gorgeous boys fawning over her platinum hair.

"I didn't know you could speak Italian," Honey tells her.

"I didn't say a word," Kit says. "They don't want me to talk."

"Let's get your stuff," Honey says, flashing teeth at the boys. "We can have a few drinks and get ready for dinner. Dinner's at ten here. Plenty of time to relax."

"Where were you?" Kit asks as we shoulder our bags. We have trouble balancing their weight on the steps. Positano is all about walking and climbing. It was settled in 800 A.D. and the streets are the same as they were then—broad steps that take you up or down the mountain on either side of the road.

"This was Vittorio De Sica's summer house," Honey says as we approach the door. "Not really his house. We have the upstairs apartment, the servant quarters. But we can at least use the garden, the garden's great. You'll love it."

It's a beauty, all right, two levels of fragrance, herbs and vegetables below, a columned breezeway above, facing the sea, its pergola roof wound with grapevines, its lawn full of flowers. The apartment, on the other hand, is just a corridor leading to a small, narrow kitchen, three bathrooms and three bedrooms, all occupied. "We're a little crowded here this week," Honey says. "You'll have to sleep in Mike's bed till Prescott leaves. Davey Boxer's here too. That's okay, isn't it? Mike can sleep with us or over at his girlfriend's." Her son had met an American girl who was here with her mother. "Two queer friends of hers pay for her school in Switzerland—you know the types. They're here too. So's Zeffirelli, you know, the director? They say Frank Sinatra is his house guest for the weekend. It's that kind of town. Fabulous. Everyone comes here. I just wish we had the space downstairs. That's what I thought we were getting when I rented this place, but the woman who bought the house keeps it for herself. She's an Austrian but she's never here. We think she might have been a Nazi. Want a beer? They're in the fridge. Why don't you get unpacked and I'll go find Grigorio."

"Can't wait to meet him," I say again.

She leaves us alone on Mike's small bed. His clothes are lying scattered on the floor. There isn't anyplace to put our things.

"Wasn't she expecting us?" Kit says.

I don't have an answer.

"I've never wanted to get high so bad in my life."

"Let's not think about it," I say.

"I'm out of meth," she says.

I can't believe it. A month's supply of five-milligram pills, the doctor had given us. I give her a tab and take another for myself. Before I put the vial away, I count four remaining.

Grigorio arrives with a bottle of tequila, Prescott close behind.

"Girls! Girls!" Prescott shouts and throws himself on the bed on top of us. He's drunk. I want to kill him. *"Buona sera!"* he shrieks.

"Prescott," Kit says. "Get off."

"Grigorio," he says, rolling up against the wall. "Pour the drinks. Tonight, we paint the town."

"Very amusing," says Grigorio. "The whole town's scared of him. They think he's kidnapped all the young boys, and the women are furious."

"Yes," Prescott says. "It is *amusing.*"

Grigorio's not what I expected, though I'm not sure what that was. Italian royalty, Honey had said in New York. A Neapolitan count. Could be. He's slight of frame with flowing dark curls past his ears and the grand sort of nose you get on certain types of nobility. The kind of guy who's relaxed around men and women alike—a dear. His dark eyes are large and have very long lashes. It's not hard to tell what Honey sees in him, especially when, after our baths, we saunter in her room. It's a salon that offers a view of the sea through two windows with double French doors. She's lying on the bed and Grigorio has a needle to her arm. They look comfortable.

Grigorio is a registered morphine addict. He gets a weekly supply of glass ampules that each contain a dose of the amber liquid. The box they come in is open on the bed. Kit can't take her eyes off it. We explain our situation. "No problem," he says and offers to fix us up with a doctor in Sorrento who runs the methadone program there. I accept this information with a sinking heart, but Kit's mood rapidly improves. We all sit on the balcony of their room, passing the bottle of tequila and watching the harbor. A few small boats bob on the surface of the water. One is rocking more violently than the rest. "They're having a good time on that boat, all right," says Honey. "It's a good town to fuck in, for sure."

But we haven't come here to fuck. We don't even do that in

New York. We came here to get away from drugs. So far, we're batting zero.

The next day is Sunday and the doctor we're supposed to see in Sorrento is off. Instead, we drive to Naples. I'm returning the rental car and Grigorio wants to cop. Because he shares his prescription with Honey, his supply of morphine is running low. I split the rest of my methadone with Kit and we pile into the car, Honey at the wheel.

"You have to see Pompeii while you're here," she says as we pass it.

"Sounds good," I say, watching it go by without interest. I'm more tantalized by the prospect of touring the cop-spots of Napoli. Anyone can do the guidebook thing; I want to know the real Italy.

We walk through the casbah in the center of town. It seems ancient. No tourists here. These shops sell no souvenirs, no postcards. People seem to be living in the narrow, hilly streets running between small stone apartment houses that are closed to the sun and dusty sidewalks that let it in. They're neither friendly nor hostile and include an unusual number of dwarfs. It's odd. We walk up and down until Grigorio spots a kid with a dirty sweet face who looks stoned. He takes us to the hospital, where we find junkies selling their morphine to get money for dope, same as they do at the meth clinics in New York. Same same.

We shoot up in the car a block from the hospital, Honey and Grigorio still in the front. The sun is beating on my neck. I'm nervous, but not about getting caught. This is the first time Kit or I have used a needle since the endocarditis, and the first time I've ever tried morphine. My entire body tingles—shooting morphine turns up the heat. We're all red as beets. Not Grigorio.

We sit quiet for a while, watching a funeral procession pass—a horse-drawn cortege laden with flowers and followed by dozens of mourners carrying hankies and more flowers, moaning to the sound of a melancholy brass band. "Just like New Orleans," I say. I was there once for a weekend with the Toast, just after the burns on my arms had healed. Those were the days. Days gone.

We drive to a café on the dock and watch the boats to Capri and the traffic around the bay. Mount Vesuvius is visible in the distance. "I'd love to go up there," I say.

"Oh sure," Honey says. "That's easy." It's a quick ride on the Circumvesuviana, she explains, the commuter train that goes from Naples to Sorrento and back.

"Yes," Grigorio says, holding a cigarette to his mouth. "It's amusing."

Grigorio speaks perfect English but he relies on certain words as a kind of spoken shorthand. "Amusing" is one of the words. "Dummy" is another. Everything absurd or repellent is dummy, everything else amusing. He's a treasury of Italian folklore, regaling us with stories about the Camorra, whose cigarette boats are in the harbor, and how Jesus really became God.

Grigorio gets a kick out of making fun of the Church, which he holds in affectionate disdain. He makes a living with political cartoons. He draws a few for us. They're unlike any cartoons I've seen before. They're not funny, not *comic*. They're amusing.

Honey gives me a nudge. "D'you think I should marry him?" I say yes.

We get on the train and head back to Pompeii. It's only twenty minutes before closing time, but Honey insists. It's too late in the day for a look at the city; instead we tour the Villa dei Misteri on the outskirts. It's all of Pompeii I'll ever see. In the eight weeks Kit and I spend in southern Italy, we never have a moment to return. We're always going to Torre del Greco, a train stop or two beyond Pompeii. Torre del Greco's at the bottom of Vesuvius. I never get to the top.

The train station opens on a tree-filled park not unlike Washington Square but without the fountain, and I come to know it well. Hundreds of dissipated couples and lone hustlers hang out there every day, to buy and sell ampules of morphine. A pharmacy across the street sells the needles—perfectly legal here. Everyone's hospitable. One couple we meet takes us back to their apartment to shoot up, so we don't have to use the station john. They live in a tiny cottage with their baby, exactly at the foot of Vesuvius. It's so small we don't want to stay, but they insist on making espresso. Each of us gets a spoonful.

Soon Positano begins to feel just as small. Kit and I want to travel—first stop, Sorrento. The doctor there signs papers that will get us daily doses of methadone from hospitals wherever in Italy we go. I'm detoxing, she's maintaining. In Venice, Florence, Siena, Genoa, Pisa, and Rome, we visit beautiful churches, beaches, museums, bars, and restaurants, but mostly what we see are emergency and hotel rooms. When we return to Rome for the trip back to New York, I've been off drugs for a week. I've grown fluent in Italian and learned quite a bit about wine. Life without drugs now seems possible. I'm fine. Then we bump into Prescott at the Pantheon. He's courting a young half-Vietnamese, half-black American named Clay who has all-too-familiar eyes, but he also has a certain je ne sais quoi and I give him money to cop. The dope he brings looks like cocoa, or the stuff they call Mexican mud, a brown shale. This isn't the way I was planning to leave the country, but it gets us home safe and sound.

As I open the door to our apartment in New York, the phone rings. I answer it. "Oh," someone says. "You *are* there! Okay to stop by?"

I cannot believe this. We haven't even kicked off our shoes. The other line beeps. "Wow, am I ever glad you're back!" says another voice. I put them both off and call Bebe. She's had all my customers for two months—I want to collect my commission. And I wouldn't mind a line to unpack with.

"You home?" I say. "I have to see you."

"Come right over," she answers. I can hear the relief in her voice. "How are you?" she says. "You good? I can't wait to see you, either."

Bebe's place is up three flights on Prince Street. Kit leads the way—she could find it blind. "*Buona sera*," I say when Bebe comes to the door.

"Here," she replies, handing me a package. "Take it."

It doesn't feel like cash. I step inside. "What's this?" I ask, dreading the answer.

"There isn't a lot of money," she says, looking away. "That Daniel," she says.

"Did he do something?"

"He's all right, I guess, but he had trouble keeping in stock. Your customers," she says.

"I thought they were okay," I say. Aren't they?

"I like them all right," she tells me. "But I have my own thing to deal with, you know. Daniel's stuff just wasn't that good and everyone kept complaining. You know how druggies complain. Actually, I haven't seen Daniel for a while."

"So what's this?"

"Oh, I know this guy, he has a friend—you know. I'm sorry there isn't more money, but that's the dope I have left."

But I don't want the business back. I only came to get a line.

"You mean, you really got clean over there?"

"Not exactly," I say. "But kind of."

"You have to take back the business. I told your customers to call you."

"They've already started."

"You'll be okay," she says.

"Honey told me you were dealing D for some time before we left."

"She said that? She shouldn't of."

"It's okay, I don't care. Is this it?"

"Yeah. It's good."

It is. She says I already know the guy she gets it from. Not the dealer, but the friend—Mark Murano? I don't know him. She offers to bring him by. I would rather buy from her, but she doesn't want to be involved. She has the other thing.

She brings Mark to see me that night. He's a slight, soft-spoken guy who lives in the Village and works in a recording studio as an engineer. He's making a record of his own, he says. He's really a musician. Sounds like a junkie to me. I buy the gram he has on him, but I know I'm going to need more. A lot more.

"Oh well," he says. "Let's see how this goes first."

"Oh well," the guy says again a couple of days later, after his third or fourth trip up my stairs. "I don't really have time for this. I can't always take off from work—sometimes I'm in the studio all night. I'm probably not doing myself any favors, but if you want, I'll speak to my friend. Maybe you should deal with him directly."

I'm down with that. There's no escaping this business now. I'm too good at it.

Mark returns with his friend, a pleasant pixie of a guy with curly black hair and an easy smile. His eyes dance as he holds out his hand.

"Hello," he says. "I'm Angelo."

ANGELO

Angelo is a very cagey guy. He keeps a certain distance. It's his dope that seems like family, and it grows. I need deliveries every day, sometimes more than once. By the end of the year, I'm bringing in a couple of thousand dollars a day, at least. Angelo gets most of it.

My people who buy by the gram get a discount. My profit is all in the little stuff, in tenths and quarters of grams, so tedious. Most of the quantity customers are other dealers—Vance, Massimo, Sylvia, sometimes Dean. There's a coke dealer named Jerome whose clients like to boost a little dope, and a small-time frog with dyed hair named Jean-Paul. The others are the regulars who can afford it, like Magna, and Claude, whose paintings are selling so well he's now, at twenty-five, a rich man.

Angelo brings me the stuff the way he gets it, in uncut ounces pressed into rock—excellent for smoking. It's so hard I have to spend a good hour each evening grinding it into powder for the customers, banging it open with a heavy hammer, shaving it down and chopping. For myself, I keep a rock.

"*Mama mia*," I say as Angelo watches me work. "This stuff is harder than diamonds."

He wets his lips. "You speak Italian?"

"*Poco poco*," I reply, under my breath.

He smiles. His mouth is small but his lips are full and inviting. His hair curls around his head like thick black smoke. I like his eyes. They're steady and open, happier than the abandoned, bashed-in look you usually see on a junkie. Angelo looks sort of normal.

In time, we find another bond—Angelo comes from the restaurant trade, too. He once owned a couple of places on an island in the West Indies, where he now lives on a houseboat. He bought those establishments with money earned from smuggling drugs and sold them for money to buy more drugs. Soon he'll buy another restaurant, maybe start a chain—maybe I'll be his chef. Ha-ha.

Angelo doesn't do drugs in the Islands. He goes down there to relax on his boat, he says, with his wife and baby daughter. Otherwise, he's in his hometown in northern Italy. But now he's in New York and this is business. He picks up a pebble that's flown off my desk, chops it with a razor. His hands are tough as a streetfighter's.

"I wish I could speak more of your language," I confess. "I love Italy." I tell him about our trip, the art-and-hospital tour of the provinces, copping in Torre del Greco's town square.

"That's very dangerous," he says, regarding me with interest.

"So is smuggling," I reply. "Anyway, once you've lived in New York, nothing's dangerous."

"We're going to make a lot of money," he tells me, smiling again. Sounds good to me.

As the months go by, our relationship never changes. We never break bread together, we don't go to movies or clubs. I never feel much closer to him than I did on the day we met. He brings the dope and I hand over the cash. We get high and talk. His English is nearly perfect but our common language is dope. Mostly, we just count money.

Sometimes I make a pickup at his hotel, where I meet an Italian friend of his or two, handsome guys with sly smiles and darting eyes who also have digs in the Islands. We talk about our drugs, our girlfriends, or the weather, how to get an apartment in New York. We never discuss the economy or politics or culture, whether what we're doing is good or bad. That's beside the point.

Every few weeks, Angelo leaves town for destinations unknown and I have to fend for myself, with Vance, or Massimo, or Daniel—I buy from them, they cop from me. We're always trading places. When Angelo returns, business continues as before, only better. I'm the best customer the guy ever had.

JUST ANOTHER DAY FOR A DEALER

July 1985. I'm standing in my office in the dark, half-dressed, hands at my sides. I can't remember where I hid the dope. I go through the usual drill, picking at the scatter under the sink, taking up the carpet in the living room, peering through the holes in the floor. Where on earth can it be? It's almost noon and I'm stumped. The phone's gonna ring any minute, then the junkie jamboree: "Are you in? Can I see you? I mean, can I *see* you?"

I head into the livingroom/bedroom, the shades are up. The room's full of sun, light the color of pale honey pouring in from the east. It takes me a minute to adjust. Kit's sitting at the foot of the bed, hunched over a guitar in her lap, unplugged, her hands absently working the strings. The cats surround her in tight little balls, furry little humps on the pillows.

"Any idea where I put the dope last night?"

She looks up. "Don't you know?"

"It's not where I thought it was."

"I never know where you put it anymore. And I have to tell you, I hate that."

"It's better you don't know," I say.

"It doesn't look that way to me."

"Come on. I know you watch me."

"You were in your room a long time last night. For all I know, you finished the dope yourself."

"I did *not*."

"Then it's here," she says, turning on the TV. "Somewhere."

I light a cigarette, racking my brain.

"I hate when you smoke," she says.

I return to the kitchen, catch myself in the mirror above the sink. My hair is thinning. I can see my scalp showing just above the tuft of my widow's peak.

Then I remember.

It's in the box of hair dye! A safe place. Dangerous, too. Kit's been sleepwalking—the Valium. The band has split up again, she's been nearly despondent. I keep finding her standing in the kitchen in the middle of the night, mixing hair dye in a cup of water. She thinks she's making Jell-O. Jell-O's her latest kick. She likes drinking it cold, without bothering to cook it. She says it takes too long to set.

"I found it," I call out.

"Let me have my share now," she barks. "Before you sell it all."

The door buzzer sounds. It's Lita, one of my first-ever customers. She moves up the stairs unbearably slowly—she could be visiting Planet Jupiter instead of me. Is she two hundred pounds or ninety? I look down through the landings. She's hanging on the rail, gasping. When she reaches the top, she looks more strung out than anyone I know. It's been a few days since I saw her last. Copping in the street again, I suppose.

She turns through the kitchen into the office, a frail bird who's lost her wings. Her black hair hangs over her ears in sodden strings, her dark eyes showing almost no whites. The large pupils swim in their place unfocused, unable to rest. Her olive skin's a urinous yellow, her long nose brims with doper's drip. She makes no attempt to hide it. She *wants* me to see how bad she is, so I'll give her a freebie, throw in an extra scoop. Too bad for her—supplies are low, and I have to pay the rent.

She lays her forty dollars on the table. The tracks on her hands are badly abscessed, just above the wrist. Her long-sleeved black T-shirt hides the rest, thank God. Looking at her is exhausting.

She stares at the money, two twenties, tries to smile. It's all she has in the world, I'm sure, but I can't let myself worry about that. Was I the one gave her this monster habit? I try to smile, too, don't know if it shows.

I hand her a preweighed pack of folded white paper. "What's this?" she asks, with a sniff. Her voice is higher than usual, thinner, like the rest of her. She puts the bindle back on the table.

"A tenth," I say. "You know."

"Don't you have to weigh it out?"

"I didn't think you'd want to wait."

"Oh," she says, doubt creasing her voice. "Okay."

Lita holds the dope in her scabby, wraithlike hand, makes a fist. I think about the others who might be over soon, what they'll say if they see her here like this, how they'll hiss and jabber about the class of people I am now compelled to serve. As if they were better off. As if it couldn't happen to them.

Lita sits with the dope in her hand, not moving. Her pupils look large enough to spill from her eyes. They're huge. Is she too sick to open the bag?

"What is it?" I ask, taking an offended tone. "You want me to weigh it again?"

"No," she whispers, wiping her nose with the back of her hand. I wish she'd take it and go. "Look," she says. "I have to ask a favor."

My back stiffens. Lita knows I don't give credit. And she knows I don't let anyone shoot up in the apartment, not since Kit's illness. But, she says, she has so little and she needs it so much, and she'd rather not have to get off on the stairs. Could she please do herself here, this once?

"You shoot up in the hallway?"

"Everyone does," she says. "Shoots or snorts."

"That's not true."

"But it is."

"I don't think so."

"There's a lot you don't know about," she says.

"Like what?" I ask. I hear the edge on my voice. I'm thinking, No wonder the super's been so nosy. The other day he said someone kicked in the building's front door; he said it was some friend of mine. Had to be, he said. I have so many.

Lita shows me the dope in her palm.

"Okay," I say. "But do it in here, in the office. I hate it when people shoot up in the bathroom."

"In here?" She's incredulous. "Isn't someone else coming?"

"Not yet," I tell her, though I can't be sure. "Stay here. I'll get you some water."

I tiptoe into the kitchen while she ties off, removing from a pocket in her jeans a spoon and cotton, and some battered gimmicks. If Kit sees this, we'll be back on the needle in no time.

I return to the office and close the door. Lita's searching her hands for a vein.

"Jesus," I say. "Couldn't you get new works?"

"And come over here two bucks short?" She's making fun of my no-credit policy. I force a laugh at myself, then she boots it. After a minute her face takes on a more natural color, her fidgeting stops. She looks at me with relief.

I don't know, she's not a pretty sight, but watching the calm settle over her now gets me hankering for the needle again, too. I'm tempted to give her a free line and cab fare if she'll go back to the East Side and get me one. Instead, I ask why she bothers with that junk from the street, it's so dirty. That's the reason she gets so sick.

"I know it's stupid," she agrees. "But I always think, better to spend twenty there than forty here. At least your stuff stays with you till morning."

"Yeah," I agree. But it never stays with me. I ask what's been going on in the hall, stress the importance of protecting my position. If we don't keep this quiet, there'll be no dealer here to complain to, no dope to relieve the complaints.

"Don't the neighbors *know?*" she asks, suddenly fearless.

I insist they don't, just Henry, who deals coke on the floor below, and Fowler, the pot-and-pill freak on the second. I tell Lita to be more careful. I start to say something about AIDS, then I don't. I offer to get her some meth.

She looks at her hands and laughs. "You're the only dealer I know who tries to talk her customers out of buying drugs."

"You think I don't know what it's like?"

"Yeah, okay," she answers. "But it's different for you."

"Not really. This drug treats me just the same."

"I don't know how to stop," she sighs. "I think I'd go nuts if I tried."

"No," I tell her. "You wouldn't. Why don't you think about buying a bigger quantity? You get a discount on larger amounts, and you won't have to wake up to an empty bag." How can I bait the poor wretch this way? Or do I just want to scare her off?

"I'd just do it all," she says with a shrug. "I've never been able to hold on to drugs."

"I'll hold them for you," I tell her. "I'll dole it out, a little less each day."

"Then I'll have to come over here every day."

"What's the difference?" I say.

She looks at me sharply. "What's the discount?"

I give her a price. "I'll think about it," she says. I give her a hug as she leaves. Her shoulder pierces mine. She's so *bony.*

Kit emerges from the bedroom. "Lita looks really bad," she says.

"I know. I spoke to her."

"You didn't."

"I had to. A dead giveaway like that, she could ruin us."

"I'm going out," Kit says, disapproving. She wants a check for the rent. I write it. "I wish you'd make some money," I say.

"Let me do some of the business then."

To this, I don't reply.

When she leaves I realize this is the first time I've been alone in weeks. I smoke a line and feel the tension run out of my body. I sit in the living-room window, in the sun. I feel nothing. I sit in the sunlight and listen. The place is silent. There's a quiet in my body too, a hush too delicate to disturb. Is it so strange to love the thing that shuts out the noise inside you? All those primitive, inarticulate, derisive sounds, that confusion of waking thought. I'm fixed to the spot. For a minute the world is new and uncomplicated, a world with no need for drugs. A world without need, period.

At four o'clock, I'm sitting in the office with Cal. He's come from a visit to a shaman who he says can help us all get off dope.

"How does he propose to do that?" I've already tried vacations, vodka, deprivation, methadone, and pills. What else could there be?

"This stuff's pretty strong," says Cal, taking a tiny snort from the mirror on my desk.

"It's the same stuff I always have. What about the shaman?"

The doorbell rings. It's Magna. Kit lets her in and they both sit down.

"Vance shot himself in the foot," she announces, plopping herself in the chair next to Cal's. She's in a terrible sweat.

"Literally shot?" I say. "With a gun?" Since when does she cop from Vance?

"With a GUN. He was waving it at ME. Can you imagine? That man is really INSANE."

"Was he smoking base?" Kit asks.

"Yes, of course," Magna says, pulling her hair across her cheek. "That's all he ever does, as far as I can tell."

"Why didn't you leave sooner?" I ask. She looks as if she hasn't slept in days.

"You don't understand," she says. "He KIDNAPPED me—I couldn't leave. It's difficult to admit, but I found it sort of *exciting*, at first. There was a THRILL to it, somehow, being around all those drugs, watching those movies. You know. Half the time I was barely conscious, which I have to say I LIKED. It was comforting. Vance was. You'd be surprised how much."

"Who's Vance?" says Cal, brushing powder off his nose.

"Oh," she says, avoiding his eyes. "This dealer-type we know." Now she looks my way. "I'm sorry," she says. Someone took her to meet Vance when Kit and I were on vacation.

"Did you have sex with him?" I ask, pushing the counter-weight on the scale to the gram mark.

Cal utters a sound of surprise. He knows I never ask questions.

Magna's eyes turn a dull gray-green. "Vance doesn't really *fuck*," she says. "But he can usually SAY the right things."

Cal is looking at me strangely. His eyes are narrow slits. "You're evil," he says.

"But," I say, "the world has a need for evil."

"You've been treating me shitty enough," Kit allows. "Everyone says so."

"I don't tell them how you are with me."

"Girls, girls," Cal starts to say, pursing his lips. He reaches in the pocket of his coat and hands me a flat, glittering piece of stone.

"What's this?" I ask. It fits snugly in my palm, has almost no weight at all. It looks like a piece of fool's gold.

"Can you see the sparkle?" he asks. "That's its magic. This comes from a very special place, it's blessed—I got it from the shaman."

"Are you giving me this in trade?"

"No," he says. "I just want you to have it. It'll protect you from the grip of evil. As long as you're in it, this stone can help take away your pain."

"But I have no pain," I remind him.

"Oh, right," says Kit with disdain.

"We're living in very dark times," Cal says. He's staring at the spine of a book on my shelf, the *Tibetan Book of the Dead*. I don't know where it came from.

Magna lights a cigarette and sniffs. "I think death must be bliss," she says.

"Yeah," Cal nods. "You haven't *lived* until you've fucked Death. We're part of the Second Coming, you know."

"When is it?" I ask. "I haven't got a thing to wear."

"That's easy," he says. "Sparkle sparkle!"

The rush hour comes and goes, and then I have to re-up. I call Massimo and say I'll be over soon. He doesn't keep me. A minute after I'm back, Lita's on the horn. She wants to see me right away. In the office, she lays her hand on the table and opens it. She's holding five crisp hundred-dollar bills. I don't ask where they came from. I measure out the gram.

"I'm going away," she says. "You'll never have to see me again."

I can't look at her now. I'm filled with envy, only one arm to feed instead of thirty. I wish her luck. I know she won't get far.

At eight-thirty, Honey calls. Grigorio's in the hospital in Naples. He's too ill to leave the country. Bad liver, they think.

Maybe cirrhosis. They started to think it was AIDS, but there are no documented cases in Italy so it can't be that. Whatever, he's too sick to move.

"I'm sorry," I say.

"Well," she says, "I'm not going to worry about it. If I have to, I'll move to Italy—I don't care. I love Italy. Okay if I come over?"

Around eleven, I hear from Claude Ballard. Can he and a buddy stop by? I want to say I'm not open, but Claude's a good friend now and I can't say no to a friend. Besides, he's a famous artist. You just don't say no to the famous.

Claude strides past me, leading a tall dark man who introduces himself as Fred. This guy's a beaut. His black satin skin fits over his cheekbones like a sheet pulled taut on a wire rack. No problem having *him* around. His eyes sparkle at the sight of me. Can't help but like the guy. I'm just not in the mood for company.

"Where's Kit? She here?" Claude asks, taking a peek in her studio.

"Not right now," I say. She's over at Bebe's getting us some coke, been gone more than an hour. Nothing unusual.

He's spotted a couple of her photographs hanging on the wall. I really ought to have one of his paintings, he says. I'd like one—his paintings appeal to me—but my cash is always tied up and his prices have gone beyond anything I can afford. Besides, I won't trade anything for drugs. I already have all the TVs, VCRs, air conditioners, and cameras I ever wanted. I have my books. I pay for my drugs in cash, so should everyone else.

"I don't trade art for drugs, either," Claude says, screwing up his nose. But he'll trade something for one of Kit's photos. He doesn't mind trading art for art.

Come to the studio, he says. Pick something out. Sure, sure, I say and weigh out his gram. Wait, he says. Just a quarter, okay? I wonder what's going on.

They want to get off in my kitchen. That's a surprise. Thought Claude was a snorter. Shit, what a day.

Since we're alone, I tell them okay. Fred ties off first, boots it up. Claude can't find a vein. Finally he pushes the plunger. His eyes fall back in his head. His color changes, his mouth droops, his knees buckle, but Fred catches him before he falls.

Oh, Jesus. This can't happen here. No way.

"Hold him up!" I bark. "Hold him, I'll get ice."

I pull two trays from the freezer but I can't get the cubes loose. Fred snatches one of them from my shaking hands, slides it upside Claude's neck, but he can't hold the ice there and keep Claude on his feet, the body's slipping. Fred drops the ice, it clatters to the floor. Claude's lips are already blue, his limbs flaccid, his eyes lost.

"How could he do this?" I say, complaining as I help Fred move Claude's body to the shower stall next to the kitchen sink. We force him in and turn on the cold. The minutes tick by, each a nail in his coffin.

"He hasn't been getting high," Fred gasps. "He just came back from Hawaii. Had a cure."

Great. Doesn't he know what kind of stuff I sell? Stupid, very stupid, shooting up God knows how much when you've got no tolerance, when you're practically clean. How am I going to explain this? Will I have to call 911? I envision the cops blowing in the door. Wait—me, call the cops? Am I insane?

"Fred," I say, swallowing hard. "We've got to get him out of here."

"I know."

"He can't stay here."

"I know."

"Conscious or not, he's gotta go."

"I know. I'll take care of it."

"How?" I ask. How is this babe going to "take care of it"?

We back Claude out of the shower, the minutes tick by. His arms and legs flop like damp rags across his body. There's no expression on his face at all, no joy, no pain, no anger. Nothing. Fred embraces him from behind, grips him across the chest. We go on trying to revive him, to walk him, but nothing we do moves him back to life.

Tears well up in Fred's eyes, his face a mask of fear. I go cold, then hot, then cold again. I force my head into calm, think *think*. Then it hits me: saline. Saline shot.

"I know what to do!" I shout. "Hold him. Talk to him. Walk him," I say. "Don't let him fall."

"Claude?" Fred pleads, his voice a whisper. "Claude, can you hear me? Don't die on me, buddy. For Christ's sake! Claude? Oh, man."

"Shut up, Fred!" I shout. I'm at the sink, dumping salt in a spoon. "He's not gonna die. He can't. We won't let him." If I say it, maybe I'll believe it.

"You think it's too late?"

"Just hold him, okay?"

Shit shit shit—I can't remember the proportions! How much salt to how much water? Do you cook it or not? Fred doesn't know and I can't remember. My brain fights my fear. I don't know what I'm doing. I have to fake it. Fake it? This is no joke. My hands quake. The salt spills over the spoon onto my shoes, there's salt all over the floor. I look over at Claude. He's gone. He's gone.

I load the syringe, the one he's just used. Fred holds him upright. I get on my knees beside them.

I can't find a vein. Claude's arms are so smooth. The clock is ticking. I hold my breath and poke his arm. No good.

"Try again."

I try again. Zilch. I give up on the vein, push the point into muscle. Fred is still holding him from behind. Now he stiffens and shakes Claude up and down, trying to shake him out of it, madly shaking, yelling Claude's name. He feels for Claude's pulse, listens for a breath. Nothing.

"That's it!" I say, too loud. "You've got to go, Fred! Get him outta here." I move to help.

"I can do it," Fred mumbles, dragging Claude's body toward the door. The goddam door. I want to pull it off its hinges.

"I'll call 911," I say. I don't want to, but I will. I know cops come along with the ambulance, but Claude is famous, after all. I better do what's right.

I make up a story in my mind as Fred drags the body through the door. "You haven't been here," I say. "If the cops happen to come, I don't know you."

"I understand," Fred says, not looking at me.

"Don't worry," I say. "He'll come around. Just get him in the air. It's air he needs now. Okay?"

We heave Claude onto the stairs. Fred's got his head and chest, I toss over the legs. I can't stop trembling. I hear the clock ticking. "You start down," I say in a rush. "I have to clean up. Then I'll come out to help you."

Fred wraps one of Claude's arms around his shoulders, grabs his waist, starts bumping down the stairs. I run back in and shut the door. No time to breathe. I dump the needles in the toilet. But the dope, what am I supposed to do with that? I can't just smoke it all and I can't simply flush it. I can't. It's not paid for.

Shit, I didn't get their money, either.

Make the call! Make the call! I shout at myself. Slowly, don't know why I move so slow, I dial 911. When someone answers, I start in. "There's a man passed out in the hall," I say. "He might be dying. Heart attack or something. Drunk, I don't know. He looks bad." I give the address and a phony name and number. "Hurry," I say. "He might be dead."

I stash the dope in three different places, wipe up the floor. The place is a mess, straws everywhere, mirrors, razor blades. Damn, the spoons! The blackened bent spoons. I throw them in the sink to wash them, but I can't get them clean, can't unbend them. Those bent stems say it all. I bury them in the garbage. What about the scale? I have to put it *somewhere*. Clock is still ticking. I lock the scale in a file drawer, then consider what might happen if I put the dope in a trash bag and drop it down the airshaft. Minutes pass. Minutes pass. I hear nothing. Funny how the phone doesn't ring.

Half an hour goes by and nothing happens, no one comes. Finally, I open the door, step out on the landing, lean over the rail.

I don't get it.

I go back inside and dial Claude's number. Fred picks up. "What happened?" I ask. "Where's Claude?" I hold my breath.

"He's here," Fred tells me. "He's fine."

"He's *fine*?"

"He woke up a minute or two after you went inside. All of a sudden, just snapped awake."

It's the salt shot, I think. It worked. It *worked*. I did the right thing.

"It must have been the salt," I say. "Took a while 'cause we didn't put it in his vein."

"Yeah," says Fred weakly. "I guess."

"Did the cops come?"

"Yeah, they came, but we were sitting on the stairs by then."

"What stairs?"

"Your stairs."

"The inside stairs? Not the stoop?" I'm almost screeching.

"Yeah, the stoop. I told them we'd been to a party, that someone must have spiked Claude's drink. All they did was laugh. They asked if I wanted an ambulance, but we got a cab instead."

"They didn't ask whose party it was?"

"Yeah, they did. I told them I didn't know, exactly. That I stopped there to bring Claude around."

"Good," I say. Fred's a good guy.

"You gotta tell Claude what happened," I say. "Or it'll happen again." Does Claude realize I saved his life?

"He doesn't know anything happened."

"You have to tell him, then. I don't think I can."

"Yeah," says Fred. "I guess."

"I'm sorry," I say. "But you know . . . you know the situation here. I can't risk the cops."

"I know. It's okay."

I hang up and make myself a promise: *no one* is going to shoot up in this apartment ever again. No one, not even a celeb. Especially not.

I used to count myself lucky because I'd learned how to make drugs work for me. I had them in my employ. I used them to govern my world. Always, I stood in it alone. I longed for a companion. I imagined it would be Death. To addicts, death is a plaything, a fascinating friend. Alive, it's us against the world. Die, and we join the ranks of millions. I see it happen every day, and I don't even have to leave the house.

Time for a vacation, I think. I have to get out of New York. I want to get away from this junk, from junkies, from myself. This room, this dark little room . . . this holed-up existence, this *dark*. The walls are closing in, there's no light in my eyes. Every time I open the door, I feel a shadow cross my soul. So when Angelo stops by at two and asks if I'll make a run for him to Thailand, I accept, without a thought.

THE GOLDEN TRIANGLE

Thailand, the Golden Triangle, the dope-smuggling capital of the East. Angelo's not coming with me. He's sending his brother, Mario, instead. I've never met Mario, and won't until we leave. "I'd feel better," I say to Angelo, "if I knew I was going with you."

We're in the office, counting money. No, says Angelo. He can't go. There are too many stamps on his passport. He shows me. It's falling apart, every page covered with visas, yellow, red, green, black, blue: New York, Tokyo, Hong Kong, Bangkok, Los Angeles, Paris, Milan, Honolulu, Bali, Bangkok.

"A collector's item," I say softly. He's been making these trips for years.

"Too long," he says, rubbing his chin. He has to lie low awhile. He puts out a couple of lines.

"Okay then," I say. "Me and Mario."

No, he says, we need another mule to carry the dope. Do I know anyone we can trust? I know Kit would go, but someone has to stay behind to take care of the business and I guess it'll have to be her. Oh, well. I can hear her moving in the kitchen, just outside the office door. She talks about a woman, another musician in an art band, who's carried several times before, Amsterdam to New York. She's not a regular user. This one smuggles just for the money. Mary her name is, Mary Motion.

She's a big-boned woman, tall, with droopy dark-blond hair falling over her pear-shaped face. Her eyes are honest brown, her mouth thin, kind of serious. She looks perfectly normal and doesn't ruffle easy. I hire her.

Angelo is happy, especially when I tell him the deal I get on our excursion-fare tickets, New York–Tokyo–Bangkok–Singapore–Tokyo–New York. Funny how this was the one thing I would never do; now I can't wait to leave. It's a dream come true: the best dope in the world at the lowest price. At last, after all these years sitting in this chair, I'm going straight to the source.

I buy a Southeast Asian guidebook, to study the local customs. Opium, it says, is growing in the hills. Watch out for tribal warfare. I feel my eyes shine.

Angelo says each of us can keep an ounce of the total we'll carry. "Maybe you can sell some of mine," Mary Motion proposes.

"Maybe," I tell her, "but I think I'll have my hands full." I'm to hold two o-z's for Angelo; the rest I'll sell at the usual price. By now I owe him big, several thousand and climbing, more than this nickel-and-dime business can pay a woman with a family of four: Kit, myself, and our two growing habits.

Angelo peels the large bills from the roll I've given him, lays them on my desk in a stack. "For the tickets," he says. I don't count it.

The night before departure, we meet with Mario at Angelo's East Side hotel. I tell them yes, I have the tickets, the itinerary. Where's the money for the stuff? Mario smiles and pats his belly, shows me a moneybelt. It's full. So is his belly. He's a little on the plump side, this Mario, about thirty-five, round and jolly in the face, thin sandy hair brushing his ears, a few inches taller than me. His eyes are the lightest of blues. He bears no resemblance to the dark, ringlet-haired bantam who is Angelo. Hard to believe they're brothers. Mario's not even much of a doper. A schoolteacher, he says. Three kids at home.

I ask where we go to make the buy. Mario knows the way, but he seems a little dim; Angelo draws him a map. Mario keeps it with the cash. Like Mary, he's doing this for the money, the easy money—the stuff there's never any of. I need money, too, but for me this is more about the dope. We do a few lines for the road and I go home to pack. Angelo's leaving town, too, leaving the country. He doesn't say where. He'll call me. He doesn't say when.

It's seventeen hours to Tokyo in a jumbo jet without a single unoccupied seat. Everyone but us is Japanese. Before the movie starts there's a newsreel. The big news is a midair crash of a Japan Air Lines plane. There are a few survivors, somehow—I don't get how, the broadcast's in Japanese. Three of the survivors, a child and two young women, appear in interviews, heads bandaged, necks braced. Fire has left one badly burned. Our cabin is quiet. This is Japan Air Lines.

Seven hours into the first leg of the trip, I get dopesick in my seat. I'm choking on my tongue, can't swallow. My skin feels loose on my skeleton, my eyes are running. So's my nose. The fellow in the seat next to me offers a pack of Kleenex, asks if I want any help from the crew. No, no, I say, and head for the john. I can see Mary Motion sitting a few rows behind me, her eyes wide and wondering, and Mario on the other side of the plane, pretending he doesn't know me.

In my bag I've got a couple of methadone biscuits, some Lo-motil and codeine, but no dope. I've been too cautious. Didn't want to travel with powder. What a jerk. What am I making this trip for, if not to carry? I stumble into the loo and bite off a piece of a meth biscuit, swallow a codeine. A minute later, it comes back up. My entire body retches, but nothing else is in it. I catch myself in the blue-green light of the tiny bathroom mirror. I have a sense there isn't a drop of fluid left inside me, no bile, no blood.

I don't know how I can still be alive. If appearances mean anything, I'm not.

I swallow another piece of meth. Before I return to my seat, a stewardess brings me the sugar I ask for in little packets; down they go. I stare at her, eyes full of tears, I'm choking on my breath. "More sugar, please," I gasp. She hesitates a moment, gets me another handful. Soon the hacking cough stops, but I'm far from feeling right. My arms seem a very long distance away, my hair feels false. Maybe this is normal, I think, as I notice the other passengers. They look green, too.

At the Tokyo airport, we change to a smaller jet for the trip to Bangkok, another five hours away. Everyone on this plane is Indian, they're going to Kashmir. Three men dressed in flimsy white leggings and long flowing blouses, their heads wrapped in white turbans, their faces hidden by full graying beards, are the only passengers in the first-class seats. I'm at a window in coach. I don't know why I feel resentful—this is their part of the world. White skin doesn't always bestow privileges. I stare out the window. The sky's black.

For dinner we get soba noodles, seaweed, and some kind of bean cake for the third time since the trip began. Breakfast, lunch, dinner, the menu's always the same. So is the entertainment: the plane-crash news. Over the summer of 1985, there have been more crashes than at any one time in the history of commercial aviation. I try to sleep. No use.

It's midnight when we arrive in Bangkok. Police are everywhere, soldiers too. There's been a coup, the borders are closed. Our cab driver says, "It's nothing."

Many more sleepless hours pass in the hotel room I share with Mary, who falls out the minute we get inside. The thin carpet is red, the bedspread is red, the curtains are red. The walls appear to be yellow, I'm not sure. We haven't bothered with the lights. The neon glow from the street outside provides all the illumination I can bear.

Mario spends the night in the hotel bar, chatting up a "sexteen"-year-old girl, one of many. I stay in my room, chipping at the codeine. I'm trying to save the meth. We don't know how long it'll be before we can score—maybe hours, maybe days. I find more packets of sugar from the plane, eat them. I pull the thin bedsheet over my head. First I'm freezing, then I'm sweating. All night long I'm turning the air conditioner off and on, on and off, opening and closing the window. The air outside is rank. I listen for gunfire, hear nothing.

In the morning I force myself into the shower. The water rails against my skin like pellets of thin steel. I order coffee from room service. It arrives in a steaming pot. I drink all of it.

At the hotel travel agency, I buy our plane tickets north. We're headed for Chiang Mai, a town in the hills near the Burmese border, popular with tourists. "It's cooler there," the ticket agent tells me. "May I arrange your hotel?" Angelo's already given me the name of the place he wants us to stay. The agent reserves three rooms.

My hands are shaking so badly I can't hold the tickets. I stuff them in my bag, approach the hotel dining room. A breakfast buffet is set up on the bar, staffed by men in olive-and-gold bus jackets, standing where the hookers had been the night before. The men are all short and all have the same haircut, styled, possibly, with an ax. They look pockmarked and sallow. I down another coffee, try to swallow a piece of fruit, settle for a few bites of sticky rice. Mario comes in, smiling, clean-shaven, wet from the shower. The girl was very nice, he says. It was fun in the bar last night. He had a nice massage. We should have come on down.

We still have a few hours to kill before plane time. In the narrow street outside the hotel, the air is so muggy and thick with smog I can hardly move my legs. Again I wish I'd brought something with me. Ridiculous, leaving all the dope at home. I'm much sicker than I ever expected, but I don't want to take a chance on buying something here from a total stranger.

We hail a cab, because it's air-conditioned. The driver wants to sell us a nickel bag of pot. I frown at this but Mario thinks it's great. I try to convince him otherwise. Everyone knows cabdrivers are cops, and besides, marijuana's not what we're here for. When I'm not looking, he buys it anyway. "Everyone does it," he whines.

"We're not everybody," I reply.

He looks dubious.

We drive along the Patpong Road, a main drag, strip joints mostly, a few jewelers. Bangkok's a stinking place. Where are the temples of gold? Families are living in the street, tending their woks over fires in the gutter, cooking breakfast. The sickening smell of frying palm oil wafts through the trees. With the auto exhaust fumes and heavy humidity, the air's nearly impossible to breathe. I bite off another piece of meth.

It's only eleven a.m., but we head for a bar and knock back a few beers. I don't taste them. My tongue feels bloody. I'm biting it. My eyes swim in my head. Mario wants a plate of French fries. They carry the stench of that sickening oil. I'll kill him, I think, before this is over.

We've all lost interest in a tour of the city's canals recommended in my guidebook. Klongs, they call them. "King Klongs," I say to Mary, who looks as glum as I feel. We walk back to the hotel.

It's almost noon and the equatorial heat has steeply escalated. All along the sidewalk, food vendors sitting under striped umbrellas display edibles we can't identify. Never have I seen food like this: strange shapes, unnatural colors, horrid odors. Shops advertise silk and linen suits made to order in a day. Men and women in thin polyester clothing rush to jobs. What about that coup? No sign of an army anywhere. I buy an English-language newspaper. The coup was a failure, but a couple of English journalists were killed and the borders are still closed. There's an article about the Thai Queen's visit to the Paris collections. A woman in low-heeled leather pumps passes by. Everyone else wears flip-flops.

The Bangkok airport looks different in daylight, clean and not too busy. The only activity on the tarmac surrounds a Vietnamese plane loading cargo. The terminal's metal detector buzzes as I pass. Two attendants approach, and a nearby guard. They want to search my bag. At the bottom of an inside pouch, I have a small plastic paper-cutter with a retractable blade. It doesn't look any more threatening than the prize in a Cracker Jack box. The blade is barely a half-inch long but it's sharp enough to cut a piece from a solid rock of dope—or a face. There's a small pocketknife in there, too, and a prescription bottle with my various pills. The guard seems more interested in my Polaroid. I waste a picture on him, and he lets me pass.

The trip north takes less than an hour. A man holding a sign with the name of our hotel takes us to a van, where a perky young woman is waiting, all smiles. I notice her skin—not a line, not a wrinkle—her cheeks are naturally rosy. She wears her hair short, cut in a subtle flip. Her dark eyes dance into mine. I haven't seen anyone like her since high school.

She says her name is Taffy. This makes me laugh and she takes me for a jolly person. I laugh again. She's a student at a nearby college and she's very congenial. How long will we be staying in Chiang Mai? she asks, very cheerful, never losing the smile. Where are we from? Would we like to take a tour of the temples?

Sure, I say. Temples? Sure. She hands me a four-color brochure. It describes several different excursions, some whole-day, some half-day, some two-day. I pick the first one scheduled for the morning, a half-day. Taffy seems happy at this. Her cheeriness is contagious. Could she be stoned? No, I don't think she's ever smelled dope in her life.

I thumb through the rest of the brochure. There are thirty-six temples within the walls of Chiang Mai, eighty more in the country around it. Taffy says if we stay another day, we can take in a few mountain villages, too. In one all they make is umbrellas. In another, silks. Which, I wonder to myself, is the one where they make the heroin?

At the hotel we drop our bags and go outside to get the lay. Mario says it's too early to check in with the connection. I didn't know we had an appointment. They have hours, he tells me. I give out an involuntary sigh. It's the same all over, isn't it?

The streets of Chiang Mai are deserted. Though it's late afternoon, there's hardly a shadow. The sky's blue-on-blue, not a cloud, the air so hot and pink and quiet it feels like a dream. I keep thinking the road's unpaved but it isn't—some kind of dusty illusion. The whole town seems built on straw. A high fence of loosely tied wooden poles runs down one side of the street, shielding the jumble of rickety houses behind it. On the other is a low line of stuccoed shops, most of them shuttered against the sun. A skinny Caucasian fellow lurches toward us with that telltale junkie buckle to his knees. His hair is long and stringy, his black jeans torn at the seat and dusty as the street. He hasn't had a bath or a meal in a while. His skin is just this side of human, his eyes have rolled back in his head. Mary makes a sound. "Well," she smirks. "We've come to the right place."

We're going to carry the dope in our intestines, packed tight in knotted condoms. We need to find a drugstore right away. The hotel concierge has told us there's one just down the road. There is. Poking through the crowded shelves, we look for laxatives and lubricants, condoms, and tuberculin spikes. Behind the counter, a middle-aged Thai man and woman, husband and wife, serve us without comment or question. No Taffy here. No "Where are you from? Do you like our town? Will you stay long?" None of that. They don't ask if we're related or what brought us. They know.

I stay many minutes at the shelves, as absorbed in the colorful boxes and shapely bottles as I was as a kid in the old courthouse that was my hometown library. George Washington had slept there; it had atmosphere. Intoxicated by the smell of polished wood and library paste, lulled by the metronomic ticks of a grandfather clock in the reading room, I lost myself then, as now, in a world of the senses, ruled by a habit of mind. But here products come from China, Egypt, Vietnam, and Germany—George Washington never saw anything like this.

My hand reaches for a small Chinese box with blue lettering. I feel a shallow breath behind my ear. "You don't want that," says a voice. The Thai man is standing at my shoulder, gesturing at the box. "That's not for you," he says.

Really? I want to know what it is. The man is loath to say. I have to be careful. I don't want to make a scene. I replace the box and pick up a tube of toothpaste. The man smiles then, trades glances with his wife; we're all very friendly. Mary Motion and I buy a tube of K-Y jelly each, several boxes of condoms, some strong laxative tabs, a couple of clean gimmicks. I pretend this is business-as-usual. In Chiang Mai, maybe it is.

Back on the street it's like a sauna, hot but dry, better than the muggy air of Bangkok, anyway. In the heat even the distant hills look pooped. In the hotel parking lot, pedicab drivers in native costume nap in the passenger seats. We stop in the hotel bar, take a table. The tourists are all out with Taffy or one of the other guides; we're the only customers, one waiter, one barmaid. Mary wonders if they know why we're here. She's too paranoid. "We're tourists," I say. "We're seeing the world."

Mario checks his watch, downs his drink. "Time to go," he says in his thin, reedy voice, forever jovial. Everything to him is a yuk. I don't trust him but he's the one with the directions, which he doesn't share with us. Orders from Angelo, he smiles. I don't.

"Don't forget to bring back a sample," I growl. He gives me a high-sign and a gap-toothed grin. When he's gone I tell Mary we should follow him.

"Not me," she says, looking around uncomfortably. "I'll wait here." We're sitting near a large picture window, just out of the sun. I watch Mario climb into a pedicab and go off. We order another round.

I can't get drunk enough. I ate my last meth biscuit hours ago, it's wearing off. After the long journey, the stultifying heat and sleepless nights, after the vodka I've consumed, I'm in a state of semi-withdrawal. Forty hours ago I was buckling my seat-belt at JFK. Now I'm staring into a glass, wishing it didn't have a bottom.

Mary and I wait for Mario and drink. We talk about New York, about the free time we'll have for shopping in Singapore, whether or not we should "lose" our passports there. Singapore is our vacation cover. The Thailand stamps dated only days apart might look funny at customs. Well, we can always get new ones. Mary says you just drop the passport in a mailbox somewhere and tell the consul it's been stolen. People steal American passports all the time.

"I wouldn't mind spending an extra day in Singapore," she giggles. "Maybe we could have some suits made." I wonder how she has the strength to laugh. I want to have cocktails on the veranda at Raffles, the hotel where Somerset Maugham used to stay. Nothing but tourists we are, after all. Taffy will never know the difference, anyway.

Other people are in the bar now, the sun's beginning to drop. We order another round. Suddenly Mario's standing by the table, again with the silly grin. Without a word we troop through the lobby to the elevators. I'm very drunk and a little stooped but at least I'm not noticeably sick. On the wall behind the check-in desk a line of clocks shows the time in every major city in the world. In New York it's about the same time as it is here, but not the same day. We've lost one or gained one, I can't remember.

In my room upstairs Mario explains that the deal is done but we've arrived too late to make the pickup. Tomorrow, he says. Two p.m.

Shit. I was hoping we'd be gone by then. Now we'll have to take Taffy's eight a.m. tour. She's going to call the room at seven.

I ask about the sample. Mario hands me a red condom balloon, its bottom heavy with perfect white powder. I dive into my bag for the pieces of aluminum foil I took from the hotel breakfast bar in Bangkok. I roll up a straw, untie the balloon, smooth out another piece of the foil. I lay down a clump of powder, light it easily. Smoke it. In a second it's gone. In a minute I can feel my eyes sparkle, my back straighten up. "I can walk!" I cry. "I can walk!" I'm suddenly in a party mood, but the other two are busy.

Mario's got a hit in his cooker, a bottlecap from a beer. He's tying off, looking anxious. Mary snorts a line off her compact mirror.

The Golden Triangle, I think, eyeing the mirror, the foil, the cooker. The Golden Triangle. We made it.

Mario boots. Couldn't I have guessed? He's down on the floor with the needle in his arm.

"Oh shit," says Mary.

Mario's going out.

"Let's get him on his feet," I say with a sigh, thinking, Here we go again. Damn.

She doesn't move. I give her a look. She's fucking stoned. Mary's no junkie, just a mule, and now she's stoned. Fucking A.

Finally she reaches over and we pull Mario to his feet. He's heavy. I curse him, take the needle from his arm. He wobbles, down he goes again, but the dope's made us powerful and we pull him up. Mario giggles. His face is scarlet. He's enjoying this! I'm yelling at Mary to wash out the spike, go down to the restaurant, steal some salt. I'm screaming at Mario; "You dumb asshole! Talk to me! Say something!" But all he can do is smile. That lazy, soporific honeymoon smile. I want to wring his neck.

Ten minutes later, Mary returns with the salt. "Forget that," I say. "Help me walk him."

It's another hour or so before we get him looking regular again. Those light eyes of his could give us away in a second. I'm so pissed I could spit. Hungry, too. I want to get some food, but while the others are taking showers I chase a little dragon instead. "I'm holding the sample from now on," I tell them. "We can't have anything like this happen again." They don't argue, I've put myself in charge. From now on, whatever I say goes.

The dead streets of daytime Chiang Mai have become a teeming river of human bodies drifting through the night. Bright paper lanterns float on the breeze, lighting the portals to windowless storefronts. Their doorways are crowded with carved wooden fetishes, some five or six feet tall. All manner of brass orientalia shines from within. Bamboo and straw mats hang everywhere. Flimsy card tables sit edge to edge on the sidewalk, laden with knockoffs of every sort of Western fashion, bending under the weight of Siamese collectibles, ivory and black lead elephants, tiny Buddhas and princesses, scores of beads and lacquerware, some pottery. Hawkers stand before every shop, their eyes shifting over the crowds thronging the street like a mall. Kung-fu music blares from loudspeakers wired to overhanging roofs. Even with all the noise and color, something's missing. It takes me a while to figure out what. It's light. There aren't any signs, no neon, no hanging shingles. None of the shops have names. Even movie houses are marked only by comic-book murals painted on the walls of corner buildings.

According to Taffy, the big draw in Chiang Mai after dark is the Night Market. It's set in a couple of large, two-story rough plank buildings, stall after stall of vegetables and dry goods of every description, fabrics, more elephants, T-shirts, shoes, statues. Each of us buys a few trinkets and a couple of cheap linen shirts.

Someone's watching us now—a sun-browned skinny Thai, a guy about thirty, unusually tall. We can call him "Joe," he says. He speaks a slangy English I imagine he picked up from American soldiers during the Vietnam War, very Burger King with a hard-on. He must have done real well in the 1960s, a street-smart kid pandering to the GIs, showing them a good time in the brothels. We try several times to shake him, but every time we turn around, he's there.

He wants to sell us pot. "Thai stick," he says. "You know Thai stick?" He puffs out his bony chest, full of pride and confidence. His teeth are chipped, his eyes hop. I think he wants to fuck me. I look at Mary. It's obvious she thinks he does, too. Mario, his eyes still lit by the dope, seems to find this amusing. Joe lets a hand hover over his cock, which I can make out pretty well through his chinos. I'm feeling good now, but not that good. I don't want him in my hotel room. I decline the pot, but Joe doesn't let up. He looks me in the eye. "I know what *you* want," he says.

"What do I want?"

"Powder," he says, whispering. "You want white powder."

Mario slides an eyeball my way. "I don't know what you're talking about," I say, looking at Joe.

"No? Okay, I show you."

"Where?" Mario asks.

"Not far, just outside town," says Joe. "Ten miles. You married?" he asks, pointing at me and Mario, Mario and Mary.

"Yeah," we all say together. "No," we say then. Joe makes a face. He asks which hotel we're in, how long we're staying, where we're from. I can see his mind work; he's a hustler. If he gets his hooks into us, we'll be spending all our available cash paying for his silence.

A lot of Thais, Mario has told us, will get real friendly, take your money, even turn you on to a major source, then turn you in to the border guards just as you're leaving the country. We might have to bribe our way out. We've talked about what it takes to buy a general—anywhere from two to ten thousand dollars, maybe more, and then that might not be the end of it, not till we land in jail.

Joe's too cunning not to play every angle. He knows we're no kind of tourists. Mario, stoned as he is, knows this too, but Joe knows a place where the girls are the most beautiful girls in the land and the heroin's the best in the world. Cheap, too, he adds. "Very good price, okay?"

"See you around," I say.

"No, wait!" he calls out, alarmed. "I'm Joe! Joe is A-OK. Ask anybody." He gestures vaguely at the street. "Come on, we have a blast."

"What is this place, exactly?" I ask.

A massage parlor. I might have guessed. They're mentioned everywhere in the guidebook. Massage parlors seem to be this country's main source of income, not including you-know-what. Mario says he really needs a massage. He rubs his ass. He bruised himself falling down earlier.

"It's a trap," I tell him, out of Joe's hearing. "This Joe-guy's full of it."

"I don't know . . ."

"We can't do this," I say.

"Maybe we should check it out," Mario decides. "We don't have to buy anything. We can just get a massage."

Mary Motion shrugs. "Maybe he's harmless," she says.

"Aren't these places just for men?" I ask Joe. Now I'm certain he means to turn us in, that he has to be an informer.

"No, no," he says, his thin hands parting the air. "Massage for women, too. You like this massage," he insists. "You ever have Thai massage?" I shake my head slowly, no. "Ah! Thai massage very special, you like it. Make you feel *good*. Very *relax*. You have a good time," he enthuses. "I show you. Okay?"

"Joe's gonna show us a good time," I say to Mary.

She laughs. "I'm done shopping," she tells me. "Might as well see a little of the country."

"Beautiful scenery," Joe agrees.

"What can we see at night?" I ask.

"Much more to see in the night than the day," he tells me. "I show you."

I don't want to go. I'm hungry again, and tired, edgy. Mary says she is, too, but now we're afraid to eat. Our stomachs have to be empty when we pick up the dope. When you're carrying fifty thousand dollars worth of heroin up your ass, you don't want to have to stop and take a shit.

Joe says we can eat at this place in the woods if we want to. It's a private club. Generals go there. Politicians. "Food good, too," he says, rubbing his belly. "Everything good at this place. Everything A-OK."

"I don't like it," I say.

Joe looks at me in mock horror. "You still don't trust me? But I am your friend, I am *Joe*. Practically *American*. Joe is A-O-Kay! Ask anyone, they tell you. Everything good with me, everything *okay*."

"He's okay," says Mario. "This is Okay Joe." He gives the guy a brotherly pat on the back. Mario's truly an innocent, I think. He comes from a little town in northern Italy where all he knows is pasta and sunshine—all he ever needs to know. "How long will it take to get there?" he says.

I shake my head. It's Angelo I'm running this trip for and I can't let his only brother go off in the woods alone, not the way he is, stoned, a stupid child. Joe says again it's okay, everything we do with him is okay. "Okay, lady?" he asks. "This is a happy place—check it out."

I don't know what to say. All I can think is, Generals go there.

"What's your name?" Joe asks me.

"Evelyn," I tell him.

He can't pronounce it. "This is Judy," I say, pointing to Mary. "She's Judy and I'm Evelyn and this is Joe."

Mario looks at me and laughs. Joe laughs, too. "Ho, Joe! Everything okay, now. Everything way okay." He says he'll get the car.

Okay Joe's "car" turns out to be whatever passing tuk-tuk will stop to take us on. The only one that will is a little three-HP truck, hardly more than a glorified scooter with a cab over the tiny front wheels. A roofed-in pickup affair is attached to the rear with two hard benches along its sides. A piece of thin pink fabric hangs where a window might be between the cab and the back. It's a Thai-sized version of the contraption Anthony Quinn and Giulietta Massina live in in *La Strada*.

"I love that movie," Mario tells me. He hops into the truck.

Our driver motions the rest of us inside. His wife and two small children cram into the front seat, three more remain in back with us. The rear end is open to the street. Vehicles similar to ours stretch beyond as far as I can see, their headlights inching along in the traffic with pedicabs, scooters, public shuttle buses, and bicycles. People on foot are everywhere. "It's the evacuation of Saigon," I say.

Joe looks at me quizzically. His hands are in his lap. "You can sit here," he offers. I'm happy where I am. Not really.

I'm sweating again. So is Mario, profusely. Mary can't get comfortable, either. She tries talking to the children, but they don't speak English. Joe talks to the driver, shouting over the noise of the traffic, the grinding of gears. In ten minutes, we move about a hundred yards.

Another ten minutes pass and we don't move at all. Horns are honking like crazy. Joe keeps up his rap—how great the Thai pot is, how fine the Thai massage, how private the club, how cool the woods, how expert the girls, how young and beautiful, how lucky we are to have met him. "I've gotta get some air," I say and climb out of the truck. Mario and Mary leave with me. We don't look back.

When we reach the Night Market, Joe's there waiting. "Hey, Ef-*leen*," he says. "Why'd you go?" He tugs at my elbow and pulls me toward an alley between the buildings. He has something to show me. Still holding my arm, he reaches in a trash can and removes a rolled-up newspaper. A spray of flowers shows at the top. "You like?" he asks. He tells me to look inside the paper. Under the flower stems I see the marijuana. "I don't think so," I tell him. He's exasperated. Mario gives a yawn.

The Night Market's closing now, it's ten p.m. We're starving. Like wolves we prowl the now-quiet streets, looking for a restaurant that will seat us. The best ones have already stopped serving. A man in the street tells us about an Italian place. We go there. I plead with the owner to stay open a few minutes more. I can't imagine eating Italian food in a place like Chiang Mai, but the thought of Thai food, everything fried, everything riced, disagrees with me more. No matter, the restaurant refuses to stay open.

"But we're from New York," I protest. It makes no impression; clearly, this isn't Italy. Calling the town as many names as we can think of, we walk back to the hotel, back to the bar, to the vodka. We buy a bottle and sit at the one empty table. The restaurant's full up now. There's a band playing, a lounge act with a girl singer doing American pop tunes in three languages. She sings a honking version of "Fever" in English, and "I Left My Heart in San Francisco" in Thai. I set aside my glass and drink from the bottle.

"I'll wake you at seven," I say to Mario when it's done.

"Don't bother," he tells me. "I like sleeping late."

Alone in my room I smoke another line from the sample. It's good stuff, all right. The best.

/ / /

Taffy's call comes at seven exactly. She's down in the lobby, waiting. "Will there be three of you?"

"No," I say, thinking of Mario. "One of us has a hangover."

Mary and I stumble down the stairs a few minutes later, find Taffy standing by a long table dressed with a pink linen cloth, a silver coffee urn, a pyramid of china cups, and a basket of hard rolls. "I'll bet you two ladies want a bagel," she says.

"Maybe later," I tell her, and knock back two quick ones, nice thick dark espressos. They get the dope going, too. I ask Mary if she wants a hit before we take off, but she declines. She needs a little time. Okay by me.

Smiling, chatty, Taffy hurries us to the van parked outside, the same wood-paneled station-wagon affair that brought us in from the airport. "We're running a little late," she explains. I look at my watch. It's three minutes past eight.

We meet the others on the tour: a retired couple from Brunei, two Chinese girls just out of high school, and a Japanese boy, a college student. Do other people find smuggling this absurd?

I wonder.

There's no sun this morning; it drizzles a little. This worries Taffy. She hopes it won't last. Some of the roads are unpaved, she tells us, and we'll have to do some walking. The van winds through the quiet streets as Taffy points out her favorite buildings, mostly temples and movie theaters. It's a pretty place, Chiang Mai, a rainbow of pastels. They call it the "Rose of the North."

All the shops are closed at this hour; only street sweepers move about. In every neighborhood, there are small temples—*wats*—their upper reaches a cross between a minaret and a pagoda. They dot the sky same as the church spires in any provincial American town. "If you listen closely," Taffy says, "you can hear the monks chanting." All we hear is the car engine. We look at Taffy. "I so love that sound," she murmurs. "So steady."

We start up the mountain. Teak forests surround us and a lot more fresh air than I've breathed in an age. "Teak is plentiful here," Taffy reports. "It's our major natural resource." Mary and I exchange knowing glances.

The road, a two-lane blacktop, ropes the mountain like a lasso around a restless bull, riding up, curving, twisting, falling back. At one point we have a view of the valley below, of Chiang Mai in the distance and a few surrounding villages. Again I wonder how many are refining opium, if that's where it's done. Mary must be thinking the same thing. "So this is the Golden Triangle?" she asks.

Taffy nods and twists in her jump seat. "Some people call it that."

A half hour later we're stopped at a roadside grocery where we change to a four-wheel-drive pickup. It's the same kind of truck we were in last night with Okay Joe, but roomier. These benches are set from one side to the other in rows. Taffy sits up front with the driver. Mary and I make small talk with the retired couple, who sit facing us. They've been all over the world, they say, everywhere but New York. In a few months they'll be in the city, where a son is engaged in business. "Where is Brunei?" I ask. I've never heard of it before.

"It's very rich," they tell me. "Oil."

"Our money is rich, too," the old man says. He pulls out his wallet to show me one of the native bills. "Isn't it beautiful?"

I study the note. It's about the same size as a dollar in a Monopoly game, maybe a little smaller. The face side, engraved in blue, features a head shot of the mustachioed sultan in a fezlike cap. The flip side is mauve and shows a picture of the sultan's palace, a glorious place. "Very beautiful," I say, handing back the bill.

"Please keep it," the man says, closing my fingers over it. "A souvenir."

I thank him.

He asks where in New York we live.

"Downtown," I say.

"Is it far from Broadway?" he asks. He wants to see *Cats*. He's already seen it in London, but he wants to see it again in New York.

"Not far in miles," I tell him. "But another world." I light a cigarette. New York is not what I want on my mind. The old lady smiles shyly. "Our son does very well there," she tells me in halting English. "He lives on Fifth Avenue." She adds a few syllables to "avenue." Mary gives me a nudge. The road in front of us narrows. No other cars pass, the woods are silent. The air thins. All I can see are clouds.

I can't believe I never knew about Brunei. There's a lot I don't know, I suppose; this is just the tip of the iceberg. I wonder why I still feel bored. At a break in the trees I look down into . . . nothing. A vast open space, filled with fog. This is about as far from home as I've ever been, but I'm enveloped in something so familiar it feels like I'm home in bed. Except there's no phone ringing, and no sad junkies filling my ear with how much they hate their husbands or wish their girlfriends were dead.

The truck slows. It's having trouble making it up a hill. "We're almost there," Taffy tells us. Then the road comes to an end.

We're in a gravel parking lot at the bottom of a mountain shrouded in mist. Rising up its side, a half-mile length of stone steps (two hundred and ninety, Taffy says) has been cut through a sloping parkside dotted with fragrant flowers. It looks for all the world like the stairway to heaven. Busloads of tourists, mostly Asian families, mill around us, coming and going. Mary walks ahead of me and I watch her disappear into the ether, mingle with the crowd. Four painted stone dragons about twenty feet tall line both sides of the base of the steps, their tongues curled, their bodies a mosaic of blue and gold. The mist drops over us like a net. It makes me shiver. I can taste the dope in my throat. I feel fine.

When I catch up with Mary, we walk the temple grounds, discovering life-size stone statues painted pink, blue, and white, their arms akimbo, their hands clasped in joy, or gratitude, or pleading, in a number of ornate peak-roofed enclosures. Several small stucco chapels surround a single big one, where they keep holy relics of the Buddha. On the roof of the structure, a gold filigreed canopy reaches through the clouds in graduated measures.

"I could kiss the sky," Mary says, staring upward.

"That tower is pure gold," Taffy says, sliding up behind us.

"It's pretty amazing," says Mary.

"It's all really gold?" I ask. "Not plating?"

"Gold, through and through." Taffy laughs. "There's a lot of gold here," she adds and drifts away. I wish I could get interested.

A few steps in front of us, squat pails filled with small gold self-stick paper squares are set around each of the painted figures that mark the pathway crossings. We watch as the Asian visitors walk up, kiss the papers, and paste them on the totems. They're prayers for good luck, we hear. I reach into a bucket and take a handful of the papers. "Can't hurt," I say, pressing them onto the statue. I don't know any prayers. I say, "Hello."

A gentle rain has started. Taffy looks at the sky, concern again crossing her dewy face. "This is really too bad," she tells me. "On a clear day you can see into Laos, almost to the Mekong River." She looks out to a point in the distance invisible to us and gives another of her sweetheart smiles. The Mekong Delta—the name always seemed so exotic to me before. Now it's empty space.

"We'll be moving on soon," Taffy says, checking her watch again. "Ten minutes okay?" She'll be waiting at the pickup.

Mary and I walk along a path by the main temple, enfeebled by the meditative hush. A row of heavy ancient bells, each about a foot long, runs the entire length of the temple wall. They hang from a pole affixed to the wall like dancers stretching at a ballet barre. They look about ten centuries old. If we don't get out of here soon, so will I.

Back in the pickup, we start up a pebbly one-lane road, in

the opposite direction from town. "Where to now?" I ask, wishing we'd brought some coffee. I've got the red balloon hidden behind a tampon in my vagina. I feel it sweat.

"A high-mountain village," Taffy says. "You can do a little shopping there, if you like."

"Sounds great," I tell her, but all I really want to see is the inside of our hotel. Mary Motion sits quietly beside me, her hands twisting in her lap. "Now I wish I'd taken a little of that sample from you this morning," she whispers in my ear. I nod in sympathy and watch the road.

"The hill people are simple but very gracious," Taffy informs us. "They might offer you a cup of opium tea." Mary presses an elbow to my ribs. "You don't have to drink it," Taffy assures us. "But it's best to be polite."

I put on my most innocent expression. "Is there *opium* here?" I do sound awed.

"Thai people are very polite," says the woman from Brunei. "Everywhere you go. Everyone is so nice."

"And," her husband adds, "the women are all very beautiful."

"Thank you," Taffy says, her eyes twinkling.

"Thank *you*," says the man. He puts his hands on his knees to steady himself. His wife gives him a look. The road's getting rougher.

We're in the trees, climbing yet another mountain, up and up. Again the fog and the emptiness, and the beauty. I sit very still and stare into the mist. Opium. It's out there somewhere.

The road turns to mud as we pull into the village, a collection of small thatched-roof shacks lining a rutted path that winds gently up a hill, then turns away once or twice.

"God," says Mary, with an expression of disbelief. "It looks just like Belize in the seventies!" She used to run cocaine out of there, she tells me. She was farming marijuana, too. "It rained a lot in Belize," she adds. "Every day, for a year."

"It's letting up now," Taffy chirps from the front seat. "Shall we walk?"

As we make our way up the muddy lane, I see the shacks are actually stalls for local vendors selling gemstones, textile prints, wall hangings, incense, and snacks. The whole village has a sodden carnival midway feel. Some of the vendors are dressed in traditional native peasant gear; the rest wear Western trousers and light shirts. "It's like the Burma Road," I say, stepping over the ruts.

"We're not very far from the Burmese border"—Taffy nods—"many of the people here cross over every day to work in the fields or sell their wares. It's illegal, of course," she says, keeping her voice low. "But it's the only way these people can eat. Most of the gem dealers are fakes," she lets on. "Later I'll take you to the ones selling genuine stones. Anyone who tries to sell you stones in the street is taking you for a ride."

Even as she says this, a twenty-something boy in a plaid shirt approaches, several strings of beads slung from his arm. He shows us a tin paintbox in his hand. Inside are a number of tiny stones— rubies, sapphires, diamonds, emeralds, pearls. He insists they're real and that they're not stolen, says we can trust him. He quotes a few prices, neither high nor low. Over the boy's shoulder I see Taffy wave us away.

Soon we're standing before a house at the top of the hill. It has a decrepit fence around it, and sits awkwardly on a rise just above the road. It appears to be sinking in our direction. Two chickens pace the yard; two roosters scratch the ground nearby. Loosely woven baskets are perched like hats on the weather-beaten stakes of the fence. A couple of paper lanterns dangle from the roof. Taffy brings us around the far side, where a woman who could be thirty or fifty is sitting on a porch step. According to my guidebook, she's wearing a traditional Meo-tribe hat over her black blouse and embroidered black skirt. We watch as she paints a piece of linen with a quill-type brush, making rows of delicate symbols. Several children surround her. Taffy makes small talk, then motions us inside.

"What are we doing?" I ask her.

"I thought you might like to see how the people here live."

"Okay," I say. But it isn't.

It takes a minute to adjust to the gloom inside, one room on a dirt floor. Smoldering wood sits in a hole dug in the middle of the room, under a makeshift stove. A large, heavily encrusted wok sits over the heat on a piece of thin metal. A few pots and a couple of enamel bowls lie on a sad wooden counter beside it. "This is the kitchen," Taffy says as if we were visiting the Grand Palais. "Feel free to look around."

I want to run out the door. It's embarrassing, gawking at the poor woman this way. What can we say? "Oh, how clever"? "How lovely"? "How delicious"? There's primitive plumbing in a corner by a rusting sink and, behind a hanging blanket, a couple of mats for beds. Long drapes of thin cotton plaid hang over the windows. Maybe there's glass there but I don't think so. There's no place to sit, except on the ground, and nothing to do about any of it.

Mary and I slip back outside while the others examine the even darker corners of the room. "It's really exactly like Belize," she says. "I can't get over it."

Behind the shack, we spot a chimney sort of structure in the ground. It might be a kiln, or an incinerator. It might be an opium refinery, too. I bend and take a sniff, hoping to catch the familiar odor, but all I find is mud and a few fallen leaves. Not the season, I guess. I pick up a twig and poke through the leaves. Mary watches me with amusement. "Anything in there?" she asks.

"I can't tell," I admit. "I don't think so." I glance down the hill toward the village. In one of these rude huts, someone is refining heroin and I want to know where. I just want to . . . *know*.

We go back and join the others. They're waiting on the porch, wondering what we've been up to. "Just looking around," I say.

We thank the peasant woman and saunter down the road past two groups of German tourists. Taffy shepherds us into the shelter of a gem dealer she says is genuine. In a minute my hands are filled with tiny pink rubies. I stare at them. So tiny. They look like candy but better, harder. I put them back on the dealer's table, where small pieces of raw jade, emeralds, and other stones are on display. I notice the scale. It's exactly like mine. It gets me thinking about the border guards again. I can't spend money here . . . and I can't walk away empty-handed. I pick out a couple of unpolished black star sapphires. The dealer weighs them in the scale—twenty dollars, she says. I buy them. Taffy approves, though she wonders why I don't take a few rubies, too. She points out larger examples. I see she's something of a shill for these people. I wonder if she takes kickbacks.

I find Mary in the next stall, considering the heft and price of a lacquered human skull in her hand. It's speckled brown, like a quail's egg. There's a brass hinge at the nape of the neck, where it must have been torn off. She plunks down a hundred and twenty dollars, American. The skull drops in her bag with a thud. "This is a sacred object here," she tells me as we merge back into the muddy road. "It's very precious." Actually, she says, it's sort of illegal to remove. She'll have to smuggle it out.

Great. Dope up the ass, Thai stamp on the passport, skull in the bag. "How are you going to get that past customs?" I ask.

"Oh," she says, "maybe this'll distract them—from the other thing."

The sun's shining now, it's almost too bright. I ask to see the skull. It's heavy as a bowling ball. "How old d'you think this is?" I'm curious.

"Old," she says. "I'll make some money on it when I get back home. There's a nice market in New York for antique skulls." A born smuggler, this Mary Motion. I can learn a thing or two from her.

/   /   /

Mario is just waking up when we get back to the hotel. He wants a snort from the sample. "No needles," I say, "no problem."

"No problem," he replies, dusting off his eyes. I go in the bathroom to retrieve the balloon. I dangle it in Mario's face. "Breakfast," he says with a grin.

"Buon appetito." I smile.

Just before two p.m., Mario cinches up the moneybelt and heads out in the pedicab. Mary and I pack our bags and walk around town looking for something to eat, something small and easy to digest. It's cloudy again, this is no fun. In a few more hours we'll be back in the pukable miasma of Bangkok. I hope the borders are open.

"Let's not stay in Bangkok," I say. "Let's go straight to Singapore."

"Okay by me," Mary says.

We step into a fluorescent-lit Formica place that resembles a McDonald's but more plastic, if that's possible. Maybe four other people are there, one Caucasian hippie couple. It's raining again. Everyone looks out the windows at the rain. We order by pointing to pictures on the wall. Who took these pictures? How long ago? They don't look very new. What does that say about the food? I've been living on chocolate milk, heroin, cigarettes, vodka, and coffee for over a year. What do I care about freshness? I wish Kit was here. What am I doing with these people?

The food comes fast; it seems warmed over. I try the Thai noodles but I don't swallow well. Mary Motion can't eat her rice either. Maybe when we're in Singapore, we say. Maybe then we'll eat. We watch the rain.

Later, Mario says he's paid for the stuff but he has to go back at six for the pickup. He wants me with him this time. A secret smile sneaks across my face—my private face, the one I never show the world, the one I keep under the skin, where this life can never betray it.

/   /   /

At five-thirty I'm in the pedicab with Mario. The driver knows where to go. I worry about that, but Mario, of course, says not to. He's paid off the driver, whose name is Chuck. We pedal onto a wide concrete bridge that crosses the River Ping. Chuck stops by a roadhouse sitting on the riverbank. Graceful trees hang low over water that appears still and glimmering in the late afternoon sun. "Wait for me here," Mario says. "I won't be long."

I'm the only customer in the bar, a rustic barnlike room with a few scattered picnic tables. The whole place is varnished knotty pine. It reminds me of the one Catskill Mountain hotel I ever went to, when I was fourteen, but without the Ping-Pong. The slight Thai barman is setting up for the evening, washing glasses, polishing the bar. I ask for a beer and go out on the back deck to wait. To pass the time I watch the traffic on the opposite shore, study the sun going down. I wish I knew where Mario was. "Three or four houses up the road," he said when he left. I wish I could see which one, but the trees—

I wish it were me making the pickup. I want to see who these people are, how they do it. Mario says it's a family and that they're very organized, very professional. Someday, I reflect, I might want to make this trip on my own. No, what am I thinking? I never want to come this way again. I want to get my dope, make my money, and get the hell out of this business, if there is a getting out. At the moment, it seems impractical.

Mario hasn't returned when I finish the beer. I'm restless. It must look strange, me sitting here drinking by the river, a white girl in black clothes, alone. I stare at my sneakers. I look to see where the barman is. He's watching me through a window. I light a cigarette, signal for another beer.

I wish I could like what I'm doing. It's not so bad, really, I guess. I'm having a vacation, I'm out of New York. I smoke and drink the beer, watch the sun, the lilies floating on the water, the bicycles gliding slowly across the bridge. It looks like the Pont Neuf in Paris. I sit in the twilight, still as a Buddha. I feel calm inside, pleased I've been handed this good dope, this good day, this good hour. I'm on a mission, that's what it is, this is important. I'm hauling back pleasure for a lot of worried people who need me.

No, it's not a mission, it's just a job. I have a business and I'm doing my job. I'm doing the right thing—I'm lucky. I'm lucky to be here. Not everyone gets opportunities like this. For a fleeting moment, I remember my life, a tiny speck on the floor of my imagination. I don't know where I am or what comes next, maybe never did. All I ever wanted was to feel swallowed whole. But in my dreams, I was always suffocating.

Even as a child I was afraid of my dreams. My parents would tuck me in bed and turn out the light, and when the door closed I'd lie there and wait for sleep and push it away when it came. When I was five, my Uncle Jack died in a car crash, killed in an instant. I began having a recurrent dream. It was a Humpty Dumpty sort of dream that began at a mortared stone wall.

My great-uncle Willie was there with me, leaning on his cane. He was my mother's uncle, but she looked to him as a parent because her parents had both died young. He was old enough to be her father but, unlike my mother, he seemed young enough to be my friend.

With Uncle Jack dead, Uncle Willie became my favorite relative. He was my favorite because we shared a secret. Whenever my family visited him and my parents went out, we stayed up late together and watched wrestling matches on TV. We didn't have a TV yet in our house. Commercial TV was only about as old as I was then and most people didn't have it. My great-aunt and -uncle had TV but no children—not counting my mother, who had been born to my great-aunt's twin sister, probably a suicide. I don't know that for sure, because my mother never told anyone how my grandmother died. "Of a broken heart" was all she ever said. "At least," I told her once, in a fit of anger, "at least she had a heart that could be broken."

This great-uncle was a believer in physical culture. When he ran from the Nazis at the outbreak of World War II, he got out of Germany and went to England, where he worked in a cousin's gymnasium. He taught swimming and weight lifting, and every day he shaved his head. He left a few hairs on top, which he would carefully comb and position with Brylcreem. At the gym he coached the wrestlers. He didn't wrestle himself, because he'd come to England with a head injury. He also acquired a cane. I never knew why; his injuries were never apparent. A lot of the time he just let the cane hang over his arm, but he didn't go anywhere without it.

Under his mattress Uncle Willie kept a silver flask that was always filled with brandy. When we stayed up to watch wrestling on TV, we drank from the flask. That was our secret. We stayed up after hours and took nips of brandy, he from the mouth of the flask, me from the cap. Then I'd fall asleep.

In my dream we stood before this high crumbling wall passing the flask. On one side of the wall thousands—thousands—of people were crowded together in the shadows, screaming for release from a pit behind the wall. They were badly dressed and many had crutches, like my great-aunt, who had a broken hip. Everyone was pushing against the wall, as if they could topple it with the sound of their screams and the weight of their agony—as if they could simply push it away, as I did the arrival of sleep.

My uncle, because he needed a cane, couldn't scramble over the wall. Also, he was too short. I, a child of five, was even shorter, but I had get-up-and-go. Also, because this was my dream, I could do anything that seemed like the right thing.

I was able to boost my uncle to the top of the wall, and I, finding toeholds between the old stones, could lift myself up after him, above the screaming minions. Whenever we reached the top and knew we could jump over, I woke up, breathing hard. I had to sing myself back to sleep. I sang a lullaby to the crippled souls imprisoned behind the wall.

Many years later, many, but before I found drugs, Uncle Willie was living in a home for the aged in the Bronx. Every now and then I'd hop a D train in the Village and go to see him. One of the last times I went, Uncle Willie wasn't in his room. My aunt was dead by then and I knew he often wandered the halls of the home talking to the ladies. They all seemed to have a crush on him. One of them was his new girlfriend. They were both in their middle seventies.

I went down the hall to the girlfriend's room to see if he was in there. She hadn't seen him since the morning. She wasn't feeling well that day. I left her alone, went into the cafeteria and then out into the garden. No uncle. Finally I went to the desk in the lobby to look for a nurse. She disappeared a moment and returned with an administrator. The administrator told me my uncle's rent had not been paid that month and what could I do about it? My uncle's expenses were usually paid by checks that came from the German government—war reparations. If they hadn't come, there wasn't anything I could do about it. All I had was a token for the D train. I didn't tell the woman about the token. I asked where my uncle was, but she didn't know. She looked at the nurse. The nurse then said my uncle had gone out for a walk and hadn't returned for lunch.

A social worker appeared from an inner office. "Are you a relative of Mr. Winter's?" she asked. I told her, Yes, I'm his niece. "Your uncle had an accident," she said. "They just called from the V.A. hospital up the road. They have him over there. Someone found him collapsed in the street. They may not let you in, but maybe you should go on up there."

The V.A. hospital was at the top of a steep hill a few blocks away. It was an old building that smelled of urine and floor wax and antiseptic. As I walked down a hall past wards of up to forty beds, I saw men without legs or teeth or eyes, lying on cots or sitting limply in wheelchairs, coughing, grunting, or staring. A lump formed in my throat and stayed there.

I found my uncle in a room with six other men lying quiet in their beds. This was the cardiac intensive care unit; they thought he'd had a heart attack. His face was red with the effort of staying alive. The stubble on his head was visible. My first thought was, If he could see that, he *would* have a heart attack.

As I sat down by his bed, a young East Indian doctor approached. They couldn't really keep my uncle in the V.A. hospital, he explained, because my uncle was not a veteran. But, he said, they were afraid to move him. They were waiting for the home to decide if it would pay his expenses. I explained that my uncle received a hefty check from Germany every month and I was certain it would pay his expenses. Well, said the doctor, they wanted to perform a spinal tap, but they needed a family member's written permission. Would I sign the form? I had just turned twenty-one. I could sign the form, but I didn't want to. I'd never heard of a spinal tap. I called my mother.

Her response was just short of hysterical. I told her not to worry, Uncle Willie seemed safe and comfortable, and maybe the spinal tap wasn't necessary. We decided to wait. When I returned from the phone, my uncle looked frightened. He squeezed my hand. He wanted to go back to the home. Would I take him? He was sure he could walk. The doctor warned me against moving him. I told Uncle Willie to sit tight, I'd be back the following day.

Next day I was on the D train again, and by the time I reached my uncle, he was just this side of conscious. I still didn't know what was wrong. The doctor handed me the permission form and I signed it. My uncle's face was still flushed and his temples visibly pounded. I was scared. I knew we were back at the wall and I couldn't help him over it. I went home.

The next morning they called me to say he was dead. Would I pick up his things, sign a few more papers? First I went to the V.A. hospital. They handed me his cane. At the home they gave me his wallet and a receipt for the reparation check, which they said had finally arrived. My father was coming to get the rest of his belongings, which were collected in a few slender cartons. The silver flask was on top, so I took it. It was empty.

At the funeral, my mother sat next to me. When the service ended, she gripped my arm. "There's no one left," she said.

"*I'm* here," I whispered.

"That's not what I meant," she said.

Two years later, she died, too. According to Jewish ritual, a family member has to identify the body. A mortician took me to her casket. In the hospital, she'd been just skin and bones, her back riddled with tumors. I could hardly look at her then. Here, I simply stared.

"Is this woman your mother?" the mortician asked. It was cold in the room and I shivered. It wasn't the mother I'd known. Her face had been round and ruddy, eyes green. Her hair had once been wavy, on the thin side, sometimes dark, sometimes fair. There had been a slight furrow to her brow, a look of concern, or dread, or expectation, I never knew exactly. Her hands had seldom been at rest. Now they were folded on her chest, frozen in an attitude she never had. Her hair was bouffant, a rusty orange, her skin had a yellow cast. The furrow in her brow was filled with putty.

"Is this your mother?" the mortician said again. I nodded, furious, a cramp forming in my belly. The mortician closed the casket.

I'm the only one left, I thought at her funeral, though I kept the thought to myself. My father was there and so was my brother and a number of my mother's friends, many of whom were weeping. They looked like the shadow people cowered at the wall in my dream. They kept calling me by my mother's name. I left them standing there, and built a wall out of drugs, drugs to keep agony at arm's length. Whenever I looked back, as I did, as I had to, those people were huddled there still, the same expressions on their faces, expectant and sad, but they had drug names and drug bodies, and when I looked back again, I saw them once more, unmoving and unmoved, in a place I couldn't change or fill. Now here I sit, expectant and sad, where the river drifts in silence and my blood travels thick in my veins, pooling as it reaches the wall.

A voice breaks my high. It's Mario. "Hello," he says, a Thai-style smile lifting his cheeks. He's standing near the rail of the deck, two brown paper shopping bags in hand. My God, how much are we carrying? These bags are enormous, almost the size of the ones you get at Bloomingdale's when you buy a full-length down coat. Mario's eyes are twinkling. I'm not even halfway through my second beer. He walks toward me and casts an eye at the roadhouse windows. I move off the deck to a dirt path that runs along the embankment, and he slips one of the bags in my hand. I look down. "Don't look yet," he says, but I've already seen it—about a dozen red condoms sitting unconcealed in the bottom. They're solid, stuffed with heroin packed tight into rocks. They look exactly like votive candles with little knots where the wicks would be.

"Why do we need these huge bags?" I ask.

Mario says he doesn't know. "I wish you could have seen how they do this," he says, still smiling.

"Me, too," I say.

"Very professional operation," he muses. "Very professional."

"Shouldn't we get a cab?" I remind him. They must have given him a snort, I think. That's why he took so long. Figures.

"Let's walk," he says.

Now *he's* dreaming. "Walk? With these? I don't think so." I'm not about to parade around the streets of Chiang Mai with a big bag of heroin knocking at my side. My eyes shift around in my head, searching for cops and possible informers. I don't see anyone, but it's dark now and this isn't my country. I don't know what to look for or where.

"They want us to get the nine-o'clock bus to Bangkok," Mario tells me.

"Bus? We're taking a bus?" I'm mystified. "What's wrong with the plane?"

Mario shrugs. The movement makes a sound in his bag as his bundles shift. "They gave me the bus tickets," he says, patting the pocket of his linen shirt. "All paid for," he smiles, pleased. "They say it's safer than the airport." He takes my hand and we stroll along on the banks of the Ping, just two romantics of no special interest, tourists with shopping bags, hunting for bargains.

"I'm not going on any bus," I tell him. "That's crazy. What do they care how we leave?"

Mario shoots me the darkest look I've seen on him yet. "I think we better do what they say," he tells me.

"How much is here?" I ask then.

"Fifteen ounces," he whispers.

Fifteen ounces? At seven to ten thousand dollars each, they're going to turn a pretty penny in New York. It's four hundred an ounce here, less than what I get for a gram, twenty-eight to the ounce. Not bad, I think. Maybe I *could* do this again. "Okay," I say. "We'll take the bus."

We go to my hotel room, where Mary Motion is waiting with

the K-Y and the luggage. "Fifteen ounces," she says. "Three of us. We'll divide it." We wrap the bundles in double layers of condoms, then separate to insert them.

For years, I've been hearing about this. They say once you push the stuff in far enough, the bundles travel naturally into your small intestines, where you can't feel them, safe from the stomach acids that kill cocaine swallowers, virtually undetectable by the Feds. Customs inspectors have probes, of course, but they don't reach up that high, and even if they x-ray the stomach, no one sees a thing. When we get to New York, all we have to do is take the laxatives we bought, and the loot will come tumbling down. These laxatives are German, much stronger than what we can get in the States. Even so, it could take a few days, or a week, even two, to bring it all back home.

In the bathroom I discover the packing to be not so different than putting in any other suppository, except these are bigger, really like wearing a candle in your ass. When the first two are in, I realize I'm going to have trouble with the rest. I apply a generous portion of the K-Y jelly, and the third ounce goes in, but no matter what I do, I can't get the fourth to stay. It looks like I'm going to need help. I don't know what to do. I can't exactly ask Mario or Mary Motion to bugger me; that would really be too weird. After I struggle a few minutes more, I pull on my jeans and knock on Mary Motion's door.

"How you makin' out?" I ask.

"I'm ready," she says, opening the door. "You?"

"I can only get three to stay in," I confess. "What do you think I should do?"

"Want me to help you?"

"Uh," is all I can say.

She offers to try to take one of my bundles inside her. We rewrap an ounce and she goes in the bathroom to try it. "Nope," she calls out a minute later. "Sorry. I'm full up."

Very businesslike then, she demonstrates a position that should help accommodate me to the process. I wish I hadn't tried to eat; I really could use a little more room. I go back in the bathroom and start again. I have to relax, I tell myself. I'm too tense. I finger myself for a while, hoping to lubricate myself naturally, but I'm too stressed to make it work. Finally, after a lot of pushing and grunting and praying, I get the fourth ounce up inside but I know there's no hope for the last.

Mario knocks on the door, says we have to get going or we'll miss the bus. In desperation, I jam the last ounce up my ass but it doesn't go in very far. I can feel it hanging, fucking turd. Well, it's not visible. I watch myself walk around in the bedroom mirror. I know I look stiff but so do a lot of tourists. There's nothing so unusual about me.

In the lobby we pay our bill and walk to the bus stop. It's not very far. Darkness has fallen and Chiang Mai is gearing up for another night of shopping. We walk close to the houses that line the road. We're afraid of running into Okay Joe. As we near the bus stop, we spot the back of a man who looks just like him. Oh, no, I think. Oh no.

But this man's Caucasian, an undernourished hippie with stringy brown hair and an unkempt goatee. How long has he been in this part of the world? To my surprise, Mario waves at him. They'd seen each other earlier, copping at the house by the river. This guy was coming out as Mario was going in. I ask where he's from. "North America," he says. Mario tells me he's Canadian, but I think he's really from Australia. We're trying to be cool and not ask questions, but Mario says the guy has made this trip many times before, and there are things I want to know. "How long is it to Bangkok?" I ask, for starters.

"About ten hours," he says.

Ten hours? Ten hours in a Thai bus with five ounces of heroin hanging out my ass? The thought stones me to silence.

The bus pulls up nearly full, no foreigners. The locals eye us suspiciously as we make our way to the rear. Mary Motion and I take seats together; Mario drops into another on the opposite side of the aisle, in front of the Canadian, who settles himself by a window and watches the street. The seats are covered in plastic, the kind you see in houses where the furniture's not paid for. They're built for Thai comfort, too short and narrow for any of us.

As we pull away from the curb, an expressionless stewardess in tight saffron cotton slacks and a drab yellow blouse starts passing out trays with "dinner"—a fried chicken leg that must have been cooked about a decade ago, a sprig of parsley, a carrot stick, and a hard, very hard, roll. "Guess we got on the no-frills run," Mary surmises. I wave the stewardess past. She seems to take this as a personal affront. She has none of Taffy's robust flair; she could be one of my customers after a bad day on the street. She could be one of us, a little farther down the road.

A few minutes later she lurches down the aisle with a tray of drinks: orange juice in plastic containers. To soften her up, I take one but don't drink it. "Good thing we ate before we came," I say to Mary.

She looks pale. Her mouth twists. She says, "I don't think I'll ever like food again."

The driver turns on a TV monitor attached by a chain to the ceiling at the top of the aisle. "Oh, good," Mary says. "Entertainment."

A kung-fu movie begins. It has Thai subtitles and consists of almost constant shouts, grunts, and screams at earsplitting volume. The villains all appear to be women. Women who die early in the film show up again later, in different costume, only to get killed again, more brutally, but still they won't stay dead. When this movie ends another begins, all the same people, same plot, new weapons. This one's even louder and more vicious than the first. Blood flows every few frames. I can't believe no one else minds, but a number of our fellow travelers are dead asleep. I try to read but it's hopeless, I can't tune out the sound of mortal combat. I look past Mary out the window. Can't see a thing. I shift in my seat; my arms stick to the plastic, and I'm cold—the air-conditioning's on full. Then the bus slows and pulls off the road into an outdoor camp kitchen set under a large and splintery teakwood pavilion. The driver turns off the TV and shouts something in Thai. We have to get off. From the window we can see waiting military police. Has there been another coup, or are we in a lot of bad trouble? I look at Mario, who's staring wide-eyed at the Canadian. "Just a rest stop," he says. "Have some tea."

I pull myself together, suck in my abdomen, tighten my ass. I don't want to have any accidents. Outside, the driver and the hostess direct us to long picnic tables, where the other passengers are already sitting down to bowls of steamed rice and green tea. The air is almost as sticky as the plastic seats in the bus but now I don't care; at least my goosebumps are disappearing. We file silently past the soldiers, who board the bus as soon as we're all at the tables. We pantomime gratitude for the meal. They're watching us, everyone is. We stick out like sore thumbs. There's only one reason Westerners like us would put themselves through this torture, and everyone knows what it is. "How on earth could anyone think this is the safe way out?" I ask Mario. He can't even speak, he's so scared. "Really," says Mary Motion.

Fifteen minutes pass before the soldiers emerge from the bus. Now they're checking over the baggage compartment. I look for a bathroom. It's an outdoor latrine. In total darkness I push the last ounce back up inside me but it still doesn't go very far. I want a cup of coffee pretty bad but I don't dare have one. When I leave the latrine, the others are already seated in the bus.

I ask the driver if he'll turn down the volume, I want to get some shut-eye. He nods and closes the door. We've taken on new passengers here; there isn't a single empty seat. I sink miserably back into mine. Mary says she's so tired she thinks she can fall asleep. "Me, too," I say, and a few minutes later I start to drift off, but suddenly the sound-track volume increases again and soon it's back to the level it had been before. I catch the Canadian's eye. "How much farther is it?" I ask.

"Relax," he says. "We're not even halfway there."

We stop two more times during the night. The other roadside rests aren't as grand as the first—one is barely more than an oversize shack—and all they serve is tea. As day breaks I begin to see road signs to Bangkok. Still the TV blares kung-fu. I can't wait to get off. I can't *wait*. When we pull into the city, twelve hours have gone by, it's nine a.m. I think only of the sample nesting in my cunt.

The Bangkok air hits us like a wall of mud. This has got to be the most inhospitable place in the world; New York is a cool mountain stream by comparison. We get our bags and tumble into a waiting cab, move out into the worst rush-hour traffic I've ever seen. The world could easily be coming to an end. And we still have to get out of the country.

An hour later we're no nearer our hotel than when we started. We seem to be driving in circles. The driver says he's looking for the quickest route. Eventually, he finds one.

At the hotel we book rooms for half a day and go upstairs to pull ourselves together. The second the door closes behind me I'm reaching for the sample. In no time I have powder in my nose. I leave the hotel refreshed.

The airport terminal now resembles a department-store bargain basement on a luggage sale day, teeming with people as anxious to leave as we are. Bags lie all over the floor in long snaking lines. We sit on ours and wait for an inspector to check them through.

The agent at the customs desk checks the passports of two English boys in front of me and gives them a careful once-over. He tells them to remove their sunglasses. Uh-oh. I hadn't intended to get high before plane time, but that bus trip . . . that air . . . the perspiring crowds. I take off my shades and hold my breath. If Uncle Willie could get out of Nazi Germany, I reason, I ought to get through a Thai airport. It's in my genes.

The agent questions the English boys about where they've been and what they've been doing. With some reluctance, he lets them pass—providing they never return in his lifetime. I hand over my passport. The agent doesn't even look at the date. He barely looks at me. In a minute, I'm on my way to the gate. Mario and Mary are right behind me.

At the gate the buzzer sounds again, and again I have to empty my bag, let the inspectors examine the penknife. They judge it to be harmless. But as we enter the boarding area, an airline official pulls us aside and my heart moves into my throat. "Excuse me," he says, "but can you wait here a minute? There seems to be a mixup on the tickets." He moves away, our boarding passes clutched in his hand.

"This is nerve-racking, isn't it?" I say.

"I wish you'd get rid of that knife," Mary pouts.

I insist I need it for the dope. She doesn't answer. We're pretty tired of each other by now, and we still have ten thousand miles to go.

Two minutes before takeoff the airline attendant returns and hands us new tickets. We've been moved from coach to first-class. "Sorry for the delay," he says.

It doesn't take long to figure out what the problem was. This is a British-owned airline, a class-conscious company if ever one was. Everyone in coach is Indian or Pakistani or Chinese; with few exceptions, everyone holding first-class tickets is Caucasian. It's a rotten situation to be party to. On the other hand, it's nice to have a comfy seat and eat on china with heavy silver service. We eat with gusto. We're going to be in Singapore two days, time enough to shit and put all the stuff back where it came from. I drink two cups of coffee and smile all the way down to the ground.

The Singapore airport is the world's easiest place for a smuggler. They seem really glad to have you in their country. They don't look at your bags or your passport, they wave you on through. And Singapore itself looks a lot like Beverly Hills without the Spanish influence. The hotel our travel agent picked for us is a four-star job on a hill covered in oleander, jasmine, honeysuckle, and palm. After Bangkok, this is truly Shangri-la.

Mary Motion and I share a room again. It's enormous, with a fully stocked bar and a view of half the island. I don't feel the least bit tired now. I smoke a few lines and climb into the tub for a soak, first removing two of the ounces. The other three are deep within the recesses of my body, and I try to push these two up to meet them, but no go.

"Yo, Mario!" I call through the door. We have connecting rooms. When the door swings back I hold out one of the ounces, put an inquiring look on my face.

"No problem," he says. More service with a smile. I hate that grin of his, that honeymoon leer, I envy it, and I don't know what I'd do without it. The other ounce I poke back wherever it'll ride and we go out in search of the Hotel Raffles.

Somehow, we never get out of the cab. This has less to do with the effects of the junk than it does the neighborhood, which has gone to seed. Raffles' striped awnings sag, its rattan porch furniture looks ragged. I figure we'll come back in the evening when the place is sure to have a little more romance. Right now it looks abandoned. I ask the cabdriver to circle it. I wonder which of these chairs was Mr. Maugham's? Did he sit there, night after night, his Singapore Sling perched on the rattan arm, listening to the characters who would people his stories of the East? We circle again. Was he here with Noël Coward? The conversation must have dazzled. Or were they just cruising the boys drifting by, eating lotus flowers? No one is as interested in this as I am. "But what about the Singapore Slings?" I point out. "We can't leave without having at least *one*."

"I'm tired," Mario says. "We can come back later."

"Yeah." Mary nods. "Let's get the shopping in before the stores close."

We drive aimlessly around town awhile, marveling at the clean streets and the neon-lit vertical malls. Eventually we go inside one, where I buy a duty-free camera and some film. I haven't been using the Polaroid much. The only pictures I've taken feature landscapes and statues, not us. I'm not keeping a diary or sending postcards, either. I don't want anyone knowing we've been here. I realize I'm happiest staying in my room, smoking my dope, pouring my drinks, and taking in the view. I can just about see Raffles from the hotel window, if I lean out far enough. I stretch out on the chaise. Finally, finally: I'm on vacation. At last, I'm away from my life.

I sleep ten hours, dead to the world. When I'm up, we get together to discuss: should we let the passports go? Mario thinks it's stupid but I want to cover my tracks. It's not so bad staying here. On the other hand, I really want to go. We go. Out comes the K-Y and in go the ounces one more time. I'm better at this now, they slide right up. Before I think about them again, we're in Tokyo.

There seem to be thousands of people waiting at the Tokyo quarantine. We have to get a health stamp before we can change planes. We stay in line two hours, then wander through the terminal. That evil ounce is threatening to escape me again. On the plane I have to go into the head to fix it half a dozen times.

The flight east is shorter, but long enough for me to think up a few stories to tell customs. I'm nervous about my passport. I'm nervous about the dope. When the stewardess announces our approach to JFK, I go in the bathroom one last time.

We go through separate lines at customs. As I set my bags on the counter, I see Mary Motion and Mario sail out the door to waiting taxis. A female agent looks carefully through the pages of my passport. I smile at her. She doesn't smile back. "You've been in Bangkok?" she inquires.

"Yes," I say, ready for what comes next. "Dreadful place it is, too."

"I see you were only in Bangkok a few days. May I ask why you were there?"

"Vacation," I say. Just be yourself, I think. Be honest and they won't see through you.

"That's a long way to go for a few days' vacation," she says.

"Well, it wasn't just a vacation," I admit. The agent is searching my face. "I'm a writer," I tell her. "I had this idea to write a guidebook for women traveling alone. A lot of women do, you know. Bangkok was my first stop."

"Why Bangkok?"

"I got a deal on the ticket," I explain. "See?" I show her the price. "They were having a sale."

"Do you often travel alone?"

"Not always. Well, yeah. I guess so."

"That's a pretty useful idea," the woman says. "A guide for women travelers."

"Well, it's a big world out there. There are lots of places to see."

She pages through my passport again. "I hear Bangkok is, well, a pretty wild place, if you know what I mean."

"It's horrid," I say. "Not wild. Unless you mean environmentally. The air stinks, the food stinks, and the hotels are completely awful." Isn't this enough now? Can't I go?

"Did you go anywhere in Thailand other than Bangkok?"

"No, I hated it too much. It made me sick. The food made me sick, the air made me sick, and frankly, some of the people made me sick, too. It's really *not* a place for women," I conclude. "It's all sleazy sex clubs, massage parlors, and cheap cheap clothes. I couldn't wait to get out of there."

"I believe you." She puts the passport down. "Did you acquire anything while you were in Thailand?"

"Just a few trinkets," I say. "Nothing of value."

"Open your bags, please."

She shuffles through them, looks at the passport again. I can see she's thinking pretty hard, but I go on explaining what everything is, the lead elephants and the linen shirts. I keep the sapphires hidden but show her the camera and the receipt.

"You seem kind of nervous," she says. "Why are you nervous?"

"I'm not nervous," I say, forcing a laugh. "I just have to go to the bathroom."

She raises an eyebrow and seems to catch the eye of someone behind me, someone in uniform no doubt. "Is there a publisher for your book?"

"Not yet," I say, "but soon."

"How do you pay for trips like this?"

I'm not prepared for this question. "This one was a gift from my dad," I say.

"Sorry your trip didn't work out the way you wanted," she says then. "Welcome home."

I could expel the ounce right there. "Good to be back!" I say happily and fly out the door.

From the cab the city skyline looks like the cradle of love, but it fills me with dread. I haven't told Kit when to expect me. I thought it would be safer if she didn't know. "Call you from the airport," I'd said, but there hasn't been time. I find myself hoping she won't be home when I get there. I have a feeling I won't want to stay.

GLAD TO BE BACK

Pack your bags," I say when Kit opens the door. She looks dressed for combat. "Hurry. We're leaving town." I head for the bathroom.

"Why, what's happened?" she says, following me, bewildered.

"Nothing," I say. She says, "Where's the dope? Do you have it?"

I sit on the toilet.

"I'm really glad you're back," she says. "You wouldn't believe what's been going on."

"I'm glad to be back. Very glad." I reach for the sample. "What's happened?"

"That's it?" she says, panic defining the shape of her mouth. "That's all of it?"

I explain we have to wait till I shit for the rest, and lay a generous line on the dresser. "Can you go to Bebe's and get me some coke? There wouldn't be any coffee made, would there?"

"I'll make the coffee. I'll go over there. Why are we leaving town?"

"I just don't want to be here for a while. I don't want anyone to know where I've been. How soon can you be ready?" I call the hotel in Montauk and book a room.

"Honey called. Grigorio's in town, they're getting married in two weeks."

"So soon? Why are you dressed this way?"

"Vance and Jean-Paul—they got into a fight. Guns and bats. It was horrible."

"They were here *together*? While you were doing business?" I won't bother to unpack.

"Last night—no one else was here. I wish they had been. I was sure someone in the building would call the cops. I'm really glad you're back."

"When are they getting married?"

"Soon. A few weeks. They can't wait anymore."

"Last night you were freebasing?"

"I know, I know. I'll never do that again. I thought cops were coming in the window. I thought there were giant bugs in my hair. I was sure we were under attack."

"Let's go *now*. I'll rent a car. Ask Bebe if she'll feed the cats."

"Honey wanted to see you as soon as you got back. I told her you were visiting your father."

My father. We haven't even spoken in a year. Thanksgiving it was, he called. So, he said, you comin'? I didn't know I was expected. Of course you are, he said. Hadn't he mentioned it? He must've forgot. I'm always welcome, he said. I supposed we could make it in time for dinner, if he picked us up at the train. No problem, he started to say, when I heard the wife making noise in the background. Was I coming alone or with Kit? With her, I said, or I don't come at all. Apparently, he said, there wasn't enough food to go around. Not enough? I was shouting by now. Not enough food on Thanksgiving? We went to Honey's instead. Lots of food, lots of fun. Plenty of love to go around.

I look at Kit's face, see the fear in her eyes, and the next thing I know we're in each other's arms. It feels strange, it's been so long. "Well," she says. "Why don't you tell me about your trip?"

Before we leave for Montauk, I meet Honey and Grigorio in a Japanese restaurant on Bleecker Street. "We have something to tell you," Honey says.

I smile. "You're getting married."

"Yes," she says soberly. "That's not it. You can't tell this to anyone. Not a soul. You really can't."

"Not even Kit?"

"If you swear her to silence." I think I know what's coming. I give a slight nod and reach for my drink.

"We've got it, hon," she says. "HIV—we've both tested positive."

My body locks. "How long have you known this?" I ask. "When did you get the test?"

"I've known awhile," she says. "We've both had lots of tests. Actually, we're not just positive. We have AIDS."

Grigorio's toying with a chopstick. I down the rest of my drink. The perfect couple, I'm thinking. Isn't this just perfect.

"There aren't too many people I can tell this to," she goes on. "For Mike's sake. He'd be ostracized at school if they knew, the way people are. I wouldn't get any work. But we have to be able to talk to *someone*."

"I have to tell Kit," I say. Did we share needles with them last summer? I can't remember.

"You can tell her, that's okay. Lute knows too. So does Ginger."

"What about Mike?"

Grigorio says they can tell him when the time comes.

"You don't look sick," I observe. Poor Mike.

"We're not sick," says Honey. "Not right now, anyway. Anyway, we're not going to go that fast, if at all. We're not going to change the way we *live*."

"That's not true," says Grigorio. "We've stopped doing drugs."

"Yes," she says. "We thought we'd try that. But you'll stick around, won't you? In case we need anything?"

SILENCE

I had a right to remain silent, Dick said so. I had a right. Silence is not held against you, not in a court of law. Silence doesn't put you in jail, but it doesn't keep you out of it, either. Not when your keeper is Dick.

He knows I sit here all day cooped up in my turkey body, suffering the junkie's maximum despair. I'm like the bridesmaid who's never a bride: always detained, never incarcerated. Why won't he leave me alone?

"I thought we should talk," he said. "About a friend of yours. About Daniel."

Oh God, I thought. Not Daniel.

"What's happened with Angelo?" I asked.

"We're trying to turn him," Dick said with a casual air. "He's stubborn, that guy, but I think he'll turn. We want him to give us his source in Thailand."

"*Thailand* is in your jurisdiction?"

"Everything is in our jurisdiction," he replied. "That's one of the perks of this job—travel. We go everywhere. The war on drugs—you know."

I wished he would take me away.

"What about Daniel?" he asked again. I took a breath.

"Dan-*iel*," I answered. "He's French."

"Whatever. We're very interested in this Daniel. We think you know where he is."

I never did know where Daniel lived. Like the others, he always made deliveries. "I think he sells antiques," I said. I don't think I sounded convincing.

"No, not antiques. We've traced him to an East Village dress shop. Do you want me to believe you've never been?"

"When have you seen me in a dress?"

Daniel, my friend Daniel. It was him I called from the pay phone up the street after Dick took Angelo away. Call Daniel, Kit said, and I did. I bought the gram from him. I did it against my better judgment, but I was clean out of judgment that night.

He chose the place we met, a neighborhood tavern on First Avenue, one step up from a dive. We huddled with Kit at the bar, a noisy crowd around us, bodies in overcoats, beery voices.

"I have to quit the business for a while," I whispered in his ear. "A friend's been busted by the Feds."

"How good a friend are we talking about?"

"Pretty good. Good enough."

"Not Massimo!"

"No, someone else."

He turned toward the window of the bar, straining to see the street through the crowd. He turned back and looked at me close. I took a sip of my drink. If Daniel knew me as well as he thought, he would have known everything then. I've never been a sipper.

"Are you sure it wasn't you they busted?"

I watched the bartender. "It wasn't me." I only wanted to warn him. I didn't want to scare him off.

Daniel finished his drink. "These cops, they wouldn't be watching you, too?"

"I don't think so."

"You don't think so? You mean, they are." His handsome face twisted up like a pretzel, anger wound up with dismay.

"I don't think so," I said. I didn't say the cops were too busy with Angelo to spare any time for us. What would that have accomplished?

"Where can we do this?" I said. "In here?"

"I want to trust you," he said, uncertain.

Part of the game, I was thinking. Risk you take.

"You have cash?"

"In my coat."

Kit stood close behind us while Daniel found my inside breast pocket. I let his hand reach around where it liked. Finally, it took the cash. "Meet me outside," he said. "Wait five minutes, then come out."

"I may need to see you again," I said when we were standing in a doorway outside.

"Okay, but you pay cash every time now—no credit, okay? I'm not taking any chances."

I put on a wounded look.

"Don't call, I'll come by on my own," he said as he turned to go. Then he wheeled back around. "It really wasn't you they busted?"

"It wasn't me," I said.

"After all I've put up with from you, this had better be the truth—you hear me?"

Who is he to make these demands? I was thinking. Just a guy I know— not really a friend. That's what I had told Dick, anyway, in those hours in that cell of a room in the Federal Building, when he was pressing me for names. "Well, there's Daniel," I said, just to say something. I've been biting my lip ever since.

Maybe it was all those stories I'd heard over the years and had to hold inside, maybe I was just sick and scared, but I couldn't be brave and I couldn't hold my tongue. When I opened my mouth that devil D flew in, and it gave up Daniel's name. After that, I fell back into silence and I never told anyone till now.

PART SEVEN

THE END

I WATCH THE RAIN

February 1986. A Sunday, gloomy Sunday, day of rest. Slept ten hours and I'm still exhausted; it's five p.m. Dark out already. It's raining again, the weather's fucked. Every weekend it rains. Weekends now *mean* rain. Can't remember when I last saw daylight. Last week? Week before? Been living in bed, in my overcoat, and pajamas, wrapped in two quilts. Always cold in here— it's the wind in the fireplace. Whoever said heroin keeps you warm must have lived in the tropics.

I feel like a long Russian novel, full of epic, tortured passion and masochistic need. In the architecture of indifference that frames the modern world, I'm a lump of forbidden clay, a cave turned inside out, petrified, hollow. Junk doesn't fill it, money either. It just sits there in the cave and digs it deeper. No wonder heroin's called Down. It sinks you.

I can't think of any reason to get up out of bed. I've tried everything I know—I haven't tried meditation. Cal Tutweiler thinks I should. He says the future depends on an alteration of consciousness today, on getting to another level. I'll wait to see what happens. As Honey likes to say, you never know what will happen, but something always will. Something always happens.

It's happened to her—both she and Grigorio are in the hospital. They have the same pneumonia, but his is worse. His lungs have both collapsed. He sits up in bed with a drawing pad, making cartoons of himself with tubes in his chest and angels around his head and she writes captions for all of them. There are balloons all over the ceiling and cartoons all over the walls.

It was in this room they finally tied the knot. People came from all over the planet to see them—they'd made that many friends. The room was so crowded it seemed more like a nightclub than a hospital. For a moment, it seemed like fun to be sick. Then she went home and he stayed in and Lute came back to be with Honey.

Without opening my eyes I pull the drawer of the bedside table and feel for the dope, lift it out. I get my fingers around the foil and straw. There's a movie on, *Key Largo*. It's raining there, too. I slump back against the pillows. I hear Kit moving in the kitchen, can't tell what's up. I listen to the rain.

"You want coffee?" she calls out.

"Yeah."

"I'll have to heat it up. You slept a really long time."

I hate reheated coffee.

"What are you watching?" Kit says, coming toward me.

Her face—she's been picking at her face. She looks like a kid with bad acne, except that she doesn't look like a kid and the acne is open sores, from cocaine. She picks at her face and I lie in bed. I smoke dope and watch movies, and wait.

"I can't believe it's still raining," she says.

"The coffee's boiling," I say.

"Does that mean you want me to bring it in to you?"

"Would you?"

"Will you give me something for it?"

"For Christ sake! It's only in the next room!"

"How far away is the dope?"

"It's not the same thing at all! Coffee's a lot cheaper than heroin."

"The phone's been ringing," she says. "I didn't know if you wanted me to answer it. Are you in today, or not?"

It's Sunday. I don't have hours on Sundays.

"Let them go," I say with a dramatic wave. "We'll be doing them all a favor."

I could be Styrofoam, the way I feel. I let Kit take the dope. I don't care anymore—let her do the business. When the day is done, Angelo's dope will be gone and I'll still owe him ten thousand dollars. Vance doesn't have anything; Daniel, either. Nobody's going anywhere but under. I heard Mr. Leather got clean, and Belle, I haven't seen her at all. I passed her on the street once, a while back, but she didn't notice I was there. She was walking mighty fast.

A customer calls who wants to bring by a friend. "Maybe you know him," she says. "Malik?"

Malik? I know him, sure—he's an old school friend of my brother's. Since when is he a dealer?

When he shows up, we don't get into any of that. We get right down to business. He produces an ounce of rock; I come to attention. He lays out a taste, and in no time I feel like myself. Maybe, I think, not all the stuff I brought back for Angelo was so pure. Who can you trust, after all? Some Thai you never laid eyes on? I ought to complain to Angelo, but then I'd have to see him and I don't know where he is. He's been gone since December, and meanwhile I've smoked all the dope. I don't care, he's done fine by me, he's made a fortune. Give someone else a chance. How many times should I have to return his investment? How many risks can I take?

"You know what?" I say, smiling at Malik. "I think you and I are in business."

The sun shines in—spring is in the air. For two weeks life

returns to normal, customers in and out, dealers. Everyone likes this stuff. Orders are large, but I know it's the end. I knew it the day it rained. Something happened to me that day. I had a feeling, a funny kind of feeling. Maybe Dick had it, too, that day, because now it's March 1986 and he's coming through the door like all the rest, asking do I have any heroin?

THE SOUND OF THE DOORBELL

"**H**ave you come up with any names?" Dick began, the third day he came around. That day was really the longest. We were running out of things to say.

"Let me ask you," he said as the sun began to set. "Do you know how to make a Welsh rarebit? The kind of places I eat in never have it."

"I don't feel like cooking," I snapped. *Welsh rarebit?* Give me a break.

"Just trying to make conversation." He shrugged. The time was barely moving. My Catapres was wearing off. I was tired of playing games.

"C'mon Dick," I said. "You can tell me—who dropped the dime? Who fingered me for the bust?"

"I'll tell you what," he answered, smoothing his tie. "Here's something we can do: why don't you try to guess? You guess the names and maybe I'll let you know when you're right."

He almost had me on that one. I wanted to know pretty bad. I almost said, "Was it Maggie?" I almost said, "Was it Massimo? Vance?" But none of them ever knew Angelo—did they?

The sound of the doorbell startled us both.

"Who's that?" Dick said with a grunt. I sat up on the edge of my bed, hands pressed flat on my thighs. My heart had jumped into my throat.

"I'm not expecting anyone," I said hoarsely. "Maybe it's the mailman."

"Go see."

My shoes seemed to have grown soles of lead. I dragged one foot after the other, sliding across the floor. Dick trailed right behind.

"Watch the door," he said to his walkie-talkie.

"We're there," said a voice.

"Hello?" I said to the intercom.

"Daniel!" I heard from below.

My hand was still on the listen button. I heard him shout, hit the ground, roll.

The walkie-talkie breathed static. "He's clean," we heard the voice say.

Dick gave me a questioning look. "Let him go," he said to his man. "But follow him."

I moved away from the door. I felt sick, out of focus, like a double exposure. Dick stayed in the hall. His eyes had narrowed, his chumminess was gone.

"You didn't happen to tip this guy, did you?"

"Who?" I said. My voice squeaked. "You mean Daniel?" I shook my head to hide my smile. What I wanted to say was, "Guess!"

WHO?

I don't understand why Dick won't say who it was set me up—haven't I been friendly? Who's he trying to protect? Someone who got caught before we did? Do we know anyone like that?

"Well," says Kit. "There's Vance."

Of course. He owes me two thousand dollars. And he was busted by city cops three months before. It cost him just a few nights in jail, after which he was mysteriously released. Later he said it wasn't anything, not anything about drugs. Maybe, I thought, wanting to believe him, maybe it was about Marcy, who had left him while he was in the Tombs. She had come over here one night to escape him. It seemed he was slapping her around. Would I help rent her some wheels? She thought I had credit cards. No, I said, I always pay cash. I pay cash for everything. "Oh," she said. "Can you spare any?"

Would Vance have nailed us to get back at me for that? He thought I knew where she was. Maybe he wanted to get out of paying what he owes. I'm not behind bars and I know why. Maybe he did it, too—cooperated.

On the other hand, it could have been Jerome, the fey weasel coke-dealing crackhead. I can't believe Bebe's gone in with *him*. They're sharing a commercial space over on Lafayette; he works there. She calls it a design studio, but Kit's the only one who produces anything there besides a crack pipe—necklaces she strings with tiny dice and religious medals, miniatures on rubber chains. She's there all day with Jerome. He could easily have dropped the dime. It was his order I had on the scale on the day of the dicks. When the mailman-cop knocked on the door, it was Jerome I had expected to see when I opened it.

"Bebe told me Jerome was busted," Kit says. "I didn't want to say anything before, but I've been wondering about him, too."

She's sitting in the chair by my desk, twisting strands of hair around her ear. We can't seem to talk anywhere but the office. "This is a bad habit, coming in this room," I say, drumming my fingers on the phone.

"Are you sure there's nothing left in here?" she asks, her voice hollow. "Nothing hidden away?"

"No drugs," I say. I've looked, many times. "Maybe there's money." I pull books from the shelves on the wall. "Here," I say. "Help me look."

"Doesn't Vance owe you money?"

"That scumbag. He'll never pay."

"Did you find anything yet?"

I shake my head.

"I wish you would call him. Call Vance."

I close the books.

"I think we should talk to him," she says.

"What's going on?" I say, when I get him on the phone. "When you gonna return that favor?"

Don't worry, he tells me. I'm not really worried, am I? I have no cause to worry, not about him. How could I be worried? About him? It's coming, he promises, any day now. He's working on something special—"a new film." Why can't I trust him? Aren't we friends?

I have many friends, I say, and none of them owe me money. I don't confess my own lingering debts. By now, they've disappeared into the bowels of the U.S. Federal Building.

"Stop this," says Vance. I can hear him smoking crack. "Don't be so hard," he says. "Haven't I always taken care of you girls?"

I tell him what's happened, sort of. Dead silence. Then, "You calling me from home?"

It's all right, I say, I only want to know who set me up. Does he have anything to tell me?

"Are you saying it was me?" he shouts. "I can't believe you'd say a thing like that! To me! A *friend*. I would never do that to anybody! Especially you—you girls! I've *never* done you dirt. What about all those times Kit came up here with those big sick eyes? I've never seen eyes like that. It didn't matter what time it was or what else I was doing, did it? I was always here for you." Now it sounds like he's going to cry.

"Maybe it was Jerome."

"Not him. Are you serious?"

He's right. It's never the first person you suspect. "Find out who it was, then. Can you?"

He says he'll ask around.

"He didn't do it," I tell Kit. "Maybe it was Betty?"

She stands up. "I don't think so. Betty's dead." I didn't know this. I feel awful. Kit's expression doesn't change. "Why couldn't it have been Daniel?"

"No," I say, under my breath. "Not Daniel."

"I don't know who did it," she says with resignation. "I guess it doesn't matter anymore."

I wish I could say what's really on my mind, but I can't seem to find the words. My mind's gone. Like Daniel.

"Vance isn't such a bad guy, really," she goes on, picking up one of the cats. "None of these guys are. These *guys*: Vance, Daniel, Jean-Paul—they'd be pretty together if they weren't so fucked up."

"Wait a minute," I say.

She stares at me. "Jean-Paul?"

That *asshole*. Was it only a week ago I threw him out? That slime. I tried to be good to him—his wife had OD'd on a trip to Asia. He loved her, I guess. I gave him a consoling bag of dope, but he wanted more. When I gave him a little more, he called me a bitch. He didn't want just a little. Why couldn't I help get him back on his feet, come on. I could do that, couldn't I?

I never did trust that Jean-Paul. Didn't like him. He would have to pay up front, I said. That was the only way. I never thought he'd do anything; sick junkies say a lot of things they don't mean. I thought, bottom line, he needed me.

"I guess you could have been nicer," Kit tells me.

There's another argument brewing, we're both getting mad. The cats have left the room. I agree with Kit about one thing, though: it doesn't matter now who did what. We can't do anything. Can we?

OUT THERE, WAITING

From the living-room window I can see the roof garden of a three-story building below. It hides part of Sixth Avenue from view. I can see the subway entrance beyond, I can hear the traffic pass. I can't see if anyone is still out there, waiting.

The stuff Dick and his crew confiscated at the bust didn't arrive by pigeon. I got it from one of those names Dick wants to hear, one who wants to be paid for that stuff. Malik.

The easy thing to do would be to turn him in. Also the hardest.

When Dick isn't around, I get a cab to Malik's apartment. He thinks I'm bringing him cash, but I'm there to tell him about the bust. He can plainly see I'm sick. He asks who set me up. A creep named Jean-Paul. Then why am I not in jail? "I have a good lawyer," I say. He accepts this. He really only wants to know one thing. how I expect to pay him.

How does he expect I can?

"That's not my problem," he says. "My problem is the guy I owe."

I let him know some of my customers are willing to pay more if I'll cop for them. That would be madness, I say, but I'll gladly turn their business over to him.

No, he says. Definitely not. No one can know he has anything to do with this stuff, or me. He has a wife, a kid, a legitimate business—painting, construction, design. Like Vance, he's trying to finance a film, but unlike Vance, he can probably pull it off. Malik used to run a theater company. He's not all talk and no show.

What can I do? I can't turn him in. He's my brother's friend.

I start going around the neighborhood on the sly, picking up money. I keep my eyes at my back. I never see any dicks. I go uptown and sit in Malik's kitchen, where I weigh the bindles and go back to make the drops. It's tiresome, and dangerous, but each time I meet with Malik, he gives me a line to relieve the sickness and another one to go.

"This has to stop," I say after a week has gone by. I'll never be able to pay what I owe. We'll both get busted.

He pats the money on the table. "We won't get busted," he says. He seems to think he's immune. He still has to pay his guy, he says, and this isn't a guy you want to mess with. This guy owes somebody, too.

"I understand the problem," I say, but I have problems of my own.

"I am going to be paid," Malik says slowly. "I am going to be paid, and you're going to do the paying." He's angry, I can see that. I also see his fear. Not of the people he owes. I'm the one making him nervous.

"You can't turn him in," says Kit when I get home. I'm scraping out a line for her. "We need this."

"It's not worth it," I say. "But I won't turn him in."

As the lawyer said, I've cooperated enough. Too much. More than I can bear.

MONSTERS

I sit on the edge of my bed and watch the cats roll around on the carpet, listen to them meow. They must be hungry. I can't move. Sweat drips from my hair, goosebumps appear on my skin. My tongue feels swollen, I've been vomiting for hours. Haven't slept in a week.

"I can't stand it," Kit says. "I can't stand it."

Cal Tutweiler calls. He knows about a rehab Kit's insurance will cover—her parents pay all her premiums. I say she ought to go. Anything's better than this.

"I'll go if I can take my own pills," she says.

The phone. Who now? Must be Dick. Can't he take a day off?

"Darling, you are out of jail!" It's Prescott. Fucking Prescott Weems.

"Yeah," I grunt.

"I hear you informed on your *friends*," he gurgles, his voice a simmering venom stew.

"Don't start," I say.

"Darling, I don't like hearing you've been a rat and I don't want to believe it. But I promise you, if it turns out to be true, I will personally destroy you and I'll do it in print. You know I can, so don't try me. Under this genteel exterior, I'm a vicious old queen, and I will make sure you never show your face in good company again. You will not be able to get a job even licking dishes, much less cooking them. Just forget it."

"I can't talk now," I say through my teeth. "I'm sick."

"You didn't turn anyone in?"

I hang up, feeling grim. The phone rings again. Oh, God. He's worse than Dick.

It's Lute. "Thank God you're there!" she bellows.

"I'm here, all right. What's up?"

"Please *please* go to the hospital to see Grigorio? Honey asked me to call you. She was there this morning but she's not in any shape to go back. Please go, there's no one else I can ask."

I'm not sure my legs will support me.

"You've got to go," she says. "Everyone else is either working or not answering, and I have to stay here with Honey. I know what Weems is saying and I don't care. I don't *care* what you did or didn't do, we've been friends too long. I'm glad you're not in jail—okay? Honey needs you. Please do this for her. Please go over there *now*. Will you go?"

I'll go. I know better now than to walk away from the sick. It empties your world, doing that. It makes your place in it small, and my spot is tight enough.

I call upon myself. I call. I hobble to the sink and splash water on my face, down two clonidines, pop an Ativan for good measure. My pupils are huge. It takes every ounce of strength to dress; I can hardly lift my coat. Kit can't believe I'm doing this. But I have to do it. I must.

I throw the coat over my shoulders and inch down the stairs to the street. The wind nearly knocks me down. I pray I'll live till I get there.

My heart jumps when I see him, a disfigured stick of a man many years older than I know he is. The long thick curly hair now hangs in thin wisps from his crown. His cheeks are sunken and his eyes bulge. They don't look real. He's barely more than a skeleton.

It's been only a month since I saw him last. He was in a different room then, the one he was sharing with Honey. It looked like a circus tent then. Now it's a chamber of death.

The tubes are gone, he's breathing on his own somehow. Two large garbage bags sit on the floor, stuffed with his belongings. They've packed him up already. Couldn't they wait? He doesn't deserve this—what did he do? He got hooked on drugs, said some funny things, and made my best friend glad to be alive. Should this be a capital offense? Death is a blessing compared to this shit. My own sickness leaves me. He calls for a nurse.

"Bitch!" he cries, and then he's out of breath. "They hate people with AIDS," he says, his voice barely a wheeze. "They turn us into monsters." The fight goes out of him and he lies still, his breathing labored as a dog's on a hot summer day. A dog's life is better.

I grasp his hand. It's cold as ice. All I see is his morphine drip. This is hell.

What is it about this life, I think, makes people willing to suffer so, just to have another moment in it? *Let go,* I want to say. His eyes flutter open and rest briefly on the TV above his bed. He still wants to look at pictures. "So stupid," he says. "So dummy." His cheeks seem to sink even deeper.

His lips move again but I hear nothing. I move close to his face and with a tremendous effort he tries again. "Have you seen Honey?"

"I'm going there when I leave here," I say. I guess I will. Nothing else to do. Wait for Dick? I'll go see Honey.

"It was all my fault," he says, his face ashen.

"It's nobody's fault," I reply, though I'm not actually sure about that.

"So dummy," he says. "There was a time . . ." He forces a smile and grips my hand. It sends another chill up my spine. "It was *amusing,*" he whispers. "Wasn't it?" An awful odor escapes his mouth, deep skank. His head falls back on the pillow.

Is this it? Is he going to die now? What if he does? I can feel the life draining from his hand like dripping paint. Will I have to be the one to tell Honey?

"Bebe said I'd find you here."

What? The voice in the doorway startles me. It takes me a minute to focus on the face. I can't quite believe what I'm seeing. It's Mark Murano—Angelo's friend. The junkie who introduced us. I let go of Grigorio's hand.

"What were you thinking when you talked to those cops?" Mark bellows from the doorway.

All the stories I've heard, all the lies I've told. I can't think of anything to say.

"That was me with Angelo that night, you bitch! He was on his way to see *you*! You ratted us out. It was you." His face is red, his hands shake. The bastard's a pillar of fury.

"Pipe down," I say, edging away from the bed. "This man is dying."

"Let him."

I wish I could faint. But nooo.

"Look," I say, "you think I set myself up? You crazy? Somebody dropped a net on Angelo and we were in it."

"Who?" He moves toward me now. I step back.

"I don't know." I still don't, not really. How could I?

"You sold us out!" Mark screams. "Why else are you walking around?"

"I don't know," I say. "Why are you?" Now we're facing each other, inches apart.

"My wife paid the bail," he says. He's shaking me and shouting. "Bebe told me *you* didn't even go in front of a judge. You did it. It was you!"

That fucking bigmouth Bebe. "Bebe is grabbing at straws," I say. Am I choking? "She doesn't know any more than I do."

"She said Kit told her you ratted."

Kit?

This is an outrage. We tussle. It isn't much of a fight. He's as dopesick as I am. I pull myself away. "You've got some nerve," I say. Wait till Dick hears about *this*. "Look," I say, "the shit I'm in is just as deep as yours. I'm not in jail, because it wasn't me they were looking for. It was Angelo they wanted and it was Angelo they got. They thought I was someone named Laura. Who's Laura? Some friend of *yours?*"

The nurse peeks in. "I have to ask you to step outside," she says. "You're disturbing the patient."

"You better watch your back," Mark says, withdrawing. "I'm not through with you yet." He pauses in the doorway. "Bitch."

A sound comes from Grigorio. I lean close. "Tell Honey I waited," he says.

I find Honey in her kitchen, rearranging the furniture, hanging a light. "Glad to see you up and about," I say, suddenly remembering that when we'd met ten years before, she was doing exactly the same thing.

"Did you see Grigorio?" she asks. I nod, a terrible black cloud.

"It's okay, hon. Don't get upset."

"I can't help it."

"I can't complain," she says, dragging herself back to bed. Now she walks with a cane. "I'm lucky I found him when I did."

"Did he have AIDS when you met him?" I ask. "Did you?"

"We both did," she says, pushing away her hair. She's feverish. "I couldn't tell anyone then," she says. "I didn't want anything to change. Anyway, it was worth it. I did what I wanted and I fell in love, too. What more could a girl ask? I only wish I could have finished my novel. That's my only regret. That, and leaving Mike."

"He knows you have AIDS now, doesn't he?"

"I'm not sure if he does," she says.

She's not sure? "What's this novel?" I say. I think I'm getting mad. "I didn't know you were writing a novel."

Her ice-blue eyes are now a soft gray. "Write that book of *yours*, hon."

"I don't know if I can. I don't know anymore if drugs should be legal. I don't know what I'd write."

"Just write your book, hon," she says.

Well, I'm writing it.

SOMETIMES

Sometimes I wonder what would have happened if what happened hadn't. Probably, it wouldn't have changed anything. It didn't change anything. Life always goes on. Time does. Heroin doesn't change that. You think it will, but it won't. It lies heavy on your chest like an unripened fruit, never finishing what it starts. Time doesn't stop and people you love slip through your hands against your will. Like Kit.

"How much are they paying you?" I whisper in her ear. The truth, I think, is always quiet. "You turned us in, didn't you?"

She jerks her head away. "Why do you hate me?" she says. "Is it because you wish you could be with a man?"

"You set us up. I know it was you. You wanted to run the business all along. I know how sly you can be. What kind of deal did you have? Did Dick promise to take me and leave you alone?"

She can't speak. She can't move. I've got her.

"Maybe Betty was right," she says then. "You are crazy."

"*You* turned us in. You hate *me*. You've hated me since you were sick. I could never give you enough. Not drugs, not sex, not money. You wanted it all to yourself. You dropped that dime, it was you. That's why Dick lets you go to Bebe's every day. That's why you still had dope when we were busted. That's why everyone excuses everything you do—it was you all along. You hate me."

She pushes me into a wall. I wriggle free and push her back. She runs in the office and throws my typewriter through the window. She crashes a chair on my desk, tries to tear the folding table from the wall. I stand in the kitchen and watch. Then she hits me. She hits me again. I look in her eyes. She hits me.

KIT'S GONE

Kit's gone. Cal Tutweiler came and took her to a rehab on Second Avenue. He's off drugs this week. Good for him.

I sit by the window and look out. Maybe I should open it. These windows have been shut for a year. I can see a few leaves on the trees outside, a ship passing on the river, people on the street below.

She did it. I know she did. She won't admit it, but she did.

I stand up and puke on the rug.

How could she do it? Why?

Two weeks pass. I get clean. Kit's still in the rehab under severe restrictions, with two more weeks to go. I haven't heard a word from Dick, but she calls every day to say she's coming home.

They aren't giving her enough methadone is what it is. They've cut her down too fast. Nearly everyone there is in for crack, and they stay up all night and pace the halls outside her room. She can't sleep, she can't eat, and they give her demerits when she doesn't show up for breakfast. They won't let her out for air. "I'm coming home," she says. "I'm gonna check myself out and go home, whether you like it or not."

I don't like it.

I wonder why Dick hasn't called. Then I wonder why I'm wondering.

I pick up the phone and call my father. He's had the operation on his heart and I want to do the right thing.

"So," I say, "have you been resting?"

"All I can do is rest," he says. "I'm so tired . . . it's a terrible thing, getting old."

"You're not old," I say. "Take it easy."

"I have no choice but to take it easy," he tells me. "You can't understand how hard this is. I'm floundering here, doing nothing."

"Dad," I say. "You're recouping. That's something."

"For instance," he says. "This morning I got up, I went into the bathroom. I picked up my hairbrush and brushed back my hair. Then I flossed my teeth. Then I was pooped!"

"At least you have hair to brush," I point out.

"Yes . . . yes . . . I guess that is something . . . to be glad of. Still, I'm a *man*, honey. I can't just sit around and powder my nose."

"I know how it is," I say.

"You *don't* know," he replies. "You *can't* know. You only think you can. You can't understand till it happens to you. It's indescribable."

"Dad," I say. "I understand perfectly."

"The doctor," he goes on—I don't think he heard me—"the doctor said I was his Olympian star patient. I'm making a champion comeback, he said. Tomorrow I can have my first shower in a week. Amazing, how having a shower is the greatest thing that can happen in a week."

I haven't had a shower in days. Can't bear the touch of water. "Life's great when it's simple," I say. "Soon you'll be running around crazy like everyone else—"

"—just another Joe Schmo."

"Not a schmo, Dad."

"I don't like doing nothing," he says.

"Look, you gotta get better," I tell him. "Okay? It's not nothing."

"I know you're right," he says. It's the first time I've ever heard him say that. "The thing is," he says, "I'm weeping so much of the time."

"Don't worry about it," I say.

"Doesn't seem like I have so much to be sad about."

"Let it out. It'll be a relief."

"I have no choice," he admits. "Out it comes, on and off, all day, when I'm conscious. Gee—imagine looking forward to a shower, like it was the greatest invention known to man!"

"Imagine," I concur.

"Haven't shaved in a week, either. Sheesh! It's terrible."

"It's not terrible, for Heaven's sake—it's trendy. My God, you are rough."

"You're a good kid," he says, "always have been. Are you eating? You're always so thin."

"Well, I haven't had much of an appetite," I tell him. "Actually, I've been ill."

"I'm sorry," he says.

"I've been poisoned," I say. My voice is gravel.

"*Poisoned?*"

I take a breath. "This good kid has been on drugs, to tell you the truth."

"You mean . . . an *addict*?"

I keep silent.

"Are you saying it's my fault?"

"No." Another silence.

"The doctor said I was his chief star patient, did I tell you?"

THAT DEVIL D

At the end of March, I'm still feeling terrible. I still tense up when I hear the phone; I still can't open the mail, but I've learned the location of every muscle in my body. Every ache and pain I have, every sleepless shudder and each nervous twitch comes right from that devil D. It's dying, at last, but it's putting up a fight, it screams in the night; I ignore it. Whoever said you could kick dope in three days must have been stoned; that's just another junkie fib. It takes a lot longer—for me, a lifetime, however long that is. Longer than five to fifteen years.

I call the lawyer. Has he heard anything? Have they set me a date in court? No, nothing, he says. He thinks the cops are losing interest.

On the thirty-first of March, that devil starts kicking me something fierce. It's bad. I'd give anything for even an hour's sleep, anything. I let myself out for a walk. Up and down the stairs, several times. As long as I'm talking or walking, as long as I stay in the light, I can breathe.

Kit calls to say she's coming home for real, they're letting her out after tomorrow. Tomorrow is her last fucking day. Could I bring her ten dollars in quarters? She owes them to a woman there who didn't make so many calls.

"I don't have ten dollars," I say.

"Call Bebe," she tells me. "Bebe always has quarters. Are you going to come and get me?"

There seems to be a brick lodged in my throat. "No," I say. "I'm not coming."

She hangs up.

A minute later, Bebe's on the phone. She has the quarters, I can come over whenever. Around dinnertime, I find myself ringing her bell.

"Uh-oh," she says. "You look unhappy."

"Yeah," I say. "Well, you know."

"Bet you'll be glad to have Kit home again."

I say nothing.

She says I look like I could use a line. I tell her no, I'm trying to stay clean. I still have a couple of pills, I'm doing okay. Then I snort the offered line. To take the edge off. If I was on methadone, it would be the same thing.

One little line—it stones me. I walk on air all the way home, eat a small dinner, my first in weeks. I sleep a bit, maybe an hour or two. In the morning, I can't raise my head. My eyes are open, but my body . . . What did I do? Just a line. One line. I can't believe what I've done. I look at the calendar: April 1. April Fool. No kidding.

HOME, TAKING A SHOWER

When Honey died I was home taking a shower. I'd been at the hospital all night—that night before Kit came home. I wouldn't have been able to sleep no matter where I was. Mike, Honey's son, and Lute were with me, Magna, and Ginger, who was taking pictures. For twelve hours we stood by Honey's bed, watching her writhe in a blue plastic diaper, listening to her gasp for breath. She had a terrible, rasping cough, and was in and out of a coma all through that sleepless night.

"I'm here for the duration," Lute said when I left, but I wasn't planning to be gone long. I didn't think the end would come soon. Grigorio hadn't let go easily and Honey was a lot like him.

I returned to see Magna nodding in a corner of the hall and Ginger standing outside Honey's room, weeping. A few others were milling around them. Honey never could feel popular enough. Lute told me when Honey died, everyone happened to be off in the lounge and she was all alone.

Mike came out of her room and I went in and closed the door. She looked good, I hope she knew that. No bags under the eyes. Good skin. I stared at her body as if from a great height. I wasn't feeling rational. Now that her wretched cough was gone, I half expected her to breathe, but nothing moved, not even the air. My eyes fell on the tattoos around her fingers. They seemed faded.

The door opened then and two orderlies appeared with a gurney, asking me to go and close the door behind me. When it opened again, they were wheeling her out in a body bag. It looked very small, child-size. How could our Honey be there? I caught Magna's eye and we both went to pieces. Fury took me back down the hall, down the stairs, to the street. I hate drugs, I said to myself. I hate them.

I hate them.

Kit was watching TV when I got home. Neither of us tried to speak. I lay down in bed and started rocking. I couldn't stop trembling, shivering. I had my overcoat on top of me; it lay on the quilts, but it didn't take away my chill. Kit took me in her arms and held me. I hated her touch, but it was warm. The rocking subsided, my legs took a rest. I drifted a little, maybe I slept, and for that day and the next and the next, Kit's arms, her warmth, her poisoned, scarred body was all that kept me from the grasp of that devil D. She was all the protection I had.

Three more days pass and nothing else happens, except I know what Kit is and she knows what I did and we live, rid of that devil D. That's all it was, I know that now, the reason she gave us up: she wanted at last to give him the slip but she had him confused with me. More days pass and we take separate bedrooms and in a month I'm well enough to get a job. First I clean yards, picking up fallen leaves, then I'm cooking again, in a restaurant serving health food. I make ninety dollars a week, before taxes. It isn't much, but it's legal, and so nothing happens. Kit goes to work for an interior designer making wall art, and more weeks pass and still nothing happens, except the days grow longer than the nights and Dick's calls get fewer and farther between. Then one day in June, I open the door and he's there.

"I was just going out," I say. "You feel like a walk?" He leads me down the stairs.

We sit on a bench on the sidewalk and smoke. "How you doin'?" he says. "How's Kit? Heard anything from Daniel?"

"Questions, questions!" I exclaim. "What are you—a detective?" He laughs, and turns his head.

"So, did you ever figure out who set you up?"

He'll never stop playing with me, never. I wonder how he's doing with Angelo, but I'm too mad to ask. When there's nothing else to say, I ask. "How's Angelo doing, anyway?"

"He's been sweating it out. Like you."

Right, I think. But I'm not in jail.

"And what does he say about me?"

"Nothing," Dick replies, very cool. "Not a word."

We share a moment of silence.

I know I'll see Angelo again someday, it's inevitable. Dick says he'll turn eventually. Everyone does. I'll be walking down the street, or sitting in a restaurant, or standing in line at a movie and he'll be there, eyes burning. Will he know me? Will we speak? I don't know but it doesn't matter; by then I'll have nothing to hide.

THE STORY OF JUNK

This isn't the book Honey thought I would write. It isn't a story I ever planned to tell. In a way, it was told to me, by all my friends and customers. I owe them. Like Sticky said, drug addicts are the best people I ever knew. I want Dick to know the same thing. I don't want him ever to ask again how "nice" people like me get into this nasty business. It's not because our lives have been so tragic, or so lonely, though that might be the case. And it's not because our parents didn't love us, though that might be the case. It's not because of any personal failures or unmet expectations, though you could count on all of it to play a part. And it's not because some of us died too young, even if it's true. It's not even because we like heroin—that's just a song and dance. There's no way to excuse or explain it. The whole story of junk is a song and dance. Everyone's got a story to tell, and most of those stories will change in some way, every time they're told. Not this one, not the story of junk. This one's always the same.

ACKNOWLEDGMENTS

I would like to acknowledge my considerable debt to those constant friends and unexpected guardian angels who kept their homes, hearts, pocketbooks, and my eyes open during the process of writing this book. For the unwitting and generous conspiracy they formed to see me through it, I am deeply, deeply grateful:

To my dear Robbie Goolrick, like whom there is no other, whose close friendship and many kindnesses have been such that my being a yankee (or a Yankee fan) will never be the same; to the wonderful Judy Auchincloss, whose delight in all things has given our human comedy noble refreshment; to Ira Silverberg, who has seen me through many a dark night and blank page; to Clarissa Dalrymple, a worldly and genuine muse, who introduced me to much of my best material; to Annie Philbin, for her understanding and unqualified support; to Mary Heilmann and Ann Rower, for being there in a pinch; to Nan Goldin, without whose encouragement I may never have made a beginning, and to Lynne Tillman, for propelling me toward the end; to my editor, Elisabeth Sifton, who knew I could write this story before I did and has been my steady compass on the circuitous journey through it; to Edward Hibbert, for his tireless efforts on my behalf; and to sweet Chris Schiavo, whose selfless dedication to my cause made this truly a labor of love.

I would also like to thank the MacDowell Colony and the Corporation of Yaddo for giving me such grand places to work, and American Pen and Change, Inc., for helping to keep a roof over my head.

I can't say enough about the essential contributions made by my best critics and readers, Brooks Adams, and Lisa Liebmann, while Rob Wynne, Charles Ruas, Keith Sonnier, Billy Sullivan, Klaus Kertess, Jane Dickson, Patty Smyth, Richard Boch, Gary Indiana, and Betsy Sussler uniquely enriched my creative life, not to mention my phone time and my place at the dinner table. I thank Leonard Drindel, Kate Simon, and Adrianne Barone for their help with my research; the forgiving staff of the Drawing Center and Phillip Munson for general assistance; Alexis Ford for donating the computer; Pat Hearn and my friends in the Wooster Group for helping me find my legs; P & J and David Becker for their patience; and all those many more anonymous souls whose stories ultimately gave voice to my own.

New York City
December 1996